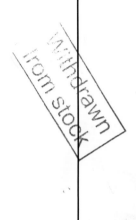

EYE FOR AN EYE

Also by M.J. Arlidge

M.J. Arlidge has worked in television for the last twenty years, specialising in high-end drama production, including prime-time crime serials *Silent Witness*, *Torn*, *The Little House* and, most recently, the hit ITV show *Innocent*. In 2015 his audiobook exclusive *Six Degrees of Assassination* was a number-one bestseller. His debut thriller, *Eeny Meeny*, was the UK's bestselling crime debut of 2014 and has been followed by ten more DI Helen Grace thrillers – all *Sunday Times* bestsellers.

🐦 @mjarlidge
📘 /MJArlidge
📷 @m_j_arlidge

EYE FOR AN EYE

M.J. Arlidge

ORION

First published in Great Britain in 2023 by Orion Fiction,
an imprint of The Orion Publishing Group Ltd.,
Carmelite House, 50 Victoria Embankment
London EC4Y 0DZ

An Hachette UK Company

1 3 5 7 9 10 8 6 4 2

A CIP catalogue record for this book is
available from the British Library.

ISBN (Hardback) 978 1 3987 0818 1
ISBN (Trade Paperback) 978 1 3987 0819 8
ISBN (eBook) 978 1 3987 0821 1

Typeset at The Spartan Press Ltd,
Lymington, Hants

Printed and bound in Great Britain by Clays Ltd,
Elcograf S.p.A.

www.orionbooks.co.uk

Author's Note

There are currently only nine convicted criminals in the UK who have been given permanent, lifelong anonymity by the courts, provided with new names and new lives following their release from prison. The crimes that these individuals committed were so notorious, so high profile, that the threat of vigilante attacks upon them in the community was deemed to be real. Because of this, the courts took the unusual step of granting them lifelong anonymity, shielding them from harm and giving them a second chance at life, under the supervision of the Probation Service.

Many applauded this decision, pointing out that most of these offenders were only children themselves when their offences were committed. But others felt it was misguided, uncomfortable that these convicted criminals were now out and about in the community, invisible and undetected. Normally if a child sex offender moves into your neighbourhood, you have the right to know about it, thanks to Sarah's Law. But not with these nine. Which some think is odd, given the grievous nature of their crimes and the fact that at least one of them has gone on to commit serious, sexually motivated offences since their release.

Over the years, several attempts have been made to 'out' these individuals, the British tabloid press in particular making strenuous efforts to track them down. None have succeeded, the nine criminals remaining concealed and protected to this day. In *Eye for an Eye*, a <u>fictional</u> take on this subject matter, I explore what would happen if someone *did* manage to release the new identities and whereabouts of these notorious offenders – not to the press, news outlets or the internet, but directly to the bereaved families themselves. Would the result be 'natural justice', these transgressors finally made to feel the full weight of their awful crimes? Or would it be an invitation to vigilantism, blood lust and mob rule?

How would *you* feel if you finally came face to face with your child's killer?

Matthew Arlidge, July 2023.

For my mother,
who made me what I am.

Day One

Chapter 1

He sensed them before he saw them. Was it a flickering shadow, the sound of shallow breathing, a clumsy footstep that gave them away? Or was it his finely tuned senses that alerted him to their presence, those survival instincts that had kept him alive for so long? Either way, one thing was certain. They had found him.

Clamping down his terror, Mark Willis kept walking. Beads of sweat clung to his forehead, his heart pounded, but he maintained a steady pace, scanning the shadowy buildings and walkways. The Rumworth Estate was a miserable place, haunted by dropouts, junkies and the terminally poor, but Mark liked it here, especially after midnight, when he could come and go as he pleased. He relished these fleeting moments of freedom, when all the misery, hurt and violence of the past seemed to melt away, when he felt invisible and secure. He'd been enjoying himself tonight, sauntering undetected towards his tiny flat, five pints of cheap lager provoking feelings of carelessness, even euphoria. But in an instant, everything had changed. Now he felt stone cold sober, his mind clear, his body tensed for flight, aware of the mortal danger he was in.

How had they located him? What had given him away? It seemed impossible. He'd been so careful, so cautious – inhabiting his new identity, making a life for himself in this new town – yet somehow they *knew*. The next few minutes would determine whether he escaped retribution or died a brutal death, his only hope the element of surprise, a sudden, unexpected dash for freedom. But which direction should he head in? Down which path should he run? Get it right and he might walk away from this unscathed, but get it wrong...

There. He *wasn't* imagining it. This time he definitely heard a footstep amidst the shadows of Lancaster House, the most run-down of the five tower blocks that marred this blighted corner of Bolton. He arrowed a look in the direction of the mouldering tenement building, expecting to see a bulky silhouette in the shadows, but to his surprise his attacker now cast off caution entirely, stepping out into the sickly glow of the lampposts.

Mark caught his breath, stumbling slightly, unable to process what he was seeing. The figure was tall and powerful, dressed in steel-capped boots, dirty jeans and a black bomber jacket. In his gloved hand, he gripped a crowbar, the sickening curve of its hook illuminated by the dull, sodium lights. This was enough to chill Mark's blood, but it was the figure's face that provoked a choked scream in his throat. Two beady, black eyes peered out from a latex pig mask, rendering his assailant inhuman, animalistic and cruel.

The figure was advancing towards him, picking up speed. Panicking, Mark spun, heading fast towards York House and the subterranean walkway that might yet lead him to safety, but he'd hardly taken a step when he ground to a halt. Another masked figure stepped out in front of him, cutting off his escape. He too was armed and hungry for violence, a triumphant hiss spilling from his snout.

'Shit...'

The word shot from Mark's mouth, high-pitched and strangulated. Turning, he doubled back on himself, hoping to retrace his steps to the Butcher's Arms, but now his attackers played their final card, a third figure emerging twenty yards in front of him, casually twirling a crowbar in his hand.

Silence. Mark stood stock-still on the gloomy walkway, his attackers ranged around him. He had walked straight into their trap and would now have to face the consequences. Violence was imminent, their blood lust palpable, their sense of triumph clear. Even now, as Mark stood there, shaking with fear, the most recent arrival snorted loudly in a crude imitation of a pig, the nasty sound echoing off the surrounding buildings. Every part of Mark wanted to fall to his knees, to beg for forgiveness, but he knew there would be no mercy here. This was the promised end.

The three men took a step forward. Then another. Still they advanced, their crowbars raised, poised to strike down their defenceless enemy. Mark could smell their sweat, hear their rasped breathing, sense their exhilaration. He knew that any second now the first blow would land, tearing skin and crack-ing bone, knocking him to the floor. After that, their attack would be relentless, his body smashed beyond recognition, in a sustained, determined act of revenge. Even now, the pig man directly in front of him was tensing his arm, preparing to attack, determined to land the first, crucial blow...

Mark lurched forward, ramming the palm of his hand into the pig's snout. His attacker hadn't been expecting resistance and offered no defence, Mark thrilling to the sound of his nose snapping, as his attacker roared out in pain. Mark's momentum carried him into the burly figure, knocking him backwards, briefly breaking their cordon. Seizing this opportunity, Mark darted forwards, aiming for the gap that had suddenly opened up. Rough hands clawed at him, grabbing his bulky jacket, but Mark tugged his arms free and sprinted away, leaving his aggrieved assailants clutching his puffa. Mark upped his speed, his feet pounding the concrete, putting as much distance as he could between himself and his attackers. A hysterical laugh rose in his throat. Having been seconds from death he was now free and clear, confident he could outrun three middle-aged men, escaping into the shadows of the grim estate he called home. All he needed was half an hour's grace, to find a safe space, make a phone call. He could survive this nightmare, live to tell the tale, make proper use of the second chance he'd been given.

Heavy footsteps behind him snapped Mark out of his reverie. His attackers had not given up, hammering along the concrete after him. He cast a look over his shoulder, to his horror discovering that one of the men was less than ten feet away, straining every sinew to catch him. Panicked, Mark raised his speed, his lungs burning, his legs aching with fatigue. He was still in grave danger, but if he could just make it off the estate, he might yet be safe.

Up ahead he caught sight of the central walkway that led to the high street and sprinted towards it, racing to salvation. But, once more, his hopes were dashed. A white transit van blocked the main entrance to the estate, its headlights blaring as if marking him out for his attackers. Even now, the driver's door was opening, another masked man emerging. Mark skidded to a halt, panicking, only just moving away in time, as a hand tore at his trailing arm. Heedless of where was going, he sprinted on, concerned only with staying ahead of his pursuers.

Mark was heading to the fringes of the estate, a maze of raised walkways, rubbish bins and flickering street lights. The passageways here were gloomy and treacherous and several times Mark stumbled, but he blundered on, keeping his pace high. Surely his attackers would tire at some point? Give up the chase? Turning a corner, he raced on, only catching sight of the upturned shopping trolley at the very last minute. Instinctively he leapt into the air, just clearing the obstacle before landing deftly on the concrete. His closest pursuer was not so lucky, clattering into the trolley before hitting the ground. Buoyed, Mark sped on. He was opening up a gap between himself and his pursuers now and if he could find a stairwell down to street level, he could lose them in the shadows below. This was his manor, his home for the last four years, and his survival depended on using this to his advantage.

He felt exhilarated, energy coursing through him, his eyes scanning confidently for his escape route, but as he skidded round the next corner, his hopes turned to ashes. In the darkness, in his panic, he had miscalculated, darting down the wrong walkway. He was not sprinting towards liberty, but in fact haring towards a dead end, the metal railings ahead that protected residents from the ring road dashing his last chance of escape. Sliding to a halt, Mark looked around for some other means of escape, but he was hemmed in by the chest-high concrete walls to the side and the forbidding black railings ahead. Behind him, he heard four sets of footsteps slow to a jog, as his attackers moved in for the kill. Resting his forehead on the cool metal railing, Mark began to cry, tears spilling down his cheeks, as his body shook with fear. No one deserved to die like this.

'Come on, lads, let's give him his Christmas present…'

They were descending upon him, weapons raised. They would take their time, feasting on his pain, *enjoying* themselves. Turning to face his assailants, Mark's eyes suddenly flashed with defiance. Was he really going to let these brainless oafs butcher him in cold blood? Was he going to let them *win*? From somewhere deep inside, a last vestige of strength, of courage, rose within the young man. His pursuers were only yards from him, poised to strike, but he was determined not to give them the satisfaction. Spinning away, he gripped the railings and started to climb.

Crying out, his pursuers leapt forwards, tearing at his jeans, but Mark pulled clear. For a moment, he teetered on top of the railings, taking in the glowing headlights that raced past on the busy road below, before throwing himself forwards.

Seconds later, his body came to earth with a sickening crunch, his head slamming hard onto the unforgiving concrete.

Chapter 2

Olivia Campbell slammed the car door shut and hurried away. The London traffic had been murder this morning, Christmas shoppers clogging every artery of the capital, and it had taken her an hour to crawl from Holloway to Tottenham. Abandoning her Corsa on a double yellow line, she raced down the street, painfully aware of how late she was. She now regretted squeezing in two client visits before the main event. Both probationers had been truculent, tardy and time-consuming, meaning she was over ninety minutes late for her first proper session with Jack. Olivia knew this wouldn't go down well – the nervous nineteen-year-old had been in a state when he arrived at his new address in Tottenham Hale last night and would probably be climbing the walls by now, convinced that her late arrival presaged danger or disaster. It was all baseless paranoia of course – she'd seen it many times before with high-profile probationers – but it wouldn't make things any easier for her this morning, which was a pity as she already felt like death.

Making her way quickly to the unremarkable two-up two-down, on whose front door hung an apologetic festive wreath, Olivia scanned the street, then knocked three times. Almost immediately a voice responded, her client stationed just the other side of the door.

'Who is it?' he asked quietly, his estuary accent punching through.

'It's me. It's Olivia.'

'Are you alone?'

'No, I've got Lord Lucan and Shergar with me,' Olivia replied, annoyed.

'Who?'

'Just open the bloody door, will you?'

Olivia's tone was harsh, but she didn't want to linger on the doorstep attracting attention and her directness had the desired effect, the door opening slowly to reveal a young, puckish face peering at her over the security chain. Softening her tone, she continued:

'Look, Jack, I'm not being funny, but it's freezing out here, so...'

Finally the teenager relented, removing the chain. Relieved, Olivia stepped inside, pulling the front door shut behind her.

'So how are you settling in?'

Stepping through the hallway into the front room, Olivia had her answer, Jack's holdall lying in the same spot he'd dropped it last night. Sensing her annoyance, the young probationer avoided her eye, staring at a spot on the floor just in front of his trainers.

'Come on, Jack, we *talked* about this. I know the transition is daunting, but you've got to make an effort. I appreciate this place isn't exactly the Ritz,' Olivia continued, running her eyes over the sickly green wall paint, the cold, cracked fireplace, 'but you can cheer it up with a bit of effort. You should unpack, make the place your own, then maybe we can see about getting some posters. What are you into? Rappers? Grime? WWF? What about football? You're an Arsenal fan, right? I'm happy to get some posters of the main guys, Odegaard, Jesus, if it would make you feel more at home?'

Olivia hated football, but she'd done her homework. Her diligence appeared to have no effect, however, the surly teenager maintaining his stony silence.

'Work with me here, Jack. I do appreciate how hard it is, but—'

'I want to go back,' he blurted out, staring hard at the bare floorboards.

'I'm sorry?'

'I want to go back to the unit.'

Olivia's heart sank. This was going to be harder than she'd thought.

'We've been through this. You can't go back...'

'I *liked* it there,' Jack insisted, ignoring her reply. 'The staff were good to me and the other lads were all right, you know.'

'The secure unit is for *offenders* only,' Olivia countered briskly. 'You've served your time, you've been passed fit for release, so you can't stay there.'

'But I'm not ready.'

'You have to be, Jack. You're a free man. This is your life now. You should enjoy it.'

Olivia was aware how lame this sounded, given their uninspiring surroundings, and was about to make a joke of it, when she realized that the spotty nineteen-year-old was crying.

'Please, just *talk* to them,' he moaned quietly, whimpering. 'Make them see. If I *want* to be locked up, isn't that best for everyone?'

'That's not for me to say,' Olivia replied carefully, shocked by this sudden show of distress. 'The rules are the rules. The Probation Service has assessed you, passed you fit for rehabilitation. I know you're scared, I know you feel lost, helpless even, but I've been down this road before, with young men just like you. And it *does* work.'

Jack looked up at her, his eyes wet with tears, disbelief in his expression.

'Honestly, Jack, you've got so much going for you. A place to stay, a job to go to, training opportunities to exploit, plus I'll be visiting you twice a day to make sure you're keeping your head above water. What d'you say? Can we make this work *together*?'

Jack shrugged, wiping his tears away, which Olivia took as a positive, so she pressed on.

'Let's go over your story again, just to make sure all the details have sunk in. Name?'

'Jack Walker,' he replied, his voice shaking slightly.

'Very good. Any middle names?'

'No, my parents didn't approve of them.'

'Excellent. Age?'

'Twenty.'

'Date of birth?'

'Third of April, 2003.'

'Where you from, Kyle?'

'Sorry? My name's Jack.'

Nodding her approval, Olivia continued, gratified to see the hint of a smile on the teenager's lips, clearly pleased not to have fallen for her trick.

'Where you from, Jack?'

'Epping originally, now Tottenham Hale.'

'Family live close by?'

'Parents are out in Spain, got a sister in Birmingham. Married, but no kids.'

'Do you get on?'

'She's all right, I suppose. All sisters are a pain in the arse basically.'

Olivia suppressed a smile. For such a recalcitrant probationer, the street-wise teenager was a decent actor.

'You in good health?'

'Not bad, got a bit of asthma.'

'What about your medical history? Any past emergencies or operations?'

'Broke my arm when I was nine. Needed surgery to repair it. I got this scar, see ...'

Jack rolled up his top to reveal a long scar on his right arm. Actually this historic injury was the result of a stabbing, but the wound was so straight and faint that you'd never know.

'Well done, Jack. That's very good. Stick to that story and you'll be absolutely fine.'

Jack looked up at her, still suspicious, but perhaps hoping she might be right.

'Before I go, I'm obliged to remind you of the conditions of your licence,' the probation officer continued swiftly, keen to get this part over with. 'No booze, no drugs. No visitors to the house without my permission. No unsupervised access to the internet, no contact with children whatsoever and no return to Southend under any circumstances.'

'Why would I want to go back to that shithole?' Jack fired back tersely.

'That's the spirit. Just make sure you abide by those rules, that's all. Because if you don't, you'll be behind bars quicker than you can fart, and it won't be a young offenders' unit this time. It'll be a Category A prison, with all the danger and unpleasantness that entails. Got that?'

Jack nodded, but said nothing. Olivia was used to this – her clients half resenting her, half needing her – so she let it pass without comment.

'There's some basics in the fridge, but I'll be back tomorrow with a batch of ready meals and some treats. For now, settle in, watch some TV and make sure you're ready for work in the morning. Here's the details of where you need to be, when you need to be there, and who your point of contact is.'

She handed Jack a neatly typed A4 sheet of paper.

'It's only labouring work, but a strong boy like you should thrive there and you'll earn a decent wage too. The foreman often employs ex-cons, but obviously doesn't know your real history. He thinks you've just finished a six-month stretch for minor county lines stuff. Don't do or say anything to disabuse him of that fact.'

Jack pulled a face, clearly confused by her use of a three-syllable word.

'Stick to the cover story,' Olivia clarified. 'An older "mate" got you into running packets, but you're well shot of him now and so on...'

Jack nodded, back on track, earning a smile from Olivia.

'Honestly, you've got this, Jack. I know you've never lived a regular life, but it's easier than you think. And it might just be the making of you. So, please, take this opportunity. Not many people are afforded a second chance, but you have been. So seize it.'

Walking back to her Corsa, Olivia wondered if her message had got through. Jack had nodded, said all the right things, and had seemed proud of his accurate recall of his new identity and personal history, but perhaps he was just telling her what she wanted to hear? Olivia sensed there was something missing, a sense of conviction, of belief perhaps that he could make a go of it. Perhaps he was just too damaged to start again, as so many of them were. He certainly seemed distressed at the prospect of his new life, a grim irony given the outrage his release had provoked in the press and social media. If they could only see him now, Olivia thought grimly, as she hurried away from the non-descript house.

Her day had been difficult enough, but it wasn't done with her just yet – a fresh parking ticket decorated the windscreen of her car. Cursing, Olivia snatched it off, climbing inside the ageing Corsa and tossing the ticket onto the back seat, where half a dozen other Penalty Charge Notices nestled. Olivia didn't give it a moment's thought, as she fired up the engine of her protesting hatchback. She was already late for her next meeting.

Chapter 3

Emily Lawrence kept her head down as she strode through the driving rain. It was a grim day in Bridgend, bitter and unforgiving, and most of the residents were sheltering inside, which suited Emily fine. She didn't need an audience for this particular pilgrimage.

Clutching her bouquet, she walked quickly down the neatly clipped pathway, casting occasional glances at the well-tended headstones on either side, some of which had been decorated for the festive season. Names, dates and family tragedies washed over her – mothers who'd died young, twins who'd been lost at birth, loving couples separated for years before their eventual reunion – but she registered nothing, barely caring for other people's disasters. Perhaps this was justifiable, as she had her own, powerful reasons for being here or maybe it was just her nature. People had always said she was selfish.

Reaching a fork in the path, she veered right, making her way to their graves as if on auto-pilot. She came here religiously twice a year, to mark Susan's, then Gwyneth's birthday, and barely paid attention to her route anymore. Her feet, not to mention her heart and conscience, took her where she needed to go. Emily never dawdled, never engaged in conversation, discharging her duty swiftly and efficiently, before heading home feeling hollow and grim. Sometimes, after a particularly upsetting visit, she would ask herself if she really *needed* to come here, to put herself through this agony year on year. But she knew the answer before the question was even posed, which is why she once more found herself in Bridgend Cemetery. It was fitting that the weather should be so grim today, Emily thought to herself, a flood of painful memories tumbling one over another.

Shaking off her dark thoughts, Emily slowed as she reached the graves, double-checking that there was no one else present before approaching them. The headstones remained immaculate, looking almost polished in the gentle glow of the winter sun. The floral displays were vivid and fresh, the dark marble gleamed and the gold lettering was crisp and clear, spelling out the details of their tragedy:

Susan Slater, born August 1991, died March 1992
Gwyneth Slater, born April 1988, died November 1992
Gone too soon. Forever in our hearts.

Emily had read these words countless times, but their brevity, their simple power, always took her breath away. A sob escaped from her, her vision blurring as tears sprung to her eyes. She clutched the bouquet tightly, seeking solace, even as the thorns dug painfully into her skin. It was too shocking, too distressing to take in, the thought of those innocent little girls dying in such terrible circumstances, but there was no ducking the reality of their torment. It was something that had to be acknowledged, fully and frequently, to keep the tragedy of their murders alive. Time did not heal, nor should it, not when their deaths had been so pointless and so wicked.

'Know them, did you?'

Startled, Emily spun round to find an elderly man looking at her. Blinking her tears away, she took in this intruder, a smart, military type, wrapped up against the cold in a heavy coat and scarf. The man's accent was local, his eyes shrewd and intelligent, but Emily didn't recognize him and his question appeared to be an innocent one.

'Not particularly,' she lied. 'Just wanted to pay my respects.'

At first, the old boy said nothing, intrigued perhaps as to why a middle-aged woman should have come out in such dire weather to visit the graves of two strangers. Then slowly his features relaxed into a sad smile.

'Just visited my Iris, but I always stop here for a minute on my way back, to offer a prayer for the little ones...'

His voice caught as he spoke and Emily turned away, undone by this stranger's emotion.

'Doesn't bear thinking about, what they went through...'

Emily nodded, but didn't turn back, bending down to place her flowers on the graves. As she did so, she noticed that there were beads of blood where she had been gripping the thorny stems and she swiftly tucked her hands into her pockets to conceal the damage.

'Beggars belief, really, what some people are capable of...'

The old man was warming to his theme, wallowing in this infamous local tragedy, building perhaps to some terrible denunciation, but Emily couldn't listen to another word. Nodding sadly at him, she took her leave, retracing her steps down the path, keen to be rid of his presence, free of this terrible place.

Every year she came and every year she was desperate to be gone, but this visit had been worse than usual. The pain, the guilt, the anguish she'd come to expect, but the pensioner's pointed intervention had summoned an emotion she had long since buried – fear. His rich, local accent, his raw emotion, his evident disgust *thirty years on* had thrust her back to a time when her name was a byword for savagery and evil, when the locals would have willingly torn her limb from limb, when she wasn't ordinary, upstanding, unremarkable Emily Lawrence. The memories terrified her even now and she could feel her whole body shaking as she hurried towards the exit. No visit to Bridgend was without risk and perhaps she had been complacent to believe she could come and go undetected. The old gent seemed kindly enough and didn't appear to be levelling a particular accusation at her, but how could she tell for sure?

Sometimes she felt people could see right through her.

Chapter 4

His eyes were fixed to the TV screen, his emotions in riot.

'Joining us on the sofa today is Alison Burnham, whose daughter Jessie was murdered in 2013 by schoolgirls Courtney Turner and Kaylee Jones. The perpetrators of that terrible crime, only eleven years old at the time, have subsequently been released back into the community. Since then, Alison has campaigned tirelessly for longer custodial sentences for minors who commit serious crimes...'

Mike Burnham shook his head furiously, unsure whether he was angrier with the BBC for exploiting their grief or with Alison for agreeing to appear on their show in the first place. He knew his ex-wife felt she was doing good, creating something positive out of an awful tragedy, but it was so painful to hear the details of that day replayed ad nauseam and, besides, what good did it do? Nobody ever listened to the victims. It was the perpetrators, the offenders, who got all the attention, the criminal justice system bending over backwards to accommodate *them*. Campaigning might take Alison's mind off their shared trauma, but in the end it changed nothing.

'Mike, are you OK to...?'

He now became aware that the showroom PA was still waiting for him to sign the sales contract. Running his eye over the inventory of windows and doors, Mike scribbled his signature, then moved away, positioning himself closer to the TV, drinking in the presenter's words:

'This morning, Kyle Peters, who murdered Billy Armstrong in Southend in 2015, was released from custody, rehoused some-where in the UK under a new identity. Alison, as someone who's already been through this, who's had to face up to the release of your daughter's killers, what are your feelings this morning?'

'Well, obviously my heart goes out to Billy's family. I know exactly how they're feeling, how angry and upset they must be. I've always believed that murder should carry a mandatory life sentence, regardless of the age of perpetrator and here, once again, we have an example of the criminal justice system letting down the victim and their family.'

Why? Why did she have to keep doing this? Every time Mike thought he might be getting back to some kind of normal, when people might see him as an everyday bloke, rather than the father of a murdered child, up popped Alison, on the TV, on radio, talking about Jessica, about Courtney Turner and Kaylee Jones, ramming it down everyone's throats. Why did she feel compelled to do this?

'Of course,' the presenter cooed. 'I suppose days like this must bring back painful memories of what happened to *your* family. The death of little Jessie, the arrest, the trial ...'

'No,' Mike hissed, angry and aggrieved. 'It was Jessica, never Jessie ...'

Heads were starting to turn in the office, but Mike couldn't help himself. The papers, the news channels had decided to call their daughter 'Jessie', because it sounded cuter, more tragic. But she had never been called that, not by *anyone*.

'Get your facts straight!' he muttered angrily. 'Do your bloody job.'

On the TV, Alison had ignored the gaffe, responding to the question, playing their game.

'It's had a profound effect on Jessica's younger sister, Rachel, but we've all suffered. I left my job shortly after it happened, then my marriage broke down ...'

When would she stop? What would any of this *achieve*, except humiliating those who'd already suffered enough. It beggared belief that Alison could be so naïve.

'Sorry, Mike, me again ...'

Snapping out of it, Mike turned to find that the sheepish PA had returned.

'It's just that your ten o'clock is waiting for you ...'

She nodded towards customer reception, where a middle-aged couple loitered impatiently.

'Sorry, I was miles away ...'

She smiled at him sympathetically, but said nothing, looking slightly uncomfortable, as if unsure how to handle him. Scanning the office, Mike now realized that several co-workers were staring at him, clearly unnerved by his angry mutterings at the TV. Suddenly Mike felt foolish and embarrassed, which only angered him further. What did he have to be embarrassed about? *He'd* done nothing wrong.

Snatching up his jacket, he tried to regain his composure, but Alison's words intruded again.

'Of course, the biggest thing is just missing our little girl. She always brought such light, such joy into any room she entered ...'

Mike shut his eyes – his aching grief rearing up once more, threatening to overwhelm him – before wrenching himself back to the present, clamping down his emotions. Turning away, he snatched up the remote control, angrily switching off the TV, before marching grimly towards the showroom, twelve sets of eyeballs following him every step of the way.

Chapter 5

He dragged the armchair across the room, placing it in front of the TV. Pausing to admire his handiwork, Jack puffed out his cheeks, frowning. Here he would have his back to the door, which unnerved him, so he returned the chair to its original position. This game of musical chairs was diverting – at the young offenders' unit every stick of furniture had been screwed to the floor. Here he could move anything he wanted, as often as he wanted, making the place reflect his desires, his needs and his personality, whatever that was.

This, however, appeared to be the only advantage of his new situation and Jack would have returned to the unit in a heartbeat, given the opportunity. It was unquestionably the best place he'd ever lived, the only place he'd ever felt *safe*. His family home had been a vortex of chaos, violence and abuse, with never a good word or deed meted out. By contrast, the unit had been a model of good order, discipline and endeavour. Jack had had a varied timetable of lessons and activities, plenty of sporting opportunities, cash to spend at the tuck shop and regular sessions on the PS5. It hadn't all been plain sailing, of course. In spite of everything he missed his family, was sad that his mum's visits had tailed off, but overall it had been a good experience. The lads, a motley crew of car thieves, arsonists and drug dealers, were decent company and trustworthy too – better brothers to him than his real ones had ever been.

It was their humour, their banter, their presence that Jack missed now. Eddie, the mixed-race kid who never backed down from a challenge, outdoing guys twice his size with his sharp tongue and total lack of fear. Tally, the inveterate practical joker and gifted artist, who did brilliant caricatures of their teachers, and of course Deano, who'd always looked out for Jack, despite having a pretty good idea who he really was. He never did get to the bottom of Deano's loyalty and affection towards him, but it'd felt good and he yearned for it now.

What was there for him here, in this strange house, in this strange city? Nothing but boredom and despair. He'd never been good in his own company, never good at sitting still and the *last* thing he needed was time to think. He wanted to be busy, active, distracted, like he had been at the unit, but here it was just him on his own, with little to do. Sure, he could turn on the TV, watch one of the carefully selected channels, but would that really fill the void? Banish those dark, nagging thoughts that threatened to overwhelm him? For it wasn't just boredom that made Jack jumpy and distracted tonight. It was fear.

He hadn't said this in front of his probation officer, the well-meaning Olivia, but he was petrified, uncertain of how he'd survive here, of what the future might hold, of what would happen if his cover was blown. There was real fury out there about his release. Tabloid journalists, members of the investigating police force, even total strangers would gladly string him up, but their bile was nothing compared to the fury of his victim's relatives. If he closed his eyes, Jack could still picture the boy's dad screaming at him as he was led away, egged on by a couple of his brothers, who looked like they wanted to tear him apart. Over the years, they'd trumpeted their belief that Jack deserved a sudden, brutal death and their damning verdict had met with considerable support in the wider world. To the general public, Jack was despicable, beyond contempt, a stain on society. He'd glimpsed the newsstands on the drive here, seen the headlines proclaiming the FACE OF EVIL, just above that hideous photo of him in that shitty tracksuit, his hair awry, his expression sullen. That was all the world knew of him – that mugshot of misery and degradation – and it's all they *wanted* to know. They didn't care about his own situation, his side of the story – no, he was inhuman, a dog that needed to be put down. This was his legacy, his reward, for his crimes: hostility, isolation and danger.

And what did he have to keep him from these morbid thoughts? To stop him slowly losing his mind? Nothing, except the crushing silence of this lifeless house. Jack was trying to put a brave face on things, to make a go of his new situation, but in truth he had never felt so lonely, so miserable, so scared as he did tonight.

Chapter 6

She could tell straight away that something was up.

Olivia had battled her way back to the Probation Service's HQ in Petty France, just a stone's throw from St James's Park, expecting to have to sit through another six-month appraisal, but she'd barely set foot on the fifth floor when she felt it – a surge of nervous energy pulsing through the department. Colleagues hurried past, phones rang incessantly and above it all throbbed a buzz of fevered conversation.

Walking to her desk, Olivia spotted Isaac Green, gesturing to him to join her. The fifty-five-year-old veteran limped over, half amused, half disappointed by the blank look on her face.

'Always the last to know, aren't you?'

'Don't take the piss, Isaac. What's going on?'

Seating himself on her desk, Isaac leaned in close, lowering his voice as he replied:

'Liam Sullivan was chased to his death in Bolton this morning. Jumped off a walkway into a busy dual carriageway to escape three crowbar-wielding thugs.'

'Who's Liam Sullivan?' Olivia demanded.

'Real name – Mark Willis.'

Now Olivia knew what was up.

'Jesus Christ, I worked with that guy,' she responded

breathlessly. 'I mean I monitored him when he first moved to Bolton. He was the twelve-year-old—'

'Who raped and murdered a seventy-eight-year-old widow. Now you're getting it...'

It was said with dark humour, but Isaac's expression belied his levity. This was a disaster, a catastrophic failure for the Probation Service, and everyone in the building knew it.

'Do we know what happened?' Olivia asked urgently.

'Just that, so far. Willis has been hidden away in Bolton for the past four years, living in a crummy flat, working in a logistics factory. He was making a go of it, more or less. Couple of minors for theft, drug use, but nothing concerning. Anyway, witnesses say he got jumped in the early hours of this morning by three men wearing pig masks.'

A snort of shocked laughter escaped from Olivia before she could stop it, drawing a disapproving look from Saul, her new colleague. Turning away, she whispered incredulously:

'They were dressed as pigs?'

'Crowbar-wielding pigs, if you can believe it. The police are investigating whether it was gang-related, something to do with drugs or—'

'Not bloody likely. Willis was a worm, a coward. He wouldn't have the nerve for anything like that, defenceless old women were more his line. This must have been a revenge attack.'

'Which is why top brass have been locked in a crisis meeting for the last two hours. A security breach like this, well... it's headline news.'

This was the understatement of the year. If it was true, if Mark Willis's cover had been blown by vigilantes or vengeful relatives, then it would dominate the news agenda for weeks. Nothing as serious as this had happened in the history of the Probation Service and it spelled serious trouble for everyone involved.

'Look at them all,' Isaac continued, nodding towards the boardroom, which was packed with the Service's directorate. 'What's that saying about a piss-up and a brewery?'

As Isaac continued to vent, bemoaning the current state of the Service, Olivia's gaze drifted to the coterie of smartly dressed men and women closeted away in the director's office. They were a mixed bag in terms of background, experience and expertise – some committed and hard-working, some mediocre time-servers, others openly beleaguered and cynical. But they all shared the same expression today – grave concern mixed with a sprinkling of panic. Olivia took them in one by one, curious to know who was speaking, what their mood was and even what they were saying, but it was hard to lip-read from this distance. She took in hatchet-faced Bridget, who adored a crisis, before moving on to Philip, the most stolid of board members, before her eyes finally alighted on Christopher Parkes, a handsome, saturnine fifty-something who was sitting very still, listening to the frenetic offerings of others. Could he feel her gaze upon him? Or was Olivia imagining it? Either way, the deputy director now turned slightly in his seat, his gaze shifting to meet hers. For a moment he held eye contact, a pulse of electricity passing between them, then he returned his attention to the meeting.

'Are you even listening to me?' Isaac complained, his torrent of complaints coming to a sudden end.

Snapping out of it, Olivia smiled goofily at Isaac, earning a weary smile from her colleague.

'Absolutely, Isaac. And I agree with everything you've said.'

'Of course you do...'

Shaking his head, he departed, hobbling back to his desk. Olivia watched him go, taking time to scan the rest of the department. This room, the cavernous remnant of better-funded days, was usually scarcely a third full at best, but today every desk was taken; probation officers, both senior and junior, fielding emails, reviewing protocols, making calls to check that their clients were safe. It was the most perfect visual expression of panic that you could hope to see – a testament to the profound shock everyone felt at Mark Willis's murder. Settling herself down, Olivia logged in, pulling up *her* files, reaching for *her* phone, preparing herself for a series of difficult conversations. There were still so many unknowns about the murder in Bolton – the who, how, why of this nasty crime – but one thing was clear: for Olivia, and everyone else in the building, Christmas had just been cancelled.

Chapter 7

'O little town of Bethlehem, how still we see thee lie. Above thy deep and dreamless sleep, the silent stars go by...'

The Salvation Army were singing their hearts out, entertaining the shoppers on Croydon High Street as they rattled their collection tins. Russell Morgan liked a good carol, had happy memories of singing in church as a boy, but this lusty rendition held no interest for him and he strolled by without a second glance. Tonight he only had eyes for Amber.

'Tell me to shut up if I'm boring you. I could go on all night about the follies of my youth,' Amber said good-naturedly, as they strolled beneath the High Street's twinkling lights.

'Are you kidding me? I love listening to you.'

Amber laughed, blushing. Russell suddenly felt foolish, as if he'd said too much, so qualified his enthusiasm:

'I mean I love hearing about you. What you've been through, what your plans are...'

He meant it, but it was also true that he *did* love listening to Amber's voice – so soft, so kind, so feminine. It was too early in their friendship to be that honest, however. The pair had only known each other for three weeks, Amber a new attendee at his twice-weekly Narcotics Anonymous sessions and though he'd been instantly smitten by the blonde twenty-something, he didn't want to come across as a try-hard or, worse, a lech.

'I'm not sure there's too much more to tell,' Amber replied, seemingly unaware of his embarrassment. 'You've heard about my long association with my old friends Charlie and Horse and, as for future plans, well I'm not sure I've got any. Surviving, I guess.'

Russell let the drug references go, didn't want to think about that, his own substance abuse a distant memory now. No, he wanted to know more about the real Amber, what her current situation was and whether *he* might figure in her future plans.

'What about Christmas? You in London or...?'

'Sure, I'll be around. Got nowhere else to go if I'm honest.'

A cloud seemed to descend on Amber now, her mood suddenly sombre. Russell immediately regretted asking – a stupid, blundering enquiry – but to be fair to himself, he was totally out of practice. He hadn't shown any real interest in anyone in years.

'Sorry, you don't need to talk about it, if you don't want to,' he suggested.

'No, it's all right,' Amber reassured him. 'I just find this time of year hard. Used to love it as a kid. Me, my mum and my sister would really go to town, buying each other all sorts of mad, foolish things. Plus there was always plenty of food and booze around. But the best bit... the very best bit was our trips to Brighton, to see the Christmas lights. I'd love to do that again, in fact I'd love to see *them* again... but I wouldn't be welcome at home, so I guess it'll just be me and the King's speech this year...'

It was said with a wry smile, but was laced with sadness.

'I'm sorry, Amber, that's tough. But if it's any consolation I know how you feel.'

'You a Billy No Mates too?' she teased. 'A Single Pringle...'

'More or less,' he shrugged, smiling.

'Well don't go all coy on me, Russell. What do they say at the group? Sharing is caring...'

Russell laughed, then replied:

'How long have you got?'

'All the time in the world,' Amber replied.

This was obviously a bald statement of fact, but was there something else in her tone too? Encouragement? Affection?

'Dad's in prison, Mum's long dead,' Russell confided. 'It's just me and my older brother, Chaz. He's an addict too, so I try and steer clear of him. I moved down to London from Luton to get away from all that shit, been making my own way here ever since. I'm a trained accountant, but hope to be a CFO soon, perhaps even start my own business one day...'

His cover story poured from him, lie upon lie, smoothly delivered and effortlessly believable. Funny to think that this process used to stress him out – trying to remember the details, labouring not to make mistakes. Now he positively enjoyed the performance, living every moment of his 'history', embellishing every event, talking up every future dream. In fact, so good was he at trotting out these fabrications, so practised at climbing inside his new identity after eighteen years, that he could scarcely differentiate the truth from the fiction anymore. Which is the way he liked it.

Slipping his arm through Amber's, he continued to regurgitate his fake life story, strolling happily through the lunchtime crowds with his new friend, bathed in the warm glow of the twinkling Christmas lights.

Chapter 8

Pulling up outside her modest house, Emily Lawrence was alarmed to see the lights blazing in the front room. Frowning, she looked at the clock. She had made good time, burning down the M4 from Wales to Reading, returning home a couple of hours before Sam was due back from school. She'd hoped to have a moment to compose herself, to process the emotions that her visits to Bridgend always provoked, in order to be her usual cheery self when he eventually returned home. But the lights that peeked through the drawn curtains set alarm bells ringing. She'd turned everything off when she left this morning, drawn the curtains, double-locked the door, ensuring the house was as secure and inconspicuous as possible. So who'd entered in the interim? Who was inside her home?

Closing the car door quietly, Emily hurried towards the door, pulling out her key. It was unlikely to be her probation officer – she only came once a month and always called ahead. Was it Paul? It was possible, but her ex-husband didn't have a key, so how would he have gained access? Could it be someone else then, someone with malign intent? But if so, why advertise their presence by leaving the lights on? Was it possible, then, that she'd been robbed? That would be a disaster, especially so close to Christmas...

A dozen terrible thoughts flooded Emily's mind, but as she hesitantly put the key in the lock, she heard laughter within. Straining, she could now make out the low thrum of male conversation and the unmistakable sound of an X-Box shoot 'em up.

'Bloody hell, Sam,' she muttered angrily, jamming her key in the lock and hurrying inside.

Closing the front door, she dumped her bag in the hall and wasted no time bursting into the front room. As she made her dramatic entrance, two teenage boys leapt to their feet. Both Sam and his best mate Gavin looked startled, then as the realization of the situation sunk in, busted.

'What the hell's going on, Sam? It's two o'clock in the afternoon. Why aren't you at school?'

There was a brief silence, then:

'Free period.'

'You're in Year 10 – you don't get free periods.'

'Spot on, Mrs Lawrence,' Gavin responded gamely. 'It was actually an inset day. Sam and I clean forg—'

'Don't give me that, you had an inset day two weeks ago. Have you been at school at all today?'

This was aimed at her son and his guilty expression told her all she needed to know.

'You bunked off?'

'To be fair, Mrs Lawrence, Sam wasn't feeling well. I offered to stay with him until you got—'

'Button it, you,' Emily countered, slapping him down. 'I've had enough of your lies and cheap charm. I can see straight through you, Gavin Williams, so take your bad attitude, your lying mouth and get out of my house. I don't want to see you round here again.'

Gavin looked stunned, as if he'd just been slapped, but Sam now leapt to his defence.

'Don't talk to him like that – he's my friend.'

'Some friend. All he does is lead you astray.'

'That's not true. It was my idea to bunk off today, Gavin tried to talk me out it.'

'To be fair, that is true,' Gavin agreed, but his hopes of a reprieve were swiftly dashed.

'Are you still here?' Emily demanded.

This time the gawky teen got the message, scooping up his bag.

'Sorry, mate,' he said by way of departure, hastening from the room. Moments later, the front door slammed shut.

'What the hell were you thinking?' Emily demanded, rounding on her son. 'Since when have you started bunking off?'

'I've only done it a couple of times, it's no biggie.'

'No biggie?' Emily exploded. 'You've got GCSEs next year!'

'And I'll do fine, OK? It was mostly science today and you know I'm good at that.'

'That's not the point. You're at school to learn and you can't do that playing Call of Duty with that prat. Plus, I like to know where you are at all times, you know I do. Speaking of which, why didn't I get a call from school, asking me where you were today?'

Now Sam looked even more sheepish.

'I ... er ... sent an email from Dad's account, explaining that I had a doctor's appointment.'

'Does he know about this?'

'Of course not.'

'Well, he will, you can be sure of that.'

'Oh for God's sake, Mum. Why are you being such a bitch about this?'

The word was out of his mouth before he could stop it. Emily glared at him, enraged, upset. Now it was her turn to feel like she'd been slapped.

'Sorry, Mum, I didn't mean—'

'I'm being a *bitch* because I have made endless sacrifices to bring you up right, to send you to that school, to ensure you turn out a decent, honest, law-abiding kid. I have *never* put myself first, always been there for you, because I want you to succeed in life. I'm being a *bitch* because I love you and don't want you to see you throw your life away. And this is how you repay me? By lying to me, insulting me—'

'I've said I'm sorry, Mum, I didn't mean to—'

'Too little, too late. You're grounded, mate. For a week. And you can kiss goodbye to the X-box for a while. At this rate, you'll be lucky to get it back by Christmas.'

Sam stared at her, stunned by the severity of the punishment. Emily sensed she'd overcooked it perhaps, but she was fizzing with anger and, besides, there was no question of retracting the sanction now. Part of her was pleased to have punished him, part of her fearful of the consequences, but she hoped he might at least acknowledge his culpability and accept his punishment. Sam, however, had other ideas, rounding on her, eyes blazing.

'I hate you. I bloody *hate* you.'

'Sam…'

Emily reached out to him, but the enraged teenager pushed angrily past her, exiting the room and slamming the door behind him. The sound, the vibration went right through Emily, jangling her nerves and compounding her misery. She'd tried so hard to be a good mum, to raise a well-rounded, polite child, to create a happy well-balanced family. And most days she felt she'd succeeded, despite the failure of her marriage and the occasional bust-up with her hormonal son. Today, however, she felt like an utter failure.

Perhaps she *was* a bitch after all.

Chapter 9

Mike Burnham walked fast down the street, trying to block out the festive joy. It was only eleven days until Christmas and the residents of Maidstone had gone to town, but Mike kept his eyes fixed on the pavement, ignoring his neighbour's cheerful greetings, the illuminated snowflakes that danced manically on people's houses. A lusty version of 'Once in Royal David's City' blared from one of the houses he passed, accompanied by raucous laughter and conversation within, but Mike pressed on, quickly reaching his front door and disappearing inside, consumed by the darkness of the one house in the street that had no decorations, no fairy lights, no life.

How Mike loathed Christmas. Once it had been the highlight of his year, he and Alison saving for months to ensure the girls had everything they wanted. The expense always outweighed their savings, and they'd often had to borrow to make up the shortfall, but it had always been worth it to see the presents under the tree, the table groaning with Christmas fare and the smiles on the girls' faces. Now, however, he despised the festive season, the whole grim charade serving only to remind him of all he had lost.

Hanging up his coat, Mike hastened into the lounge. It was dark and quiet, which is how he liked it. Normally he would collapse onto the sofa, losing himself in the mindless colour of Sky Sports, transporting himself to a sun-kissed golf course in Saudi Arabia or a raucous football stadium in Manchester, but tonight he set about tidying the place, clearing away takeaway cartons and discarded newspapers. This evening, he was expecting company.

Flicking on the lights, Mike drew the curtains, turning to survey the scene. The rubbish was gone, the cushions straightened, but the place still looked cheerless and cold, so Mike fussed about, lighting the lamps, switching on the radio, doing whatever he could to make the place seem more welcoming. When he and Alison had been together, this had been her domain – she had a natural eye for interior design and had always been the more sociable of the two. Now that he was alone, these domestic duties fell to him and he realized to his dismay how dusty everything was, a thick line of the stuff clinging to every surface. Grabbing a cloth, he set to work, sending great plumes spiralling into the air.

Time was of the essence and he set to it like a dervish, building up a sweat, but as he dusted the small collection of framed photos on the sideboard, he slowed, pausing to look at his favourite picture of Jessica. It was taken at her school fair, Jessica sitting in her wheelchair, her face painted, grinning broadly at the camera. It was a picture that he loved more than life itself and he drank in the details. Her wonky glasses, her rosy cheeks, her impish smile – they were all part of what had made his daughter so special. His little fighter, who'd never been able to walk because of her cerebral palsy, but who'd never let it hold her back, living life to the full, always with a cheeky grin on her face. This treasured photo seemed to define her, seemed to bring her back to life and looking at it, Mike felt his heart burst with love, with pride, with grief. If only he could turn back time, so he could hold his angel in his arms once more...

The sharp buzz of the doorbell cut through these fond dreams. Wiping away his tears, Mike quickly replaced the photo and hurried into the hallway. Taking a moment to compose himself, he opened the front door to find Graham Ellis waiting outside.

'Graham, how nice to see you,' Mike said, trying to sound composed and cheerful.

'You sure you're expecting me?' his visitor replied amiably. 'I've been ringing for five minutes.'

'So how have you been keeping?' his visitor asked.

The two men were seated at the kitchen table, beers in hand.

'Muddling along. Work's fine, though it's always mental at this time of year.'

'Seeing much of Alison and Rachel?'

'When I can,' Mike replied carefully. 'Things are still difficult with me and Alison, but I try to do right by Rachel. She's had lots on. Christmas productions, parties and what not...'

'Tell me about it.'

Graham Ellis smiled as he said this, his genuine affection for every member of the family clear. Back in his former incarnation as a detective inspector with Kent Police, Graham had led the team that had brought Jessica's killers to justice and Mike knew he still looked in on Alison and Rachel. He was grateful for this, but it also made him feel uncomfortable, worrying that the retired police officer knew more about his daughter's life than he did.

'And how are you in yourself?' Graham asked, running a hand through his thinning hair. 'Are you OK, Mike?'

'Sure, why not?' Mike responded evasively. 'I'm getting on with things. Once Christmas is done and dusted, I'm going to sort this place out.'

Graham nodded, taking in the stained Formica surfaces and

faded kitchen units. Mike suddenly felt idiotic, embarrassed by his empty promises. Graham had been visiting him here for years now and knew full well that Mike had made no attempt to decorate the place in all that time. Mike turned to his old friend now, feeling the need to justify himself, to explain his lack of effort, but the retired inspector's gaze was elsewhere, fixed on a copy of the *Sun* that Mike had tidied away before his arrival. On the front cover was a police mug shot of a truculent twelve-year-old boy and above it the strap line:

The Face of Evil. Sadistic Killer Kyle Peters released

Mike took in the headline, once more feeling a stab of anger, then looked up to find Graham staring directly at him.

'It must be hard for you,' the policeman said sympathetically.

'Is that why you've come round? To check up on me?'

There was a harsh, accusatory tone to his question, but Graham Ellis ignored it.

'Partly. I know it must bring back painful memories. I remember the anger you felt when Courtney and Kaylee were released, God knows I felt it myself, so I just wanted you to know that you're not alone, that I'm here for you if you need to talk.'

'I'm sorry, Graham, I shouldn't snap at you,' Mike responded, suddenly feeling petty and unworthy of his kindness. 'But you're right, it is hard. It's *bloody* hard.'

Mike wanted to stop there, to swallow down his bile, but he couldn't.

'*It's just not right*. People like that should never be let out.'

'With respect, Mike, that's not for you or me to decide, whatever we may feel about it personally.'

'Well, it *should* be. Those animals ...' Mike spat back, his voice thick with emotion. 'Those animals who murdered my little girl got seven years in a young offenders' unit, before being released. Seven years. Is that all Jessica's life was worth?'

'Of course not, Mike. But that's not how it works.'

'And where are they now? Living nice lives, in a new town, with new names, getting ready to enjoy a lovely Christmas no doubt, while the rest of us are left to suffer, to wallow and rot in our own misery *because of what they did*. It'll be the same for this piece of shit...'

He nodded aggressively at Kyle Peters' mug shot.

'...living the life of Riley somewhere – happy, carefree. Where's the *justice* in that?'

'I know and I sympathise. If I'd had my way, they would have stayed behind bars for longer, *much* longer.'

'Well then...'

'But don't think that it's easy street for them either. They are very damaged individuals, who'll have to live with what they did for the rest of their lives.'

'That's a joke,' Mike shot back. 'Do you think they care two hoots about us? About what they did? You were there, Graham. You saw those girls laughing and joking in court.'

'They were eleven years old, Mike. They didn't know what they were doing.'

'Bullshit. They knew *exactly* what they were doing. And what's to stop them doing it again?'

'They are very closely monitored,' the ex-police officer protested. 'And have to abide by very restrictive licence conditions.'

'Really, Graham? Do you *really* believe that? The Probation Service is a shambles, you know it is. Meaning that these creatures are at liberty to do what they like, when they like. And you may be fine with that...'

'I'm not. Of course I'm not.'

'…but I think it's outrageous, dangerous, criminal. Those girls, this Kyle Peters, could be living next door to you, spying on your kids, plotting their next crime and you'd know nothing about it. The courts, the police, the Probation Service bend over backwards to help them, rehousing them, giving them new identities, new histories, helping them to lie, to cheat, to get away with murder. It's not right, but more than that, it's not *safe*.'

He fired out the last word, glaring at Graham Ellis. But still his guest refused to lose his cool.

'Mike, what you went through, the pain you've endured, is unimaginable. I know you've lost so much, so many people you loved, and that as a result your trust in people, in institutions, has been very badly shaken. But you can't live like that forever. You can't always assume the worst. Jessica's killers were passed fit for rehabilitation, just like Kyle Peters, so we have to hope, to assume, that they're living safe, productive lives.'

'Don't be so naïve. Rehabilitation is a meaningless concept to these animals; they don't feel a shred of guilt for what they did. You interviewed them, for God's sake. To them it was all a big joke, a game…'

'You're right,' Graham Ellis replied, shaking his head sadly. 'I never saw any remorse, any regret from either of them. So I *do* understand your anger. But however much grief and pain you still feel, you mustn't let this rage consume you. It's not what Jessica would have wanted.'

It was a low blow, but it struck home, Mike painfully aware of how shocked his little girl would have been to see him so vengeful and bitter.

'It's already cost you so much. Your marriage, your relationship with Rachel. I know you feel that you'll never get over this, but somehow you have to try and look *forwards*. Take up those offers of counselling, make arrangements to see Rachel, re-connect with your parents, your friends. Get out there, try and have some fun, perhaps even meet someone...'

Mike shook his head dismissively.

'And land all this baggage on them?'

Mike looked up now, expecting some sympathy, some acknowledgment of the scale of the task. But his old friend's expression was stern and unforgiving.

'If that's what it takes to turn your life around, then yes. It's vitally important that you concentrate on the things that *matter*,' he responded slowly. 'Alison, Rachel, your work. Christmas is coming too. I know this is always a tough time, but why don't you go to town this year? It's been a good year for you financially, so why not enjoy the fruits of your labour? Spoil Rachel. Spoil *yourself*.'

'It's not that easy.'

'Only because you insist on punishing yourself, Mike. I know you blame yourself for what happened to Jessica—'

'How could I not?' Mike interrupted brusquely, his anger flaring. 'If I hadn't been late picking her up, those animals would never have taken her. If I'd been five minutes earlier, if I'd arrived when I said I was going to—'

'No,' Graham warned. 'You can't carry on doing this to yourself, Mike. It wasn't your fault, it wasn't Jessica's fault, the only people to blame were those girls. They've been tried, found guilty and punished for their crime. As much as they can be anyway...'

Mike shook his head witheringly, but Graham Ellis pressed on.

'You have to focus on the future. On the things that really matter.'

Graham's eyes bored into him, earnest, beseeching.

'Please, Mike. If you can't forgive them, at least forgive *yourself*.'

Chapter 10

She stared out into the darkness, drawing deeply on a cigarette. Olivia was working hard to cut down her nicotine habit, but still allowed herself one Marlboro Red a day. She liked to enjoy it whilst looking out of the window, taking in the glinting London skyline. The view over the capital was one of the few positive features of her flat in Tooting and she always enjoyed this moment, the reassuring buzz of nicotine calming her after a stressful day.

Tonight, however, she was finding it hard to settle, her emotions in turmoil, her mind a whirl of questions after Mark Willis's murder. She was desperate to know what the fallout would be, what effect it would have on them all, and right on cue her intercom buzzed noisily. Hurrying over, she let her visitor in without bothering to check the monitor. She knew exactly who it was. Moments later, there was a gentle tap on the door. Pausing to check her appearance in the mirror, removing a stray hair from her forehead, Olivia opened the door. Christopher Parkes stood outside, brooding and darkly handsome as always. Olivia felt a pulse of lust shoot through her, but concealed her fervour beneath a veneer of irritation.

'You're late,' she scolded.

'You're lucky I came at all,' Parkes replied, entering the flat and tugging off his coat. 'It's bloody chaos back at base.'

'Go on,' Olivia replied, encouragingly. 'Don't keep me in suspense.'

Shaking his head good-humouredly at her excitement, Parkes crossed to the sideboard, helping himself to a generous whisky, before he replied:

'There's not much to tell, that's the problem. We're still trying to piece it all together ... What we *do* know is that the three sons of Mark Willis's victim are currently in custody in Bolton. They've flatly denied any involvement, say they were at a lock-in last night back in Hartlepool, but one of them's got a freshly broken nose, so do the maths ...'

'Bloody hell. Do we know how they found him?'

Parkes shrugged, suddenly looking much older than his fifty-two years.

'Willis kept himself to himself, had no mates, no girlfriend, followed the rules of his licence. We spoke to the local MAPPA team up there, they said there'd been no inkling of trouble, no concerns raised. Obviously they would say that, but on the face of it, it doesn't look like an accident or fuck-up on Willis's part.'

'Which means the Probation Service is going to be in the firing line.'

'Exactly. Firth is having a prolapse as we speak and with good reason. If Willis's name and location *were* leaked, if a relative or journalist got hold of them, then ...'

He didn't need to spell out the circumstances, the pair silently contemplating the potential consequences of this setback, before he briskly downed the rest of his drink.

'Anyway, I'd better get on. Just wanted to fill you in.'

'Stay. Have another ...' Olivia said quickly, crossing to pick up the bottle. 'You've only just got here.'

'I shouldn't. I've got to drive.'

'That's never stopped you before,' Olivia countered brightly, topping up his glass.

Parkes shook his head, smiling knowingly, taking a swig. As he did so, Olivia moved in close, slipping her hand between his legs. Instantly, she felt a reaction, her visitor reacting to her touch. Olivia could tell Christopher wanted to resist, but was finding it difficult.

'You're a *very bad* influence...'

'You better believe it,' Olivia replied, leaning in for a kiss, enjoying the taste of whisky on his lips. 'But because you've been a very good boy this year, I've got a surprise for you...'

She broke off, crossing quickly to the sofa and lifting a cushion to reveal a beautifully wrapped gift. Scooping it up, she hurried back to her lover, entwining her leg around his as she offered it up to him.

'Happy Christmas, my love.'

Parkes hesitated to accept it, but Olivia beamed at him, willing him to play along. Putting his glass down, Parkes removed the wrapping to reveal a box stamped with the Omega logo.

'Olivia...'

'Shh, just open it. Take a look.'

Parkes' reluctance was clear, but slowly he opened the box to reveal a brand-new Omega Seamaster inside. Olivia stepped in, pulling the expensive timepiece from its holding.

'It's the very latest model and look...'

She turned it over to reveal a date inscribed on the back: *13/2/21.*

'The date of our first kiss.'

She was trying hard to keep it fun, but her good humour did not reach her guest.

'You know I can't take this.'

'You don't have to wear it at home. Take it to the office, wear it there.'

'Why are you doing this, Olivia?' he pleaded.

'Because it's Christmas. Because I wanted to buy you something nice,' she replied, her voice catching. 'Because I bloody love you.'

'And I'm very fond of you too,' Parkes replied, his expression pained. 'But we *agreed*, we drew a line under things, for *both* our sakes.'

'What if I don't want it to end?' Olivia countered, her volume rising now. 'What if I want all those months of creeping around, all those stolen moments to actually lead somewhere, to *mean* something?'

'They meant something, you know they did. But you also knew from the start that I was married, with two teenage boys who rely on me...'

He closed the box and handed it back, but Olivia turned from him, refusing to accept it.

'Listen, Olivia, what we had was real and meaningful.'

'*Have*,' she hissed pointedly.

'But it was always going to be a temporary thing.'

'Except things got a bit more complicated than that, didn't they?' she countered bitterly.

'Be that as it may,' Parkes pressed on. 'We talked about it, we made a plan and came to a joint decision to move on. Pulling stunts like this is out of line.'

'Stunts like this?!'

She was virtually shouting now, but didn't care.

'That cost me the best part of a month's wages. Money I don't have! But I bought it because I love you, because I want you to have something nice from me.'

Tears were running down her cheeks, but this didn't move her former lover, who appeared annoyed rather than sympathetic.

'Oh, this is pointless,' he blurted, snatching up his coat.

'Go on, run away. Run back to Penny and your *beautiful* children...'

'You're the one making this difficult, Olivia, not me,' he complained. 'I'll talk to you tomorrow, when hopefully you'll be feeling a bit more sensible.'

'Oh, piss off.'

She didn't mean it. She wanted him to stay, for things to be right between them, but the evening was ruined now and they both knew it. Placing the gift on the coffee table, Parkes hurried to the door, pausing on the threshold. As he turned back to his ex-lover, his expression had softened to something close to regret.

'I never wanted things to end up like this, Olivia. I really didn't. If we can be friends, I'd really like that, but whatever, I...'

He hesitated, struggling to find the right words, before adding: 'I'm sorry.'

Then he left, pulling the door shut behind him.

Chapter 11

'Apologies for pulling you in so late, Chandra, but I'm afraid this couldn't wait.'

'No problem, sir. Anything I can do to help.'

This was not how she really felt, of course. Detective Inspector Chandra Dabral had been due home an hour ago, to relieve her husband from the rigours of childcare, but you didn't refuse a summons from the detective superintendent. Which is why she now stood in his office on the top floor of Scotland Yard, hands behind her back, game face on.

'I'm sure you've heard about the incident in Bolton in the early hours of this morning,' Detective Superintendent Terry Draper continued briskly.

'Only the rough details. Not our jurisdiction.'

'Well it is now,' Draper replied dryly. 'As you know, Willis was convicted of raping and murdering seventy-eight-year-old Valerie Bridge, eleven years ago. Her three grown-up sons – Vince, Steven and Mick – are currently in custody in Bolton, being questioned by local CID. They're denying everything and seem to have several witnesses who can place them at the...'

Draper paused to check the report on his desk.

'...Dog and Whistle pub in Hartlepool at the time of the

attack. They're probably lying, though whether that can be proved or not is another matter.'

'Why are they so sure it's them?' Chandra asked, braving a direct question. 'Do they have witnesses? Cell site info? DNA?'

'Nothing like that so far, I understand. The three men were careful: disguised their identity, wore gloves, drove a van that was stolen from Hartlepool, which they later dumped. No, it's their mobile phone communications that are intriguing, specifically that of the eldest son, Steven. Six weeks ago, he received an anonymous text from a pay-as-you-go phone in London, revealing Mark Willis's new name – Liam Sullivan – and the address of his flat in Bolton.'

Chandra whistled, shocked.

'So there was nothing suspicious on the ground in Bolton leading up to this attack then?'

'Nothing obvious,' Draper replied soberly. 'No traffic on vigilante forums, no local gossip, no reports of concern from Willis himself. This attack was a bolt from the blue and a pretty nasty one at that.'

Draper gestured to the photos on his desk, hastily scanned images of Mark Willis lying spreadeagled on a dual carriageway, a pool of blood encircling his head.

'So we're thinking that the Bridge brothers got the info,' Chandra suggested, drinking in the disturbing images, 'staked Willis out, then ambushed him . . .'

'That's pretty much the size of it. Which brings us to *your* involvement. This was no accident, no chance sighting. Someone deliberately leaked confidential information to Steven Bridge, presumably with the express purpose of provoking an attack, perhaps even Willis's murder. As the culprit leaked the info whilst in the Metropolitan area, it falls to us to investigate. It's possible a member of the public, a journalist or a vigilante got hold of his details, but it's highly unlikely. Which is a problem because only a handful of people in the entire country have access to this kind of highly confidential intel – basically his Bolton MAPPA team, the top brass at the Probation Service and, of course, the Minister of Justice.'

'So we're looking at a potential case of misconduct in public office?'

Draper nodded, grim-faced.

'For obvious reasons it's imperative that we get on top of this ASAP. The Ministry of Justice and the Home Office are going berserk, plus news of Willis's murder has already filtered out onto social media.'

Draper turned his laptop round, so Chandra could see the Twitter feed he was monitoring.

'A group calling itself Justice Never Sleeps leaked the news within an hour of his death, posting photos on Twitter and Instagram of Willis's corpse, pictures that were taken by local drivers near the incident. This self-declared vigilante group are clearly delighted by Willis's demise, as are many of their fol-lowers…'

Chandra grimaced as she watched the tally of 'likes' below the images mounting fast. Celebrating someone's murder – even someone as notorious as Willis – was beyond sick.

'I don't need to tell you that this murder is going to be *big* news, so let's try to get ahead of the curve. Let's find out how this information was obtained, who leaked it and why.'

'Of course, sir.'

Draper had sounded determined, resolute and Chandra echoed his tone, keen to repay his faith in her. But as she marched away down the lonely corridor, she felt far from confident. In fact, she felt like she was about to walk into a shitstorm that might have profound implications for policing, the criminal justice system *and* her own career.

Tugging her phone from her pocket, Chandra swiftly typed out a message to her husband.

'Can you put the twins to bed? I'm going to be working *late.*'

Chapter 12

The street was deserted, save for the two figures huddled together against the cold. The wind was biting tonight, flecks of sleet whipping through the air, but Russell didn't care, pleased to feel Amber's body against his. They had chatted all the way from the high street, ranging the territory from friendships, to education, to hobbies, but were now deep into suburbia, away from the throng. Here the locals were tucked up safe at home, or closeted in one of the cosy pubs, leaving the two friends free rein of the streets, which pleased Russell greatly. It felt like they were in their own little cocoon, cut off from the rest of the world. It was as if this night existed for them alone.

'You're honestly telling me you've never seen *Reservoir Dogs*?'

'Nor *Pulp Fiction*,' Amber replied, smiling at his incredulity. 'Not my cup of tea.'

'I think I may have to reconsider the basis of our friendship,' Russell teased, withdrawing his arm from hers. 'In fact, I think I may have to let you go ...'

'They're too violent, I don't see why anyone would want to watch them,' Amber replied, laughing.

'Because they're *bloody* good.'

'If you say so.'

'So what do you like then?' he demanded. 'Films with Judi Dench?'

'Give me some credit. I'm not even thirty...'

'Lily James then...'

She punched him playfully, shaking her head.

'Typical bloke. Always think you have the monopoly on good taste.'

'Well, I'll hold my hands up to that,' he replied, smiling. 'But seriously, you've got to give me something to work with...'

'I liked *Joker*. Does that pass the taste test?'

They strolled on, chatting easily, eventually reaching the smart block of flats that Russell called home. Slowing, Russell turned to Amber.

'Are you sure you don't want me to walk you home?'

'No need,' she answered. 'I'm literally a stone's throw from here, it's fine.'

'Still doesn't feel right, normally the guy walks the girl home, not the other way around.'

'Well, I'm not a normal kind of girl...'

Her face lit up as she spoke, breaking into a cheeky smile, rendering her more beautiful than ever. Russell wanted to grab her, kiss her, but he held back.

'Look, it's really cold, so why don't you come up, order a cab? We can have a coffee before you go, if you like? Chill out for a bit?'

The slightest tightening of her smile. Instantly, Russell knew he'd pushed it too far too fast.

'Another time maybe,' Amber replied gently. 'I really need to get home.'

'Of course, no problem.'

Russell felt annoyed and angry, as if he'd lunged at her and been knocked back.

'Call me tomorrow though?' Amber said quickly, offering an olive branch.

'First thing.'

A brief silence, then Amber leaned forward, kissing him gently on the cheek.

'Night then...'

Turning, she headed off down the street, wrapping her arms around herself to ward off the biting cold. Russell watched her go, furious with himself for having overplayed his hand, yet excited too, his eyes glued to her curves, her tight backside, her long legs. She was so damn hot that all he could think of was losing himself in her. Despite his misstep tonight, he was resolved to do whatever was necessary to have her. It would take patience and determination, but he was more than ready for the challenge.

He had waited too long for this.

Chapter 13

Summoning her courage, Emily knocked on the door.

'Sam?'

There was no reply. She knew Sam was still awake, could hear the gentle throb of his music, so she persevered.

'Please, love. I just want to talk.'

Pushing down the handle, Emily eased the door open. Stepping inside, she saw Sam lying on his bed, his face turned to the wall. Once more she felt a sharp stab of sadness – she couldn't bear it when he was upset, especially when she was the cause of his distress. With a heavy heart, she picked her way across the floor, seating herself on the end of his bed.

'Look, Sam, I'm sorry if I overreacted, if I embarrassed you in front of Gavin. I didn't mean to ... I just ... I just don't want you to throw away the opportunities you've been given. You're a clever boy with a bright future ahead of you, *if* you make the right choices. Bunking off school, spending time with boys who ... who perhaps don't have your abilities, your options, well that's the first step on a slippery slope. I'm not trying to be cruel, or a killjoy, or what-have-you ... I just want you to fly high, that's all.'

She faltered to a halt, not sure what else to say. Every word of this was true and she hoped that it might somehow cut through

Sam's anger. To her immense relief, her son now turned to her, looking uncomfortable, even a little ashamed.

'I'm sorry, too. I shouldn't have said those things.'

'It's already forgotten.'

Emily couldn't resist leaning in and giving her teenage son a big hug. She didn't care that he felt awkward in her embrace, she just loved holding her best boy.

'Mum...'

Emily disengaged, intrigued by his tone. Sam sounded tentative, even a little nervous.

'What is it, love?' she asked, suddenly concerned.

'Gavin and me... well, it's a bit complicated, but... we don't just bunk off together for the sake of it. We... we've both been a bit picked on at school...'

'Bullied?'

Immediately, Emily felt anger rising within her.

'Kind of,' Sam continued quickly. 'It's not too bad, but sometimes we just like to get away from it, you know...'

'They're bullying both of you?'

'Yeah, quite a lot actually.'

'But why you two specifically?'

Sam hesitated, then replied:

'Because of our friendship. Because of the way we feel about each other.'

Emily stared at Sam, wrong-footed, then gathered herself quickly.

'I see. I didn't realize. Are you two... are you an item or...?'

'Well, I don't know if Gavin's my boyfriend or anything,' Sam said, avoiding his mother's eye. 'But I'd like him to be. Are you OK with that?'

'Sure, of course. I'm just surprised that's all, because you were seeing Amy for a while and—'

'That wasn't a real thing. I'm gay, Mum.'

It was said with such certainty that momentarily Emily didn't know how to respond.

'Sorry for landing this on you,' he continued, more confidently. 'I wanted to be honest.'

'Of course, darling. And I'm very grateful... The only thing is that...'

Sam looked up, wary. Emily was tempted to backtrack, to abort this line of thinking, but persevered nevertheless.

'...sexuality is fluid at your age. You're only fourteen. It's very early in life to be saying definitively what you *are* and what you're *not*.'

'I don't agree. I've never liked girls, not in that way. And now I've met Gavin...'

'Just give it time, that's all I'm saying. Explore who you are by all means, but—'

'I *know* who I am, Mum,' Sam countered, bristling. 'That won't change.'

'Everyone changes, love. Nothing is set in stone. You grow, you develop, you find out new things about yourself,' Emily insisted. 'Who you are as a child is not who you are as ad—'

'I'm not a child, so don't treat me like one. I'm gay and that's the end of the story. If you've got a problem with that, then...'

'I don't, Sammy,' Emily reassured him quickly. 'I really don't, OK?'

Sam stared at her, clearly still angry and uncertain whether to believe her or not.

'I'd never judge you like that. Please believe me.'

Sam shrugged, but her evident sincerity and emotion appeared to have mollified him a little, so she pressed on.

'Look, it's really late and you've got school tomorrow, so let's talk about this some more tomorrow. But please know that I have nothing but love and admiration for you, always.'

Reaching forward, she squeezed his hand, then rose.

'Now, lights out in ten or you'll be good for nothing tomorrow...'

Slipping out of his room, Emily closed the door behind her. It had been a difficult, draining day and now she just wanted to be in bed. Heading into her bedroom, she drew the curtains, turned on the radio and began to undress. She was desperate to switch off, to forget the cares of the day, but the news bulletin on the radio stopped her in her tracks.

'Bolton police have now confirmed that the man chased to his death in the Daubhill area of the city in the early hours of this morning was Mark Willis. In May 2012, twelve-year-old Willis was found guilty of the brutal rape and murder of pensioner Valerie Bridge in Hartlepool. Released four years ago, Willis is believed to have been living under an assumed name, working at a local logistics depot in the central Bolton area. Police have so far declined to comment further...'

All hope of respite was now gone. Emily remained rooted to the spot, barely able to breathe, shocked to the core. This was her worst nightmare made flesh.

Chapter 14

'Head will roll for this, you mark my words.'

Mike Burnham shook his head in dismay, annoyed by the MP's macho posturing. Ever since he'd heard the news of Mark Willis's murder, Mike had been hooked to the TV, watching bulletins on Sky, BBC and ITV, before turning over to *Newsnight*. Guy Chambers, a junior minister at the Ministry of Justice and a very familiar face on political talk shows, was the main guest, fulminating against the Probation Service.

'Obviously we don't have all the facts,' the MP continued, making a feeble attempt at circumspection, 'but if we *are* looking at a catastrophic breach of security, then there will have to be change, *from the top down*. The depth of the Probation Service's incompetence was revealed during the enquiries into Usman Khan and Joseph McCann and it appears nothing has changed, despite their claims of extensive reform...'

Mike switched the TV off, unable to take any more. He'd heard dozens of politicians claim to be tough on crime over the years, promising to shake up the criminal justice system, to put the victims of crime first, but nothing ever changed. It was all hot air, ambitious MPs jumping on the bandwagon, hoping to bolster their leadership credentials, appealing to the party faithful, whilst doing *nothing* to help those who'd really suffered. What did these people know about justice? About doing what was *right*? They, the civil service, the system, *protected* law-breakers and killers. It fell to ordinary men and women to keep the public safe, as events in Bolton had proved. Some would chastise the perpetrators for their attack on Willis, branding them renegades or vigilantes, but many more would applaud them, celebrating the fact that those three boys had finally got justice for their mum. Mike certainly wouldn't criticise their actions – what else were they supposed to do when the scales were so heavily tipped in favour of offenders? – but in truth he didn't really *feel* the sense of triumph he was hoping for. Somehow he never could relate to somebody else's pain, however hard he tried.

Cresting the landing, Mike headed to the bedroom. As usual, he switched on Classic FM as he prepared for bed. He couldn't bear the silence that descended after dark and would often let the radio play all night, rather than lie alone in the crushing silence. He missed his ex-wife, he missed his family, but most of all he missed Jessica. In waking hours, he had work, shopping and chores to keep him busy, but there were no such distractions after dark. The nights were always the worst.

Lying on the bed, Mike tried to lose himself in the music, to follow the rhythm, the melody, to keep his brain active and alert. But fatigue was stealing over him now and try as he might, he couldn't keep his eyes open. He fought it, fought it with all his might, terrified of what horrors might visit him in the darkness, but moments later he was asleep.

Immediately, she came to him. Memories of Jessica. Howling with laughter, making a cheeky aside, arguing with her sister, shouting at her mother – mixed moments of familial joy and tension that he would give anything to experience again. But soon, darker thoughts, darker images began to intrude. The terror on Jessica's face as two raggedy girls pushed her wheelchair up and down slag piles at the deserted quarry, their leering, triumphant expressions as Kaylee Jones filmed the petrified eleven-year-old begging for mercy, as Courtney Turner tipped her defenceless victim out of her wheelchair onto the cold, hard ground, goading her, kicking her savagely, moving in for the kill...

Mike sat bolt upright, gasping for breath, his eyes brimming with tears. He wanted to scream out his anguish, roar out his fury, tear this world asunder, but he knew he would only be howling at phantoms in the night. So instead he lay back down, eyes wide open, defying his aching fatigue, fighting the darkness that threatened to engulf him.

Day Two

Chapter 15

If she could, she would have slept for days. Olivia had dragged herself from her bed to the shower, then to the coffee machine, hoping to slug off her lethargy, but still she was dead on her feet. She'd hardly slept, her mind flitting from her faithless lover to her panicking charge then back again, anger and frustration growing all the while. She'd risen feeling even less refreshed than when she went to bed and was struggling to get herself going, which was a problem, because once again she was running *late*.

The whole thing was unsustainable. Six members of Olivia's department were currently on sick leave through illness or stress, meaning the rest of them had to pick up the slack, monitoring *their* probationers whilst also tending to their own. It was impossible, ridiculous, inhumane, but the work had to be done, hence Olivia's packed schedule. Slinging her half-drunk coffee into the sink, Olivia gathered her files, ramming them into a tote bag she'd picked up at some farmer's market, when she'd briefly flirted with going organic. Amazing, the fantasies she'd once entertained about living a trendy London life, when the reality was eye-watering rent, obscene council tax charges, awful traffic and the bargain shelf at Aldi. Annoyed by her own naivety, Olivia shoved the last file into the bag. But in her haste, she snagged it on the handle and the folder opened, spilling several pages of closely typed A4 onto the floor.

'Oh, for God's sake...'

Getting down on all fours, Olivia snatched up the pages, shoving them back into the file. As she did so, however, her eyes fell upon the text, much of which was heavily redacted. This was Jack Walker's file and even though she'd read it dozens of times, she paused now to take it in. It was a pointless exercise – what could she learn now that she didn't already know? Yet somehow she felt compelled to drink in the sordid details, plumbing the depths of his degradation.

The early sections of the report were about his background. His family in Southend, his terrible school attendance record, his minor brushes with the law. It also featured Jack's testimony about events within the home. His absent father, his neglectful mother and, of course, the sexual abuse. This took up three pages of the file and though the names of the offenders were blacked out, it wasn't hard to divine who Jack was referring to when he outlined the catalogue of rape and casual violence he'd been subjected to. His older brothers, who themselves were now behind bars for a mixture of serious offences, had preyed on him several times a week, pinning him down, assaulting him, degrading him. There were suggestions that Jack had in turn meted out similar treatment to his younger brother, Danny, though Jack strenuously denied this. Olivia wasn't inclined to believe him, feeling that at the very least he had bullied his younger sibling. If there was one thing she'd learned over the years, it was that violence always begets violence.

Now her eyes strayed to the latter sections, where Jack's own crime was dissected. This made for difficult reading, but Olivia never shirked from the task, would be failing in her duty if she *did*. Again names and locations were redacted, but in reality this was pointless obfuscation, the grim details well known to everyone in the UK. The report outlined how Jack had abducted a young boy from Southend Pier, luring him to an abandoned house with the promise of sweets. There he'd tortured, raped, then bludgeoned the four-year-old to death, in what the judge described as a 'sickening and sustained attack'. Despite her experience, Olivia felt the bile rising in her throat, the savagery of Jack's crime laid out in black and white. It was not, however, the appalling catalogue of injuries – the shattered ribs, the broken eye socket, the smashed teeth – that really sickened her. No, it was the sexual element of the crime that turned her stomach, the boy's post-mortem revealing that Billy Armstrong had both semen *and* candy floss in his mouth when his broken body was found.

Dropping the file, Olivia bolted for the bathroom. Flinging open the door, she fell to her knees and vomited into the toilet bowl, bitter coffee stinging her nose and throat. She heaved three times, then was done, rolling away to lie on the cold linoleum. Why did she do this? Why torture herself with details that were seared in her brain anyway? Lying on the floor, Olivia stared at the stained ceiling, wondering now about the wisdom of having taken on this particular case. Should she have refused it? Asked for Jack to be reassigned to someone else? Probably, though then she would have had to explain *why*, which would have opened another can of worms. Maybe that *would* have been the better route, though, whatever ructions it might have caused. Perhaps she should have been honest with her superiors and let the safeguarding protocols do the rest. After all, the Probation Service would *never* have assigned her Jack Walker's case if they'd known she was pregnant.

Chapter 16

Mike stared at the mirror, barely recognizing the man looking back at him. He'd once been a handsome, strapping bloke, a catch Alison was proud to have landed. She loved showing him off, hitting the pubs, bars and restaurants in Maidstone together. Alison was no slouch in the looks department herself and they *had* made a striking couple. But that guy, that cheeky, swaggering lover was long gone, replaced by a hollow-eyed ghoul, who looked ten years older than he was.

Mike's hair was flecked with grey, there were dark rings under his eyes and a lived-in sadness in his features that always made people cautious of engaging with him. And that was just strangers. Those who *did* know him, who knew his history, took even greater care to avoid him. What, after all, do you say to a man whose child has been murdered? Whose brutal, sadistic death still plays out in the tabloids, feeding the public's grim fascination with extreme violence? Nothing. You say nothing.

Slapping on some aftershave, Mike winced as the alcohol stung his tired skin. Every day he went through this rigmarole, as if on auto-pilot, but who was this man staring back at him? This empty husk in a smart shirt and tie? This automaton who spent his days extolling the virtues of double glazing? It seemed comical to Mike that he still bothered getting up each morning, donning his suit, heading to the showroom. He knew he only did it to keep busy, but it was still a farce, playing at being a normal human being who cared about his career, prospects and salary. He was acting a role, with no interest in whether he made the sales or not, yet it was still better than the alternative. He'd tried that before and it had nearly killed him – two bottles of vodka a day is likely to do that. No, this was the best way forward, the only way, but some days the absurdity of it hit home, Mike doomed to repeat the same routine day in, day out, to engage in the same meaningless enterprise with no interest in its outcome. He often said that *he'd* got the life sentence Courtney Turner and Kaylee Jones should have received. Today he felt it with every fibre of his being.

Taking one last look at himself, Mike departed. He was presentable at least, some semblance of pride forcing himself to make the effort. He wasn't popular at work, nor particularly successful, but he worked long hours without complaint, so they were happy to keep him on. Sometimes the prospect of pursuing this path for the next fifteen, twenty years robbed Mike of all energy, conviction and desire. Could he really do it? In his darkest moments, he'd thought about ending it all, checking out in an orgy of booze and pills. But something always held him back. He refused to be thought of as a coward and, besides, what would that do to Rachel, who'd already endured so much? No, there was nothing for it but to swallow his despair, his boredom, and simply carry on.

Snatching up his suit jacket, Mike marched to the hall table. As he did so, his phone pinged loudly and Mike scooped it up. Work never contacted him this early and Alison tended to message late at night, once Rachel was in bed. So it was probably spam, a reminder that the car was due for its MOT and Mike was tempted to ignore it, but curiosity won the day. He was surprised to see that the message was from an Unknown Number and even more confounded by the contents:

Courtney Turner is now living under the name Sharon Wall at 24 Meadow Lane, Colchester, CO1 1AP.

Mike stared at the message in disbelief, his heart beating sixteen to the dozen. Who had sent him this message? What did they stand to gain by doing so? And could it actually be *true*? Was the bitch who'd tortured, humiliated and murdered his little girl really living just an hour's drive away?

Chapter 17

'How did they find him? How *on earth* did they know where he was living?'

Emily had only agreed to meet her ex-husband under duress and was already regretting it. Paul was in a right state, bombarding her with questions – questions she couldn't answer.

'I've no idea,' she replied tersely. 'They don't talk to me about these things. It's nothing to do with me.'

'You're both protected by the same system, the same people—'

'That's not true, Paul. The team in Bolton has nothing to do with the team in Reading. For obvious reasons, these kind of cases…' Emily hesitated, hating referring to herself as a 'case', then carried on: '…are kept entirely separate from one another. My handlers would have no idea what was going on in Bolton and vice versa. That's how it works, that's how everyone is kept safe.'

'Except they're *clearly* not. You've seen the reports, the mobile phone footage. They were lying in wait for him, Emily. They ambushed him, chased him to his death. He was only lucky they didn't get their hands on him.'

'Strange way to define "lucky".'

'You know what I mean. He was a hair's breadth from getting

73

his head caved in and only avoided that by throwing himself into four lanes of moving traffic.'

He was virtually shouting and suddenly checked himself, aware that other customers in the café were listening to his angry outburst. Lowering his volume, he continued:

'Look, all I'm saying is you've got to talk to them. Find out what's going on. See if you and Sam need to be temporarily moved, or even relocated. The poor kid's just starting Year 10, his school work's really ramping up. He's got a lot going on.'

You don't know the half of it, Emily thought to herself. Paul liked to play the doting parent, but it was *she* who'd brought Sam up, she who knew him best and she bridled at the insinuation that she would willingly expose her son to danger through her own negligence or lack of interest.

'You're overreacting.'

'By caring for my son?'

'Don't you pull that one with me, Paul. It was *you* who left me...'

'Oh for God's sake...'

'*You* who took up with someone new, *you* who was absent for *the first ten years* of Sam's life.'

'You pushed me away!'

'No, you *ran* away. Ran away from me.'

'Well, can you blame me?'

'Do you really want me to answer that, Paul?'

She said it aggressively, but in truth she didn't entirely blame him for leaving. With her history, her criminal record, her notoriety, she was a lot to take on, not least because shackling yourself to 'Emily Lawrence' necessitated colluding in a fiction. No, it was the way Paul had left her that still stung, abandoning mother and child, taking up with a woman half his age and moving to the other end of the country. Yes, they'd moved back down south now, taking an active interest in Sam, but it was far too late to play the doting father.

'Look, this isn't getting us anywhere,' she continued, swallowing her anger. 'We have no idea what happened in Bolton. Perhaps Willis got drunk, told a friend who he really was? Perhaps there was a girlfriend who got too close? Could be *anything*.'

'They're saying on the TV that someone deliberately leaked the information to the victim's family. There was a guy on *Newsnight*, an MP, who said—'

'It's just speculation, guesswork and until we know what actually happened, it's vital that we both remain calm,' Emily insisted. 'You're right, this is a big year for Sam, so the last thing he needs is to be uprooted from his school, his friends, his family. I'll bet you whatever happened in Bolton is a local cock-up, a stupid mistake Willis made which ended up costing him dear. I don't make those kind of errors; I don't take risks...'

Paul looked as though he was about to interject, so Emily pressed on.

'...and I have been successfully hidden in the community for over twenty years as a result. *Twenty years*, Paul. Think about that. Think about how successful I've been, how successful the system has been in keeping me and Sam safe. It works, it's secure, so *please*, can we try not to panic, when there is absolutely nothing to worry about? I do my best by Sam every day, helping him to grow, to prosper and it isn't easy, let me tell you. I have a life of my own, a job, responsibilities to friends and colleagues, a To Do list as long as your arm and, frankly, conversations like this are not helpful. I've had to get my deputy to cover for me today in order to be here, so do me a favour and dial it down, OK? I've got this, there is *nothing* to worry about.'

Her blood was up and, predictably, Paul backtracked under

the weight of her spirited defence. His bark was worse than his bite and he'd never been able to match her for sheer force of personality. She sent him on his way, if not reassured then at least pacified, leaving her to get on with her life. Hurrying back to her car, she allowed herself a fleeting moment of satisfaction at having nipped Paul's tantrum in the bud, before it could properly impact on her, or worse, Sam. Yet in spite of her relief, Emily felt a nagging sense of worry. She'd talked a good game to Paul, dismissing his concerns as idle fears, but was not nearly as relaxed as she made out. The truth was that she *had* been shaken by the news of Mark Willis's murder, spending a sleepless night conjuring up all sorts of terrible scenarios. As soon as she was home tonight, she'd call her probation officer, see if she could cast any light on the situation, because currently she was going out of her mind, imagining the very worst.

Perhaps Willis's exposure was due to a local aberration, a chance sighting, but what if it wasn't? What if someone *had* deliberately betrayed him to his death? His crime was no more notorious than her own, so could it happen to her too? Could she be tracked down, attacked, killed? Could Sam find himself in the firing line? It was a thought that shook Emily to the core, the settled calm and optimism of the last fourteen years evaporating in an instant. She'd worked hard to convince Paul that there was nothing to worry about, but she didn't believe it, not really. Darting a look over her shoulder as she hurried back to her car, Emily had to admit that for the first time in years she felt unsettled and scared, as if the net was slowly closing in on her. *Was* she being stalked? Hunted down?

Was someone watching her right now?

Chapter 18

It was a bitter morning in Coombe Park, the icy dew crunching beneath Russell's feet as he strode across the grass. Years ago, when he was still finding his feet in Croydon, learning to inhabit a new identity, a new life, his meetings with Isaac Green had always taken place behind closed doors, away from prying eyes. Now, however, he liked to meet his probation officer out in the open, so he could combine exercise with pastoral care. Green was a slow walker, leaning heavily on his walking stick as the result of an historic injury, but claimed he enjoyed the fresh air.

'Sounds like you're flying at work?' Isaac said as they turned a corner, heading for a gaggle of dog walkers.

'Two promotions in the last five years can't be bad,' Russell replied confidently. 'Jacob said that if I keep this up, then CFO might be an option in the future.'

'That's very impressive. And you're still enjoying it?'

'Absolutely. I like the numbers – keeping an eye on the profit margins, the projections. And I like the fact that we're growing, creating new markets every day...'

'Then I'm happy for you. You've worked hard to get where you are.'

Russell acknowledged Isaac's compliment and they walked

on, the veteran probation officer just about managing to keep up with the younger man's stride.

'What about family? Have you spoken to your dad?'

'A few weeks back.'

'And your mum?'

'Now and again, you know how it is.'

Isaac did and knew not to push it, so he moved the conversation on.

'What about NA? I hope you're still attending twice a week?'

'Religiously.'

Isaac Green looked up at his client, scenting sarcasm. But Russell was swift to allay his fears.

'Honestly, I haven't missed a session. They're good for me and, actually, I enjoy them now.'

'You've changed your tune.'

'Well, there's a reason for that...'

Russell slowed to a halt, turning to his probation officer, who also checked his pace, seemingly glad of the rest.

'I've met someone.'

'A girl?'

'D'uh. I'm not like some of you London types,' Russell replied, laughing, letting his mild Bedfordshire accent punch through.

'How long's this been going on?'

'Only a week or two. But I'm hopeful it might lead somewhere.'

'Does she have a name?'

'Amber. Nice kid, from Brighton originally. Had a hard time with heroine and coke, but she's on the straight and narrow now. Got a placement as a trainee graphic designer, lives in East Croydon, so only a stone's throw away from me.'

'How well do you know her?'

'I don't really, but she's mint.'

'And do you think this is wise?'

Now a frown creased Russell's brow.

'Sorry?'

'You know what I mean. Given your history, do you think it's wise to let someone get close to you?'

'I'm not a bloody monk, Isaac. If I fancy someone, I fancy them.'

'I understand that, but even so …'

'What's the issue? You think I'm going to *confess*? You think I'll forget who I am now?'

'Of course not, you've always protected your identity scrupulously.'

'What then?'

Isaac stared at his charge thoughtfully, as if trying to choose the right words. Russell watched him closely, a slow realization dawning.

'Oh, I get it. You think I'm a danger to *her*?'

'I didn't say that.'

'Your bloody face is.'

'I'm just saying that you haven't shown interest in anyone, haven't been intimate with anyone *in years*. You've no idea how you'll react, what feelings it might provoke …'

'I know *exactly* how I feel and you're wrong. This is good for me. It's the last piece of the jigsaw. You're always saying that I'm fit to live a normal life, well this is a normal life, with a job, a bit of cash and a pretty girl on my arm.'

'OK, OK,' Isaac said, holding up his hand in surrender. 'I understand that and you're right, of course you're right.'

'But?'

'But … just take it slow.'

'For her sake or mine?'

'Both, if I'm being honest.'

'Well, I'll give it a whirl, but I'm not promising anything. I've waited a long time for this and, fuck it, I deserve some happiness, right?'

Nodding, Isaac said nothing, keeping his counsel. The two men moved off, walking on in uneasy silence, blending in with the morning crowds, before slowly disappearing from view.

Chapter 19

'What's going on, Jack? Why aren't you ready?'

The teenager stood in the kitchen, wearing only his boxer shorts, awkward and exposed. Aware that he had messed up, he avoided Olivia's eye, as she laid into him.

'This is your first day at work, you can't be late.'

'I'm sorry, I overslept. Must have been more knackered than I thought.'

'Did you set an alarm?'

'I thought I did.'

'Jack, we talked about this. Your happiness, your progress, your future is *your* responsibility, right? So if I say you need to be up and ready first thing, then you need to be up and ready. The world won't bend to accommodate you, you have to fit in with *it*.'

'I'm sorry. I just couldn't get to sleep last night.'

'What was the matter? First night nerves? The bed's OK, right?' she asked, concerned.

'Yeah, that's all fine. I just didn't feel too well. Stomach ache. To be honest, I don't feel great now...'

'No, no, no. You might have been able to pull the wool over their eyes at the unit, Jack, but I've been around the block. Don't kid a kidder.'

'Honest to God, I've got cramps, proper pains...'

'And I'm next in line to be Pope.'

Scowling, Jack turned away, but Olivia continued, unabashed.

'I get it. Today's a big day, a massive step for you. Going out into the real world, dealing with real people, real situations. It's natural to be apprehensive, but running away from things is *not* the answer. Get today out the way and tomorrow it'll be much easier, I promise.'

Jack looked up at her, sceptical, saying nothing. Crossing to the sink, Olivia picked up a glass and ran the tap, as she continued:

'Now, you remember where you're going?'

'Oak House, Enfield.'

'That's right. George Simmons, the foreman, is expecting you. He's tough but fair. Don't let him ride you and you'll be fine. The cab should be here in five minutes sharp, so if you move it, you can have a quick wash before you get dressed. I can make you a sandwich to take with you. Cheese OK?'

Jack nodded wearily, but made no attempt to move.

'Come on, crack on then, I'll keep an eye out for the taxi.'

Filling her glass, Olivia took a large draught, enjoying the hit of the icy cool water.

'Are *you* OK?'

The question took Olivia by surprise, her response swift and unconvincing.

'Top of the world. Why wouldn't I be?'

'Well, you look kind of pale. And, no offence or anything, but you're sweating.'

Flustered, Olivia ran her palm across her forehead, sweeping the sweat from her brow, noticing as she did so how hot and clammy her armpits felt. Worse, she now felt another wave of nausea sweep over her.

'Is anything wrong?' Jack said, taking a step towards her. 'Do you need to sit down?'

He took another step and now Olivia held up her hand to stop him, aware of how inappropriate it was to be standing so close to this semi-naked, young man.

'I'm fine.'

'No, you're not – you're white as a sheet.'

'I said *I'm fine.*'

She rasped the words at him, angry and unsettled. But he seemed completely unfazed by her discomfort, continuing to stare at her. Wild thoughts filled her head. Was it possible he *knew*? That he could *tell* she was pregnant? Pushing these idle fancies away, Olivia straightened up, towering over the diminutive teen once more.

'And *you're* late. So post haste. I want you back out here and ready to go in two.'

He looked at her for a moment, intrigued, then slowly turned and left the room. Exhaling, Olivia tried to gather herself, to master her growing nausea. Turning, she re-filled her glass, chiding herself for being weak and foolish, urging herself to regain her composure. But this was easier said than done, and as she raised the glass to her lips, Olivia was surprised to find her hands were shaking.

Chapter 20

Her stomach was doing somersaults as she made her way to the centre of the room. This was the most high-profile investigation Chandra Dabral had ever led, the biggest operation her team had ever been assigned, and all eyes were on her, both within the incident room and beyond. Bring it to a successful conclusion and she might yet dream of further promotion. Failure would dash those hopes forever.

'I expect by now you all know what we're dealing with,' she said, commanding the room, keeping her voice strong and steady.

Twenty expectant faces nodded, the rumour mill having done its job.

'Misconduct in public office. It's a very serious offence, one which several of your former colleagues have fallen foul of over the past few years, so our investigation, our methods, our behaviour need to be *squeaky clean* on this one. We must work calmly, professionally and with purpose, until the perpetrator is arrested and charged. Given the gravity of the offence, I know this won't be a problem for you.'

Chandra paused, pleased to see many purposeful responses from the group. The team seemed energized, committed, loyal, but how could she tell for sure? She'd inherited most of them from her predecessor and had no idea how they'd respond to being part of such a newsworthy investigation. Could they be trusted to be discreet? Or might one of them be tempted to get into bed with an ambitious journalist, taking advantage of the financial opportunities such a case might afford?

'Confidentially is paramount in an investigation such as this, so no talking out of school – to partners, friends or the press. What's said in this room, stays in this room.'

Again, Chandra paused, letting her gaze play over every face, until she was sure her message had sunk in. Then she crossed to the incident board.

'So, six weeks ago, at 10.15 a.m. on the seventh of November, a message was sent from a Samsung Galaxy phone in London. Cell site tracking puts the phone somewhere in the vicinity of Shepherds Bush. There's numerous residential properties and shops there, but also a conference centre which I'll come to in a minute...'

She stabbed a circled area of West London on the map, before continuing:

'The phone and SIM have no registered owner, but we do have the phone's serial number, which could prove useful when we have a suspect in custody. The message was sent to Steven Bridge, resident of Hartlepool, and read "Mark Willis is living under the name Liam Sullivan, in Flat 2, York Tower, on the Rumworth Estate, Bolton". Short, but very sweet, as far as Mr Bridge was concerned. As you'll know, Mark Willis raped and murdered Valerie Bridge, a seventy-eight-year-old widow, when he was only twelve years old. He served seven years at a young offenders' unit, before being passed fit for parole, at which point he was moved to Bolton, where he was given a new identity and a second chance. Valerie Bridge's family were not happy about this and it's not hard to see why...'

Chandra took a breath, then continued:

'Valerie's ordeal was lengthy, her injuries severe. Fractured skull, two broken arms, not to mention a perforated bowel, thanks to the severity of the sexual assault.'

Chandra saw a junior officer look away, but she pressed on:

'Her three sons, Steven, Vince and Mick have often claimed that they'd tear Willis apart if they could get their hands on him, trumpeting their ambitions on Twitter, Instagram and so on, despite repeated police cautions. In the early hours of yesterday morning, they got their chance, ambushing Willis on his way back from the pub. It's not our job to bring the Bridge brothers to justice, that's Bolton CID's remit. *Our* job is to find out who provided them with confidential information about Willis's whereabouts, thus instigating the attack.'

'Are we definitely saying it's a leak?'

This from DS Buckland, an experienced, plain-speaking officer. He was nominally her deputy but Chandra wasn't ready to trust him yet, as over the past few weeks he'd told anyone who'd listen that it should have been *him* who got the promotion to DI, not her.

'That's our working theory.'

'There must be other possible explanations? Perhaps someone saw him on the estate, recognized him. His mugshot often appears in the tabs, so it's got to be possible?'

Chandra was curious as to why DC Reeves, one of the newer officers, was so keen for it not to have been a leak, but she didn't comment on this, responding:

'It's possible, but eleven years have passed. Twenty-three-year-old Liam Sullivan looked very different from twelve-year-old Mark Willis. Back then he was a pudgy, fresh-faced lad, whereas in later life … well, look for yourselves …'

She tapped his photo.

'Gaunt, unshaven, peroxide hair, earrings, tatts. I'm not sure *I'd* recognize him.'

'He looks like a poor man's Phil Foden,' DC Lucy Drummond offered, to general amusement.

'Also, there was absolutely no traffic re Mark Willis on vigilante forums in the run up to the attack,' DS Buckland added, keen to keep the team on track. 'There've been a couple of alleged sightings of him over the years, but things had been quiet on that front for several months now.'

'Exactly, and given that Willis had not expressed any specific concerns and was seen by multiple witnesses drinking and chatting in the Butcher's Arms that night, seemingly without a care in the world, I think we can assume that his unmasking came as a complete shock to both him and his MAPPA team. Talking of which...'

She pivoted once more, directing her team's attention to six faces pinned to the board.

'The upper echelons of the Probation Service would obviously have known where Willis was, but the day-to-day monitoring, the close work, was handled by the six members of his Bolton MAPPA team. As you know, a multi-agency public protection arrangement involves several organizations, which in this case boils down to this tight-knit group of six. Their number includes a senior police officer, a senior probation officer and representatives from social services and the local district council. It was *their* job to ensure Willis played by the rules, behaved responsibly, contributed to society and generally kept himself safe. Ultimately, his welfare was in their hands.'

'Are we saying it's one of them, then?' DC Cooke asked, intrigued.

'That's what we need to find out. You'll find their names and details on your briefing sheet, and I want us to run the rule over *all of them* – communications history, financial situation, political bent, family set-up, professional standings, the works. But I want us to pay particular attention to this man…'

She indicated a man of late middle age, with heavy, dark eyes and a greying moustache.

'Detective Inspector Martin Coates, a long-serving member of Bolton Constabulary, who's a year or so from retirement. He's the only member of this MAPPA team who was in London on the day the message was sent to Steven Bridge. In fact, he was at a conference organized by the Met and Ministry of Justice at the Excel Centre in Shepherd's Bush.'

She rapped the cell site circle on the map.

'I've asked him to attend the station this morning and I plan to interview him shortly. Maybe he's innocent, but the coincidence of his whereabouts that day has to be worth exploring. So get me intel on him, anything that could link Martin Coates to the leak.'

'Big call,' DS Buckland piped up. 'Putting a serving officer in the frame.'

'They've been known to break the law before, Detective Sergeant, and we're only following the evidence. So I'd suggest we put aside any political concerns and get on with the job.'

Some of the officers were already rising, but Chandra held up her hand, stopping them.

'One final word. This will undoubtedly be a very challenging investigation, not least because a significant percentage of the general public will *applaud* what Steven and his brothers did. I don't, and I'm sure no one here does either. A crime has been committed – two crimes, in fact – and it is our job to ensure whoever set this tragic chain of events in motion is apprehended and prosecuted to the full extent of the law. Whatever we may think of Mark Willis, however appalled we were by his crime, we should remember that he has parents, siblings and friends who are grieving now. They deserve justice. They deserve to know who condemned Mark to his death. So for them, for the good of us *all*, let's find the rat who played God with someone else's life.'

Chapter 21

'I'm just not sure it's the right thing to do.'

She hesitated, glancing at her husband, before continuing:

'I mean we've been talking about it for years, but it's so expensive. And with Christmas coming, I'm nervous about what the eventual bill will be.'

The middle-aged doctor turned back to Mike, hoping for some reassurance, perhaps even a discount. Normally Mike would have seized on this, sensing the door was ajar, but today the words washed over him, hardly registering at all. Annoyed, her husband took up the baton.

'But think of the savings we'll make on our energy costs. Over time, these windows will pay for themselves. That's right isn't, mate?'

'Absolutely,' Mike replied, nodding absently.

'I don't know,' the doctor countered. 'Perhaps we can take a brochure and think about it?'

'Sure, they're on the front desk,' Mike replied helpfully. 'Pick one up on your way out.'

Perplexed, the couple departed, the husband casting angry looks in Mike's direction, annoyed by his lack of engagement and the unsatisfactory outcome of their visit. Mike shrugged it off, his mind elsewhere, but turning, ran straight into Simon, his energetic boss.

'What's up, fella? Losing your touch?'

It was said with a smile – jovial office banter – but his edge was hard to miss.

'There was a sale begging there. Normally, you'd have had it signed and sealed by now.'

Beneath the bonhomie, there was genuine confusion, even concern.

'She wasn't ready,' Mike replied, trying to sound authoritative. 'He'll work on her and they'll be back in the New Year, mark my words.'

'Let's hope so, because those targets won't reach themselves, Mike, and Head Office are asking me to make efficiency savings…'

Mike was tempted to tell him where to go – he was fifteen years older than this low-grade David Brent – but instead he smiled and replied, 'I'd better get to it then.'

Snatching up his suit jacket, he grabbed his car keys.

'Where are you going?' Simon queried. 'I thought you had clients scheduled this morning.'

'Next one's an on-site visit,' Mike lied. 'Old lady who can't get out. I said I'd go round.'

'I didn't see it on the roster.'

'She rang first thing this morning and I took pity on her. Could be a big sale, she sounds a bit desperate and you know what I'm like, a bleeding heart…'

'Well make it quick, we're going to be rammed this morning.'

'I'll be back before you've missed me.'

Winking at him, Mike hurried away. He could see in the reflection of the display window that Simon's eyes were glued to him, clearly convinced that something was 'off' about his behaviour, but Mike didn't care. Ever since he'd received the anonymous text message that morning, he'd been able to think about nothing else, his mind full of visions of Courtney Turner leading a happy, untroubled life in Colchester. What did she look like now? What was she up to? Had she been in trouble with the police again? It seemed highly likely as she had always been the more dominant, more sadistic of the two girls, the driving force behind Jessica's senseless murder, but suddenly he *had* to know. He knew it was risky, that it might all come to nothing, but there was no way he could ignore the message. Which is why, even though his boss had obviously seen through his flimsy cover story, he didn't backtrack now, marching fast out of the showroom. There was no point hesitating, no point putting this off.

He had a date with a killer.

Chapter 22

'I don't care what you've done, or what you haven't done. I give everyone a fair chance on my site, right?'

The burly foreman towered over Jack, his eyes boring into him.

'In return, I expect punctuality, professionalism and hard graft, understood?'

Jack nodded, but said nothing, unable to find his tongue.

'This is a major new housing project, months of work, so if you play your cards right, you could be onto a good thing here. You've got your NVQ in bricklaying, correct?'

'S'right,' Jack managed, his voice tight and reedy.

'Good, then I'll start you off on the bungalows. Got a decent bunch of lads working over there, you should fit right in.'

The foreman pointed to the far corner of the site. Jack hesitated, nervous, then took a tentative step forwards, but George Simmons reached out, stopping him, confiding in a low tone:

'Nothing to be worried about, lad. We've all crossed the line at some point in our lives.'

This was said knowingly, in the spirit of solidarity.

'Work hard and everything will be all right. This is the first day of the rest of your life.'

Patting him firmly on the back, the foreman sent him on his

way. His send-off was energetic, optimistic, upbeat, but Jack felt none of it. He was disoriented and uncertain, viewing events as if at a remove, looking down on this curious scene from above. Everything today had been unsettling and unfamiliar, not least being raised from his bed by his irate probation officer. The journey to the site had been no less disorientating, staring out the window of his taxi as the world passed by. Commuters hurrying to work, parents pushing prams, children in their smart uniforms – everyday scenes, yet he felt so cut off from it all, as if these workaday pursuits were for everyone but him.

His arrival at the site was little better, the taxi driver dumping him and heading off without a word. He'd had to find his own way, making several wrong turns, before locating his point of contact. George Simmons had been friendly but brisk, which is why Jack found himself walking through the heart of a noisy building site. He'd never been in a workplace before, having spent his nineteen years in an abusive home, a prison cell and a secure unit. How did it work? What were the rules? How did you get along without pissing anyone off or provoking unwanted attention? He'd never had a dad to take him to the football, to teach him how to socialise, how to front up to other people, any of that shit. What was he supposed to *do*?

'Look out fellas, we've got fresh meat . . .'

Embarrassed, Jack realized the burly builder was referring to him. Several others looked up, intrigued by his arrival.

'Not much to him, but we could always use an extra brickie. What's your name, handsome?'

'Jack.'

'Jack the lad, eh?'

'I guess.'

'Don't look so scared, boy. I'm not going to eat you. Get over there next to Jez, show us what you got . . .'

EYE FOR AN EYE

EYE FOR AN EYE

Jack did as he was told, aware that several knowing looks were passing between the rest of the gang. Positioning himself next to Jez, a lanky flame-haired bloke, Jack picked up a brick and trowel, following his colleague's lead.

'So where you from, Jack?' Jez asked amiably.

'Epping,' Jack mumbled, concentrating on laying the mortar evenly.

'A forest dweller, eh? You into loads of weird shit, Jacky boy?'

'Don't think so,' Jack responded weakly.

'You don't sound too sure,' Jez laughed, slapping on some fresh mortar. 'What's your thing then? Football? Birds? Weed?'

'Football, I guess.'

'Which team?'

Jack hesitated for a moment, then replied:

'West Ham.'

Jez puffed out his cheeks in disgust.

'Jesus Christ. Lads, we've got a bloody Hammer here...'

A volley of abuse drifted Jack's way, then people returned to work, the novelty of his arrival wearing off. Soon he was all but forgotten, the rest of the crew chatting amongst themselves.

'D'you see those pictures on Twitter?' Jez asked, excited.

'What?'

'You know, the guy in Bolton. An internet group – vigilantes and that – posted them. The pics were only up for a bit, but they were sick, man. You could see the bloke's head split open, blood everywhere.'

Jack froze, the brick suspended in his hand. He had no idea what Jez was talking about, but he didn't like it.

'Who was he then?'

'Mark Willis. The guy that spit-roasted that old dear, then smashed her head in, when he was only a nipper. Some folk caught up with him last night, chased him through a housing estate. He jumped thirty feet from a bridge apparently, just to get away. Landed on the ring road in the middle of the traffic. He was opened up like a jam pudding.'

A noise was growing in Jack's ears. Was this really *true*?

'Still too good for him,' another builder piped up. 'I bet those guys are gutted that they didn't get their hands on him, give him a *proper* send-off.'

'They'd have ripped him apart.'

'Too bloody right. You rape old biddies, what do you expect? That guy was an animal...'

Jack tried to block out the voices, tried to focus, but his vision was blurring and he felt dizzy.

'If someone told me where one of these sickos was, I'd be straight round there. Gut him with a fucking trowel,' another brickie declared.

'Trowel? You want bolt cutters, mate. Snip his knackers off...'

'Spot on. I'd take them all out, one by one. Make them suffer. Kiddie fiddlers, rapists, the lot.'

This provoked general agreement and now Jez's voice cut through.

'What about you, Captain Jack? Want to be part of the lynch mob?'

Jack couldn't speak. His chest felt tight, his legs unstable and his hand was shaking, mortar sliding off his trowel.

'Sure,' he said loudly, feigning a smile. 'Sign me up.'

'That's the spirit. Got the bloody terminator here, lads.'

Laughing, the builders returned to their theme, outlining the ritual violence they would inflict on those they deemed beyond the pale. Their anger, their blood lust filled Jack's head, rendering it impossible for him to concentrate on his work, the bricks landing unevenly on each other as he manically applied the mortar. He wanted to blot out their hate, to zone out to somewhere happier, but he was surrounded on all sides by bile and vitriol. He was tempted to flee, to hare from the site and keep running, though there was no question of drawing attention to himself in that way. So, instead, he remained quiet, piling brick upon brick, confused and scared, praying all the while that the angry young men wouldn't notice the devil in their midst.

Chapter 23

'For God's sake, do you *want* me to have a nervous breakdown?'

Olivia knew it was pointless losing her rag like this, but her frustration was boiling over. Eyeballing the recalcitrant ex-burglar in the armchair opposite her, she continued:

'How long have you been doing this, Eric? Surely you've learned the rules by now.'

'Course I have,' the probationer replied, scratching his belly. 'But it's all bullshit. I ain't no threat to society anymore, so why should I jump through hoops? I'm not a circus dog.'

'I wish you bloody were, you'd be easier to train.'

Olivia wanted to put him in his place, furious that this oaf, who wasn't even her client, was being so obstructive. But to her annoyance, Eric burst out laughing.

'That's pretty good, I like that. Perhaps you could come more often, instead of that other one. He's fat as butter and reeks of—'

'Not if I can help it,' Olivia interrupted. 'If Charlie's not back at work by Monday, I'll go round there myself, smoke him out.'

More laughter, which only annoyed her further.

'As you know, you've got to complete three purposeful activities per week in order for me to sign you off,' she continued, as if speaking to a child. 'What shall I put on the form?'

Silence, the portly ex-con staring thoughtfully at the stained ceiling.

'Did you attend your AA session?'

'Missed it this week.'

'What about your community reconstruction programme?'

'They keep changing the times ...'

Olivia was losing the will to live, but pressed on.

'What about training, then? You were doing a course in ... in carpentry, weren't you?'

'Tiling, actually.'

'OK, well that's good,' Olivia responded, raising her pen to tick the box.

'Only the bloke was off sick this week.'

Defeated, Olivia withdrew her pen.

'So what *have* you done? Have you done anything productive this week?'

A long silence, before Eric finally responded.

'Well, I did tidy the kitchen.'

Olivia hesitated. It wasn't even close to being enough, but it would have to do. Ticking the box, she replied:

'Well, that's one down. Let's see if we can muster two more before Friday, OK?'

Walking back to her car, Olivia felt more washed out than ever. Every probationer on her list, from harmless burglar to child killer, was a mess – slovenly, careless, despairing, panicking, suicidal or just plain lazy. Could none of them give her a break? Make her day a little easier? Things had started badly and were getting steadily worse. The nausea had gone, but had been replaced by crushing tiredness and a splitting headache. In the past, Olivia had pushed through these frequent lows with coffee, alcohol and cigarettes, the latter providing the necessary motivation to get her through the working day. How she craved one now – to give her the necessary pick-me-up, to drive her headache away – but she was trying to give up, had been down to one cigarette a day for weeks now...

Her eyes alighted on the newsagent opposite.

'Bugger it...' she muttered, crossing the road and heading inside.

Making her way to the counter, she was greeted by the owner, an Eastern European guy in a Paris St Germain shirt, but she ignored his small talk, cutting to the chase:

'Twenty Marlboro Red, please.'

He obliged, opening the discreet cupboard behind him and ferreting about. As he did so, Olivia clocked the stacks of newspapers ranged in front of her. Immediately, she forgot about her cigarettes, her eyes drawn to the front pages. Every title ran with the story of Mark Willis's death, his chilling twelve-year-old mug shot staring out at the reader. Olivia knew that endless pages would be devoted to yesterday's events, relaying sensational details of the probationer's death, whilst taking the opportunity to revel in his shocking offences once more. She flicked through the *Mirror*, which contained numerous grainy shots of the crime scene, before moving onto the *Daily Mail*. It doubled down on the sensational aspects of Willis's murder too, but also devoted its entire opinion piece to a withering attack on the Probation Service, singling out embattled director Jeremy Firth for particularly close attention. Happy to pour fuel on the fire, the tabloid seemed intent on making the situation intolerable for everyone involved.

'Terrible, isn't it?'

Olivia looked up to see the shopkeeper staring at the headlines.

'Who's the winner in all that? Nobody...'

Taking the cigarettes from him, Olivia said nothing, running her eye over the headlines one last time. Maybe he was right – there were certainly many editorials here that would take the same line. But Olivia suspected that the general public would take a different view, might believe that justice had finally been done. Several of the tabloids had adopted this line of thinking, but it was the *Mirror* that summed up this feeling best, with its simple but arresting headline:

AN EYE FOR AN EYE

Chapter 24

'Have you seen the papers?'

Jeremy Firth sounded casual, blasé even, but Christopher Parkes could tell his boss was intensely interested in his response.

'I glimpsed them, but haven't fully digested them yet,' Christopher replied evenly.

This was not true. Christopher had pored over every major paper and newsfeed in his office this morning and, whilst he hadn't been surprised by the criticism of the Service, he had been taken aback by the level of vitriol aimed at its long-serving director.

'I didn't see anything in them that should particularly alarm us,' Christopher continued brightly. 'Though obviously we're going to get a huge amount of criticism over Willis's death. Dress it up how you like, it *was* a major cock-up.'

'Not by us,' Firth said quickly. 'The Bolton MAPPA team had total jurisdictional control and responsibility for Mark Willis. This was Alice Dunne's fault, no one else's.'

'Is that the party line then?' Christopher asked, looking up from the selection of newspapers smeared over the boardroom table.

'It's the truth. Unless you think there's someone else who should carry the can for this debacle?'

It was another test, another challenge, one that Christopher wasn't prepared to rise to.

'So we're saying it's a local issue?' Christopher asked by way of response.

'Absolutely. And it's vital that *everyone* understands that. It's going to be tin hats on for a few weeks now. Journalists, commentators, government ministers are all going to make hay with this story, so it's vital we appear credible, steadfast and united. We can't have any deviation from our central message. Any hint of weakness or division and they'll take us apart piece by piece, undo all the good work we've done over the last fifteen years...'

The exact duration of Firth's tenure as director, Christopher noted, though he said nothing.

'Solidarity is key, now more than ever,' Firth added. 'I take it I can rely on you to ensure that that message filters down to the rest of the management team?'

Firth's eyes locked onto Christopher's as if trying to read his soul. The pair had never been close and Firth had always been suspicious of Parkes's ambition. Never more so than today.

'You can count on me, Jeremy,' Christopher said warmly, breaking into a smile. 'I'll make sure everyone understands the gravity of the situation and is ready to play their part.'

'I'm glad to hear it,' Firth replied firmly, patting Christopher on the shoulder. 'Loyalty is so important in this place. If you want to get ahead...'

'I couldn't agree more,' Christopher replied, his smile still in place.

'I'm glad we understand each other.'

The director's gaze remained fixed on Christopher. Whether this was to cement their bond or root out disloyalty, Christopher wasn't sure. But he gave away nothing, maintaining eye contact, until Firth himself moved away.

'Oh well, back to the coal face,' the director said jauntily, leaving the boardroom and sauntering off down the corridor.

Christopher waited until Firth was out of sight, before returning his gaze to the hatchet job on the table. His eyes ran over the damning headlines, before pausing on a comment piece in the *Daily Mail*, which was strongly critical of Firth. The deputy director drank in the text, enjoying its excoriating tone, before alighting on the journalist's byline, which displayed her contact details, urging readers to get in touch if they had a story.

Madeleine Barker: madeleinebarker@dailymail.com

Christopher paused, his eyes fixed on her email address. Then, checking the coast was clear, he picked up the newspaper and, secreting it in his briefcase, swiftly left the room.

Chapter 25

'What exactly are you accusing me of?'

Detective Inspector Martin Coates glared at Chandra Dabral across the table, his hostility palpable. Interviewing a fellow police officer is a fraught affair and Chandra had tried to be polite and diplomatic in her questioning, but Coates had been impatient, touchy and aggressive from the off. Now he seemed to be losing it all together.

'I'm simply trying to ascertain whether you can help us with our enquiries,' Chandra replied calmly. 'I'd like to get to the bottom of this as quickly as possible, as I'm sure would *you*.'

'Spot on,' he shot back. 'I should be back in Bolton, with my Force, rather than down here dealing with your half-cocked fantasies.'

Chandra raised an eyebrow, unimpressed by this blatant attack on her authority.

'Inspector Coates, you're here at my request, for which I thank you. But be under no illusion. Regardless of your rank and your status, I will arrest you, let you cool off in the cells, if I feel you are deliberately trying to obstruct an ongoing investigation. Is that clear?'

He glared at her with contempt, but did not push back.

'Good, so let's pick up where we left off, shall we? On the

seventh of November, you were in Shepherd's Bush at a Ministry of Justice conference, arriving in London on the 06:53 train from Manchester, returning home on the 21:53 train from Euston? Am I right so far?'

'Yes,' Coates replied testily.

'Did you send or receive any messages during the time you were in London?'

'Of course. Dozens.'

'From which devices?'

'From my phone and my laptop, both of which you currently have in your possession.'

'Any other devices?'

'No! How many more times do you want me to say it? I've never owned a Samsung Galaxy.'

'You're absolutely *sure* about that? Because this is your last chance—'

'Why would I do what you're suggesting?' Coates interrupted brusquely. 'Why would I risk my career, betray my vocation, to endanger the life of someone in my care?'

'I was hoping you'd tell me.'

'I was on his MAPPA team, for God's sake. I'd been monitoring Mark Willis for over two years, checking that he was safe, ensuring he was rebuilding his life. Why would I suddenly turn on him for a cheap moment of revenge?'

'Maybe you had doubts about him? Perhaps you felt he was mugging you off, pretending to toe the line, whilst actually re-offending? There *were* incidents early on in his probation when concerns were raised about his behaviour, weren't there?'

'That was ages ago, and it was just a misunderstanding. Mark Willis had been good as gold recently.'

'Perhaps you thought he hadn't been punished enough in the first place, then? There are plenty of officers in your neck of the woods who thought a few years in a secure unit was meagre justice for the Bridge family.'

'Maybe, but I've never met anyone expressing that opinion and I certainly wouldn't condone it.'

The police officer sat back in his chair, folding his arms, as if bringing the conversation to its natural end. But Chandra wasn't having that.

'Tell me about Ian Blackwell.'

Now she saw a reaction. Coates recovered quickly, but Chandra had definitely seen a moment of uncertainty, of fear even.

'He's my cousin,' Coates explained, before adding quickly, 'but we're not close.'

'He was sacked two years ago for misconduct in public office.'

Chandra let these words hang in the air.

'Nasty incident, wasn't it? Blackwell released confidential information whilst still a serving police officer. Incited the public to attack a suspected paedophile living in the Burnley area. Correct?'

'Yes.'

'Isn't it also true that he's the brains behind Justice Never Sleeps, an online vigilante group that specialises in outing so-called "dangers to society"? A group that seemed to be ahead of the curve on Mark Willis's unexpected murder, posting pictures of his corpse within an hour of his death. They were way ahead of the major news networks, other social media—'

'So you've put two and two together and concluded that I committed career suicide to help Ian and his motley crew of have-a-go heroes?'

Chandra said nothing, watching him shrewdly.

'Jesus Christ, this is lunacy!' Coates snapped, losing his cool. 'I have no respect for Ian and certainly wouldn't assist him in any way. He betrayed himself, his vocation, not to mention our family, when he went rogue. It beggars belief that I would help him.'

'So you're not in contact?'

'Of course not, he's a bloody pariah! Within the Force and within our family.'

'That's curious because we've been looking at your phone records – the phone you admit to possessing – which show that you've spoken to him quite frequently in the last few weeks.'

Another marked reaction; Coates caught out again. Chandra pulled two sheets of paper from her file, turning them round for the suspect to see.

'Once on the second of December, once on the twelfth of December, then again on the fourteenth of December.'

'He called me.'

'So you *did* speak then? You admit it?'

'Yes, but—'

'What did you talk about?'

Coates hesitated, searching for the right words.

'Look, I'll admit that he was trying to get me onside, pressurising me to give him titbits of information, anything he might use to raise the profile of his group.'

'I see.'

'But I told him where to go. Said he was endangering my career as well as his liberty.'

'So you just said no and hung up?'

'Yes!'

'But your conversation on the second of December was nearly ten minutes long. And the subsequent one just under five. Seems a long time to me, if all you're doing is telling him to sling his hook.'

Coates was sweating now, fidgeting uncomfortably in his seat.

'Look, the first time, he buttered me up a bit, before coming out and asking me. The second time, he apologized, then turned the screw, implying that the family were all on his side, that they felt he'd done the right thing, which was patently untrue.'

'And you just politely listened? Very good of you.'

'It wasn't like that. I loathe that selfish bastard; I loathe everything he stands for. I would never conspire with him – it's absurd.'

'Well, I don't believe you.'

Coates stared at her, shocked that his emphatic rebuttal had cut no ice.

'You are the clear link between Mark Willis, the leak *and* the Justice Never Sleeps group. You knew where Mark Willis lived, what his routine was, where he liked to drink and, for reasons that I cannot fathom, decided to betray him to his death. The only outstanding questions for me are when you hatched this plot and why you felt compelled to go through with it.'

'No!'

The word exploded from Coates' mouth, harsh and percussive.

'You're *not* pinning this on me. I know your type – ambitious, impatient, keen to make a name for yourself. You may think this is your hot ticket to promotion, the high-profile case that'll make your name, but mark my words, Inspector Dabral...'

His words dripped with scorn and contempt, as his eyes locked onto hers.

'...you'll not climb the ladder by making a scapegoat out of *me*.'

Chapter 26

He remained stock-still, his gaze locked onto the front door. It had taken Mike Burnham just over an hour to make it to Colchester, cutting a swathe through the city on his journey to Meadow Lane. Ensuring he had the right number, Mike parked further up the road, on the opposite side of street. Aware that he'd be visible to anyone passing by in the sleepy residential street, he climbed out and opened the bonnet. He hoped people wouldn't register someone tinkering with his engine, buying him time to watch the terraced house opposite. He just prayed no one asked him what was *wrong* with his vehicle, as he knew absolutely nothing about cars.

Minutes passed, then an hour, then another. Still there was no sign of life in the shabby property opposite. Was this a wild goose chase? A hoax? Part of him hoped it *was*, that this whole escapade would turn out to be a stupid mistake, so he could return to his humdrum life of lethargy and despair. But whilst there was still doubt, whilst there was still a chance that Courtney Turner *was* living here, he had to stick it out. He was, however, finding it increasingly hard to identify things to fiddle with under the bonnet, feeling more and more a fraud. What would he do if someone challenged him? A local busybody, or worse, a police officer? How would he justify his presence here?

Anxious, Mike glanced at his phone, clocking the time. Two hours he'd been here. Even if he left now, he'd still have to explain to Simon why he'd vanished for several hours, missing multiple appointments. Mike felt himself slowly deflating, a wave of depression sweeping over him. Perhaps it *was* madness to have come here on the basis of a random message.

A loud bang made him look up. Someone had left the house, slamming the door behind them. A female figure in leggings and hoodie, heading fast down the street. Was that Turner? Had he missed her? Panicking, Mike eased the bonnet down, clicking it back into place, before locking the car. Waiting until the scurrying figure had made it to the end of the road, Mike then set off in pursuit.

The woman darted round the corner, hurrying away down the high street, occasionally shooting anxious glances at her watch. Following a hundred yards behind, his phone clamped to his ear in mock conversation, Mike strained to get a proper glimpse of her, but it was impossible. Her hoodie was up, her back to him and, besides, he had no concept of how tall she was now, whether she was fat or thin, having last laid eyes on her as an eleven-year-old girl. He couldn't even see her hair colour from here, meaning it was highly likely he was pursuing an innocent stranger. But still he didn't relent.

She strode on, picking up speed. The figure darted down one street, then seemed to cut back on herself, heading sharply in the opposite direction. Had something spooked her? Did she know she was being followed? Mike pressed on regardless, dogging her footsteps, so close now that he could smell the heavily floral perfume she left in her wake. This might be the only chance he'd get to see if the anonymous messenger was telling the truth. The woman was definitely speeding up now, breaking into a light jog, shooting another look at her watch. This cheered Mike. Perhaps she was just running late, heading to an unfamiliar house or restaurant, unaware that anyone was following her.

Now, to his relief, she slowed as a pub came into view. The Rat's Castle didn't look much, with its grubby windows and battered saloon door, but the woman didn't hesitate, disappearing inside. Lowering his speed, Mike made sure that two minutes had passed, before he took a deep breath and stepped inside.

The interior was dingy and tired, the preserve of shirkers, drunkards and students. Feeling self-conscious in his smart suit and crisp shirt, Mike hurried to the bar, gesturing to the barmaid, who reluctantly tore herself away from her phone.

'What can I get you?' she said without interest.

He scanned the taps quickly, selecting Carlsberg, even though he never drank lager.

'Two pounds fifty, mate.'

He paid her quickly, the coins rattling in his shaking hand. Eyeing him curiously, the barmaid took the money and headed for the till. Moments later, she was once more engrossed in her phone, oblivious to his presence.

Mike took a couple of sips, remembering how much he hated tasteless, fizzy beer, then turned to afford himself a better view of the interior. For such a tired establishment, it was surprisingly busy, but he could still make out his quarry, sitting with a crowd of mates in the far corner. She had her back to him, so he took a moment to appraise her companions. They were a rum crowd, all in their late teens and early twenties, dressed in cheap fashion, ornamented with plenty of bling. Baseball caps, earrings, patterns cut into shaved heads, they seemed to be playing at being LA gang members in a tired Essex pub. Rolled up cigarettes perched unlit in a couple of the young men's mouths, signalling their desperation to make a pilgrimage to the smokers' yard.

Mike took another couple of gulps, surprised to find that

he had nearly finished his pint. He was nervous, feeling oddly vulnerable in this unfamiliar watering hole, but he urged himself to keep calm, to remain vigilant. He had come here for one reason and one reason alone. Once he'd worked out if this was a hoax or not, then he could go home. There was no reason why he should come to any harm. At least that's what he kept telling himself.

Mike looked up sharply. There was movement at the back of the pub. The smokers were on the move, heading towards the rear exit. His quarry remained where she was, however, but now shifted in her seat, raising her hand to remove her hood. Mike held his breath, watching intently as she shook out a mass of black hair. Black, raven black hair, the same colour as his daughter's killer.

Could it really be her? On cue, she turned to her friend, affording Mike a view of her profile. Time seemed to stand still, her movements and gestures appearing to take place in slow motion, as memories, bitter, hateful memories, came flooding back. It *was* her, no question about it. It was Courtney Turner. Now she was laughing, that nauseating, high-pitched laugh that he'd heard so often during the trial, as she joked around with Kaylee Jones. From nowhere, it hit Mike like a tidal wave, overwhelming him, consuming him.

Hatred. Pure, undiluted hatred.

Chapter 27

Emily smiled to herself. Driving away from her annoying discussion with Paul, she'd decided to do something she'd never done before in all her years as a professional. She was going to bunk off work.

Normally she'd never have sanctioned this. She had strong views on personal responsibility and the importance of leadership, but she knew she'd be no use today. Mark Willis's murder, Sam's revelation about his sexuality, the fear in Paul's eyes had all come together to leave Emily feeling distracted and on edge. There was no way she'd be able to concentrate on work today, no question of her interacting meaningfully with her colleagues, her clients, her beady-eyed boss. Hang it all, her new deputy was a decent accountant who'd keep things ticking over – *she* could take the strain today.

Emily had called the office, claiming to be sick, revelling briefly in the buzz of this uncharacteristic misbehaviour, then started to make plans. As she drove homeward along the busy A415, she mapped out the rest of the day. She'd go home for a coffee, change out of her work things, then head into Reading town centre. She'd do some clothes shopping, pop in on a friend, then call in at M&S Food for some treats. The last twenty-four hours had been difficult and upsetting and she was determined to spoil Sam tonight, to put their relationship back on an even keel, to let him know how much she loved him.

Cheered, she hummed along to the radio, enjoying the familiar melody of 'Rocking around the Christmas Tree'. She always loved this time of year, going completely over the top, as single parents are wont to do. She knew it was ridiculous, extravagant, but having never enjoyed a proper family Christmas as a child, she felt she was owed a little indulgence. Sam, ever thoughtful, made sure to buy her a nice present, which always moved her deeply. Opening his gift, as he watched expectantly on, was the high point of her year.

Excited, Emily drummed her fingers on the wheel, wishing the traffic would ease up so she could get home. Now that she'd decided on a day of leisure, she was keen to make the most of it. Happily the jam started to ease and the road cleared. Speeding up, Emily slid into the outside lane and, taking advantage of a sudden gap in the traffic, swung off the ring road, just as the lights turned from amber to red. Pleased, she teased the accelerator, racing away. She knew all the back routes, would be home in less than ten minutes now.

As she sped away, however, Emily noticed something. A steel-grey Audi saloon in her rear-view mirror. It was forty feet behind her, keeping a steady pace, but how had it got there? It must have come through on red, but what was the urgency? And now as Emily scrutinized it in the mirror, she felt a tremor of alarm, a flicker of recognition. Was she imagining it or had she seen the same Audi this morning, as she drove to meet Paul? Of course, grey Audi saloons were fairly common, but was there something about the number plate that she recognized from earlier, the OV23 at the start indicating that it was a new vehicle. *Had* she clocked it earlier or was her mind playing tricks on her?

What to do now? Should she speed up, test whether it really

was following her? Or should she slow down, try to see who was at the wheel? The sun was low today, glaring off the Audi's windscreen, so Emily opted for the former, pressing down on the accelerator. She was doing forty, now forty-five in a 30mph zone, but she didn't care, feeling suddenly scared. The car behind seemed to raise its speed too, keeping pace with her, Emily's anxiety rising with each passing second. If she *was* being tailed, who was pursuing her? Making a snap decision, Emily pumped the accelerator, the car behind following suit, before abruptly swinging to the right, skidding to a halt in a bus lane. She lurched forward in her seat, the seatbelt biting into her chest, before falling back into her seat. The Audi shot past, pulling up sharply at the T-junction ahead, before turning left onto Chequer Street and driving away.

Emily watched it go, sweat creeping down her spine. What was that all about? Was she being paranoid? Steadying her breathing, she watched the clock rack up a couple more minutes, then moved off, turning right at the T-junction and speeding away. As she drove, she kept a close eye on her rear-view mirror, but happily the Audi was nowhere to be seen. Soon she was back in Woodley, the neighbourhood she'd called home for the best part of twenty years now. Parking was always easy in her street and normally she'd claim a spot right outside her modest semi-detached house. Today, however, she decided to do things differently, completing two laps of the block, before parking up a hundred yards from her home. She knew she was probably overreacting, but given everything that was going on, she wasn't prepared to take chances.

Better safe than sorry.

Chapter 28

'What's the matter? Is everything OK?'

Russell smiled, amused by Amber's evident confusion and alarm.

'There's nothing wrong. Why should there be?' he replied evasively.

'Well, it's just you said you needed to see me urgently and it's the middle of the working day, so ...'

'So you assumed I was in a crack house, sending you an SOS?'

'Not exactly,' Amber laughed, relieved. 'But I did wonder whether you might need to talk about that, or family stuff or whatever ...'

'No, everything's fine.'

Amber smiled, reassured, but still seemed confused. They were in a busy Pret near her office, which was packed with office workers grabbing a quick sandwich.

'So ...'

'So why did I ask you to come here? During the working day?' Russell said, picking up her thread, pretending to be outraged on her behalf.

'Yeah, kind of.'

'I wanted to see you.'

'Well, that's very sweet of you, but ...'

'And it needed to be *now*.'

He didn't elaborate further, enjoying her confusion.

'Russell, what's going on? Why are you acting weird with me?'

'OK, I'll come out and say it. I need you to bunk off work early today.'

'Right…'

'In fact, it would be better if you didn't go back to the office at all.'

'Because?'

'Because I've got plans for us, but it means leaving soon. You could go back to the office, do the last couple of hours, be a good girl… but it would be more fun if you didn't.'

And now Amber seemed to relax.

'What is it?'

'No, no, no. I need an answer first. Are you prepared to skip work and spend the rest of the day with me? Yes or no?'

Amber stared at him, shaking her head at his cheek, then broke into a smile.

'Well, I am owed time off, plus I did stay late on Monday…'

'That's my girl.'

'I'll say I'm working from home, they'll never know.'

'Right then,' Russell said, rising. 'Let's get cracking.'

Surprised, Amber followed suit, picking up her bag and phone.

'Do I at least get to know what we're doing? Where we're going?'

Russell pretended to consider this, before smiling coyly in response.

'Absolutely not. I've got a little surprise for *you*.'

Chapter 29

'You're just too good to be true. Can't take my eyes off of you ...'

The song blared from the radio, the builders entertaining themselves by joining in. Jez in particular was getting into the swing of it, using his trowel as a microphone and swinging his hips provocatively, as he belted out the words. Jack tried to ignore him, to concentrate on his work, but his mind continued to race with thoughts of Mark Willis, lynch mobs and worse. He desperately wanted to keep his head down, keep focused, but Jez seemed determined to distract him, sliding past now, singing suggestively, whilst delivering a firm slap on his bum. Jack hadn't been expecting it, jumping out of his skin, dropping his trowel in alarm.

'Leave him alone, that's sexual harassment!' one of Jez's mates called out.

'Not in my world. He's *begging* for it,' Jez replied gleefully, before turning his attention to another victim.

Smarting, embarrassed, Jack reclaimed his trowel and continued working. He knew that some of the lads were looking askance at him, curious as to why he was mute in their presence, seemingly determined *not* to be part of the fun. He knew he should join in, be one of the lads, but he couldn't do it. News of Mark Willis's murder had knocked him for six and he felt tongue-tied and sweaty. Besides, what was he supposed to say? What did he have in common with them, with their easy, uncomplicated lives? Fearing his mouth might seize up, or worse that he would gabble and make some mistake in his cover story, Jack decided to say nothing, hoping to appear an industrious worker. However, he knew that he cut an odd, distracted figure, which only made him more anxious.

He tried to reapply himself, but once more he heard footsteps approaching.

'Please, Jez, I'm trying to work,' he pleaded, turning to the joker.

But it wasn't Jez. It was the foreman, George, who did not look pleased.

'What the hell are you playing at, Jack?'

'What do you mean? You told me to come over to the bungalow site and Jez asked me to start work on the short wall—'

'Is that what you call that? I can see that thing's jerry-built *from the other side of the site.*'

Jack stepped back, his heart sinking at he took in the uneven construction.

'Your stacks aren't aligned and the pointing's all over the place. Any load bearing on that and it's done for.'

To illustrate his point, George stepped forward, kicking at the brickwork, which immediately collapsed to the ground.

'What the fuck did you do that for?'

Jack was in George's face before he knew what he was doing. 'That took me all morning!'

If the foreman was surprised by Jack's sudden aggression, he didn't show it, deftly grabbing him by the collar. Tugging the probationer towards him, it was now *his* turn to assert himself, pulling Jack closer and closer, until their noses were almost touching.

'And it'll take you all afternoon to do it again. Understand?'

He glared at Jack, daring him to push back.

'I want it done again from scratch. And I want it done properly. You got a problem with that? Then you can walk, mate. We don't carry *anyone* here.'

Jack wanted to headbutt him, spit in his face, tell him exactly where to go, but there was a steel in the foreman's eyes, a threat in his tone, that suggested this would be a *bad* move. So even though a crowd was watching them, even though he'd have to back down in front of everyone, he dropped his eyes, nodding his compliance.

'That's better,' George said, releasing him. 'I'll be back in an hour to see how you've done.'

Turning, George stalked off, receiving a fist bump from Jez, alongside many approving glances from the lads. Humiliated, Jack turned away to begin his task, snatching up his bucket. He could tell the others were all looking at him and he urged himself to get a grip. He had nearly messed things up on his first day, letting his rage, his anxiety, get the better of him. What the hell was he thinking? He was supposed to be a minor drugs mule, a county lines victim who had been exploited, not some violent, uncontrollable thug.

Suddenly Jack felt ill-equipped for the task, at sea in a world suddenly full of pitfalls and danger. Mark Willis had been killed, *exposed and killed*, yet no one had seen fit to tell him. Instead Olivia had sent him here, waving him off with a cheery smile, to do hard labour with a bunch of mindless oafs who seemed intent on persecuting him. Even now, they were laughing at him, mocking him, insulting him behind his back. He had been someone's plaything before, their whipping boy, their *victim*. He hadn't liked it then and he didn't like it now. So, even as fear continued to grip him, as anxiety coursed through his veins, another emotion began to stir inside him, as he laid one brick on top of another.

A dark, simmering anger.

Chapter 30

He stared at her, consumed with rage. Mike struggled to believe it, but the evidence was right in front of him. Here was Courtney Turner, the girl who'd butchered his little girl, all grown up, flourishing, having fun. The very notion was unspeakable, immoral, obscene. This piece of shit should be burning in hell, not sitting here laughing, joking and drinking. Even now she was flirting with some ripped guy next to her, running her finger over his biceps. The sight made Mike feel sick to the stomach. What right did *she* have to be living life, enjoying herself, when his little girl was lying six feet underground?

Turning away, Mike stared hard at his empty pint glass. His blood was boiling, he wanted to scream out in anger, heralding the injustice of this world, but some semblance of common sense remained, counselling caution. So instead he gripped the bar, squeezing the sticky dark wood until his fingers stung, battling to regain his composure.

But it was hard. So hard. This was everything he'd feared and worse. Ever since their conviction, the lives of the two girls who'd murdered Jessica had been shrouded in secrecy, the police and Probation Service going out of their way to protect them. Even so, the odd titbit of information had made its way into the popular press, revealing how Courtney Turner had led a cushy life in a plush young offenders' unit, indulged, cossetted, given whatever she wanted. This situation had been a step up from her home life and the convicted criminal must have thought she'd hit the jackpot, taking advantage of others' naivety and generosity of spirit. She hadn't been punished for her crime, she'd been *rewarded*, taught that you could commit an act of barbaric cruelty and somehow prosper from it. Who in their right mind thought this was the right way to deal with these thugs? They should be made to face up to their wrongdoing, to understand the appalling damage they'd done, but instead they were reaping the dividends, laughing in the face of justice.

Right on cue, there it was again. That hideous, sneering laugh. He'd heard it in his nightmares countless times, replaying the grim scenes from the courtroom where Courtney had giggled and joked with her younger accomplice, Kaylee, even as the details of Turner's appalling savagery were relayed to the shocked jurors. Mike gripped the bar harder, his fingers burning with agony, as he remembered their disinterest, their self-absorbed amusement whilst those present were forced to watch mobile phone footage from the attack, Kaylee filming her accomplice as Courtney mocked and belittled Jessica, as the young girl lay on the ground, crying and begging for mercy. Even now he could hear the sound of Courtney spitting on her, degrading his daughter in the vilest terms, outlining exactly what was going to happen to her. He recalled with equal clarity the nervous giggling behind the camera, Kaylee's weak protests, before Courtney put her protesting sidekick in her place, picking up a rock to begin stoning their helpless victim. But what killed him, what ensured that he'd not had a moment's peace since, was the sound of Courtney's heartless laughter as she attacked her prone victim, each rock that landed sending a jolt of pure rage right through him …

A peal of nasal laughter rang out once more, Courtney throwing her head back as she opened her lungs and this time Mike was on the move. Shoving his bar stool aside, he made directly for her, marching across the floor. His mind was raging, he could barely see, but he knew exactly what he was going to do. He'd yank her backwards by her raven hair, pin her down, then punch her wicked, braying face until all that was left of her was—

'Watch out, mate!'

The warning came too late, Mike barrelling into a burly bloke carrying four pints of lager. Such was the force of the collision that one glass fell to the floor, smashing, whilst the rest of the lager cascaded over Mike's white shirt. His progress brutally arrested, Mike stood there in shock, his anger doused by the ice-cold liquid dripping down his front.

'That's four bloody pints gone.'

Mike stared at him, surprised that this guy could be so worked up over a few drinks. But now he became aware that the aggrieved customer was not the only interested party, other drinkers turning to see what all the fuss was about. Brought to his senses, Mike pulled out his wallet, pressing a twenty-pound note into the man's hand.

'Get yourself some more. I'm very sorry.'

Turning, Mike hurried away, ignoring the vile verbal abuse that pursued him. Having been on the point of committing a serious crime, in front of a sea of witnesses, it was time to retreat, to lick his wounds, to try to regain some kind of equilibrium. He'd burned to know if Courtney really was here, if she was living a comfortable life in Essex, but now he had his answer, he just wanted to be away. It had been a mistake to come here and he made haste, pulling open the pub door to make his escape.

But as ever Courtney Turner had the last word, as she had done in real life and in his nightmares, for as Mike stepped out into the freezing night air, he heard it once more.

That awful, mocking laugh.

Chapter 31

Amber shrieked with laughter as the Waltzer spun round and round. Clinging on for dear life, Russell loved every second of it, drinking in her abandon, her joy, loving every second of it. He wasn't normally one for fairground rides, but Amber adored them and her unbounded excitement about being back on Brighton Pier was enough to convince him to overcome his misgivings. Normally, he'd have been praying for the nausea-inducing ride to come to a swift conclusion. Tonight, however, he didn't want it to end.

Things had worked out perfectly. He'd refused to say where they were going, only that they needed to take a train. Once they'd made it to Blackfriars, however, Amber had spotted the Brighton train on the display and knew exactly where they were heading. To his surprise, she had teared up at this, couldn't believe Russell would be so thoughtful, so kind as to arrange this trip down memory lane. He detected a note of sadness underneath; the sense that in an ideal world, her family would be here with her, but this did not detract from her excitement at the prospect of some proper festive fun.

They'd eaten candy floss, ridden rollercoasters, tried and failed to win cuddly toys, even had an abortive slow dance at the end of the pier, an enterprise that lasted seconds before they dissolved into fits of giggles. And now they were on the Waltzer, surrounded by the laughter and screams of dozens of festive revellers, a computerized rendition of 'Frosty the Snowman' fading in and out of focus as they hurtled round. Amber was in her element, having the time of her life, but now her smile started to fade as the ride began to slow.

'Awwww,' she moaned theatrically, putting on a sulky child's voice. 'Can we go on it again, Dad?'

'Not on your life,' Russell laughed. 'Once was definitely enough.'

'Spoilsport,' his date retorted, punching him on the arm.

The ride slowed to a halt, the rusting metal arm that had held them in place lifting. Amber was first out the blocks, leaping down and hurrying away towards a hot drinks concession.

'Hot chocolate and marshmallows?' she called over her shoulder, darting to the front of queue, just in front of a large family.

'Not a chance. I'm never eating or drinking again. I feel sick as a dog.'

Laughing, Amber placed her order and moments later they were strolling towards the end of the pier, finally putting some distance between themselves and the throng.

'Thank you, Russell,' Amber said quietly, slipping her arm through his. 'This means a lot.'

'You don't need to thank me,' he replied quickly. 'I wanted to do it. I just hope it's as fun and enjoyable as you remember.'

'It's better,' she cooed, snuggling up to him.

They walked to the end of the pier in silence, Russell thrilling to her touch. Such an outcome would have seemed impossible a few years back, when his name was still a byword for depravity, yet here he was strolling along with a beautiful woman, drawing admiring glances from passers-by. For years he'd been dismissed as evil, as pondlife, yet here he was sticking two fingers up at the lot of them. He had a sexy girl on his arm, who liked him, who *wanted* him. Pausing at the safety rail, he turned to look back at the festivities, realizing that they were now perfectly framed by the glowing Ferris wheel behind.

'Quick selfie.'

Pulling out his phone, he leaned into her, firing off half a dozen shots.

'Let me see,' Amber urged. 'I'll probably have hair over my face, or my eyes closed...'

But she didn't. She looked bloody gorgeous, the lights of the Ferris wheel bestowing a sparkling festive glow on her features. It was the perfect image, perhaps the best photo he'd ever taken and he felt exhilarated to have captured it. Russell hadn't known how tonight would pan out, if Amber would play ball, but the warm, lithe body pressed against him quelled all his doubts.

It was all going completely to plan.

Chapter 32

'Thanks, Mum, that was great. *More* than great.'

Sam pushed his bowl away and leant back in his chair.

'Are you sure you don't want another helping?' Emily urged. 'There's plenty left.'

'Are you kidding? I've got athletics tomorrow. I shouldn't have had one helping, let alone two.'

'Well if you're sure – it won't be as good tomorrow.'

Smiling, Sam held up his hands in surrender, so Emily relented, picking up the remnants of the bread and butter pudding and carrying it over to the island.

'Hey, Mum…'

She turned, wondering what else he might want.

'You sit down,' Sam continued, rising. 'I'll do the dishes.'

'You don't need to do that.'

'Least I can do after *that* meal.'

Acquiescing, Emily handed over the bowl, watching on with pride as her son, her precious boy, set about doing the dishes. Taking him in, she marvelled at his maturity, his kindness, his sensitivity, wondering what she had done to deserve such a blessing. How foolish all the hurt and anguish of yesterday seemed now. She had been disappointed by his truanting and shocked by the reasons behind it, but it had been *her* fault that things had got so testy and awkward. Sam had just been trying to be honest with her about his situation and she had twisted things, complicating them with her own baggage, her own hang-ups. Her son was just a regular teenager, making his way in the world. No, he was better than most teenagers, having a wisdom, a generosity of spirit, a thoughtfulness that most boys his age lacked. She should remember that, letting him make his own way, giving him space to breathe, without bringing her issues to bear on the situation.

Picking up the plates, she crossed to the dishwasher.

'I told you to sit down,' Sam protested, laughing. 'Can't you stay still for a minute!'

'You know I'm not very good at doing that. I like to keep busy.'

'Have the night off, open some wine, reward yourself for once.'

His words hit home. Maybe she did deserve a treat. She had spent the afternoon making a beef and ale pie, a bread and butter pudding, buying an X-Box voucher to top up his account, ensuring that all was ready for Sam's arrival. He'd returned home in a thoughtful mood, but when he'd seen the effort his mother had gone to, he'd responded with real enthusiasm. He'd been allowed extra time on the Xbox, spent a little while messaging his friends, then enjoyed a meal with his mum during which they'd talked, really talked, about anything and everything. It had gone completely to plan, been a great success and a cool glass of Pinot Grigio did sound good... but old habits die hard.

'Let me just sort out your athletics kit and then maybe I'll have a drink...'

'You're a lost cause,' Sam replied, shaking his head good-naturedly.

Ignoring his gentle censure, Emily left the room, padding

upstairs to the first-floor landing. The drying racks were in the spare bedroom and she soon found herself plucking items off it, gathering shorts, sports vests and socks. She knew many parents found the dull grind of laundry monotonous, even soul-destroying, but she'd never felt that way, always getting a gentle, warm charge from providing clean clothes for her son. It was the same feeling she got when cooking meals, sewing on labels or picking him up from a friend's house. It meant she was being a good parent, a good mum. Which was very important to her.

Hearing a noise, she looked up to see Sam crossing the landing to his bedroom, pulling off his t-shirt and tossing it in the laundry basket.

'Think I'll have a shower before bed, if that's OK,' he said, turning to her.

'Sure. But don't leave the towels on the floor.'

'As if I would.'

Winking, he walked off to the bathroom. Emily watched him go, her eyes picking out the faint scar that peeked out from just above the waistband of his trousers, the product of a burst appendix when he was eleven. It had been horribly distressing and scary at the time – her little Sammy in real pain and anguish – but now the memory cheered her. Though he'd been in considerable discomfort, there'd never been any real danger and there had definitely been some fringe benefits, Emily revelling in the time she'd spent nursing him back to health, spoiling him rotten. If that uncomfortable incident was the worst thing that had happened in the first fourteen years of Sam's life, then she had to be doing something right. Her childhood had been very different, steeped in violence, poverty and neglect, which had left their mark. She'd been terribly damaged by her upbringing, her mind, her emotions, her soul warped by mistreatment, propelling her towards some very bad choices and some wicked deeds, but it hadn't destroyed her. She had done many bad things in her life, made numerous mistakes, but Sam – caring, loving Sam – wasn't one of them.

He was the only thing she had got dead right.

Chapter 33

He had made his choice in life. Now he had to see it through.

Everywhere he went, Ian Blackwell seemed to be surrounded by people who still believed that happiness was possible, who clung to the old-fashioned notion that marriage, kids, consumer products and a Netflix subscription made for a successful, contented life. He saw it in the faces of Christmas shoppers on the busy streets, in the loved-up expressions of young couples dragging their first Christmas tree home. Hell, he even saw it in the faces of the other customers in this run-down internet café, immigrants messaging their loved ones back home, telling them that they would send money in time for the festivities, that their grand adventure in the UK was working out. Once Blackwell would have been happy for them, would have shared their excitement. Now he thought that they were deluded.

Pulling his baseball cap down further, Blackwell turned away from his neighbour, a voluble woman from the Philippines, to look at his monitor. The café was a dump and the tech slow, but it suited his purposes. No one questioned your business or showed the slightest interest in what you were doing, allowing the former police officer to work unmolested, with little chance of detection. Even if the police did manage to track his activity to this particular café, hidden away in a remote corner of

Brixton, they'd gain precious little intel from the portly Turkish owner, who seemed far more interested in watching porn than vetting his customers. For now, this out-of-the-way dive was the perfect headquarters for Blackwell's operations and he intended to make the most of it.

Sliding his data stick into the port, Blackwell opened up the server. Moments later, he was on the Justice Never Sleeps site, logging in via the admin section. Now he set to work, swiftly uploading two new photos of Willis's body. Unlike the earlier pictures that had been taken by passing motorists, these latest images had been snapped by an attending WPC - one of his followers and a true believer – and they were magnificent in their clarity and detail. If people out there had enjoyed the first snapshots, they'd go crazy for these.

A loud noise made Blackwell look up. The door had swung open, allowing a blast of cold air to rip over the disgruntled patrons, as two teenage boys barged in, laughing and chatting. Innocent though this interruption was, it was a reminder to Blackwell not to linger, so he moved onto the site's private message board. He was amazed to find ten new messages, each with potential sightings of lowlifes up and down the country. He skimmed them, dismissing several as the work of time-wasters and fantasists, but flagging three sightings that had real promise: a rapist who'd skipped bail in Glasgow, a disgraced Scout leader spotted in Blackpool and an eighteen-year-old mum who'd beaten her baby to death seen drinking in a Wetherspoons in Plymouth. All worthy of further investigation when he had the time.

Logging himself out, Blackwell reopened the site, this time accessing it as a normal punter. As he did so, his mouth fell open. The thumbs-up count, the appreciatory comments, were rising second on second, hundreds, no, thousands of ordinary people reacting to his postings, responding to his clarion call for justice. Blackwell had known that Willis's death would be box office, but nevertheless the level of engagement took his breath away. This was more than he'd expected – way more – and it thrilled him to the core. All those sacrifices, all the abuse he'd taken from colleagues, friends and family had been worth it. They'd laughed at his mission, ridiculed his ambition, but the boot was on the other foot now. He only wished his ex-wife could have been here to acknowledge how wrong she'd been about him. He was a success, he was making a difference, he was winning the war.

Having wallowed in the shallows for too long, having been too cautious, too conservative, Ian Blackwell was in the Premier League now. Mark Willis was the first big fish, but he wouldn't be the last. And with each exposure, each victory, Blackwell's following would grow, until the momentum was unstoppable. Willis's death that had lit the blue touch paper that would set this people's revolution in motion. Blackwell loathed any criminals who thought they could mug off the system, committing crimes, then walk away scot-free, but it was those who committed sexual crimes for whom he reserved a special brand of hatred. They were the lowest of the low, those animals like Mark Willis or the recently released Kyle Peters, who preyed on old women and vulnerable children. These rapists and paedophiles, who had thumbed their noses at justice for far too long, were now in the firing line themselves, thanks to *him*. He would see that they were punished for their crimes, enduring the anguish that they had inflicted on their victims. They would feel the terror, the agony, the *fear* that was their due.

For these animals, death, when it eventually came, would be a sweet release.

Chapter 34

'Why didn't you tell me? You should have told me...'

Jack spat the words at Olivia, upset and angry.

'Mark Willis's murder has got nothing to do with you,' Olivia replied firmly, labouring to placate him. 'It's a local issue, some cock-up in Bolton, it's *not relevant*.'

'Not relevant?' he replied, incredulous. 'They found out who he was, they hunted him down. Three bloody guys with pig masks and crowbars. I've seen the footage...'

'How?'

'What do you mean "how"? Every bloke on the site was watching it on his phone. Loving it, laughing about it...'

And now his fear, his anxiety, cut through. Responding to this, Olivia replied gently:

'Look, I'm sorry, Jack. Maybe I *should* have told you, but I didn't want to rattle you on your first day and, honestly, it doesn't affect your situation. You're perfectly safe here.'

'Am I?'

'Yes,' she insisted. 'Obviously we'll review all our security procedures in the wake of this, but I'm certain that when we get to the bottom of it, we'll find that someone in his MAPPA team messed up, or Willis got complacent, gave himself away.

Which is why it's so important to be calm, to act normally and embrace the new you. How did you get on today?'

Jack dropped his gaze, staring angrily at the floor.

'Badly. The foreman said my work was shit and everyone else was banging on about what *they'd* have done if they'd got their hands on Willis. It... it was bloody awful.'

'That must have been very tough,' Olivia replied sympathetically, placing a comforting hand on his arm. 'But it's just bad timing, that's all. The Bolton thing will calm down, you'll get the hang of things and everything'll turn out fine, I promise. You passed your NVQ with the highest marks possible, you're good at what you do, you could really make a career out of it.'

'As if. I'll be lucky to make it to the end of the month, the way things are going.'

'That's crazy talk, Jack. You're not in any danger, I promise you. The best thing you can do is have a quiet evening, get a good night's sleep, then start again in the morning.'

'Easy for you to say. You're in the know. I'm being told *nothing*.'

'I'm telling you now.'

'Someone could be posting my new identity, my address *right now*. But how would I know? I'm being kept in the dark.'

'Ask me anything you want. I'm here fo—'

'It'd be all right if I had a phone,' Jack interrupted. 'Or a tablet. Something where I can keep an eye on the news—'

'Sorry, Jack, I'm not falling for that one.'

A flash of anger in Jack's eyes now.

'If you want news, you can watch the TV or listen to the radio.'

'That's not where the real shit goes down,' Jack replied, working himself up. 'You want to know what's really going on, you need social media. There's that group, Justice Never Sleeps—'

'You know you're not allowed any access to social media,' Olivia intervened firmly, cutting him off. 'So don't go there.'

He glared at her, unrepentant, fizzing with fear and frustration, but Olivia refused to be played. She was too long in the tooth for that.

'Look, I know this is difficult,' she persevered. 'But I'm going to have to ask you to trust me. It's my job to keep you safe, to help you flourish in your new situation, so if there is even the tiniest chance that you might be in danger, I will intervene. I will move you, get you a new identity, whatever it takes. I'm on your side, Jack, but I need you to work with me. And more than that, I need you to trust me. Can you do that?'

'I'm just so isolated here. It freaks me out.'

'I know it's hard being alone. You're used to having people around you and—'

'I mean, how can I protect myself if it's just me?'

'You don't *need* to protect yourself. Nobody knows you're here.'

'But what if they find out? What if they come here? Who's going to protect me? *You?*'

'If I have to, yes. But it won't come to that.'

Puffing out his cheeks, Jack walked away from her, unconvinced.

'Honestly, Jack. You are one hundred per cent safe here, so try not to worry. There's a microwave curry in the fridge, poppadoms on the side and some chocolate yoghurts. Have dinner, watch a bit of TV, relax, then get some rest. I know things seem bad tonight, but honestly you're at the start of a great adventure, Jack. I'm convinced it'll be the making of you.'

Silence, then a brief, surly nod. Stealing a glance at her watch, Olivia continued:

'Look, I'd better run now, but I'll be back first thing tomorrow.

Any problems, any concerns, you have my number. You can call me night or day.'

Another sullen nod. It wasn't much, but it was the best she was going to get.

'Until tomorrow, then.'

She left, closing the living-room door. Crossing to the window, Jack teased open the curtains, watching as she hurried away down the street. He stared out, tense and unhappy, then dropped the curtains, returning to his bag. For a moment, he stood there, surrounded by the deathly quiet of the empty house, then he calmly unzipped his rucksack. Inside, were eight cans of maximum strength cider. He was trying to be a good boy, to do as he was told, but tonight he *needed* oblivion.

Chapter 35

'You're late.'

Mike's ex-wife was not one to mince her words and Alison didn't even bother to greet him before launching in. It had been like this ever since their divorce, a bitter, distressing split that had taken place less than a year after Jessica's murder. They'd had many happy years together prior to that, but the memories of that golden time were harder and harder to summon, especially in the teeth of Alison's naked hostility.

'I'm sorry, got a lot on at work,' Mike lied. 'But I'm here now. Is she ready?'

'Has been for nearly an hour. Honestly, Mike, if you're going to continue seeing Rachel, you're going to have be more reliable. We've all got busy lives to lead, especially at this time of year. I ... We can't be here hanging around, waiting for you.'

'Got somewhere nice to be, have you? You and Dave?' he responded bitterly.

'That's my business. You just hold up your end of the bargain.'

'Here she is!' Mike said brightly, turning away from his wife, to face Rachel who was now padding down the stairs.

His sixteen-year-old daughter smiled sheepishly at him, as she descended the stairs, joining them in the hall.

'You all right, kiddo?'

Another brief, flashed smile. He loved it, but it was a sight that always undid him, Rachel's smile a carbon copy of Jessica's broad grin.

'You OK, Dad?'

'Never better.'

He said it with as much conviction as he could muster, but in reality he felt dreadful. His trip to Colchester had left its mark; Courtney's laugh, her smile, even her scent seeming to cling to him. She was all he could think about, yet somehow he had to force himself to focus. His access to Rachel was limited enough as it was, he didn't dare make a mess of this rare visit.

'But I tell you what – I'm bloody starving. Shall we get cracking?'

She didn't need a second invitation, the atmosphere between the trio tense and heavy. Before long, it was just the pair of them, heading down the street, hand in hand. Mike kept the conversation light, commenting on some of the more absurd light displays in people's front rooms. The mood lightened slowly, Rachel warming to his presence, but he was still relieved when Mac's All Night Diner came into view. It was one of Rachel's favourites and she always enjoyed her visits there.

Safely installed in their booth, they set about attacking the menus. Moments later, burgers had been ordered, sides decided upon and both had large strawberry milkshakes perched in front of them.

'So how's school? How are rehearsals for the Christmas show?'

'All good. Got a decent part this year, which means I've got loads of lines to learn.'

'You'll be fine. You always are.'

'You are coming, aren't you?' she asked, sounding suddenly doubtful.

'Of course, kiddo. Wouldn't miss it.'

He meant it too, though in truth he always found these events hard to take. Couldn't bear the endless looks of sympathy he received, couldn't stand seeing happy couples with their healthy, loving broods. The whole thing made him feel at odds with Christmas, with life.

'What's it about this year?'

'Well, it's the nativity story, but set in a refugee camp in Calais.'

'Different.'

'It's actually all right. It's got music, bit of dance. I'm doing this duet with Charlie. We've practised loads of times, but the moves are like so complicated and we have to do it all while singing and acting. It'll be a miracle if we get it right. Of course, everyone watches while we do it, which makes it *way* worse...'

Rachel was in full flow, gabbling happily about the trials and tribulations of teenage life. Mike let her talk, losing himself in her excitement and enthusiasm, happy that *she* was happy. He liked the energy, the sheer amount of incident and information she was able to rattle out. There was so little going on in his life that it was a pleasure to listen to someone whose life appeared to be a never-ending whirl of highs and lows, triumphs and disasters. He liked to watch her as she spoke, the words sometimes barely registering, enjoying the rapid movement of her mouth, the sparkle in her eye, the dimples that appeared when she smiled or laughed. He was drinking her in now, the words flying at him, staring at her intently, losing himself in her enthusiasm. The outside world, the waitresses and customers, seemed to fade away, his attention locked on his daughter. But as Rachel continued to recount her adventures, something strange began to happen. Her face started to change, slowly at first, then with greater urgency, Jessica's distinctive features replacing those of her sister. Mike blinked, trying to fight it, but he couldn't halt the transformation.

'She thinks I should ask for a solo, but honestly I wouldn't have the nerve...'

Mike looked away, closing his eyes to try to dispel this waking nightmare, but when he looked up once more, it was Jessica talking to him, her sixteen-year-old eyes beaming with excitement and happiness.

'You know what it's like when the spotlight's on you, when everybody is looking. Half the time I want to freak out, half the time I want to dance and sing and go crazy...'

Jessica laughed as she said this, throwing back her head, unleashing that magical smile. Mike felt tears prick his eyes. Here she was, his beautiful daughter, all grown up.

'Honestly, I don't know where I get it from. Mum would run a mile and I can't see you on the stage...'

Mike felt a sob rising in his chest. He wanted to hug his baby girl, hold her close, weep on her shoulder.

'Dad?'

Mike felt a tear roll down his cheek, then another.

'Dad, are you OK?'

Suddenly, Jessica's face vanished to be replaced by Rachel's once more. She looked deeply uncomfortable and, worse, upset.

'Sorry, yes, I'm absolutely fine,' he said, brushing the tears away. 'Just been a long day, that's all. Anyway, don't stop, I'd like to hear more.'

'Have you even heard a word I said?' she demanded angrily.

'Yes, of course. You were talking about your singing and...'

He petered out, unable to continue, undone by his emotion.

'I think we should go,' Rachel said, tears filling *her* eyes now.

'Don't be silly,' Mike protested. 'Our burgers will be here in a minute.'

'*I want to go.*'

Said with a finality that crushed him. Suppressing her tears, Rachel rose, picked up her bag and headed fast for the exit. Gutted, Mike pulled out his wallet and, ignoring the waitress's enquiries, slammed thirty quid on the table before hurrying off. By the time he made it out of the diner, Rachel was already halfway down the street, hurrying home.

The evening was ruined, the party over and there was nothing to do now but hare after her, feeling more than ever like a failed parent.

Chapter 36

Chandra crept across the landing, talking quietly into her phone.

'He's continuing to deny everything, sir, but honestly I think we're onto something.'

She broke off briefly, peeking into the kids' bedroom. Inside, twin toddlers Diya and Pari were slumbering happily, a sight which always melted her heart, but pushing aside her maternal guilt at having missed bedtime, Chandra stepped away from the room, taking care to avoid the creaky floorboard in the middle of the landing.

'What we need now,' she continued, 'is more time. We need to find a concrete connection between Martin Coates and Ian Blackwell. I'm certain that the Justice Never Sleeps group is connected to whoever leaked the confidential intel, given how quickly they were onto the story. So far we've got repeated phone calls between Coates and Blackwell in the days leading up to the attack, which is obviously helpful, but not the *content*, so that could be argued either way in court. Positive, digital communication between the cousins would be helpful, something that *proves* Coates was intent on leaking highly confidential information with the express purpose of exposing and harming Willis.'

She had reached the bedroom now. Stepping inside, she

kicked off her shoes, smiling apologetically at her husband, Nimesh, who lay on the bed reading an Ian Rankin novel.

'And are you confident we can find it?' Detective Superintendent Draper asked pointedly.

'I'm very hopeful, sir. I've got the tech team poring over his laptop, his phone, his desktop computer, plus we've circulated Blackwell's details to every ward in London. We believe Blackwell's currently operating in the capital and obviously his arrest could bring this whole case to a swift conclusion.'

'I'll let you get on, then. Call me the minute you have anything.'

He rang off abruptly, leaving Chandra hanging. Exhaling, she pocketed the phone, then collapsed onto the bed. She felt wrung out, exhausted beyond belief. And this was only day one of what promised to be a gruelling investigation.

'Are you able to tell me what's occurring?' Nimesh asked, doing a very poor impersonation of Nessa.

Despite her tension, his foolishness raised a smile. Whatever Chandra was going through, her lovely, loyal, silly husband always managed to cheer her up.

'No ... though if you've been following the news at all today, you can probably guess what it's connected to.'

'Which means it *must* have been a leak. If you're involved, I mean.'

'I can't confirm that and you're not to speculate, you naughty man.'

Nimesh mimed sealing his lips, raising another smile.

'Have you eaten?' her husband continued. 'I saved you some, can heat it up if you like ...'

'You're a doll,' she said, reaching out and taking his hand in hers. 'But honestly I couldn't eat a thing.'

'Starving yourself isn't going to help. You've got to eat.'

'I know, but honestly I feel sick as a dog.'

'You're not pregnant, are you?' he asked, feigning horror. 'Because if you are, I'm going to kill the bastard who—'

Laughing, she hurled a cushion at him, which he deftly deflected.

'Why are you always so happy?' Chandra asked, amazed.

'Why are you always so stressed?'

Chandra's smile faded. This was a familiar refrain in their relationship, though she never really begrudged the inference, because she knew he was right.

'Because I've just been handed the proverbial poisoned chalice.'

'Great…'

'And I'm fairly sure my future depends on getting the right result and *quickly*.'

'You'll do it. You always do.'

'This one's different,' Chandra replied, shaking her head anxiously. 'I'm going to have to lift a lot of rocks, kick up a real stink, and even then we might not get a conviction. Draper will be watching my every move, the press too, meaning I'll be quietly going out of my mind with worry, working all the hours God sends, whilst you and the girls have to fend for yourselves.'

'We'll be fine. We'll miss you, but we'll cope. I'm not a complete noob.'

'I know, but it's so much to ask of you, they're so little.'

'They're more robust than you think. We can manage without you for a bit.'

'But I don't want you to. I want to be here with you.'

'And you will be again soon, but you *have* to do this.'

Chandra didn't respond; she knew he was right. Her futile notion that she could somehow avoid the beartrap that had been set for her was born partly of a desire to spend time with her young family, but also partly due to fear.

'What if I mess it up, Nims?'

'Don't be daft.'

'I mean it. I've pushed for this. God knows, I've been battering down the door, asking to be given something significant, something high profile. But I never expected *this*.'

She looked up at her husband, real fear in her eyes now.

'What if I'm not up to it?'

Chapter 37

'He has to accept some of the blame, some of the responsibility, yet he seems determined to wash his hands of the whole affair.'

Christopher Parkes' words dripped with contempt, as he eyed his boss across the room. Jeremy Firth seemed in oddly good spirits tonight, holding forth to his colleagues, even making jokes. The Service's Christmas party had gone ahead as planned, in spite of the situation in Bolton, though those present had assumed it would be a rather sombre affair. Firth, it appeared, hadn't got the memo.

'Can you blame him?' Olivia responded wryly. 'He's, what, a year away from retiring? The last thing he wants is a major scandal threatening his pension.'

'Even so, he's in cloud cuckoo land,' Christopher responded, puffing out his cheeks. 'He seems determined to land this on Alice Dunne, even though ultimately every member of the Service is effectively *his* responsibility. If someone fucks up, then it's his fault. He's at the top of the tree, for God's sake.'

'And how do you think he's stayed there for so long? By making sure that nothing ever sticks to him. Every success was at his instigation, every cock-up an aberration by someone else.'

'Even so, you should hear him talk,' Christopher responded tersely. 'He's aware of the shitstorm heading our way and seems far more interested in protecting himself than in getting to the bottom of what actually happened. We spent half the meeting last night discussing whether Dunne could be relied on to go quietly or whether she'd kick up a stink.'

'Perhaps he's just trying to protect the reputation of the Service.'

'There's only one thing he's trying to protect – his position. Something he's done very effectively for the last fifteen years. Jesus, how many scandals have there been during his tenure? Multiple operational cock-ups, not to mention that unpleasant thing with his PA, and yet *still* he clings on, despite being utterly out of step with the modern world, with no interest in innovation, better practice or the public image of this place. He's totally betrayed every decent, hard-working officer here and he needs to be replaced.'

He hissed the words, frustrated ambition lacing every syllable.

'Your time will come.'

'Maybe sooner than you think.'

'What do you mean?' Olivia asked, suddenly intrigued. 'What are you up to?'

Smiling, Olivia was about to stroke his arm, to tease the information out of him, when suddenly she spotted Christopher's wife across the room. Though deep in conversation with Firth, Penny clearly had one eye on the pair. Smiling broadly, Olivia raised her wine glass, a friendly gesture that was reciprocated by Mrs Parkes.

'Your wife is watching us,' she whispered, still smiling.

'Then act natural. We're just two colleagues discussing recent events. Talking of which, how is your charge? Do you think you can keep him afloat?'

'I've no idea, he's completely freaking out,' Olivia replied grimly. 'And don't change the subject, we were talking about you and your wife.'

'Olivia...'

There was a warning tone in his voice, her former lover clearly concerned she was about to make a scene. But Olivia had had a shitty day and wasn't in the mood to be bullied.

'Planning a nice family Christmas, are you?'

'Do we have to do this?' he replied, looking suddenly deflated.

'How *are* the boys by the way?'

'OK, you've made your point.'

'And what point's that, Christopher? Oh, you mean, how you got me pregnant, but are leaving me to spend Christmas alone, whilst you live it up with your perfect nuclear family?'

Checking that his wife wasn't watching, Christopher took Olivia by the arm, steering her to a discreet corner of the room by the bar.

'Oh, that's perfect. Hide me away, out of sight, out of mind.'

'It's not like that, Olivia.'

'That's *exactly* what it's like. You'd love all this to go away, wouldn't you? Swept under the carpet, so you can return to lovely Penny, whom incidentally you said you found boring and suffocating...'

'We talked about this, we agreed that it would be best for everyone—'

'No, *you* talked and *you* agreed. But guess what? Maybe I don't want to have an abortion.'

'Don't lay that on me,' Christopher countered quickly. 'I was very clear about the need for us to be careful.'

'Accidents will happen.'

'It wasn't an accident and you know it,' he fired back, testily.

Olivia stared at him, dumbfounded.

'You think I got pregnant on purpose? That I'm trying to *trap* you?'

He avoided her eye, but his silence confirmed it.

'Fuck you, Christopher.'

'For pity's sake, keep your voice down,' he implored.

'You really are incredible. There's never any comeback with you, is there? Just onwards and upwards, without so much as a glance at the people you leave in your wake.'

'It's not like that, you know it's not. I had ... I have feelings for you, but I just can't do it. Despise me if you want to, but I can't break Penny's heart, can't destroy my boys, by walking out on the family. I know I've fucked up and I'm sorry about that. More than anything I want to try and make things right between us. Will you give me that chance, Olivia? I will make this right, *I promise.*'

She wanted to call him out, rail at him for his selfishness, his arrogance, but her lover was visibly upset, his expression riven with sadness and with regret. Suddenly Olivia felt the fight go out of her, feeling nothing but a profound sense of emptiness and loss.

'How, Christopher? How?'

He held her gaze for a moment, searching for an adequate response, then suddenly broke off, walking away in the direction of his wife. Hollow, devastated, Olivia wanted to break down right there, to cry her eyes out in front of the whole bloody room, but some vestige of common sense, of her dignity, remained, so she marched to the bar instead.

'Double vodka, please. In fact, make it two ...'

Casting around, she looked for her partner in crime. The room was packed with badly dressed civil servants and probation officers desperate to forget the bitter present, to pretend that the endless carousel of funding cuts and resultant cock-ups was just a bad dream from which they'd awaken one day. Olivia wanted no part of their delusion – tonight she wanted to drink with someone as caustic and embittered as herself. Isaac Green could be relied upon to get tanked up at these events, before insulting his colleagues, or if it was a particularly good night, his superiors. But hard as she searched the sea of familiar faces, she couldn't find him. Perplexed, Olivia frowned. It wasn't like Isaac to turn his nose up at free booze. Where the hell was he?

Chapter 38

He shuffled quietly down the corridor, listening intently for any signs of life. He was pretty sure the whole department had vacated the building, heading to an overpriced bar in Westminster for the annual festive celebration that was as pointless as it was forced, but it wouldn't do to take any chances. Not tonight.

Reaching the end of the quiet corridor, Isaac Green buzzed himself into the office, cautiously opening the door and peering inside. To his relief, the vast open-plan area appeared to be deserted, a sombre, lifeless space illuminated by a few glowing monitors. Shutting the door carefully behind him, Isaac didn't waste any time, struggling across the tired carpet towards the private offices of senior management, propelling himself forwards with his walking stick. Security staff would be patrolling the building and would be bound to poke their head in at some point, so there was no question of lingering. The sooner he was in and out the better, especially if he wanted to show his face at the party, which seemed a sensible precaution.

'Well, aren't you a sight for sore eyes?'

Isaac froze, shocked by this sudden voice in the darkness. Turning quickly, he spied Saul Behr hunched in front of his monitor, smiling up at him.

'What the hell, Saul? You scared me half to death.'

'Sorry, mate,' Saul replied, laughing. 'Just pleased to see you. I've been on my lonesome here for over two hours now...'

'What are you even doing here this late?' Isaac demanded, his tone laced with irritation.

'Oh, just catching up on a few emails. I'm so behind, what with everything that's going on. And I really want to stay on top of things.'

Isaac stared at him, staggered that frontline experience had not yet destroyed the young man's idealism and enthusiasm. Perhaps there *were* people in the department who still believed? Then, recovering himself, he asked:

'Not going to the party then?'

'Not really my thing, to be honest,' Saul replied. 'So I was leaving it as late as possible. I suppose I probably should show my face...'

'No chance of getting promoted if you don't. That's lesson number one, mate.'

This seemed to decide it for the ambitious young man, who rose, snatching up his jacket.

'You coming? I can wait for you in the lobby, if—'

'No, you go on,' Isaac responded quickly. 'I've got to check in on a couple of my clients, so I might be a while. See you there later?'

'Don't bet on it. One drink, then home for Netflix in bed.'

Pulling a goofy face, Saul sauntered off. Tense, Isaac watched him go, barely moving a muscle until he'd heard the door shut and his colleague's footsteps recede. Then he was off again, limping over to Christopher Parkes's private office. He tried the handle, which turned easily, revealing the deputy director's private domain. Despite his gnawing anxiety, Isaac felt a surge of adrenaline, excited to have the run of the place once more. Casting one last look over his shoulder, Isaac took a deep breath, then slipped inside the hushed office, securing the door quietly behind him and gently dropping the blinds.

Chapter 39

This was it. This was his moment.

Russell hadn't held back on their journey home to London. Hidden away with Amber in a two-seat berth at the rear of the carriage, he'd given full rein to his desire, kissing her passionately, whilst letting his hands wander over her slender body. From East Croydon Station, it was a fast march back to his flat and the pair now stood on the doorstep in expectant silence. Determined, hungry, Russell pressed home his advantage.

'I'd invite you in, but I know you're not that kind of girl,' he teased.

'I could be persuaded,' Amber responded gamely.

Leaning in, Russell gave her a long, lingering kiss, before breaking off, breathless, buzzing.

'After you,' Amber whispered.

Russell opened the door and ushered her inside.

Once they were in his flat, things moved swiftly. The ruse of a nightcap was dispensed with, Russell pressing Amber up against the front door as they kissed some more. Moments later, they were in the living room, Amber dumping her bag on the floor and falling back onto the sofa, inviting Russell onto her. He didn't need a second invitation. Tearing off his shirt, he ripped hers open, exposing her gym-toned body beneath. Leaning down, he kissed the top of her breasts, watching as goosebumps rose on her soft skin. Now they were sliding onto the floor, entwined around each other. Her tongue sought out his, a charge of pure electricity passing between them. Now he had her on the floor, biting her ears, her neck, before tugging her bra aside to attack her nipple with his tongue.

He was exhilarated, as hard as rock. It had been so long since he'd been intimate with a woman and he yearned to tear Amber's jeans off and fuck her right now on the unforgiving wooden floor. But as his hand scrabbled towards her belt, she stopped him in his tracks.

'Slow down. No need to rush.'

Russell looked up at her, annoyed. But Amber smiled, adding: 'We've got all night...'

Disengaging, she kneeled in front of him. He leaned forwards, hungry to kiss her, but she placed a hand on his chest.

'My turn first.'

He was tempted to ignore her, to force himself on her, but something restrained him. Perhaps she was right, perhaps it *would* be better if he took his time.

'Close your eyes,' she continued.

'Sorry?'

'Close your eyes – I've got a little surprise for you.'

Russell obliged, expectant. Moving forward, Amber ran her finger through his hair, gripping his thick curls, even as she reached into her bag with her spare hand. Russell's breathing was short, his mouth clammy, his excitement reaching fever pitch. Amber looked at him smiling, then, yanking his head back sharply, ripped a kitchen knife across his exposed throat. The blade sank deep into an artery, a wicked arc of blood shooting high into the air. Russell crumpled in on himself, collapsing to the ground, gasping. He couldn't breathe, his vision was blurred, his heart pounding. Lying on the floor, blood pooling around him, he reached out to Amber, appealing for help, but instead she stood over him, knife in hand, her expression one of pure hatred.

'Do I look familiar to you, *Andrew*?' she demanded.

The use of his real name shocked him to the core and now, even in his dire distress, he began to notice something familiar in her impish features, a tiny flicker of recognition. But before he could fully process this thought, Amber struck hard, falling to her knees and driving the knife straight through his right eye socket.

Chapter 40

She slammed the front door shut and slid on the chain, before bending down to pick up the mail. Straightening up too quickly, Olivia suddenly felt dizzy and unstable. Exhausted beyond measure, she'd had too much to drink at the party, in a vain attempt to drown her sorrows, and was regretting it. She was already despondent, washed out and lonely. How much worse would she feel tomorrow with a raging hangover?

Dumping her bag on the floor, Olivia scanned the post. Masses of junk mail advertising everything from pizzas to handymen, but amidst the detritus were a couple of Christmas cards. Momentarily cheered, Olivia tore the first one open, discarding it quickly when she realized it was a generic missive from the local furniture store. Moving onto the second one, which looked more promising, Olivia hastened to the contents, keen to see who the card was from. The message was brief and to the point.

'Happy Christmas from Mum.'

Olivia chuckled darkly, how bloody typical. No energy expended, no affection afforded and certainly no mention of love. There had never been any mention of love, her mother having let it be known many times over the years how disappointed she was not to have had a son. Shaking her head, Olivia turned to look at the cover design and immediately burst into raucous laughter. It was a picture of the Madonna and child, an angelic image of all-consuming motherly love. It was hilarious, beyond perfect, given Olivia's situation and she suddenly found herself howling with laughter at the cosmic fuckery of it all. It seemed incredible to her – incredibly amusing – that her mother, her wretched, loveless mother, had chosen this bloody card of all cards to send her at Christmas. What was she *on*? Had she no memory? No conscience?

Olivia leaned heavily against the wall, gripped by laughter, wild, crazy laughter, her whole body convulsing with mirth. What a joke it all was. What a joke her *life* was. A sad, sorry joke. And now, slowly but steadily, the peals of laughter started to fade, replaced by deep, gasping sobs. In a flash, manic amusement turned to anguish, Olivia clutching the offending card as she slid down the wall to sit on the carpet, crying her heart out.

Day Three

Chapter 41

She teased the key into the lock, listening intently as she opened the front door. Satisfied that her arrival had not been detected, a bone-weary Olivia slipped inside, pulling the door shut behind her. Inside, the house was as quiet as the grave. On the one hand, this was reassuring. If Jack wasn't aware she was in the property, then he'd have no time to conceal any illicit substances, non-approved devices or other evidence of rule-breaking. On the other hand, the crushing silence of the house probably meant that he was still in bed, and that he once more risked being late for work. Olivia shook her aching head in dismay, as she padded towards the bedroom. How many times did he need to be told?

Wrenching the door open, she marched inside. Immediately, the slumbering form, half obscured by an Arsenal duvet, shot upwards, startled.

'What the hell...?' Jack demanded angrily, as he realized who the intruder was.

He snatched up a towel, wrapping it round himself to conceal his skimpy boxer shorts.

'This is my bedroom – you can't just barge in here unannounced.'

'Actually I can. I told you there would be random drug and alcohol tests and today's your lucky day.'

'Oh man...'

'Besides, you're running late for work. The taxi will be here in ten minutes and you're not remotely ready. Sling some things on, let's do the tests, then you can get going.'

Jack stared at her, hostile and recalcitrant.

'Well, chop, chop,' she chided.

'Get out then.'

'Sorry, no can do, rules are rules.'

Muttering, Jack threw on the rest of his clothes, before spraying himself with an obscene amount of Lynx Africa. Choking, Olivia ushered him out.

'Can I brush my teeth first? I can eat on site.'

'Well you can, but I'll have to accompany you to the bathroom and, anyway, it won't do any good. Your bedroom smells like a bloody brewery and I can guess why. So maybe grab something to eat first, then do your teeth?'

Scowling, Jack pushed past her into the kitchen, filling a tall glass with ice-cold water.

'What did you have?' she demanded angrily, pursuing him.

'You're off your head. I had a quiet night like you said.'

'Then you won't mind if I raise my voice,' she said, increasing her volume until she was nearly shouting.

'All right, all right, give it a rest, will you?'

'What did you have?'

'Just some cans of cider, that's all. To wind down...'

'That all?'

'Sure.'

'Drugs?'

He shook his head, avoiding her eye.

'Look at me, Jack.'

'I swear, that's all it was, just a bit of booze, nothing special.'

'You think breaking the rules is *nothing special*? I could have you inside for this kind of breach. Fancy that, do you?'

'Don't be mad.'

'Then *obey the rules*. You're only out on licence, remember that. And don't you dare think of lying to me again. I haven't got the time or the patience.'

'But you encourage me to lie,' Jack protested, livid. 'Every day you tell me to lie – about who I am, where I'm from. How am I supposed to know when to turn it on, and when to turn it off?'

'You offer your cover story to everyone else,' Olivia replied firmly. 'But you are always open and honest with me. That's how it works.'

Shrugging, Jack slumped into a chair, picking at a slice of plain white bread, tearing small pieces off to eat.

'Look, I do understand how hard it is,' Olivia continued, trying to soften her tone. 'Having to play at being someone all day. But it will become easier over time, so natural you won't even know you're doing it.'

'That's easy for you to say, but I'm shitting myself all day, and then I'm back here by myself all night. I'm... I'm going out of mi' head. Got nothing to do, no one to talk to. I bloody hate it, can't *stand* being by myself...'

A flash of self-hatred, of abject loneliness, which was swiftly covered up, Jack rising to refill his water glass. Olivia watched him carefully, before responding gently.

'I know and I sympathise, but these are the cards you've been dealt. This, frankly, is the best hand you're going to get, so you need to try and make it work. There *is* no alternative.'

Jack said nothing, staring into the sink.

'Given recent events, it's even more important that you follow the rules we've set out. Your best defence, your best bet in life, is to *become* Jack Walker. If you do, then I promise you everything will be all right. Please, Jack, for your sanity, for mine, do the right thing, become the man I know you can be.'

She was working hard to sound positive and finally she got a shrug of acceptance. Not before time either, as Olivia knew the taxi could only be moments away.

'Now let's do these tests and get you off to work, shall we?'

Jack reluctantly consented to be breathalysed – close, but not over the limit thankfully – and provided a urine sample, protesting all the while about being watched. Completing the formalities, Olivia sent him to the bathroom to do his teeth, before heading into the kitchen, pulling off her latex gloves to toss them in the bin. Inside, nestled amidst the sticky black plastic were eight empty cans of Diamond White. Grabbing the liner, she pulled it from the bin, before heading towards the back door, dismayed at Jack's weakness and stupidity. She'd given her speech dozens of times, reminding her clients of their responsibilities, but did it ever really sink in? Did they understand the precariousness of their position? Did they not appreciate the glorious opportunity they'd been given? Against the odds, these offenders had had redemption, happiness, hope handed to them on a plate, yet Jack, like so many others before him, seemed intent on sabotaging this escape route, of throwing his last chance away. It was as depressing as it was predictable. Yanking open the back door, Olivia stalked towards the bins in a black mood.

Sometimes she was convinced these people actually *wanted* to get killed.

Chapter 42

'Not a pretty sight, is it?'

Chandra Dabral turned away from the corpse to see a man in an ill-fitting suit approaching. Offering a sweaty hand, he continued:

'Bill Jones. I'm SIO here.'

He puffed out his chest as he spoke, pleased to have landed such a high-profile murder.

'Normally, I wouldn't let another officer set foot on my crime scene...'

Chandra noted the use of 'my', but didn't react.

'...but top brass told me that you had an interest in this one, so here you are...'

His welcome couldn't have been more loaded. Perhaps he didn't like her because she was fast-track. Perhaps he resented her because she was a woman, or Asian, or both. Either way, she didn't care, her only concern now the latest, shocking development in *her* investigation.

'Who found him?' she asked, cutting to the chase.

'His probation officer, Isaac Green,' Jones said, sniffing loudly. 'You're welcome to chat to him once he's finished his formal statement, but basically he checked in on his charge early this morning and found him like this.'

Steeling herself, Chandra turned back to the corpse. Naked and defiled, the thirty-five-year-old man lay in a large circle of congealed blood. His right eye had been destroyed by a savage blow, his right cheek a riot of bruising and blood spatter, whilst his throat hung open, the lolling flap of skin revealing his severed windpipe.

'Real name is Andrew Baynes, though he'd been living here as Russell Morgan for the last eighteen years. I guess revenge *is* a dish best served cold...'

'I'd keep that kind of speculation to a minimum, if I were you,' Chandra replied sharply. 'As yet, there's no concrete link between this attack and what happened in Bolton.'

'Bit of a coincidence though, isn't it?' Jones grinned knowingly. 'Given this guy's history. "The Cannibal Killer"...'

Jones wrapped his mouth around the words, enjoying the theatricality of the moment. Chandra was tempted to tear a strip off him – the idea of anyone gaining pleasure from this brutal crime was obscene – but she held her tongue. Jones was warming to his theme, relaying Baynes's misdemeanours, but Chandra didn't need reminding. Baynes's murder of fourteen-year-old Alice Rose had been national news. Aged only fifteen, the drug-addicted, occult-obsessed teenager had lured his wannabe girlfriend to remote Bedfordshire woodland, where he'd slit her throat, then stabbed her forty-three times, before drinking her blood and attempting to eat her flesh. As with Kyle Peters, Andrew Baynes's subsequent release had caused a media furore, but over the years his case had drifted from public consciousness. Now, however, it would be splashed across the front pages again, specifically linked to the recent murder in Bolton. The perpetrators were no doubt different, probably completely unconnected in fact, but the journey of travel was the same. Somehow, for reasons unknown, these ex-offenders were being exposed and betrayed to their death. This conclusion, despite Chandra's bluster, was inescapable, meaning her life, and that of her team, had just got much harder.

'Yup, this is going to be a big one,' Jones added, echoing her thoughts. 'Kind of thing that comes around once a decade, so I ought to get to it. I think for clarity's sake it would be best if your involvement was kept under wraps. Don't want to confuse the public with a major murder investigation in play, so perhaps you could slip out the back when you're done?'

Jones was already heading to the door, presumably preparing himself for his first media appearance, but Chandra let him go without comment, her attention glued to the body. She hadn't believed DS Buckland when he'd called her this morning with news of Andrew Baynes's murder, couldn't take in the pace at which events were moving, but there was no denying it now. What had initially appeared to be a specific incident of betrayal and revenge in Bolton was fast becoming a national emergency, a conspiracy that threatened the credibility of the entire criminal justice system, not to mention the preservation of law and order itself. The root cause of these catastrophic breaches of security remained opaque, but the attacks themselves were clearly personally motivated, a wanton and pointed act of retribution. Baynes's killer had clearly spent a significant amount of time with his corpse, inflicting innumerable stab wounds on his devastated torso in a sustained and determined assault. To Chandra, the message this relayed was crystal clear.

Andrew Baynes's past had finally caught up with him.

Chapter 43

Emily strode down the street, her spirits soaring. She was still enjoying the afterglow of a wonderful evening with Sam, brimming with gratitude at her good fortune. The last couple of days had been upsetting and disquieting, but now life seemed to be back on track. The memory of her visit to Bridgend was fading, there had been no developments in the tragic Bolton case and, most importantly, she and Sam were reconciled. How stupid their argument seemed now, how clumsy her attempt to push her son away from his identity and sexuality. She may have been a messed-up child, with no boundaries, morality or concept of self-worth, but her boy was not like that. Watching him walk off to school this morning, chatting and joking with his pals, Emily had felt a real flush of pride and hope.

Life seldom allowed her to indulge in such moments of happiness, however. She'd always kept herself busy, taking on extra responsibilities and leadership roles at the modest accountancy firm that had employed her for the last ten years, making sure not a second was wasted, that she was always contributing, helping the firm in numerous small ways. She was never fully remunerated for her industry and dedication, but this had never bothered Emily – she enjoyed giving back, helping others out, gaining a real sense of satisfaction from simply ensuring that the office ran smoothly and efficiently, day in day out.

Time-keeping remained a challenge for her, however, so once more she found herself hurrying down the street. She now regretted having parked her car so far from the house; usually she just shot out the front door straight into the driver's seat. Today, however, she was having to half walk, half jog down the narrow pavement, laden as ever with bags of files. Hot, sweaty, she nevertheless refused to let this dampen her mood, aware that such petty problems were to be laughed off, enjoyed, as the stuff of a happy, normal life.

Struggling on, she juggled her various bags with mixed success, one tote bag now sliding off her shoulder, depositing a clutch of files onto the pavement. Sighing, she bent down to scoop them up before continuing on her way. As she did so, however, she noticed something. A car slowing, then speeding up again, apparently in time with her movements. She heard it first, the fall, then rise of the engine, then glimpsed it out of the corner of her eye, a dark shape dogging her progress. Instantly Emily was on high alert, but telling herself not to be paranoid, she sped up, breaking into a gentle canter in her eagerness to get to her car. Ahead of her, a Morrison's van approached and Emily took advantage of this, straining to see the pursuing car's reflection in the van's windscreen. As the supermarket vehicle passed by, she clocked the vehicle behind her and immediately her heart skipped a beat. It was a dark grey Audi saloon.

Emily hurried on, now only thirty yards from her car. The pursuing vehicle remained close behind, keeping pace with her. She chanced a glance over her shoulder, taking in the OV23 number plate, then swiftly turned away. It *had* to be the same car, the coincidence too great to dismiss. But what should she do? Should she run to her car and speed off? Should she call her probation officer? No, that seemed too alarmist, too extreme, when she might yet be mistaken, her equilibrium disturbed by recent events. What then? Reaching her car, Emily hit the key fob, preparing to disappear from view, to hide from her mystery pursuer. But as she pulled open the driver's door, something made her pause. This was lunacy, running from a phantom driver, with no idea who was at the wheel, what they wanted or whether they had any idea who she really was. From nowhere, Emily felt a surge of defiance, of anger. She hadn't spent two decades rebuilding her life to run scared now. No, it was better to face her fears, confront this strange presence, than spend the rest of the day conjuring up all sorts of dreadful scenarios. Tossing her bags into the passenger seat, Emily suddenly pivoted and marched towards the road, heading directly for the dawdling Audi.

Immediately, the driver reacted, the car slowing to a halt, even though the road was free of traffic. Suspicious, Emily strode on, only fifteen yards or so from the vehicle now. The glare continued to render the windscreen opaque, so she hurried down the line of cars, keen to dart a look through the driver's window. She was closing in on her quarry, ten yards away, now five...

Suddenly the car leapt forward, roaring past her, knocking her sideways into a parked car. Shocked, Emily craned to see through the glass, determined to unmask her pursuer.

And now she clocked him. It was only a fleeting glimpse, a fraction of a second at the most, but the sight made her blood run cold, the recognition instant and chilling.

It was a face she'd not seen in the flesh for nearly thirty years. Her older brother, Robert.

Chapter 44

He watched closely as the young man approached the house. Mike had been stationed in his car since 9 a.m., perusing a copy of the *Daily Mail* whilst also keeping a close eye on the comings and goings at 24 Meadow Lane. The newspaper had helped pass the time, the inside scoop today majoring on Jeremy Firth, the embattled director of the Probation Service, who'd been photographed last night staggering along a road near St James's Park, drunk and unstable following an office Christmas do. Mike was too jaundiced to be angered by this, the article merely confirming everything he thought about the Probation Service, and he had quickly flicked past it to lighter fare. It had kept his mind active at least, as he watched the comings and goings in the quiet suburban street, occasionally looking up from his paper when there was a sudden burst of activity.

The postman had turned up at Courtney's house at half past nine, ringing and knocking fruitlessly, before moving on, resentfully replacing the bulky parcel back in his sack. Forty minutes later, this courier had turned up, slewing his battered Movano across the kerb, before hurrying to the front door. Thirty seconds of bell ringing followed, before he too gave up, taking a picture of the item before tossing it behind the bins. Now he was heading back to his van, his mind already on his next delivery. But

Mike's attention was fixed on the terraced house – a house he was now certain was empty.

Waiting until the courier sped off, Mike looked up and down the street. The morning rush was over, parents and workers alike having headed off for the day, so the road was all but deserted. Reaching into the backseat, Mike picked up a holdall and was about to open the door, when his phone buzzed loudly on the dashboard, making him jump. Pausing, he took in the caller ID, his heart sinking. Simon, again. His boss had already left one snippy message asking when Mike was *thinking* of turning up; this time Mike imagined he would be considerably less polite. He let it ring out. He'd need to invent some excuse in due course – a dash to A&E, an ailing relative – but that was for later. Now he had a job to do.

Climbing out of his car, Mike hurried across the road, barely breaking stride as he darted into Courtney Turner's front garden, before angling sharply right to duck down her side access. The metal gate that had once barred access was rusty and defeated, rocking back and forward on damaged hinges, and Mike eased past it, disappearing from view. He was wearing a coat he'd bought from a charity shop, with a baseball cap pulled down over his face, but still he didn't want to linger.

He scurried down the passage, keeping low, scanning for potential entry points. There was no side door, which was a disappointment, but halfway along the wall, he found a frosted window, which presumably concealed a downstairs toilet or bathroom. Pausing by it, Mike ran a gloved hand round the tired, yellow casement. No doubt this double glazing had once been cutting edge, heralded for its durability and security, but it was old and neglected now, the rubber seals tired and the plastic hinges loose. Smiling to himself, Mike quietly unzipped his holdall, retrieving a hammer and chisel knife from inside. Easing the blade under the seal, just below the locking mechanism, he took aim and struck hard with the hammer, the chisel sliding cleanly forward. Mike smiled to himself – ten years as a window fitter had left their mark. He could still install or break open windows in his sleep. Slipping the hammer into his pocket, he now worked the chisel blade back and forth, once, twice, three times. On the third tug, he put a bit of extra force into it, and obligingly the lock snapped, the window falling open. Gripping the rim, he pulled hard, the aged window groaning slightly as he opened it wide. It had clearly not been opened in years, which suited him fine. Once inside, he could pull it tight shut again, ramming the locking mechanism back into place, ensuring it looked as though it hadn't been opened. If he was clever, if he was careful, nobody would ever know that he'd been in the house at all.

Gripping the frame, he placed one foot on a nearby wall tap and pushed up. First one foot landed, then another, and moments later he was stepping down quietly into a small ground-floor shower room. Immediately, he paused, listening for signs of life, for the first time feeling a stab of nervousness. He'd debated long and hard about coming here, but what choice did he have? Now that he knew where Courtney Turner lived there was no question of staying away, of carrying on as usual. So even though his head was pounding and his stomach turning circles, he slipped his tools back into his holdall and teased open the bathroom door, before taking a breath and disappearing inside.

Chapter 45

'I'm sorry.'

Olivia looked up from the kitchen bin to see a penitent Jack lingering in the doorway. Replacing the bin liner, she straightened up.

'We can talk about it later. Your taxi's waiting so...'

She gestured for him to go, but still Jack hesitated.

'I didn't *want* to break the rules, not on the first day. But I just felt so shit, you know. It's this place, it's so quiet, so dead. It gets to me.'

'I know and I've been thinking about that. Let me see if I can find something to keep you out of mischief. There's a handful of second-hand games consoles that get spread around various properties. If I can get you one of those, would that do?'

If Olivia was expecting excitement or enthusiasm, she was sorely disappointed. Jack barely reacted, continuing to stare at his feet.

'Look, I really think we ought to discuss this later. You're in danger of being late for—'

'I wanna see Danny.'

'I'm sorry?'

Olivia wasn't sure she'd heard him right.

'I want to see my little brother.'

'That's out of the question.'

'Why? It's Christmas, isn't it? And he *is* family…'

'Are you taking the piss, Jack? You've only just got here, just started to take your first baby steps in your new life – why would you want to risk all that by making contact with your family?'

'Because they're all I've got.'

It was said with real feeling, which took Olivia by surprise. She knew Danny was the one member of the family Jack had ever said a good word about, but even so this display of emotion wrong-footed her.

'And I miss them,' Jack continued earnestly. 'You got family, right? You must know what I'm going through.'

Olivia side-stepped this invitation to share personal information, responding:

'Look, I do appreciate how hard it is, especially at this time of year, but your family… well they belong to the old you, don't they? Seeing them again, opening up that can of worms, well, it can only upset you and could, in the wrong circumstances, place you in danger.'

'I'm not talking about going back to Southend. I'm not that stupid. We could hook up in London somewhere, we'd be safe enough there.'

'But why, Jack? Why do you want to see Danny?'

'Because I love him. Because he's my little bro'. The others… well you know what they were like, but Danny always looked out for me, we were *mates*. He'd still come out and see me, I know he would.'

'But what would meeting him achieve?'

'It would make me feel a bit less alone. Like there's *one* person in the universe who doesn't think I'm a piece of shit…'

Olivia said nothing, shocked by his passion. There was anger there, but real vulnerability too. It was a combination that was hard to dismiss.

'You tell me I've got to make this work,' he continued, 'that this is my best chance, well I can't do it. Not alone anyway. People out there...'

He gestured towards the window, indicating the cruel world beyond.

'...they wouldn't piss on me if I was on fire, and here, well, here I've just got myself for company. And that generally doesn't work out too well...'

Olivia was alarmed by his tone, bitter, dark, but said nothing.

'I'm going to go mad here all alone. I need someone to talk to...'

Olivia hesitated, uncertain how to react to this cry from the heart. She couldn't believe she was even considering it, given everything that was going on, but Jack looked close to the edge and she wasn't entirely sure what the outcome might be if she *refused*. Scenting her hesitation, Jack pressed home his advantage.

'Half an hour. That's all. I could meet him during my lunch break, in a pub, or a park.'

'No parks, absolutely not.'

'A pub then. There'd be no one in them in the middle of the day. You could come along if you like. Make sure I stay on the wagon.'

'I haven't got time to go traipsing round London after you. But perhaps that's what you were banking on?'

'Piss off,' Jack shot back angrily. 'I made the offer, if you're too busy that's your outlook.'

'Be that as it may, I still think this is a really bad idea,' Olivia replied firmly, 'and I would strongly advise you to—'

'You can't stop me though, can you?'

Jack was angry, staring at her darkly. She'd been wrong to accuse him of trying to pull the wool over her eyes, losing what little sway she'd had with him.

'Well, no, but—'

'There's nothing *legally* stopping me contacting, meeting my brother, if we do it well away from Southend?'

Jack had her now and he knew it.

'It's actively discouraged, but, no, I can't stop you seeing your brother,' Olivia conceded.

'There you go then.'

'But I can withhold privileges, make changes to your licence, do everything in my power to make your life uncomfortable.'

'What the fuck?'

He was about to explode, so Olivia held up her finger, silencing him.

'So, if we *are* going to do this, we do it my way.'

Surprised, appeased, Jack instantly backed down.

'Whatever you say. You're the boss.'

'Dead right. So, here's the drill. We will do it at a venue of my choosing, somewhere in London. You will call me immediately before and immediately after your meeting, which will last no more than thirty minutes. You will not drink, take drugs, buy or exchange *anything*. You will head straight back to work afterwards, interact with no one else and, above all, you will be *fucking discreet*. Is that understood?'

Olivia was laying it on thick, coming down hard on him, but in truth she was rattled and concerned. This whole scheme was madness, but she had the strong sense that if she refused, he would do it anyway, perhaps even heading back to Southend. Her best bet was to curate this family meeting as best she could and hope that the brothers had lost any closeness they once had, that it would not be something Jack would care to repeat.

'Is that agreed?'

'One hundred per cent.'

'Right then,' Olivia continued, shooting a despondent look at her watch, 'let's make the call.'

Chapter 46

She stabbed wildly at the phone, hammering the buttons. Emily had one eye on the road, the other on the keypad, with the result that she twice entered the wrong number, before finally succeeding in entering the correct digits. Hitting 'Call', she prayed that it wouldn't go straight to voicemail.

Moments later, she heard the call connecting, the ring tone pulsing in the car.

'Please pick up, please pick up...'

Still it rang. What was going on? Why wasn't she picking up?

'Hello, Marianne Jeffries speaking.'

'Marianne, thank God. It's Emily. Emily Lawrence...'

'Are you OK, Emily?' her probation officer responded, concerned. 'What's going on?'

'I've just seen Robert.'

There was a pause on the other end, then:

'Robert, as in...'

'Robert, as in my older brother, who'd rip me apart as soon as look at me. Robert *Slater*...'

Emily's voice trembled as she spoke, tears threatening.

'How sure are you?'

'One hundred per cent. I looked him straight in the eye.'

'Did he approach you?' Marianne asked, seriously worried now.

'No, he was in a car, but he drove right past me. It's him, no question. He's been following me for the last couple of days, I'm sure of it.'

There was a long silence on the other end.

'What the fuck should I do, Marianne?'

'Where are you now?'

'Driving to Sam's school.'

'Good. Pull him out. Make up an emergency, spin him a line. Just get him out. I'll go to your house, get clothes, toiletries and other essentials. We'll meet at the Marriott Hotel, Heathrow, just off junction 5 of the M4, right?'

'Heathrow Marriott, junction 5,' Emily repeated dutifully.

'And, Emily, if your cover is blown, we've no time to waste. Do it quietly, do it carefully, but do it *now*.'

Chapter 47

His nerves were jangling, his breathing shallow, but still he pressed on. Mike had never broken the law before, never trespassed on someone else's property, but somehow he had to be here, had to see what manner of woman this animal had become.

The floorboard creaked loudly as he stepped into the hallway and he froze, his heart in his mouth. But the house was as quiet as the grave, his intrusion undetected. Exhaling slowly, Mike took a few steps forward, poking his head into the kitchen. It was a mess, washing up lying undone in the sink, a plastic bowl coated in congealed porridge sitting on the counter, but there was nothing to detain him, so he moved on.

The front room also contained little of interest, so he padded upstairs, taking care to tread on the sides of the stairs, so as not to trumpet his presence. Cresting the landing, he considered where to head next. There were four doors off, one of them lying ajar to reveal a shabby, family bathroom. Ignoring this, he moved left, pushing at the first door he came to. This revealed a handsome master bedroom, spacious, sun-lit, with an ensuite to the rear. Had the property been owned by someone more houseproud, it could have been a fantastic room – high-ceilinged, airy, with nice Victorian features – but like the kitchen, this room was a tip. Women's underwear littered the floor, alongside discarded magazines and the odd crisp packet, plus there were a number of ashtrays overflowing with joints. It was gross, slovenly, careless, yet even amidst the degradation, there were signs of affluence too. A pair of Nike Jordans sat proudly on the dresser, next to a groaning jewellery box. Alongside that was the box for a new iPhone 14, complete with its contract. Mike picked this up, clocking the hefty monthly fee with interest, making a note of Courtney's phone number. Replacing it, he moved on, his eyes roaming to the bedside table, on which lay a half-eaten bar of Galaxy, a hair scrunchy and a packet of condoms.

The sight of this repelled Mike; the mucky, everyday detritus of this woman's life. Eating, sleeping, fucking. Anger immediately flared in him – why should Courtney be enjoying these simple earthy pleasures, when Jessica never would? He stared down at these discarded personal effects, his rage growing by the second. He'd told himself he was just here out of curiosity, to see what kind of creature Courtney was now, but already his mind was wandering to darker places, fantasising about lying in wait for the unsuspecting young woman, scaring the hell out of her by jumping out at her, confronting her, attacking her...

Suddenly Mike snapped out of this dark reverie. He'd heard something, a noise downstairs. Tensing, he listened closely, his heart in his mouth as he heard the front door shutting, then voices. Two voices, a man's and a woman's, chatting and laughing. Now there was movement, the sound of floorboards groaning, the stairs creaking. Someone was coming fast up the stairs, taking them two at a time, getting closer and closer...

Had he given himself away somehow? Had his presence been detected? There was no time to ponder that now for the footsteps were heading directly for the master bedroom. Panicking, Mike turned, hurrying into the ensuite, just as the bedroom door opened. Stepping behind the bathroom door, Mike pressed himself up against the cold tiles, seeking what little cover he could. And there he remained, holding his breath, now just seconds from discovery.

Chapter 48

He looked so shaken, so bereft, that Chandra wasn't sure he'd heard her.

'Mr Green? I was asking when you last saw Andrew Baynes?'

The veteran probation officer suddenly came alive, turning to Chandra as if seeing her for the first time. They were closeted together in her aged Mondeo, outside Croydon Police Station. It wasn't an ideal interview space, but Chandra reasoned that Green might be more relaxed in an informal environment, plus she didn't want Bill Jones peering over her shoulder. So, as time was of the essence, her Mondeo would have to do.

'Yesterday,' Green muttered, shaking his head sadly. 'We went for a walk in the park.'

'How did he seem?'

'He was his usual confident self. He seemed positive about things, happy even.'

'He didn't express any concerns about his safety?'

'No, not at all. It was probably the most relaxed I've seen him.'

'Did you notice *anything* odd during your interaction yester-day? Anything that struck you as unusual or suspicious?'

'Not really.'

'And is it normal that you would check in with him *every* day?'

Now Green paused, unnerved by the question, so Chandra was quick to follow up.

'I mean, you had a good long chat with him yesterday. What prompted you to turn up at his flat first thing this morning? Were you worried about something?'

'No, I...'

Green, hesitated, as if trying to find the right words.

'In... in the course of our conversation yesterday, he mentioned that he'd met someone – a woman – and that he had developed feelings for her. I was surprised by that; it was the first time Andrew had ever mentioned anything like that in all our years together.'

'So there *was* something unusual about your chat yesterday then?'

'I suppose so,' Green conceded, shifting uneasily in his seat. 'It certainly wasn't a welcome development. I was worried about him, and her too if I'm honest, so I wanted to continue our conversation.'

'To tell him *not* to get involved with her?'

'Potentially. Although obviously it's his life at the end of the day, so...'

'And that's why you were at his flat this morning? That's why you found him?'

Green nodded, but said nothing, staring bleakly out of the windscreen.

'You seem shaken by this death, Isaac?' Chandra observed.

'Wouldn't you be? You saw him, right?'

'I did.'

'Well, then...'

'You were his principal probation officer.'

'His *only* probation officer.'

'You were close to him then?'

'I wouldn't say that. He was a client. But over time you get to know someone, fall into a rhythm with them.'

'You *did* like him then?'

'Like is a strong word. It was important that I never forgot, never glossed over, what Andrew had done.'

'You were troubled, then, by his past actions?'

'Of course. He killed a young girl in cold blood, then mutilated her corpse. That was the context of our relationship, the reason we continued to meet.'

'And by the sounds of it, you felt he might still be a threat?'

'It pays to be careful in my line of work. Look, where is all this going? I've already been grilled by DI Jones. I've agreed to talk to you out of courtesy, but I don't really see—'

'I'm investigating the possibility that someone in authority is deliberately leaking the whereabouts and identities of high-profile ex-offenders.'

'And you think *I* had something to do with it?'

'We'll be interviewing everyone who was privy to confidential information concerning Andrew Baynes. You were the senior probation officer on his MAPPA team, the only person who saw him regularly.'

'This is insane. I was *helping* him.'

The words exploded from Green, laced with anger and irritation.

'Whether I liked him or not was immaterial. I was doing my job and I was making progress. Andrew had got a good job, a nice flat, had kicked the drugs. He was making a go of it, and I was by his side every step of the way. You've no right to accuse me of anything.'

'I'm simply asking you some straightforward questions—'

'Well, you're barking up the wrong tree,' Green interrupted

tersely. 'He was moving on with his life, embracing new opportunities.'

'Like this woman? The new girlfriend?'

Green shrugged, annoyed, receding back into himself.

'Can you describe her to me?' Chandra continued calmly.

'Blonde, tall. A great rack by all accounts…'

He was deliberately goading her now, trying to get a reaction, but Chandra ignored him.

'We've had a look at Baynes's digital footprint, to see if he was messaged by anyone unusual – threatened, warned off, whathave-you. We didn't find anything of interest, but we did find *this*. It's a photo taken last night in Brighton. It's of Baynes and a young woman, apparently on some kind of date. Could this be his new girlfriend?'

Green took Chandra's phone from her, drinking in the image of a loved-up Baynes smiling with a pretty blonde in front of Brighton's Ferris wheel. Instantly, he reacted, his face clouding over.

'What is it, Isaac? What have you seen?' Chandra demanded.

'That's her, all right.'

He sounded stunned, almost lost for words.

'What's more, I know who she is.'

Chapter 49

'Who the fuck do you think you are?'

Jack stared at the irate foreman, but said nothing.

'What makes you think you can turn up an hour late and get away with it? Are you taking the piss?'

'It was the traffic,' Jack lied.

'Bullshit. Everyone else got here on time. Fancied a lie-in, did you?'

Jack stared at his feet, simmering. What the hell was he supposed to say? He couldn't tell the truth, but he couldn't think of a lie quick enough. Now George jolted him out of his deliberations, ramming a fat finger into his chest.

'You don't get a lie-in in this game,' he spelled out. 'You don't get to rest up. You get to work like a dog morning, noon and night, doing what I tell you, when I tell you. Because if you don't, you're out on your ear. Understand?'

Jack wanted to scream. Why were people always lecturing him? But instead he nodded.

'Say it, then,' the foreman demanded. 'Say, yes George, I understand.'

'Yes, George, I understand,' Jack mumbled.

'I'm glad to hear it,' George continued, enjoying himself. 'Because I need to be able to rely on you. I need to able to *trust* you. And, let me tell you you're a long way from that at the moment, mate.'

Who was he kidding? Jack wasn't his mate. Never would be.

'But I'm a fair man. I'm prepared to let you *earn* my trust. I'm pulling you off bricklaying today, you can be my mule instead. See that pile of blocks ...'

He indicated a large pile of bulky concrete blocks.

'...I need them all over the other side of the site. Cooky wants them. You know where I mean, don't you?'

He was being deliberately patronising, determined to humiliate his latest recruit. Jack could see the other builders watching, enjoying the show, his anger flaring once more.

'Now be a good boy and run along. Those blocks won't shift themselves.'

George patted Jack on the head, chuckling, before heading off. Furious, Jack was tempted to haul him back, beat him to the ground, smash his teeth down his stupid, fat face, but he reined in his anger. He was on the edge, aggrieved, unsettled, but he'd promised to make a go of this, to embrace this new life, so swallowing down his anger, he started to load the blocks into a battered wheelbarrow. There was fire in his blood, his mind was racing, but he could just about keep his rage in check. For now.

Chapter 50

He peered through the crack in the door, his anxiety rising with each passing second. The occupant of Courtney's bedroom was the ripped guy Mike had seen her flirting with at the pub. He now lay on the unmade bed, scrolling idly on his phone, apparently unaware of the intruder concealed just a few feet away.

Turning away, Mike wiped the sweat from his brow as he considered his options. There was no way he could make it out of the bedroom without being seen. Should he then front up to the situation, presenting himself and trying to talk his way out of the house? But what the hell could he say? How could he possibly explain his presence here? And what if the guy tried to stop him?

Mike's breath was short, his mind cloudy, but now his eyes fell on the cracked bathroom window. Could he escape? What if he were to tease the window open? Could he climb through it without disturbing the numerous bottles of shampoo on the window sill? Could he leap down to the ground without breaking his ankle? Carefully Mike made his way over to it, one measured step at a time. In his mind he could hear the floorboard creaking noisily, screaming out his presence, summoning the massive hulk next door to fall upon him. But, miraculously, he made it to the window undetected. For a moment, his spirits soared, but as he gripped the upper sill and prepared to push, they plummeted again. The dirty window was painted in, presumably hadn't been opened in years.

His mind reeled. What to do now? He still had his holdall on his back, he had tools he could use to release the window. But such a task would take twenty, thirty minutes at least and would be far too noisy to go undetected. No, he was trapped in the small bathroom. But where did that leave him? What the *hell* should he do?

A sound next door made him look up. Someone else had entered the bedroom. Padding back to his hiding place behind the door, Mike made out Courtney's voice, talking in hushed tones to her man. There was brief chat, laughter, then the sound of the bed groaning as she joined her companion. Mike couldn't believe it, shaking his head in silent consternation. With each passing minute the situation was becoming more alarming and surreal. Courtney Turner was just feet away from him now, lying on the bed in the arms of her lover. It was crazy, dangerous and disorienting all at the same time. Worse than that, it was all his fault.

Silence in the bedroom. For a moment, Mike dared to hope the couple had nodded off, but now he heard a sound that turned his stomach. Kissing. Hungry, moist kissing. Closing his eyes, Mike turned away, wanting to block it all out. But the movement within the bedroom was growing more intense, sheets rustling, clothes being ripped off, the sound of a belt hitting the carpet. Now the duvet was discarded, sliding onto the floor. And then he heard it – a slow, sensuous moan of pleasure. He tried to blot it out, but there was no mistaking the sounds of Courtney's pleasure, which grew steadily louder with each passing second.

'Please make it stop, please make it stop...'

He whispered these words to himself, but if anything, his

silent entreaty only made things worse, a heavy, rhythmic knocking ringing out now, as the bedpost collided noisily with the wall. The guy was talking, terse and assertive, which seemed to heighten Courtney's enjoyment, her moans of pleasure getting louder and louder. For a minute, Mike thought he was going to vomit, the sound of her ecstasy too sickening to bear, and he clamped a fist to his mouth in pure agony. But now, thankfully, his ordeal came to a sudden end, Courtney climaxing loudly just a few feet away from him.

Mike remained stock-still, as the lovemakers gasped and sighed. It had been months, years, since Mike had had sex himself and in other circumstances he might have been turned on by someone else's passion. But the sound of Courtney's enjoyment produced entirely the opposite effect in him. As he stood there, shaking in the bathroom, Mike wanted to tear the house down, set the whole world ablaze. He was seething with bitterness and rage, almost unable to process what he'd just heard. It was awful, beyond awful, seeming to mock his grief, his agony, his loss. How dare she. How dare she enjoy herself like that.

His mind was pulsing, his heart thundering, overcome with emotion and distress. He couldn't believe what he'd experienced, what he'd had to endure, but now to his horror, he realized that the worst was yet to come. For even as he stood there, seething and shaking, he heard movement, Courtney slipping out of bed, crossing the messy floor and pushing straight into the bathroom.

Chapter 51

'What the hell's going on, Mum?'

Sam was staring at his mother as if she was mad. They were standing in the school corridor, ranged opposite each other, isolated yet conspicuous in the mid-morning hush.

'It's nothing bad, but you need to come now.'

'But I'm in the middle of a lesson. Plus, I've got football club at lunchtime...'

'Don't worry about any of that. I've squared it with your teachers, and football club will still be here when you get back.'

'But why do I need to come? I don't understand...'

His confusion was laced with growing anxiety. Emily felt terrible, upset by his obvious concern as he mentally scrolled through the various possible emergencies.

'Is it Dad?'

Emily stared at him, saying nothing. Should she do it? Should she go there?

'Has something happened to him?'

'Nothing bad,' she lied, feeling like a horrible fraud. 'He's just had a bit of an accident at work. He's going to be fine, he's at the hospital now, but I think it would be good if we could go and visit him straightaway.'

'Can I call him?' Sam asked, pulling his phone from his bag.

'Not yet. He said he'd call us as soon as he can.'

Emily smiled gamely at him, feeling guilt-stricken. Sweat was trickling down her back and she felt a throbbing in her temples. Sam seemed to sense this, challenging her:

'What are you not telling me? Why are you acting so weird?'

'I'm not.'

'So why can't I call Dad? I don't understand.'

'He's in with the doctor, that's all. You can speak to him soon, I promise.'

'Are you sure?'

This was her moment to come clean, to admit that Paul was fine and that *she* was the problem. But how could she do that, here of all places? She felt terrible deceiving Sam about his father, but what else could she do? How else could she get him to come with her? As far as Sam was concerned, her parents were dead and she had no siblings, so who else *could* she use to explain her sudden appearance at his school in the middle of the day?

'Trust me,' she found herself saying. 'Everything's going to be OK. But we need to go now.'

Finally, to Emily's enormous relief, Sam relented, the bond of trust between them, built up over many years, prevailing. Fixing a smile on her face, she took her beloved boy by the arm and led him fast down the corridor, pushing through the heavy double doors and away.

Chapter 52

His hands were burning, his legs protesting, but he was nearly there. Just a few more metres and his task would be complete, his torture over. It had taken Jack most of the morning to haul the hundred-odd blocks across the building site, struggling under the enormous weight as the wheelbarrow hit ruts, trenches and other small obstacles. Several times the barrow had tipped over, depositing its weighty load onto the ground, sending up huge plumes of dust. No one had come to his aid, the other builders laughing and cat-calling as he sweated to get the bulky blocks back into the barrow. Jack had sworn bitterly under his breath, wishing them all sorts of misfortune, but had somehow managed to keep his temper, keen to complete his punishment in the shortest time possible.

He was pushing ten circuits now, his hands blistered, his fingers raw, the soles of his feet aching and numb, but he was nearly done. Surely then George would have to relent, bring an end to his humiliation, restoring him to his rightful place amongst the brickies. Taking heart from this, Jack pushed forward, almost sprinting the remaining yards to the swollen pile of blocks, depositing the last load alongside them with a flourish, before dropping to his knees, exhausted, but relieved.

He stayed there, breathing heavily, gathering himself, mentally preparing what he would say to his overseer, how he would frame his genuine regret and renewed commitment. But before he could muster the words, he heard footsteps approaching. Looking up, he saw George Simmons sauntering his way towards him.

'There you go, boss,' he said, rising wearily. 'All moved, like you asked.'

'Well done, Jack. I'm impressed.'

'Happy to help. But honestly I think I'd be more use to you—'

'Thing is, I've changed my mind.'

Jack stared at him, alarmed by his crooked smile, the glint in his eye.

'I *actually* need them where they were this morning, after all. Sorry about that.'

George turned away, smiling, but Jack wasn't having that. Grabbing his arm, he stopped the foreman in his tracks.

'What the fuck are you playing at?'

'Get your hands off me, boy.'

But Jack wouldn't relent. Wouldn't do a damn thing this liar said.

'You asked me to move them, I moved them.'

'And now you'll have to move them again, if you know what's good for you,' the burly foreman replied, plucking Jack's hand from his arm.

'Or what?'

Jack was fizzing with anger and this was an open challenge. But his employer seemed amused by the question.

'Can I let you into a little secret, Jack?' he hissed. 'Only the desperate and the criminal are sent to work with me. Which one are you, eh?'

Immediately, Jack broke eye contact, keen to avoid George's scrutiny.

'My lads are all on skid row, their lives in the toilet, hoping, praying, for one last chance. Well I *am* that last chance, the only one they'll ever get. They do what I want, when I want, and they're grateful for it.'

Smirking, he moved in closer, getting up in Jack's face.

'They're my bitches. Just like you.'

They were almost nose to nose now, stale whisky strong on the foreman's breath.

'Are you ready to roll over then, Jack? Are you ready to be my bitch?'

He smiled, revealing a hideous collection of yellowing teeth. George was enjoying every moment of his dominance, his power ... but he'd picked the wrong cat to kick. Fronting up, Jack rammed his knee into George's groin, once, twice, three times. Taken by surprise, the foreman slumped to his knees, groaning furiously. Jack was tempted to follow up, downing him, stamping on the fat fuck's swollen head. But catching himself, he managed to wrench himself away, tugging off his hi-vis jacket and tossing it to the floor before marching off angrily towards the gates.

Jack could see the shock on the other builders' faces, could hear the vile curses issuing from the floored foreman, but he kept on going, never once looking back. He'd been given his opportunity, a fresh start, and he'd blown it.

There'd be no coming back from this.

Chapter 53

His legs were aching, his muscles burning, but he remained motionless, not daring to move. As Courtney had made her way to the bathroom, Mike had made a split-second decision, stepping into the cracked bathtub, and sliding the shower curtain in front of him. It was thin and cheap, a hideous apricot colour, yet it provided just enough of a barrier to shield him from view, as Courtney stalked in, pushed down the toilet seat and plonked herself down.

Mike was seconds from disaster now. The flimsy curtain had protected him from instant discovery, but Mike knew his bulky silhouette would be instantly visible if Courtney looked his way. He knew this for certain because he could make out *her* shape as she sat in front of him, urinating. This day, which had begun with a very bad decision, was fast becoming a living nightmare. Mike had been surprised, trapped, had eavesdropped on those two animals having sex and now he was hiding in a scummy bathtub, listening to Courtney cleaning herself up. Once more, Mike felt a wave of nausea sweep over him, but he clamped it down. Even if he did manage to get out of this unscathed somehow, God knows what he could be charged with – trespass, breaking and entering, stalking. It beggared belief that he could have been so stupid, but there was nothing to do now but ride it out, so he remained stock-still behind his scant cover, drinking in the strange odour of perfume and marijuana that filled the little room.

Rising, Courtney flushed the toilet, then turned to wash her hands. Seconds later, she was gone, returning to the bedroom. Relieved, Mike exhaled slowly, quietly sucking in much needed oxygen, as he shifted his feet and rotated his aching shoulders. Courtney, meanwhile, hurried back to her bed and Mike strained now to hear her urgent whispers, expecting her burly boyfriend to burst in at any moment. But to his immense relief their chat soon subsided, to be replaced moments later by gentle snoring. Mike couldn't quite believe it, finally sensing a change in his luck, but he remained where he was, letting one minute pass by, two, three…

Now he could hear two sets of snoring, one deep and sonorous, the other light and gentle. Knowing he had to move, that this was his only chance of salvation, he teased the curtain aside and stepped down onto the lino. It took his weight, barely protesting, so he moved quickly to the doorway. Here he paused once again, peeking through the gap in the door, fearful that he was mistaken, that he'd overplayed his hand. But the lovers *were* fast asleep, lying in each other's arms. This was it then. It was time to go.

Gripping the holdall tightly, Mike tiptoed out of the bathroom, making his way steadily across the room. The floor was cluttered and messy, but soon he was at the head of the bed. He was only a few feet from the door now and, if he could just get there, he felt certain he could make it out of the house unscathed, even if the occupants became aware of his presence. He was so close to escaping, to putting this whole nightmare behind him… but now he paused, turning back to the bed. At first, he didn't know why he'd done it, but somehow he felt compelled to linger and, now, looking down at the slumbering pair, he understood. There she was. Courtney Turner, entirely at his mercy.

Instinctively, his hand moved to the holdall. His hammer was so close at hand. How easy it would be to slide it out, raise it above his head and bring it crashing down. He'd dreamed, *fantasized* about this moment, when he would unleash all his fury, his grief, his pain on the animal who'd butchered Jessica. Why not seize it? Right here and now? He hadn't planned it this way, but suddenly it seemed the obvious path to take. Nobody had seen him come or go, so who'd be able to say that he was responsible? Courtney lived in a rough area, so he could make it look like a robbery. Sliding down the zip, he reached inside, locating the reassuring bulk of his hammer. Slipping it out, he weighed it in his hand, surveying his sleeping victims.

Which one should he do first? Everything was propelling him to bring it down on Courtney's skull, but what if he only injured her, or worse, failed to connect? That would alert her boyfriend and then where would he be? He could be injured or killed himself. Should he do the guy first then? But could he be confident of felling him with one blow? Or would he need several, allowing Courtney to wake up and intervene? Could he really subdue them both before being confronted?

It was madness, of course it was. He wouldn't pull it off and, anyway, perhaps someone had seen his car in the road, made a note of the number plate. Also, he had his phone on him, surely his movements could be tracked by the police? No, it would be insane to commit such a rash act and yet... there she was. The phantom of his nightmares, slumbering, unaware, defenceless. Who cares what might happen to him, as long as she couldn't live, love or laugh anymore. That was all that mattered. The *only* thing that mattered.

He must stay the course, clamping down his nerves to see the job through. Mike knew in his heart that part of him had hoped for exactly this scenario when breaking into the property. And here it was, handed to him on a plate. Muttering darkly, Mike raised the hammer again. This was it. It was time to honour Jessica's memory. To see that justice was done. Fixing his eyes on Courtney, Mike screwed down his courage, then brought the hammer down.

As he did so, a piercing scream rang out, causing Mike to suspend his strike in mid-air, the hammer stopping just short of its intended target. At first, he was utterly confused. Courtney had not moved, nor had her boyfriend, so who...?

Mike spun round, expecting to see someone in the doorway, but it was empty. Now another cry rang out, shrill and reedy. Mike turned again, more disorientated than ever, but now he spotted it – a baby monitor lying amidst the detritus on the floor, flashing red. It was a baby, a baby that was crying. Courtney's baby?

The infant's cries were growing louder. Mike turned back to the bed to resume his attack, but now the bulky man was stirring. Courtney too, her eyelids flickering, as she turned in his direction. It was now or never, the danger growing with each passing second, he had to *act*.

As Courtney's eyes started to open, Mike turned and fled, hurrying noiselessly from the room. Gliding down the stairs, he teased the front door open and slipped out, shutting it quietly behind him. Now he was down the path, then onto the street, walking first, then jogging, before finally sprinting back to his awaiting car, breathless and scared.

It had been a mistake to come here.

Chapter 54

It was time to go.

Flinging open her suitcase, Caitlin Rose grabbed great armfuls of her clothes, stuffing them inside. She was careless, barely registering what she was selecting, determined to cram in as much as she could, as quickly as she could. Now she was scooping up her make-up bag, a phone charger, a packet of Nurofen, two pairs of trainers, tossing them in too, before picking up the framed photo from the dresser. This she handled with more care, wrapping it carefully in a cardigan, before placing it gently in the suitcase. It was the best picture she had of Alice, her beloved little sister, and she wasn't prepared to damage it.

Zipping up the suitcase, she crossed to the bedside table, yanking the drawer open. She knew her passport was in there, but it was still a relief to see it staring up at her. She flicked it open, double-checking that it was still in date, that everything was as it should be. Momentarily her eyes flicked to the photo, taking in her natural, unadorned features and her trademark cropped cut. How different she seemed in that photo compared to her current incarnation, with her flowing blonde locks and heavy make-up. Strange how things work out. Truth was, she had enjoyed her brief time as 'Amber', her more confident, more ruthless alter ego. She'd enjoyed the male attention she provoked, her golden hair and lithe figure attracting many approving glances. She had also enjoyed the deceit, effortlessly fooling that sadistic fuck into thinking she was attracted to *him*. And she'd enjoyed the pay-off, driving that kitchen knife through Baynes's eye. She could vividly recall his look of shock, of horror, of fleeting realization, the memory still making her tingle with pleasure.

But that was then. Now her task was to get to Luton Airport before her involvement in his murder was detected. She felt sure that she would achieve this, for the simple reason that not a soul in the world knew what she'd been up to. She had planned, prepared and executed this whole thing herself and planned to be long gone when – *if* – they ever worked out who the lovely 'Amber' really was. Baynes certainly didn't have any real friends and his family had long ago disowned him, so with any luck it might be a matter of days before his body was discovered, by which time she would be in Southern Spain, perhaps even North Africa, living under a false name, enjoying her liberation from the curse of Andrew Baynes.

Plonking the heavy suitcase on the floor, Caitlin took one last look around the room. Once upon a time, she'd shared it with her older sister, until Alice turned thirteen and decided she needed her own room. To Caitlin, this had felt like a gross betrayal, but this was the only blemish on their friendship, their love. She had adored, idolized her older sister, right up until the moment she was lured into those woods. The ensuing trauma, the media frenzy, that gut-wrenching trial had cost them dear, her mother most perhaps, but they'd all suffered. Caitlin knew she'd become difficult – wilful, violent, easy prey for those who wanted to sell her drugs – but one element of goodness had survived. Her love for and loyalty to Alice. This had spurred her on, had given her strength to wreak revenge for the terrible wrong done to that innocent girl. Stroking the wall with her finger, Caitlin drank in the happy memories contained in this room, the late-night chats, the midnight feasts and, of course, waking up on Christmas Day, bottling them for the future.

Picking up her suitcase, Caitlin dragged it onto the landing. But as she did so, she heard something. Faint at first, but growing steadily louder. Sirens. It couldn't be, they *couldn't* have got onto her that fast. It had to be some local emergency, a fire or road traffic accident. And yet, there were a *lot* of sirens. A cacophony of them, in fact. Panicking, Caitlin abandoned her suitcase and raced into the front room. The sound of sirens was almost deafening and through the net curtains she now saw a police car pull up sharply in front of the house. Then another, then another. They'd found her.

Bolting, Caitlin charged from the room, hurrying down the stairs. There was no way she could make it past the uniformed officers out front – even now she could hear heavy footsteps thundering towards the door – so instead she swung round the banister and sprinted into the kitchen. Skidding to the back door, she grabbed the key off the top of the microwave, spilling it now, a loud thump behind her making her jump. Snatching it up off the floor, she tried to guide it into the lock, her hands shaking as she did so.

'Come on, come on...' she pleaded, panic assailing her.

The thumping on the front door was growing louder, but now finally the key found purchase, sliding into the lock. Caitlin turned it roughly, then flung the door open, racing away. She tore over the straggly, neglected grass, making it halfway to the back gate, before she heard the front door splinter under the weight of the police assault. Haring on, she made it to the back gate in seconds, teasing the combination lock to the right setting, then yanking it off and opening the door. Stepping out into the rear access passage, she closed the gate behind her, then peered down the long alley. This narrow alleyway connected all the houses on this street, eventually leading out onto Montgomery Road. Mercifully, there was no police presence here, so Caitlin took off, tearing over the cobbled alley towards salvation.

She'd had to leave her clothes, her toiletries and, worst of all, her picture of Alice, but she still had her passport and a cash card, which would be plenty for her. Now she just needed somewhere to hide out, to make plans, to see if someone could be persuaded to take her to Ireland, France, Norway, anywhere for a big dollop of cash. It was crazy, and certainly not what she'd planned, but it was better than a lifetime behind bars, so she upped her pace, eating up the ground to the mouth of the passage. She felt excited, scared and exhilarated all at the same point. She'd had a close shave, but she would get away. She would be free at last, and more than that, at peace.

But now, just as victory was in her grasp, life slapped her in the face once more. A police car, blue lights flashing and sirens blaring, slid across the mouth of the passage, blocking off her escape route. Skidding to a halt, Caitlin turned on her heel, racing towards the other end of the passage. She'd barely taken five steps, however, before this too was closed off by another police vehicle. Hesitating, she turned back to the original car, intent on charging at them, fighting her way out of this desperate situation.

But three armed officers were now ranged in front of her, their semi-automatic weapons aimed directly at her chest.

'Armed police! Down on the ground!'

She stared at them, shocked.

'Down now!' the officer screamed, his finger gripping the trigger.

And now Caitlin obliged, dropping to the ground and laying

her face in the dirt. She had had a good run, done what she set out to do, but at the very last she'd fallen just short. As she was hauled off the ground, searched and cuffed, she screwed up her eyes and summoned up an image of the one thing, the one person, that had made all this worthwhile.

Her beautiful sister, Alice.

Chapter 55

'Well, isn't this nice?' Olivia teased, casting an eye over the opulent interior, taking in the hundreds of vintage books, neatly stacked on pristine oak shelves.

The Cinnamon Club had once been Westminster Library and retained many of the original features, giving it a sophisticated, old-world feel. Olivia had never eaten here before and was determined to drink in the atmosphere, running an eye over the politicians, aides and journalists for whom this was a regular haunt. Momentarily, the cares of the day seemed to melt away and she smiled as she turned back to her lunch date.

'One of the perks of the job,' Guy Chambers replied, winking at her.

'Even for a *junior* minister,' she replied, teasing.

'Well the gravy train hasn't entirely stopped, despite the best efforts of the *Telegraph*.'

'I bet.'

It was said with mock-disapproval, but in truth Olivia didn't care a fig. She'd have done the same given the opportunity and somehow it was very Guy. Ever since they'd first met at Durham University, he'd had both an air of refinement and an unerring ability to land on his feet. This applied to both his life and his career – despite several foot-in-mouth gaffes, he was hugely popular with the Conservative grass roots and seemed to be forever getting promoted, now the deputy to the Minister of Justice.

'So what are we having? Wine or beer?' Guy continued, pulling a handkerchief from his pocket. 'I've got a stinking cold, but you know what they say, a snifter a day keeps the doctor away...'

'You choose.'

Blowing his nose discreetly, Guy consulted the menu, then ordered a bottle of Riesling. Within moments, their glasses were filled with crisp, aromatic wine and Guy was leaning back in his chair, eyeing her mischievously. It was a look Olivia knew well – over the years Guy had always been the naughtiest of her university mates.

'Let's get down to business then. I'll show you mine, if you show me yours.'

'Not much to tell so far,' Olivia replied, laughing. 'Firth seems determined to ride it out, pinning the blame on the top woman in the Bolton MAPPA team. I think he's hoping that if he can keep this contained, see out his last year in office, he can retire with full honours.'

'He'll be lucky, especially after today's piece in the *Mail*,' Chambers replied, dismissively. 'The minister thinks he's a useless plonker and who's to say he's wrong? I mean, what was Firth thinking? Staggering down the street, pissed as a lord, whilst Rome burns. I'll be amazed if he sees out the day – everyone can see the rot starts at the top.'

'That's not how he sees it. He talks about the whole Bolton thing as if it's some inconvenient bureaucratic issue. He hasn't once expressed sympathy for the victim, even though this is a man's *life* we're talking about.'

'Oh, spare me the bleeding heart, Liv,' Chambers snorted, taking a swig of his wine. 'I know you have to say that because of your profession, but do you really feel sorry for Mark Willis? His victim suffered worse than he did, *far* worse.'

'Even so, he was hunted down, chased to his death.'

'And didn't it make for good TV?' Chambers quipped.

'You don't fool me, Guy – you're not as hard-hearted as you make out.'

'Aren't I? Genuinely, I feel no remorse, no sadness over Willis's death at all. And I'm not alone. There was a poll in the *Sun* today that said sixty-three per cent of people thought Willis had got what was coming to him.'

'Oh, so you're just following popular opinion. That makes more sense.'

'Make a joke of it, if you will,' Chambers countered. 'But it's what people out there feel, and who's to say they're wrong?'

'And how's it playing your end?' Olivia replied, moving the conversation on.

'Well, we're not going to make a big song and dance out of it, but the enquiry into the leak will have its own momentum,' Chambers replied calmly. 'If Martin Coates *is* fingered for it, if it can be proved that it was just one bad apple, then I suspect it will die down soon enough. If it was a leak, a more profound security breach, then it could be rather more serious for everyone. Either way, the minister will be looking to use this to engineer some kind of regime change within the Probation Service. So much dead wood at Petty France...'

'Will Christopher be affected?' Olivia asked quickly. 'I know Firth is probably for the chop, but Christopher is the coming man. He's got real ideas for how to shake things up.'

She petered out, aware her lunch date was laughing at her. A flash of anger pulsed through Olivia, but Chambers was undeterred.

'Still sticking up for him, eh? After everything that little shit's done to you.'

'It's not like that. I genuinely think he could make a difference.'

'And isn't that you all over?' Chambers replied affectionately. 'You always did try to see the best in everyone. Then again, that's *Guardian* readers the world over, isn't it?'

'Tell me,' Olivia retorted, annoyed. 'What is it you like about the *Torygraph*? Is it the cartoons or the photos of the Royal Family?'

'Both,' Chambers laughed, blowing his nose again. 'Sometimes it's the only fun I get in the whole day. The minister's an absolute nightmare at the moment.'

'Go on,' Olivia cooed. 'Tell me more.'

They were back on safer ground now, Olivia always enjoying the titbits of Westminster gossip that Guy provided. Smiling, her old friend was about to respond, when his phone started ringing, causing several heads to turn. Clocking the Caller ID, his face fell.

'Speak of the devil. I'd better take this.'

He rose, scurrying away to a quiet corner. Olivia watched him retreat from view, talking urgently into his phone, before turning her attention to the other diners. She picked out the shadow Health Secretary, a former Chancellor, before spotting Emily Maitlis in urgent conversation at another table. Olivia enjoyed her visits to Westminster, it always seemed a world away from the front line, a blessed relief from the mean streets of Tottenham and Dagenham. Guy was now hurrying back to the table and Olivia turned to him once more, keen to carry on their gossiping. But immediately she clocked that this wouldn't be possible. Her lunch date looked ashen and distressed, in a palpable state of shock.

'You'd better get back to base,' he rasped breathlessly. 'There's been another attack.'

Chapter 56

Emily walked fast through the lobby, Sam a couple of steps behind. He was full of questions, quizzing her about why they'd pulled up at a hotel when they were supposed to be going to the hospital, but Emily batted them away. This was not a conversation she was ready for yet, nor one she *wanted* to have. Once they were safe and sound, she could start to broach the subject with him, but not until then.

Reaching the reception, she waited nervously for someone to arrive, checking the latest text from Marianne, before pouncing on the first available member of staff.

'Hi, I've got a twin room booked,' she said, trying to sound as relaxed as she could.

'What's the name?'

'Simpson, Louise Simpson.'

She trotted out the name Marianne had given her, as if it was entirely natural. Out of the corner of her eye, she saw Sam react, but she laid a hand on his arm, warning him not to make a fuss. Thankfully, he obeyed, the receptionist appearing not to notice.

'Great. I can see that's all been paid for. All I need is a credit card for incidentals.'

'We won't have any, so can I just get the key, please?'

'Well... it is company policy.'

'I know, but we've had a really long journey and we're dog tired, so *please*...'

The young receptionist looked at her, then at Sam, before deciding to take pity on them.

'Here you go, then. You rest up.'

Resisting the urge to snatch the key, Emily accepted it, turning to head towards the lift bank. She'd barely got three steps, however, before Sam grabbed her arm.

'What the hell's going on, Mum?'

'Not now, Sam.'

'Why are you checking in under a false name? Are you in some kind of trouble?'

How the hell to answer that? Her whole life had been nothing *but* trouble.

'Look, I'll explain all soon, but the important thing is that actually Dad's fine.'

'I'd figured that much out for myself,' he replied, witheringly.

'I'm sorry, I needed to get you out of school and I couldn't think of another way to do it.'

They had reached the lift bank, Emily stabbing the call button viciously.

'But *why*? I don't understand what's so urgent—'

'Like I said, in time, you'll understand, but for now you're going to have to trust me.'

The lift doors pinged open, but as she made a move to enter, Sam stepped in front of her, blocking her path. She tried to circumvent him, but he grabbed both of her arms this time, forcing her to face him.

'No, no way,' he replied, firmly. 'You're going to tell me what the fuck's going on. And you're going to tell me *right now*.'

Chapter 57

He stared at the image, scarcely believing his eyes. There she was, in the flesh. Janet Slater had achieved almost mythic status in the vigilante community by staying below the radar for over twenty years, with not a single sighting of her anywhere in the country. But here she was at last. The photo couldn't have been more mundane, a snatched image of Slater outside a Tesco Metro, but the impact was breathtaking. This child killer, this phantom, who had remained concealed from her vengeful family for two decades, had finally been outed, in Reading of all places. There would be no hiding now.

Darting a look around him, Ian Blackwell set about uploading the image. His pulse was racing, sweat beaded his brow, his fingers slick and slippery as he typed. He half expected the door to burst open, for the police to pour in, bringing an end to his adventure, yet another part of him knew he was entirely safe. He had been ultra-cautious, operating now from Willesden, in the north of the capital, changing his accommodation every night and never using the same internet café twice, but this wasn't the real reason behind his assurance, his confidence. No, it was more the sense that his project – his *mission* – was unstoppable. It was as if the world had suddenly turned, as if the scales of justice had rebalanced, as if the time of the good and the true had finally come.

Willis was dead. Baynes was dead. Janet Slater was exposed and on the run. News of these triumphs had had an electrifying effect on the vigilante community, not least on the Justice Never Sleeps website. It had crashed twice today under the weight of sightings, rapists, paedophiles and terrorists up and down the country being publicly outed. It was all that Blackwell could do to keep the site operating, to keep the portal open for lovers of justice everywhere.

Of course sightings did not always equate to a just reckoning and, unfortunately, Janet Slater had escaped retribution. However, with this photo, Blackwell could ensure that her punishment was simply postponed, that in time she would pay for her crimes. The former police officer watched the upload bar carefully, thrilling as it inched slowly forwards, damning Janet Slater pixel by pixel. With a satisfied ping, the admin server announced the upload complete, confirming that the picture was now live.

It was time to go now, time to seek out another anonymous B&B, to keep one step ahead of the law. But even though caution and speed were of the essence, Ian Blackwell allowed himself a brief moment of triumph, staring lingeringly at the snatched image.

It was the end of the road for Janet Slater.

Chapter 58

She pressed her face up the against the glass, desperate to see what Caitlin Rose would say. Would she deny everything, protesting her innocence? Or would she revel in her crime, celebrating the fact that justice had finally been done?

Chandra watched intently as the suspect leaned back in her chair, picking at her nails. Caitlin Rose seemed hostile, resentful and Chandra longed to be in the interview suite, riling her, provoking her, cracking her open. But this was Croydon CID's investigation, so there was no question of that. The SIO, DI Donna Parks, had been much more welcoming and collaborative than Bill Jones, however, so Chandra and DS Buckland could at least watch proceedings through the two-way mirror, drinking in the drama.

'Do you deny attacking him?' DI Parks asked.

'Absolutely not,' Caitlin replied calmly, leaning forward theatrically to talk directly to the recording advice. 'I killed him fair and square. And what's more, I *enjoyed* doing it.'

As she spoke, she glanced at the two-way mirror, as if sensing their presence.

'To clarify, you're admitting that you stabbed Andrew Baynes to death at his flat in Croydon last night.'

'Correct. Go to the top of the class.'

'In fact, according to initial pathology reports, you stabbed him a total of forty-three times. Exactly the same number of injuries your sister Alice sustained when *she* was murdered.'

Caitlin smiled, sending a shiver down Chandra's spine. On the face of it, Caitlin Rose appeared to be a nice, law-abiding girl, who'd looked after her ailing parents and generally been a good citizen, but today she looked deranged, the ghost of 'Amber' still present.

'For the benefit of the tape,' DI Parks said. 'The suspect is smiling and nodding.'

'Yes, it was me,' Caitlin responded, picking at her nails. 'I can't say I enjoyed that bit, but needs must. I can't get rid of the *taste* of him, you know. His grim, sweaty skin. And I can still feel his tongue thrashing round inside my mouth, like some fucking dog.'

She wiped her mouth with her sleeve, looking momentarily repelled, before recovering her sardonic smile. Parks ignored the diversion, continuing calmly:

'And the attack was something you'd planned in advance?'

'Sure, been hunting this guy for three weeks now.'

'And this was following a text message you received?' Parks continued, consulting her notes. 'Outlining Andrew Baynes's whereabouts, his new identity?'

'Yes,' Caitlin shot back, annoyed. 'You have my phone, so ...'

'Do you know who sent you the message with that confidential information?'

'It doesn't matter who sent it,' the suspect countered quickly. 'The fact was that I now knew where this little prick was hiding. That was all I needed. I watched him, worked out what his routine was and then I made plans. That's it. No great mystery, Sherlock.'

'You enrolled at his Narcotics Anonymous group deliberately to befriend him?' Parks replied, ignoring the jibe.

'What do you think?' Caitlin replied witheringly. 'I've done a bit of drugs, but nothing like this guy. He was a mess, or had been at least. He went to the group twice a week and was bloody *desperate* to share.'

'So you befriended him, went to Brighton with him, came on to him...'

'Well, actually he came on to me, but that suited me fine. I had my red lines – there was no way I was going to let that animal fuck me – but I could play the game to get what I needed. Stupid prick was on his knees, eyes closed, waiting for me to touch him. Well, I *touched* him all right...'

Chandra reacted, unnerved. She was at one remove from the conversation, but the young woman's venom was hard to stomach. By the look of things, Gary Buckland felt the same way, perhaps picturing the knife smashing into *his* face.

'And why, Caitlin?' Parks asked, undeterred.

'I'm sorry?'

The suspect sounded genuinely perplexed, so the detective clarified.

'Why did you kill him?'

'Are you kidding me?' Caitlin laughed. 'You're *seriously* asking me why?'

'Well, I'm assuming it's because of what happened to your sister, Alice—'

'And the rest,' Caitlin interrupted tersely. 'My dad's an alcoholic because of what Baynes did. And my mum's six feet under, topped herself two years ago, couldn't handle the guilt. So yes, in every way, it's about what he did to Alice. The way he preyed on her trust, lured her to those woods, took pleasure in tormenting her. It's because of the huge fucking hole he left in our lives, the beautiful soul he snuffed out, because of his own twisted desires. That's why he *had* to die and I challenge you, or anyone else, to say different.'

Caitlin sat back in her chair, exhausted but defiant. Parks regarded her, then continued:

'Well, you've been very clear so far. But there's one outstanding issue I'd like to clarify.'

'Fill your boots, love,' the suspect mocked. 'I'm not going anywhere.'

'Who sent you the information about his whereabouts? Who told you his name?'

Chandra held her breath, her eyes fixed on Caitlin Rose. The suspect seemed to take an age to respond, considering her words carefully, before replying:

'I've absolutely no idea. It was anonymous. But let me tell you this...'

She turned to the two-way mirror, staring directly at Chandra.

'...Whoever they are, they're on the side of the angels.'

Chapter 59

'Do you believe her?'

Chandra and Gary Buckland were hurrying towards her Mondeo. It was imperative that they now got back to base ASAP, to start processing these latest developments.

'No reason not to,' Chandra replied calmly, trying to conceal her rising anxiety. 'Caitlin's phone shows she received an anonymous text three weeks ago, spilling the beans on Baynes. It was sent from the same Samsung Galaxy phone that leaked Willis's details, but a different SIM was used. So whoever's doing this is being very cautious.'

'Did Caitlin respond to the message?'

'Once, straight after she got it, asking who'd sent the message. But she never got a reply.'

Buckland digested this, then asked:

'Do we know where the message was sent from?'

'Somewhere in the vicinity of Oxford Circus.'

'And the date, time?'

'Friday the twenty-eighth of November at 9.45 a.m.'

Buckland exhaled heavily, puffing out his cheeks.

'Well that buggers everything. I've been over Martin Coates' movements with a fine-tooth comb, going back weeks now. He was only in London twice during the last couple of months. On the 8th of November and the 11th of December. Every other day, he's got a cast-iron alibi – multiple witnesses who can place him in Bolton. I'll get the guys to double-check his movements for the twenty-eighth, but it'll be a bust.'

Chandra digested this, her mind turning, before she responded:

'So are we saying Coates *wasn't* involved in the Bolton leak?'

'Looks that way. He strenuously denies it and thus far we can't link him to the phone that leaked Mark Willis's information.'

'Plus, there's a pattern developing here that doesn't seem to fit,' Chandra said, picking up his thread. 'An anonymous leaker, maybe based in the capital, who's deliberately releasing classified information. I guess it's *possible* that Coates has an accomplice, someone based down here—'

'But it doesn't seem very likely,' Buckland cut in, trying to be as charitable as he could.

Chandra took the hit and they walked on. Reaching her car, Chandra zapped it open.

'So what now?' Buckland asked, as they both climbed in.

'Well, they'll charge Caitlin with first-degree murder, no doubt provoking a huge public backlash. Meanwhile, it's *our* job to unearth a concrete link between the two murders, find out who's pulling the strings.'

Firing up the engine, Chandra was about to move off, when her phone buzzed. Placing it carefully in the cradle, she hit receive.

'DI Dabral.'

'Sorry to bother you, boss, it's DC Cooke.'

'Can it wait? We'll be back at base in twenty minutes.'

'Not really, no.'

Instantly, Chandra was on edge.

'We've just taken a call from the deputy director of the Probation Service, Chris Parkes.'

'Right...'

'It appears there's been another leak.'

Chandra stared at the phone, stunned.

'Who? When?'

'Emily Lawrence, real name Janet Slater. She's been living under a false name in Reading for twenty-odd years now. Has made a good fist of things apparently, got a decent job, a teenage son. Anyhow, she was surprised by her older brother, Robert, outside her home. She got away OK, is in hiding with her son, but there's no doubt her cover's blown and that her brother intended her harm. Anyway, just wondering what you want us to do?'

There was real nervousness in the DC's voice, but for once Chandra could think of nothing to say to comfort her. This was way beyond anything she'd dealt with before and Chandra suddenly felt scared, ill prepared and totally out of her depth. What was going on here? What kind of twisted nightmare had she been thrust into?

And where would it all end?

Chapter 60

This was the conversation she'd prayed she'd never need to have. But there was no avoiding it now. Sam was staring at her, silently imploring Emily to put him out of his misery. If he'd been simply angry or confused, perhaps she could have persuaded herself to leave him in the dark for a little longer. But her son, her loving, devoted boy, looked scared and sad, something she couldn't abide.

'I want you to know,' she began falteringly, picking at the blanket on the narrow twin bed, 'that everything I've done, I've done to protect you, to protect us. That's always been my first, my only, priority.'

Sam said nothing, blinking nervously as if expecting the worst. Swallowing down the nausea that was fast gripping her, Emily falteringly continued:

'And I hope, in the days and weeks ahead, that you'll re-member that. I never wanted to lie to you, I hated doing it, but honestly I had no choice.'

'Lied about what? What are you talking about, Mum?' Sam demanded, his voice shaking.

There was no avoiding it, no running from it now. Closing her eyes, Emily replied:

'My name is not Emily Lawrence. My… my real name is Janet Slater.'

She heard his sharp intake of breath, but she pressed on.

'I'm from Bridgend originally, not Cardiff. I've still got family there in fact. My father, three brothers, a sister…'

'But you said your parents were dead! That you were an only child.'

'I know I did and I'm *trying* to explain, OK?'

She opened her eyes and was immediately poleaxed by what she saw. Sam was staring at her, shell-shocked, tears pricking his eyes. She'd never seen him look so frightened and it was like a dagger to her heart.

'Part of the reason I've never told you all this was because… because I had a terrible time as a kid. My ma walked out on us when I was six, left my dad with seven mouths to feed. She never looked back, even though she only lived two streets away…'

Suddenly Emily's chest felt tight, emotion swelling within it, the sharp sting of rejection still raw.

'It… it was a very bad time,' she continued falteringly. 'Dad worked all day and drunk all night. We were left to fend for ourselves, to look after the baby who cried and cried and cried. It was… it was God awful, is what it was. We never had enough money for food or rent, hardly went to school and when we *did*, we were bullied. We were dirty, dressed in hand-me-downs, our hair crawling with lice… It was disgusting, humiliating.'

Without thinking, Emily smoothed down her long, dark hair. She washed it every day without fail now, had done for twenty-plus years. But still the memory of her lank, itchy scalp remained, goading her.

'School was bad enough, but home was even worse. We never had any idea what mood Dad was going to be in. He used to sit in that bloody armchair, beer in one hand, fag in the other, bawling at us, ordering us to keep the baby quiet. If you did as you were told, all well and good. But if you didn't...'

Sam was looking in horror, but she couldn't stop now.

'He would beat us with whatever came to hand – his belt, a rubber hose, the poker from the fire. The nurses at A&E got to know us pretty well, but nothing was ever done about him, so he did what he liked. Caught me stealing his cigarettes once. Made me eat the whole packet in front of him, gagging on that hideous tobacco, then he stripped me, threw me out on the street. I must have stood there for hours, naked and humiliated, banging on the door, begging to be let back in...'

Her voice caught, the sad little girl she once was punching through again. Crying silently, Sam laid his hand on her arm, but she gently removed it. She didn't want his sympathy.

'You have to understand that I was in a very bad place. I was angry and sad and hurting. My mum didn't want me, my dad wanted to hurt me, my siblings ignored me, I had no one, Sam, no one at all. I'd have killed myself if I'd had the courage, but I was a coward, a worm...'

'Please, Mum, stop,' Sam pleaded, sobbing.

'I can't, love, you need to hear this,' Emily insisted, her own voice shaking. 'It's who I am. It's *what* I am.'

'What do you mean? What happened?'

Emily knew she had to keep going now or she would never be able to say it.

'One day... one day it got so bad... I don't even remember what happened to make me so angry... but it got so bad, that I... did a very wicked thing. My dad was drunk, sleeping, even though the baby was wailing upstairs. It was just me in the living room, watching him slumbering, beer and fag still in hand. And... to this day I don't know why I did it... but I... I picked up that cigarette and I placed it on the carpet next to his chair.

It started to smoulder, then it caught fire, and the chair went up, the carpet with it. It only took a couple of minutes for the fire to spread and in all that time I ... I did nothing. I just stood and watched. Only snapped out of it when my brother Rhys grabbed me by the arm, telling me to get out, that the house was on fire ...'

'What ... what happened then?' Sam asked, white as a sheet.

'The whole place went up and that was that.'

'Were you hurt?'

Emily shook her head dolefully. She suddenly felt utterly overwhelmed, as if she had a great weight pressing down on her.

'I was OK, most of my brothers and sisters too. My dad was hurt, though, had quite serious injuries actually. And ... and the baby didn't make it.'

'The baby died?' Sam gasped, horrified.

'Yes, Susan died.'

Three simple words, but devastating to say.

'You've got to believe me when I say I didn't *mean* to harm her. I wasn't thinking really, I just wanted to do something, to hurt *somebody*.'

'Were you ... were you arrested?'

'No. Nobody knew you see. My brother thought I'd discovered the fire and had frozen, the police thought my father had fallen asleep, dropped his cigarette, so ...'

Sam nodded, but looked as though he'd been slapped. It was too much to take in, Emily knew that, but now she'd started she couldn't stop, wanting to vomit the whole thing up.

'We got taken into care, fostered, me and Gwyneth ending up with this couple, Mr and Mrs Thomas. It seems strange to say it now, but ... those next few months were some of the happiest of my life.'

Sam was frowning, so she carried on quickly:

'I know that seems heartless, cruel even, and I *was* genuinely sad about Susan ... but you see we got so much attention, so much sympathy after the fire. Everyone wanted to make a fuss of us kids, we were *special*, they were falling over themselves to help. I suppose it was the closest thing to love I'd ever experienced and I couldn't get enough of it.'

She faltered briefly, knowing the next step would be the worst.

'The first six months or so went well enough for us, but then people got on with their lives. The Thomas's worked long hours, it was just me and Gwyneth a lot of the time. Even though we were close in age, we'd never really got on. She used to whine all the time and was always trying to get me in trouble ...'

She was aware that she was speaking ill of the dead and could tell from Sam's expression that he had an inkling where this was going, so she persevered:

'In all honesty, I think I was probably jealous. She was a cute little thing who got all the attention, which I missed, I *sorely* missed, having never really enjoyed any kind of—'

'What happened, Mum?'

His interruption shocked her, his tone so terse and solemn. She didn't want to tell him the rest, she really didn't, but she had no choice.

'I ... I set another fire. I don't why I did it, I was in a real mess. But I started another fire. Mr and Mrs Thomas were fine, so was I, but ...'

'Gwyneth died too?'

He sounded so appalled, so shocked, that it was all Emily could do to nod her head. If the earth could have opened up and swallowed her, she would have welcomed the release.

'How old was she?'

Emily swallowed hard, before replying:

'Three and a half.'

Sam stared at her, horrified.

'Please believe me, Sam, I've regretted what I did, lived with the consequences every day ever since. The papers crucified me, my older brothers have spent the last twenty years hunting for me, but it's the *guilt* that really cripples me. It's like the little girl who set those fires was someone else, a child from my worst nightmares, but I know it was *me*. I know I did those things and I will never, never stop trying to make amends for it.'

She hoped her words would cut through, but her penitence had no effect on her son. Sam was staring at her, ashen, his whole world collapsing. He'd known perhaps that it was going to be bad, that he was going to learn things he couldn't unlearn, but his shocked expression revealed that nothing could have prepared him for *this*.

Chapter 61

'We are facing the biggest crisis in the history of the Probation Service.'

Olivia stole a look at Christopher, who stood at the far side of the room, staring at his feet, as if distancing himself from the speaker. Olivia could see why – Jeremy Firth looked shocked, panicky, a man out of his depth. But at least he wasn't underplaying the situation anymore. Then again, how *could* he? His character assassination in the *Daily Mail* seemed like small beer now, compared to the avalanche of bad news that had just descended upon both him and the Service. In the last forty-eight hours alone, two high-profile ex-offenders had been murdered and Emily Lawrence's cover had been blown. Rattled, Jeremy Firth continued:

'We will have to accelerate our review of *all* our security protocols. First thing is to make contact with your clients, assure yourself that they're safe, whilst giving them whatever support, comfort and advice they require. There's a lot of fear and speculation out there, it's our job to try and calm the situation.'

Good luck with that, Olivia thought to herself. The Ministry of Justice was in a state of tumult, gripped by outrage, paranoia and blame-gaming, and would no doubt lash out shortly, casting the Probation Service in the role of villain. The press were already camped outside Petty France, battering down the doors in their hunt for fresh information and once the news of Andrew Baynes's murder broke, the shit would *really* hit the fan. Nothing remotely like this had ever happened before.

'I know it's Christmas and that you all have family commitments, but I need your total focus now. I need you to work round the clock to protect those whose care has been entrusted to us. There will obviously be a strong public reaction to this, lots of press interest, but we can't allow ourselves to get distracted. Top priority now is to protect our people, co-operate with the police investigations into the murders of Mark Willis and Andrew Baynes and, perhaps most pressingly, ensure the safety of Emily Lawrence and her son. They are currently safe, thank goodness, and are now in hiding with Probation Service staff in attendance, but we can't afford to get complacent. It gives me no pleasure to say this, but following Emily Lawrence's exposure, it is clear now that someone in a position of authority is leaking highly confidential information directly to the bereaved families.'

A ripple of disquiet and anger flared across the room. Olivia sought out Isaac, his gaze briefly meeting hers, before he turned away. All around them, colleagues both old and new were reacting to this crisis, some with defiance, but most with pure, unadulterated shock.

'Inspector Dabral, who's conducting an investigation into these leaks, informed me earlier that a week ago someone anonymously texted details of Emily Lawrence's new identity and current whereabouts to her older brother, Robert, in Bridgend. The message was sent from a phone that was active in central Reading, near to Emily's home, so the perpetrator had been close to her and her family, following her, stalking her even. An hour ago, the internet group Justice Never Sleeps published a recent image of Emily outside a Tesco Metro in

Reading, presumably taken by the same person who's responsible for these security breaches. Obviously this makes the situation far more complicated, as most of the country will know exactly what Emily looks like. Obviously we can take measures to deal with that, specifically as regards her appearance, but I'm afraid it raises the stakes still further. Which is why we all need to be hyper-vigilant, extra discreet and utterly professional. No sharing of information unnecessarily, no talking to friends, family or even colleagues and *absolute silence with the press.*'

He hissed these final words, his gaze drifting across the room in the direction of Christopher Parkes, before returning his attention to the massed ranks once more.

'It's horrible to think that someone we trust, perhaps even someone in this room, is deliberately betraying our clients to danger, but until we find out who is responsible, we must operate a complete information lockdown. Lives are on the line here, because, honestly, until we root out this mole, I cannot guarantee that more blood won't be shed.'

Firth's dire prediction hung in the air as the meeting broke up, dozens of probation officers scurrying back to their desks, phones clamped to their ears. Olivia spotted Christopher abandon the director, walking swiftly back to his office, and she fell into step with him, the pair walking in comfortable silence, until they were well out of earshot.

'Strong stuff, though I'm not sure anyone was convinced he's got a handle on the situation,' Olivia said quietly.

'It was entirely pointless. A classic case of someone shutting the gate after the horse has bolted. But it was stirring enough, as valedictory speeches go.'

Olivia looked up at him, surprised.

'He's for the chop then? Definitely?'

'The Minister of Justice said as much on the *Today* programme this morning. Apparently he was apoplectic when he saw the article in the *Daily Mail*. Still, at least he now knows what we're dealing with. That our beloved director is a lecherous, incompetent drunk.'

'Should I assume...' Olivia said cautiously '...that it was no accident Madeleine Barker was stationed outside Petty France last night, ready to pounce?'

'Accident or no,' Christopher responded, ducking the question, 'it was very useful that she was. Should make the coup de grace swifter, cleaner. Then we can get on with the business of sorting this place out. This whole department needs root and branch change, shock and awe tactics, if we're ever to recover our reputation with the public. With some decent investment, we could be a proper, functioning institution again.'

'And has anyone spoken to you about the position? About what happens *after* Firth goes?'

'Not yet, but I've scheduled a call with the minister for later today, so...'

They had reached his office and stepped inside.

'I'm pleased for you,' Olivia said warmly. 'I know the circumstances aren't ideal...'

'That's one way of putting it.'

'...but this could play well for you. Keep your head down, avoid the incoming fire and then, when the moment's right, present yourself as the saviour of the Service.'

'It's as if you can read my mind.'

It was said with affection, a smile creasing his lips, as he turned to her.

'Though I must say I'm amused by your ambition for me, given your history of refusing promotions – promotions that were warranted and which should have been taken.'

'Oh, don't start, you know I'm happier at the coalface. I don't want to be running things, steering the ship, but you could do it with your eyes closed and do it a lot better than Firth.'

'A three-year-old child could do it better than Firth.'

Laughing, Olivia took her lover's arm, giving it an affectionate squeeze.

'Well, I'm pleased for you, Chris, you deserve it.'

His reaction was subtle, but marked, returning her smile, whilst gently removing his arm and heading to the desk. His secretary was just outside and now that he was so close to a long-held ambition, there could be no room for silly mistakes. The rejection smarted, Olivia suddenly feeling a rush of sadness and regret, but she masked it, talking briskly as she changed the subject.

'Whilst I've got you, I wanted to ask you about Jack.'

Parkes had been checking his emails, but now looked up.

'What should I do with him?' Olivia continued. 'There's obviously a risk he's already been compromised, so should we move him? He's only just settling into the new place, and not very well at that, but maybe we *should* move him, just to be safe.'

Parkes took a moment, weighing up the options, before replying:

'No, keep him where he is for now. There's an almighty fight going on over available safe houses, of which we've precious few. Sit tight and say nothing until we have a proper contingency plan. Though God knows when that will be. At the moment, it's headless chickens leading the blind.'

Olivia was still mulling on this proposed plan of action as she stalked the dingy corridor back to the main office, tugging her phone from her pocket. She tapped feverishly and, moments later, the call connected:

'Hi, this is Jack. Leave a message.'

Cursing under her breath, Olivia tried again, but once more it went straight to voicemail. This time she waited for the beep, before leaving a message.

'Jack, it's Olivia. Call me the moment you get this.'

Ending the call, she punched in another number. Seconds later, the call was answered.

'George Simmons.'

'George, it's Olivia Campbell.'

'I was wondering when you were going to call.'

Immediately, Olivia felt a shiver of alarm.

'Why? Is there some kind of problem?'

'Yes, there's a bloody problem. Your boy kneed me in the nuts, in front of all the lads.'

'Oh Jesus, George, I'm sorry…'

'Then he rips off his jacket and stalks off, hasn't been seen since. I don't need that kind of aggravation, and I certainly can't have anyone treating me like that, so you can tell him not to bother—'

'Where's he gone?' Olivia interrupted.

'Well, thanks very much for your sympathy.'

'I'm sorry, George, he shouldn't have done that, but honestly I do need to find him.'

'I've no idea where he is, nor do I care. Honestly, if I never see that wanker again it'll be—'

But Olivia had cut him off and was already running towards the lifts.

Chapter 62

'Look what the cat dragged in.'

Jack looked up sharply, alarmed. The deep, sneering voice belonged to a muscular young man who was now bearing down on him. It took Jack a couple of seconds to process this strange sight, to comprehend that this strapping bloke was his little brother.

'All right, Danny.'

'All right.'

His response was cool, measured, leading Jack to wonder whether there was *any* residual affection there. They had once been close, but time and tide had taken their toll. He hadn't seen Danny in years and certainly couldn't read him as well as he used to.

'Looking good, mate,' Jack said admiringly.

'Gym four times a week. I can see you're not doing much – you're getting fat, mate.'

Danny laughed, provoking an instant, angry reaction from Jack. His little brother had always been his lapdog, his punch bag, now he seemed comfortable *goading* Jack.

'I could still take you, one hand tied behind my back.'

'I'd like to see you try.'

Jack was sorely tempted to rise to this challenge, to wrestle the little scrote to the ground, but they were standing in a beer garden in the middle of Romford. Their 'affectionate' stand-off was already attracting glances, so instead he ushered his brother to a nearby table.

'Can I get you something to drink?'

'No, it's all right. I'm not staying,' Danny replied.

'Well, fuck you too. Haven't seen you in years, and you can only spare me five minutes?'

It was said with a fixed smile, a smile which didn't reach Jack's eyes.

'You called me, remember,' Danny fired back. 'Twice actually. Whilst I was working. You're lucky I made it here at all. I had to beg my manager for an extended lunch break.'

'What a good little boy you've become. Speaking of which, have you got it?'

Nodding, Danny reached inside a plastic bag, producing a battered iPad and charger.

'Cheers, mate, you're a brick,' Jack said as he took it from him. 'What do you want for it?'

'On the house.'

'Don't be daft!'

'Seriously, I don't want your money. But if you get busted, you didn't get it from me.'

'Fair enough,' Jack said, slipping the iPad and charger into his rucksack. 'I owe you one.'

'Forget about it. This one's for old times' sake.'

It was said with a smile, but Jack noted Danny's determination to avoid any form of relationship with him, even one where Jack was in his debt. Disguising his irritation, he replied brightly:

'I guess that's family for you. How are the rest of the gang?'

'All right, I guess.'

'Dad?'

'The same.'

'Never mind. What about Mum? How's she keeping?'

A marked reaction this time, Danny shrugging and looking away.

'Danny?'

'Up and down, you know how it is.'

'No, I don't, that's why I'm asking,' Jack responded, insistent, annoyed. 'I haven't seen her in over a year, you in more like five. No one's been to see me recently, hence why I'm asking. What's going on?'

'Nothing's going on. Honestly. Look, I'd better be getting—'

But Jack had already advanced towards him, grabbing him by the sleeve. Danny tried to shake him off, but Jack pulled him in closer, towering over him. Ever since they were little, he'd always been able to intimidate Danny and, despite his brother's muscular physique, things hadn't changed completely.

'You're not leaving here until you tell me what's going on.'

Still the younger man squirmed.

'I mean it, Danny,' Jack hissed, tightening his grip.

'She's got cancer, OK?'

'What?'

'Lung cancer, had it for a while.'

For a moment, Jack was speechless. Some days he loved his mum, some days he hated her, but still this news hit him like a train.

'How's she getting on? I mean, is she going to be OK?' he asked.

Danny's sombre expression told him all he needed to know.

'Jesus Christ, is she in hospital then?'

'No, they've let her come home. They wanted to send her to a hospice, but she wouldn't have it.'

'Hospice? So...'

He couldn't quite say the words, so Danny obliged for him.

'It's stage four. They say she's got weeks, but I'd be surprised if she lasted that long.'

Danny looked gutted, as if he was about to lose his compass, his rock. Jack felt a wave of sadness sweep over him. Why did it have to be cancer? Why did it have to be *her*?

'Look, she didn't want you to know,' Danny continued softly. 'Doesn't want anyone to know really. But I guess it's your right.'

'And you're looking after her on your own?' Jack asked, incredulous.

'No one else around, is there? And she wanted family, you know...'

'I'm so sorry, Danny.'

And he meant it. He was sorry for *everything*.

'Nothing to be done, mate. Life's shit and then you die, right?'

It was said with such crushing despondency that Jack felt another surge of guilt.

'Anyway, I'd better go. Look after yourself, Jack.'

Danny turned on his heel and walked calmly away, out of the beer garden, out of Jack's life. Jack watched him go, his throat constricted with emotion, tears stinging his eyes, feeling as low as he'd ever felt. He'd come here hoping to chat, joke, reminisce, to conjure up good times from the past. But watching his brother disappear from view, Jack was suddenly painfully aware of all he had loved and lost.

Chapter 63

It cut deep to hear the woman he'd once loved scold him like an errant child.

'What's going on, Mike? Rachel came home in a right state the other night and since then nothing. No calls, no message, no apology. I don't know why you think it's acceptable to—'

Mike hit the red button, killing the voicemail. Alison's irate message had followed hot on the heels of several from Simon and he couldn't take any more. He felt got at, mistreated and utterly exhausted. He had barely been able to keep his eyes open on the journey back from Colchester, the comedown following the drama in Courtney's house robbing him of energy and he rested his head on the steering wheel, praying for oblivion, for a moment's peace.

A sharp rap on the window made him jump. Shocked, alarmed, he turned to find Graham Ellis peering through the window, evidently concerned about him. Pasting a smile on his face, Mike climbed out of the car.

'Sorry, did I miss something, Graham? Were we *supposed* to be meeting today?'

'No, no,' the ex-inspector replied cheerfully, concealing his anxiety as well as he could. 'I was just passing and thought I'd pop in.'

'That's very kind,' Jack replied, knowing full well that Graham had probably been waiting on his doorstep for an hour. 'Why don't you come in?'

Mike made the tea, surprised to find that his hands were shaking. Was this fear following his close shave or the after-effects of his intimate proximity to Courtney Turner? Steeling himself, he placed the two cups on the table, concentrating hard on not spilling any hot tea. Graham seemed in sober mood and, after the customary pleasantries, cut to the chase.

'There's been some more developments, Mike, and I wanted you to hear them from me, rather than via the news or social media.'

Mike looked up. Despite his bone-crushing exhaustion, he was intrigued.

'Last night, Andrew Baynes was killed in his flat in Croydon. He'd been living under an assumed name there for several years.'

'Andrew Baynes? He was the guy that—'

'The Cannibal Killer, the tabs called him.'

'I remember.'

He kept his tone neutral, but already Mike's emotions were churning.

'Do they know who did it?' he asked tentatively.

'Caitlin Rose, the younger sister of his victim. She's in custody now, has made no bones about her involvement. She stalked him for three weeks apparently, before making her move.'

'Jesus Christ...'

'It's obviously a terrible tragedy,' Graham continued, look-ing fixedly at Mike. 'But this, and other recent events, suggest that someone within the government or the Probation Service, someone with top-level access, is deliberately leaking the identities and whereabouts of these offenders to their victim's families, with the sole intention of causing them harm.'

Mike said nothing, staring directly at him.

'You're going to hear *a lot* about this in the coming days,' the ex-police officer continued briskly. 'It's a bloody shit show, a national scandal. But...'

He slowed now, enunciating every word carefully.

'...I want you to ignore it all, Mike. I want you to blot it out – the media frenzy, the endless commentary, the opinions on both sides of the argument. A lot of people will try and exploit this situation, and I don't want you getting sucked into it. So if a journalist or blogger contacts you, asking for your opinion, send them on their way. Also, if you receive any message that purports to offer information regarding Courtney Turner or Kaylee Jones, I want you to delete the message, then call me straight away. Can you do that for me?'

For a fleeting moment, Mike was tempted to confess all. But how could he own up to hiding in Courtney Turner's bathroom, listening in as she had sex? It was pathetic, it was degrading. But more than that, Mike wasn't ready to give up his secret knowledge. For once, probably for the first time since that horrific day ten years ago, he was ahead of the police, the Probation Service, the press. He had insight, information that nobody else had. And he wasn't going to give it up easily.

'Of course,' he found himself saying. 'Whatever you say, Graham.'

The ex-copper looked at him shrewdly, nodding thoughtfully, before responding:

'Trust me, it's for the best.'

Mike said nothing in response, picking at his fingernails.

'Anyway,' the ex-policeman continued, 'I've taken up enough of your time. Do you have any plans for tonight or...'

It was obviously asked more in hope than expectation and Mike took great pleasure in surprising him.

'Actually, I'm going to go out tonight.'

'Right, well, that's good,' the police officer replied, wrong-footed.

'Yes, it's the firm's Christmas do. I wasn't going to go, can't usually face these things, but this year I will. Why not have a bit of festive fun, right?'

Mike kept this up for the next five minutes, ladling on the forced bonhomie and optimism before ushering his unwelcome guest out the front door. Peering through the crack in the curtains, Mike watched Graham Ellis hesitate, looking back at the house, as if intrigued by what Mike would do next, before eventually heading on his way. He watched the ex-police officer disappear from view, then hurried upstairs into the sanctuary of his bedroom. The office's Christmas party was due to begin shortly, but instead of making his way to the wardrobe, Mike paused in the middle of the room, tugging out his phone. Scrolling through his in-box, he quickly located the anonymous text message.

Courtney Turner is now living under the name Sharon Wall at 24 Meadow Lane, Colchester, CO1 1AP.

A moment's hesitation, a sharp intake of breath, then Mike pressed 'Delete'.

Chapter 64

Things were spiralling out of control, the investigation failing to keep pace with events, but Chandra knew that she couldn't show any weakness in front of the team. They needed her leadership now, whether they liked it or not. So her voice was commanding and clear as she outlined the latest shocking developments.

'Emily Lawrence, real name Janet Slater. Outed by text on the fifth of December, surprised by her brother this morning. She's safe for now, but had a narrow escape. Her older brother, Robert Slater, has repeatedly told any press outlet that'll listen that he won't rest until Janet is dead. You'll see from the documents in your file that the Slaters hail from a rough part of Bridgend, the family well known to local police even *before* those two tragic fires, and that generally the family prefer to settle things *personally*, rather than relying on the authorities. All of which means we have a third leak, a third very damaging, very dangerous leak.'

Concerned faces stared back at her. The team were only just processing information relating to Andrew Baynes's murder, but now faced a whole new line of investigation.

'The information was sent to Robert Slater from the same Samsung Galaxy mobile as previously, but once again a new pay-as-you-go SIM was used. Obviously, then, we are dealing with a determined and organized threat here, someone keen to remain below the radar. Moreover, the person, or persons, responsible for these leaks are methodical, precise and ruthless, intent on spilling as much blood as possible in a way that attracts maximum publicity. The exposure of Janet Slater is another hammer blow for the Probation Service and the criminal justice system, but for us it provides another strand of investigation that might yet throw up vital clues. Where are we at with the Reading MAPPA team?'

DC Reeves was quick to respond, recognizing the urgency of the situation.

'Nothing doing, I'm afraid. I can't see anyone from the Reading team being involved. None of them attended the conference where Mark Willis's info was leaked, nor were they in Oxford Circus when Andrew Baynes's identity and whereabouts were released. Also, I've had a look over their HR files and none of them have any record of insubordination, they haven't filed any complaints – they seem to be committed public servants. Obviously, I'll keep digging, but honestly, guv, there's nothing ringing any alarm bells.'

'Keep on it. What about the London team that were monitoring Andrew Baynes?'

'I'd like to have a closer look at Isaac Green,' DC Drummond piped up. 'He *was* at the conference DC Reeves just mentioned and he was certainly in London when Baynes's details were sent to Caitlin Rose. No idea of his movements on that day, but I'd like to check them out.'

'Why him specifically?' Chandra challenged. 'There were several other people on Baynes's MAPPA team.'

'Well, it's partly because he's the only probation officer on the team, a veteran of the service with open access to and lots of contacts in Probation Service HQ, but it's more about his history and attitude.'

'Go on,' Chandra replied, intrigued.

'You should have a look for yourself, but his file reads to me as if he's at war with the Probation Service. Numerous complaints, accusations of racism, a clear sense that he feels his skin colour has held him back, that others have been promoted faster and higher. Several issues too over pay and pensions, but the big ticket item is an historic injury – a stabbing in the line of duty – which he never felt he was adequately compensated for.'

'I noticed he was limping when I met him earlier. What's the story?'

'Got a knife in the abdomen from one of his clients,' Cooke replied quickly, drawing a reaction from DS Buckland. 'A sometime burglar and dealer who was high on drugs at the time. Severed a nerve in Green's leg and he's never been fully mobile since. Green received a modest payout, but has constantly petitioned for a review and extra cash.'

'You think he's bitter, burnt out? Maybe even actively hostile towards the Service?'

'Possibly,' the young DC responded. 'He still turns up, does his hours, but you have to wonder if his heart's in it, especially as he's currently the subject of a disciplinary review. He had a bust up with his line manager a couple of months back that got way out of hand...'

Chandra nodded, digesting this. She had sensed something 'off' about Green when she'd spoken to him earlier.

'Good work, let's pull him in again. I'll talk to him. In the meantime, make contact with Probation Service HR, get the lowdown on his running battle with them. And tell the digital team that we need a minute-by-minute breakdown of his movements and communications on the seventh of November, the twenty-eighth of November and the fifth of December.'

'But would he have had access?' DS Buckland interrupted,

keen to make his mark. 'Yes, Green knew Baynes's whereabouts and identity, but would he have known about Mark Willis? And Janet Slater? He has absolutely no connection with the Bolton or Reading MAPPA teams as far as I can see, so how could he have obtained the info?'

'That's what we need to find out,' Chandra replied calmly. 'The whereabouts and identities of offenders granted lifelong anonymity is encrypted on the Probation Service's Delius system, on Limited Access Only files. The list of people who are able to access these is incredibly short: Jeremy Firth, Director of the Service; his deputy Chris Parkes; The Minister for Justice and his deputy Guy Chambers; and a small group of high-ranking civil servants—'

'My point exactly,' Buckland interrupted. 'Isaac Green isn't in their league. He's a foot soldier, nothing more.'

'A foot soldier with decades of experience as a probation officer. Perhaps he has ties to people now working in Bolton or Reading; perhaps he's actively cultivated those connections, sharing titbits of gossip here, an indiscreet word there.'

'Or maybe he's got to someone within the Probation Service HQ who can access the files?' DC Drummond offered. 'I know you're supposed to be able to trace who's accessed the files, but there must be ways round that if you're technically minded?'

'That's certainly possible and we should look into it. But I'd like our principal focus to be on Green's connections to other officers handling the very highest-profile offenders. I'd like files on every probation officer handling these sensitive cases ASAP.'

'Good luck with that,' Buckland responded. 'The Service is tighter than a gnat's chuff when it comes to handing out *that* sort of info.'

'Well then, we'll just have to be persuasive,' Chandra shot

back, her voice laced with steel. 'This is a *murder* investigation after all.'

She held Buckland's gaze, just long enough to best him, the junior officer dropping his gaze, then turned back to the team.

'Whilst we're waiting for that, I want us to drill down on the timings and locations of the leaks themselves. We know all three leaks were made from the same phone, albeit with different SIMs. We can assume therefore, I think, that the perpetrator is an individual who discovered the current identities and whereabouts of Willis, Baynes and Lawrence, then released that information, twice whilst in London and once whilst in Reading.'

'That's the bit I don't get,' DS Buckland asserted. 'Say this guy is based in London, as the first two leaks suggest. Why go all the way to Reading just to send the message?'

'Presumably to take this photo,' Chandra responded quickly, tapping the snatched photo of Emily Lawrence outside Tesco Metro. 'Perhaps our leaker wanted to confirm that Emily Lawrence really *was* Janet Slater or perhaps they wanted the photo as insurance, in case she managed to evade her brother's attentions. By publishing that online, our perpetrator could ensure that Emily Lawrence has nowhere to run.'

'Are we saying that this photo was taken on the same day that the info about Emily Lawrence was leaked?' DC Reeves asked.

'That's what we've got to find out,' Chandra replied. 'You can tell by the Christmas posters in Tesco's front window that it was taken recently, so it's possible it was taken on the fifth, but we need to be sure. Let's put this photo out there, in the newspapers, on social media, see if we can get an exact date and time when it was taken.'

'Isn't that rather dangerous?' DC Drummond asked. 'Won't everyone know what Emily Lawrence looks like then?'

'We'll pixelate her face, make her unrecognizable. The

important thing is to show the public the image, see if they spot themselves in it. There's an old lady in the photo, also a young mum – perhaps they can help us pinpoint when it was taken. Meanwhile, the important thing for us right now is the timing and location of the leaks themselves. We need chapter and verse on people's movements. Isaac Green's of course, but everyone else on this list too. If we can link any one of them to the Excel centre on the seventh of November, Oxford Circus on the twenty-eighth *and* Reading on the fifth of December, then I think we've got our man. So let's get to it.'

Galvanized, the team dispersed, hurrying back to their desks. Chandra watched them go, relieved, but as her eye fell on the list in front of her, her spirits waned. She had got the investigation back on track, but the task ahead was a daunting one. She hoped that her theories about data breaches might be correct, yet the more obvious explanation was that someone with top-level access was deliberately leaking highly confidential information, betraying their calling to ensure natural justice was done. Counterintuitive as it seemed, they were *all* suspects and would *all* have to be checked out.

Running her eye down the list of high-ranking civil servants, directors, ministers and their deputies, Chandra felt her spirits plummet and her stress levels soar, this small handful of names a veritable Pandora's box of potential career suicide for a lowly detective inspector. Isaac Green was a key suspect, but all these important figures would need to be interviewed. It was not a task Chandra relished; she knew she would be placing her head on the block by doing so, but there was no putting it off. If it had to be done, it was best done quickly and with a personal touch, Chandra making the appointments herself. So, sighing, she turned and headed swiftly back to her office, closing the door firmly behind her.

Chapter 65

Retreating to the bathroom, Sam closed his eyes, hoping that his nightmare would end, that he'd wake up in his bed at home, that all this hideousness and pain would suddenly melt away. Yet he knew in his heart that this was real, that it was happening, hence why he was hiding out in the bathroom of a Heathrow hotel.

The last couple of hours had been horrible. He hated seeing his mum like that – agonized, guilt-ridden, in physical pain as she recounted her grim story. But he also hated what she'd told him – the terrible sequence of rejection, anger and violence that had marred her childhood and cost two innocent children their lives. But worse than all of that, if such a thing was possible, was the fact that *everything he thought he knew was a lie.* For years he had grown up trotting out the fiction that his mother had given him, how her parents had died in a car accident when she was young, that she was an only child who'd always yearned for a sibling. It was lies, all lies.

Sam felt his stomach lurch and he dropped to his knees, vomiting violently into the toilet bowl. It was swift and painful, three strong heaves, then he was done. Immediately, he heard gentle knocking on the door, but he ignored it. He didn't want to talk to her, didn't want to face her yet. He needed to be alone.

Propping himself up against the bath, Sam tried to gather

himself. What the hell should he do? How on earth was he supposed to deal with something like this? Should he confront his mother, ripping her to shreds for her cruelty, her violence, her duplicity? Or should he take pity on a woman who was so clearly broken by the day's confessions? Should he abandon her and run away? Or should he try to prop her up, reminding himself of the years of love and devotion she'd lavished on him? It made his head explode and he was sorely tempted to call Gavin, to vent a little and ask for comfort, but would that place *him* in danger too?

The thought was electrifying and devastating. The idea that there were people out there who were determined to harm his mother, perhaps even him too, was mind-boggling. The idea that their anger was so great, even after all these years, that they actively wanted to shed blood, beggared belief. Who *were* these people? And how much of a threat *were* they? Sam now found himself pulling his phone from his pocket. A moment's hesitation, then he googled 'Janet Slater'. He wasn't ready for this, wasn't sure he could face it, but he had to know what they were dealing with.

The first thing that sprung up was a photo of young Janet, aged nine. It hit Sam like a train, the sweet image of the buck-toothed girl in her unkempt school uniform. He'd never seen this photo before, any photo of his mother as a child in fact, and in normal circumstances it would have swelled his heart. But here it was presented as the face of a criminal, a double murderer smiling craftily at the camera. It didn't make any sense, it couldn't be true, but the reams of text surrounding the image made clear that it was, as did the photos of the charred houses, the children's funerals and the court sketches of little Janet sitting in the dock. He'd seen this kind of thing on documentaries before – but this was his own mother.

He was scrolling fast, taking in the particulars of the crimes, the shocking details of which were recounted by the sickened firefighters who attended the scenes, sharing images that would haunt them for the rest of their lives. Now he was reading details of the investigation and trial, accounts of Janet giggling in court, her testimony in the dock that she 'enjoyed hurting things that couldn't fight back'.

Sam dropped his phone, the device hitting the tiles with a sharp crack. He couldn't read any more, couldn't process any more, dropping his face into his hands. He thought he knew his mother, thought he loved her, understood her.

But who the hell *was* this woman?

Chapter 66

She was like a magnet pulling him home. Jack didn't have many fond memories of his mum – she'd neglected him and turned a blind eye to his suffering – but there *were* fleeting moments of love that he could recall. The scooter she'd given him for his fifth birthday, the smiles she bestowed on him when he went to the corner shop for her, the attention she'd lavished on him when he cut his knee on broken glass in the park. These simple acts of kindness, these brief flashes of maternal love exerted a powerful sway over him, hence his pilgrimage to Southend now. She was his mum, after all, so he had to see her.

He had been full of misgivings on the train journey down, his nerves rising steadily as he got closer to his home town. He was travelling alone, Danny ignorant of this rash journey, which suited Jack fine. He could avoid drawing attention to himself as a solo traveller and, besides, he didn't want his little brother telling the family that he was coming, didn't want them forewarned or forearmed. He was in control of the situation, but still he felt wired and anxious, as if danger lurked around every corner.

He kept his head down, cap over his face, as he passed through the ticket barriers. But nobody was interested in him, he was just another body moving through. Stepping out onto the street, Jack felt a sharp pang of emotion. Just the smell of the place, the cry of the seagulls, transported him back to his childhood, a period of turbulence, violence and occasional joy. The shop faces had changed, but the streets remained the same and it was with something approaching pleasure that he hurried down them now. He *knew* this place; it was as familiar to him as his own face. He knew all the back streets, all the cut-throughs, where to go, where to avoid. He felt powerful, in control, feelings heightened by the secrecy and illegality of this visit. He felt alive again, no longer on the back foot, once more in control of his destiny.

Jack made swift progress, avoiding the seafront, ducking the crowds, sticking to the lonely streets away from the tourist hub. This was his Southend, the unseen roads and back alleys that visitors never knew existed. He liked these streets, they were real, honest in a way, but as he made his way steadily towards Marlborough Road, he felt his stomach begin to tighten. His decision to come here had been so instinctive, so impulsive, that he'd never really thought about what he might say or how he'd be received. It wasn't too late to pull out, of course, he could head back to London, full of lies and apologies, but his feet kept on moving, almost in spite of himself, propelling him homeward.

Ten minutes later, he was there. Standing outside 43 Marlborough Road, a neglected Victorian terrace that had seen better days. For a moment, he was a child again, pushing through that peeling door, shouting and arguing, laughing and fighting. It hadn't all been bad, had it? Angrily, he pushed that thought away. It had always been shit. But it was still his birthright, it was who he was, so climbing the steps, he knocked sharply on the door.

Silence. Then the sound of coughing within, but no movement. He knocked again. More coughing, but again all was still.

So bending down, Jack picked up the mat. There, as always, was a rusty latch key. Smiling to himself, Jack opened the door and slipped inside.

The front room was dark and gloomy, thick with the odour of cigarettes. It was a smell he always associated with his mother and he felt a surge of emotion within him. Here she was, in the flesh. Initially, she had visited him at the young offenders' unit, turning up when time and money allowed, seeming to take some pleasure from their meetings. Latterly, those visits had tailed off, with the result that he hadn't seen her in well over a year. And now he understood why. Once broad and powerful, she was now a shell of a woman, hunched, shrivelled, hollowed out by a pernicious, aggressive disease.

'Who is it?' Pam Peters croaked, warily.

Jack hesitated. How to answer that question? Stepping forward into light, he answered:

'It's me, Mum.'

He saw his mother start, shocked by his sudden appearance in the family home. She stared at him blindly, as if disbelieving her own eyes.

'Sorry to turn up out of the blue, but I had to see you. Danny told me, about your illness and that...'

'Is it really you?'

She gasped the words, lack of oxygen and a swelling of emotion rendering her breathless. Jack moved in closer, kneeling down in front of her.

'Yes, it's me,' he countered, smiling through tears.

'My Kyle,' she whispered, stroking his cheek with her bony hand.

And now he broke, sobbing as he rested his head on her knee. Nobody had called him that in years and it felt so sweet, so right, that he completely lost it, weeping without embarrassment. He was with his mum. He was home.

He couldn't say how long he cried for, but eventually she lifted his head, drying his tears.

'Stand up, son,' she croaked. 'So I can get a better look at you.'

He did as he was asked, wiping the tears from his cheeks, smiling awkwardly as she inspected him.

'A fine lad now. A fine, strapping lad.'

Jack nodded, but said nothing, too emotional to speak.

'How are you getting on then? I heard they let you out.'

As she spoke, she ferreted in her housecoat, locating a packet of Lambert and Butler.

'OK, I suppose. I'm living in—'

He caught himself just in time.

'I've got a house now, a job. Things are OK, you know.'

'Good, good,' his mother replied, lighting up and drawing deeply on the long cigarette.

'And how about you? Those don't seem to have done you too much good...' Jack joked, provoking a wry smile.

'Well, you have to take your pleasures where you can find them.'

Jack was still smiling, but felt a stab of anger inside. His mother had been *all about pleasure* – drink, men, drugs – anything that took her away from her responsibilities, her children, her life. She knew what had been going on in her house, the hideous abuse that was taking place under her roof, but she'd done nothing, preferring oblivion instead. Clamping down his rising bile, Jack continued:

'What do the doctors say? Are you getting treatment or what?'

'Packed all that in,' she replied dismissively. 'Too little, too late, and it was only making me feel shit. I reckon you made it in the nick of time.'

She laughed bitterly, before breaking into a coughing fit. Nasty, hacking coughs that went right through Jack.

'Don't say that, Mum. You can fight this thing.'

'Are you kidding? The fight went out of me years ago.'

She eyeballed him as she spoke, her tone knowing and pointed.

'Don't be daft, you're as strong as an ox.'

'Maybe one day, not now. Now all I've got are fags and whisky. But that's OK, they'll see me home.'

'You can't think like that. You've still got Danny. You've still got me. The others too. Plenty to live for.'

'Maybe, maybe…'

'I mean it,' Jack continued, kneeling down by her once more. 'There's no need to give up, not yet. You've got to enjoy your time. You should try and get out. Danny can help you. And…'

He hesitated for a moment, suddenly nervous, then added:

'…and if you want, I can pop down too, take you out. I know it's against the rules, but if we're careful…'

'No.'

The word was shocking, final.

'I don't mean regularly or anything,' Jack said, backtracking. 'But I'd like to help.'

'No, Kyle. This is your last visit.'

He stared at her, mute, in shock.

'Don't look at me like that,' she scolded him, suddenly angry. 'You shouldn't even be here in the first place.'

'But I wanted to see you.'

'Well, you've seen me. So now you can go.'

Jack was floundering, taken aback by her sudden coldness.

'Why are you being like this?' he protested. 'I came here because I was worried ab—'

'Why am I being like this? Are you *seriously* asking me that?'

The words sprang out, crisp and eloquent, anger sharpening her tongue.

'Do you have any idea what you've *done* to this family?'

'Course I have. I know I fucked up—'

'No, you have *no* idea. No idea at all. Because you're only interested in yourself, always were...'

Speechless with the injustice of this accusation, it took a moment for Jack to find his tongue.

'How can you say that to me? You of all people?'

'Oh spare me. You're a selfish little shit and you know it.'

'Fuck you,' Jack rasped, angry and upset.

'No, fuck *you*, Kyle. For coming here, for destroying this family, for ever having been born.'

He stared at her, aghast, overwhelmed.

'I know you think you've suffered, well, let me tell you, you were the *lucky one*. You got away. The rest of us had to stay here. Had to suffer the insults in the street, the bricks through the window, the dog shit smeared all over the front door. We used to be known round here, liked even. Now people wouldn't spit on me if I was on fire. I used to have friends, Kyle, family, a life. Now I'm the slut, the stupid cunt, the fucking monster at the end of the road. People have spat at me, crossed the road to avoid me, called me every name under the sun. Danny's been attacked three times, your sister twice... so don't you dare call me selfish. It's you, Kyle. You and your violence and your sickness and depraved desires. My son, the kiddie fiddler. Well, I hope you *enjoyed it*, boy, because it cost us, cost us dear.'

Jack staggered backwards, shocked, sickened. He felt dizzy and breathless, reeling from this sustained verbal assault.

'Please stop, Mum. Just stop,' he gasped.

'Truth hard to hear, is it?' she goaded. 'Well, it's about time you heard it. Time you realized what you did to us. Because of you we can't set foot outside our own house, can't go for a drink, a dance, nothing. We're pariahs in our own bloody town, *all because of you.*'

Jack scrambled to his feet, he wanted to blot out her viciousness, to get away. But she wasn't finished yet.

'I still love you I suppose, that's a mother's curse. But you ruined my life, son. You ruined *all* our lives. So go now and don't ever darken our door again.'

She eyeballed him viciously, as she concluded:

'You should *never* have come here.'

Chapter 67

He glared at her as he struggled across the room, collapsing into the plastic chair with an exasperated sigh, banging his walking stick loudly down on the table.

'Good to see you again, Mr Green,' Chandra Dabral said evenly.

'I wish I could say the same,' the probation officer replied angrily. 'I should be back at base, trying to sort this mess out, not going over my statement for *a third time.*'

'Then you'll be pleased to hear that I actually have some fresh questions for you. I'd hate for us to rake over old ground.'

'What do you mean "fresh questions"?' Green asked, disturbed.

'I'm trying to get an overview of your movements during the last six weeks.'

'Why?'

'In particular, I'm keen to establish where you were on the seventh of November,' Chandra continued, ignoring the question. 'Am I right in thinking you were at a conference at the Excel Centre in Shepherds Bush?'

A brief pause, then Green nodded, on his guard now.

'Good. And how about the twenty-eighth of November? Were you in London that day?'

'If it was a weekday, then yes. I was probably visiting clients.'

'Anyone in the Oxford Circus area?'

'Not that I'm aware of.'

'Were you working the whole day?'

'Like a trooper.'

'Only your phone seems to have been switched off that morning, no signal at all between 8 a.m. and 10 a.m. It was my understanding that probation officers of your rank and experience had to be contactable at all times, given your special responsibilities?'

'Can I help it if my phone occasionally loses signal? I was probably on the tube...'

'For two hours?'

'Or in a black spot. You know what it's like in London.'

It was said evenly, but there was no mistaking Green's hostility now.

'How about the fifth of December? Were you in London then?'

'I assume so.'

'You never have cause to visit other towns? Specifically, is there any chance you were in Reading that day in the course of your duties?'

'No. My clients are all London-based. *Janet Slater* is somebody else's responsibility.'

There was a twinkle in Green's eye now, as if he'd stolen a march on Chandra by guessing the reason behind her question.

'Who looks after her then?' the police officer demanded.

'I've no idea. Her Reading MAPPA team, I suppose. It's none of my business.'

'Unless you made it so...'

'Look, I've already told you I was in London that day.'

'All day?'

'*Yes.*'

'Only you seem to have stumbled across yet another "black spot" that day. No messages, no calls, no signal in fact, between

11 a.m. and 2 p.m. Plenty of time to get to Reading and back if you'd needed to do so...'

'Where is this going, Inspector?' Green hissed, leaning forward aggressively. 'I've done nothing wrong, yet you persist in harassing me. Well, tread carefully, because I've had plenty of experience of this kind of thing and I *never* take it lying down...'

'Yes, I was going to come on to that,' Chandra responded crisply. 'Your one-man war against the Probation Service...'

As she spoke, she opened her file, revealing numerous pieces of paper.

'I've had a little look at your HR file. I see you're currently the subject of serious disciplinary proceedings following an altercation with your line manager, plus so far I've counted *seven* separate complaints against your employers, but the main one pertains to your historic injury. Would you like to tell me about that?'

Green hesitated, for the first time looking uncertain.

'What is there to say?' he eventually answered, angry and bitter. 'It's all there in the file. The guy wasn't even my client, I was just covering for a colleague. He was high as a kite, paranoid, said he heard voices *telling him* to attack me. The ambulance took the best part of an hour to turn up, by which time my leg was fucked. I spent several weeks in hospital during which I received one phone call from HR. *One phone call*. Nobody visited me, no one talked to me, I had to pay for my own cab to get home.'

'You were obviously very angry about that...'

'I was bloody furious. But that wasn't the worst bit. That came later, a brief letter of apology and £20,000. Twenty grand! That doesn't even begin to cover what that bastard cost me...'

'What did it cost you?'

'Everything. I couldn't move properly for months, couldn't sleep because of the pain. My confidence was in bits, I was bitter, distracted. My wife stuck it out for a year, then left me and you know what, even though I called her every name under the sun at the time, I don't blame her, because of what I'd become, because of what they'd made me.'

'I'm sorry, Isaac, I had no idea.'

'Well, there you go then. Seems you don't know everything.'

He sat back in his chair once more, flustered but triumphant.

'Would you say you have a personal animus against the Probation Service?'

'In English please.'

'Would you say you actively despise the Probation Service? That you have an ongoing vendetta against them?'

'Absolutely not. I want justice. I want what's owing to me.'

'And if you felt that wasn't going to happen? That you were going to be cheated of what you were owed?'

For a moment, Green looked like he was about to respond, but then suddenly reeled himself back in.

'I have every confidence that I'll get what I'm due. Right always prevails in the end,' the probation officer concluded, leaning back and folding his arms.

Chandra eyed him keenly, sensing he was starting to close up on her.

'One last thing then. Have you ever accessed internal Probation Service systems or files that you had no authorisation to view?'

Green blinked, surprised by this sudden change in direction. 'I'm sorry?'

'It's a straightforward question. Have you ever broken internal protocols to access confidential information that you should not have been privy to?'

'Absolutely not. That's a sacking offence.'

It was said quickly and with conviction, but Green's eyes told a very different story.

'Now can I go, please? I've got a lot work to do.'

Chapter 68

Where the hell *was* he?

Olivia scanned the streets, desperately hoping to catch a glimpse of Jack's hunched form shuffling home. She'd done two circuits of the roads around the building site, stopping multiple times on the second pass to check out the local pubs and off-licences. But this had yielded nothing, so she'd raced back to Tottenham Hale. She'd searched the house top to bottom, then set out again, driving past the house a couple more times as she did fruitless laps of the surrounding streets. But the house remained dark and deserted, the whereabouts of its sole occupant a mystery.

She punched his number in again, but the result was predictable.

'Hi, this is Jack. Please lea—'

She ended the call, declining to leave a message. His voicemail was already full of her irate offerings – what good would one more do? If he would just turn his phone on, just answer the call, then they could sort this out. But Olivia had the strong sense that Jack had turned his phone off for a reason, which made her nervous. He had presumably met his brother as planned, somewhere in London, but that encounter should have taken place hours ago. Night was falling, it was already dark, so where had he subsequently gone? And with whom? Was he still with Danny? If so, what were they up to? They had once been close, but Jack had definitely bullied his young brother, perhaps even abused him, so who was to say that their encounter wouldn't have turned nasty, even violent?

Going against all protocols, Olivia had tried to ring Danny. She knew it was foolhardy, and part of her had been glad when it went straight to voicemail. Hanging up without leaving a message, she'd told herself to pursue more conventional routes, not to constantly imagine the worst. This was easier said than done, however.

Slowing at a red light, she punched in a familiar number and seconds later the call was answered.

'Saul Behr.'

'Saul, it's me again. Have there been any sightings?'

'Nothing concrete, I'm afraid.'

Olivia's heart sank. She'd hoped that mobilising her colleagues, especially those who were young and still believed wholeheartedly in the cause, might help her get out of this hole. But luck was against her today.

'We had a couple of case workers operating in that area. They've been doing the rounds. There was a potential sighting of Jack at the Coach and Horses in Romford, but that was at lunchtime, so he'll be long gone by now. Sorry...'

'OK, that's better than nothing. Stay in touch and if you hear anything.'

'You'll be the first to know.'

She rang off, speeding away from the lights, before executing a perfect U-turn. She would head for Romford, hoping that Jack was still in the area. Right now she'd take him being holed up drunk in some boozer there, even though this would be a flagrant breach of his licence. But even as she raced there, she sensed that this was a fond hope. Jack had been in a bad place this morning and clearly his day had not improved – a violent altercation with his boss leading to him severing ties with work after only two days. From there he had presumably headed to meet his brother, a concrete connection to his violent past. Cursing herself for ever having sanctioned the meeting, Olivia sped on, beset by worry. She wanted Jack to come back safe and sound, to return to her orbit where she could protect and, if necessary, control him. But her instinct told her he was about to do something stupid, something reckless, perhaps even something fatal.

Chapter 69

He staggered through the streets, oblivious to those around him, barely heeding where he was going. Tears filled his eyes, his legs felt like jelly, but he kept going. He had to get *away*.

Crashing into a passer-by, Jack cannoned sideways, hitting the wall before carrying on. A volley of abuse pursued him, but he didn't stop, stumbling onwards. Nothing, none of it, mattered anymore. He had reached rock bottom and nothing could touch him now. How stupid, how naïve he'd been coming here. He'd craved company, craved family, something to make this Christmas feel a bit less bleak and what had been his reward? Rejection and humiliation. Danny couldn't get away fast enough and his mother hated him. If only he could turn back time, so that he didn't have to endure those awful, bitter accusations. He had suffered so much, been endlessly vilified and insulted, but he'd never felt as bad as he did today.

He needed to get home. London was bad, but Southend would be forever seared on his brain as the stuff of nightmares. He knew now that he wouldn't feel safe, wouldn't be able to focus, until he was on a train travelling away from this hideous place. Why had he ever come here? Didn't he know it was his fate to be alone and despised? Why had he imagined that anyone would actually want to see him? He was a stain, no more, no less.

Wiping the tears away, Jack tried to get his bearings, ignoring the intrigued glances of passers-by. The streets looked strange to him now, but slowly he began to realize where he was, instinct propelling him down a side alley that he knew would cut minutes off his journey to the train station. He sped up, fear and anger driving him forward. He would get out of this shithole and never come back. He would never think about, never mention this place again – it would be as if the town, and everyone in it, had been wiped off the map.

This thought cheered Jack and he broke into a trot. He was reaching the end of the alley now, would soon be spilling out onto the main drag. From there it would only be a two-minute jog to safety. 'Fuck 'em all,' he thought gladly, 'I'm done with the lot of you.'

'Where's the fire, mate?'

The voice cut through his musings, sharp and nasal. A rangy teenager in jeans and a hoodie loitered at the end of the alley, eyeing him curiously.

'No fire, just need to be on my way.'

'Understood, brother. Understood.'

Jack slowed now, looking at the young man with interest. There was something about his face that was familiar. Were they at school together? Had he lived in the neighbourhood?

'Need anything to take with you?'

Jack had been about to depart, but now paused.

'Dope, blow, speed?' the teenager continued, sensing a sale. 'It's good shit, mate, fresh off the boat.'

Jack eyed him, intrigued, as the dealer pulled his merchandise from his pocket, displaying it for his enjoyment. Jack knew he should turn and go, spurn this lowlife. But the drugs were just there, sitting in his palm, beckoning to him.

'All right,' he said quickly.

'All right what?'

'Speed, blow, weed,' Jack replied urgently.

'Fair enough, but it'll cost you. £100. You good for that?

Jack responded by pulling a small wad of notes from his rucksack.

'Yes you *are*...' the dealer said, impressed. 'Give me the dough and get your blow.'

Methodically, Jack counted out the notes. It was dangerous to be back in this space, but there was no denying it felt good. He was already quivering with excitement, the blood pumping in his veins. Handing the money over, he held out his hand expectantly. But, to his surprise, the teenager kept hold of the drugs, and looking up, Jack now saw that the young dealer was staring at him intently.

'Hey, fella,' he said, screwing up his eyes curiously. 'Don't I know you?'

His mother had been right. He *shouldn't* have come here.

Chapter 70

Why the hell had he come here?

Was it to get Graham Ellis off his back? To push Courtney Turner from his thoughts? Or was it simply to prove to himself that he could still lead a normal life? If it was the latter, a foolhardy attempt to enjoy some festive fun, then it had been a massive miscalculation. Looking around the function suite of the Maidstone Marriott, Mike saw nothing that raised his spirits or cheered his heart. It was populated by scores of badly dressed sales staff, in various states of drunkenness, dancing, joking and shrieking with laughter. It was like a scene from Hell, shrill, disquieting and utterly alien to him. One guy had already vomited in a potted plant, right next to a couple who were snogging furiously, yet everyone seemed to be behaving as if this was entirely normal. As if it was *fun*. Mike had always hated these events, sales teams from all over the south-east brought together in a grim charade of forced jollity, but tonight's gathering was even more unbearable than usual. What did all these people have to celebrate? What was so great about their lives that they were partying so hard? It was desperate, overwrought and he hated every second of it.

'Another double, please.'

As the barman obliged, pouring another generous glass of

Bell's, Mike caught Simon's eye across the room. He'd already had a brief chat with his boss, deliberately approaching him whilst he was surrounded by senior sales reps, hoping that his claims of illness wouldn't be unpicked in front of colleagues. Mike knew, however, that it was only a matter of time before his boss called him on his unscheduled absences, his repeated failure to respond to calls. He just hoped he could stay one step ahead of him tonight.

Turning away from the bar, Mike took a long, slow swig, savouring the burn in his throat. His only hope of enduring the evening now was to get properly pissed, then make his excuses and stumble home for a night of sweet, drunken oblivion. Part of him was actually looking forward to it, as long as he *could* sleep. But in reality what chance was there of that? His mind was overcooked after the shocking events of the day, one half of his brain fleeing the awful memory of Courtney Turner's sexual ecstasy, whilst the other half continued to turn on Graham Ellis's surprise visit.

Why had Graham turned up suddenly, today of all days? Just hours after Mike had trespassed on Courtney's property? Was it, as the ex-police officer had suggested, to warn Mike not to get sucked into the growing public clamour for revenge on those who'd committed acts of unspeakable evil? Or did Graham's sudden appearance have a more sinister purpose? He had *specifically* urged Mike to delete any message connected to Courtney Turner's current whereabouts. Was it possible that he already knew Mike had received this message, because *he* himself had sent it? Was Graham Ellis covering his tracks now, knowing that Mike had taken the bait?

It seemed impossible, Graham had always been such a sensible, calming influence. And yet... he *had* turned up the day before Mike received the text message, stoking his anger, awakening old feelings, and now he'd turned up again out of the blue, as if he already knew what Mike was up to. There was no question that Graham had shared Mike's indignation at the girls' meagre sentence, that he had burned with anger at their seven-year stint in a glorified holiday camp, whatever he might have said in public at the time. Was it possible then that he was somehow involved in all this? Was even the *source* of these leaks?

Graham had seemed sincere in his insistence that Mike swallow down his anger and try to make a new life for himself. Yet he must have known that that was an impossible task, that Mike's thoughts strayed constantly to that dark day ten years ago. Whether in daydreams or nightmares, Mike's mind constantly fixated on those few, terrible hours when everything changed. Frequently – too frequently – Mike tried to drink those visions away, to blot out the horror, but alcohol often only made things worse, Mike's overheated brain pulsing with awful images, replaying the events of that day constantly, as if on a loop. Mike could feel those memories, those rapier thrusts of guilt and self-hatred, circling now. Draining his whisky, he clamped his eyes shut, desperate to force these phantoms away, but as he did so, he saw himself again, sprinting through the lonely corridors of that leisure centre, searching for his missing daughter, crying out her name. 'Jessica, Jessica, Jessica…'. But he was too late. He was *five* minutes too late and those evil bitches had already pounced, wheeling his daughter away, promising to take her home.

A sob erupted from him, as Mike's eyes snapped open. He was clinging to the bar, drunk and distraught, the bartender eyeing him with concern. Tossing the empty glass back onto the counter, Mike turned away, hurrying fast towards the exit. His legs felt unsteady, shaking beneath him, but he kept moving, clawing his way through the crowds, desperate to escape. He had been mad to come here, the din of the drunken carnival appearing ever more obscene. Sweaty bodies, spilled drinks, drunken flirting, party streamers, he wanted none of it. He wanted to tear it all down, kill the music, bellow out his misery, but instead he blundered on, slowly zeroing in on salvation. He was close to the exit now, so close...

Suddenly he was careering sideways, cannoning off another partygoer. Stumbling, Mike righted himself to find the guy staring at him, beer in hand, quizzical but not hostile.

'Easy there, fella. Too much Babycham?'

He was smiling, a hideous toothy grin, amused by his predicament. Mike had no idea who he was, a rep from another branch probably, but he was instantly repelled by him, his eyes glued to his freckly face, his loose tie, the dark sweat patches under his arms.

'Feeling festive, are we, mate?' the reveller continued, laughing loudly.

Why wouldn't he go away? Why was he leering at Mike, as if they were drinking buddies? What did he want from him?

'Tell you what, mate, let's shake hands and I'll buy you a drink. I'm in the mood to *party*...'

He did an obscene hip jiggle, before taking a swig of his Budweiser, grinning wolfishly at him. Sickened, Mike turned away, but his companion grabbed him, hauling him back.

'Don't be like that. I'm just being friendly like...'

'Get off me,' Mike barked, tugging his arm free.

'Fair enough,' the reveller responded, aggrieved. 'But you should lighten up, mate. It is Christmas after all.'

Mike turned away, though he yearned to hurl abuse at this mindless idiot. He just wanted to be alone, away from this place, but before he'd taken two steps, his tormentor added:

'Come on, cheer up, fella. It might never happen.'

Before Mike knew what he was doing, he'd turned, advancing on the man and flooring him with one punch. The sales rep crashed to the floor, his beer bottle tumbling from his hand, his head colliding hard with the polished wood floor. Stunned, reeling, he barely took in the words, as Mike grabbed him by the collar and rasped:

'It already has, *fella*. It already has.'

Chapter 71

Chandra Dabral marched back to her office, deep in thought. Her skirmish with Isaac Green had been inconclusive – the probation officer was clearly hiding something, yet had played his hand carefully, revealing nothing incriminating. Green would be a hard nut to crack, wily, experienced, canny, but Chandra never ducked a challenge. They would have to be targeted, precise and methodical, however, particularly as regards Green's movements. He had clearly dropped off the grid several times in the last few weeks, which was intriguing, not to mention a blatant breach of the terms of his employment. Why risk disciplinary action, even dismissal, unless it was something important? What did Green have to hide?

Chandra was already formulating a plan of action, mentally plotting out the next twenty-four hours, when DC Cooke rose from her desk, flagging her down. The junior officer looked flushed, excited, so Chandra slowed, intrigued.

'Got another possible name for you,' Cooke said breathlessly. 'Guy Chambers. He's a junior minister at the Ministry of—'

'I know who Chambers is.'

'Yes, of course, sorry. Anyway, I think I can link him to both London *and* Reading on the relevant dates.'

For a moment, Chandra said nothing, surprised. Her thoughts

had all been bent towards Isaac Green, but if DC Cooke's assertions were correct, it clearly warranted further investigation.

'How sure are you?' she demanded.

'One hundred per cent,' DC Cooke replied. 'I spoke to the BBC producer this morning and she emailed me over their schedule of guests. Guy Chambers was definitely on the *Today* programme on the morning of the twenty-eighth of November, so would have been in the vicinity of Oxford Circus when Caitlin Rose was sent Andrew Baynes's details.'

'And we know he was at the conference in Shepherds Bush on the seventh of November, standing in for his boss.'

'Right. Plus, he's the MP for—'

'Reading South,' Chandra interrupted, anticipating her colleague. 'Have we checked his diary for the fifth of December?'

'Doing it now, but the House of Commons wasn't sitting that day, and he usually spends Fridays in the constituency, so…'

In spite of herself, Chandra felt a tingle of excitement.

'Would he have known Emily Lawrence was living in his constituency?' Cooke asked.

'Totally,' Chandra replied. 'The MAPPA teams have to inform local MPs and sometimes they even sit in on the meetings if they have a special interest in the case.'

Cooke nodded, but said nothing, troubled.

'What are you thinking?' Chandra queried.

'No, nothing. I'm just processing it, that's all,' the young officer replied. 'Are we definitely saying then that Chambers is a suspect? I mean, he's a serving MP, a junior minister at the Ministry of Justice…'

'I know it seems like a bit of a stretch,' Chandra replied carefully. 'But the coincidence is too big to ignore. Guy Chambers was in the right place at the right time, when the details of Mark Willis, Andrew Baynes *and* Janet Slater were leaked. Plus he has form. You've heard him on the radio, on TV. He loves presenting himself as a voice of the people, constantly claiming that offenders aren't punished enough, that victims' families are being failed by a broken system. Every time something goes wrong, you'll find him on *Newsnight*, lambasting the police, the Probation Service. I used to think he did it to tickle the Tory grassroots, now I think he genuinely *believes* it. He's a dog whistle politician who actually buys into his crazy ideas, which makes him very dangerous indeed.'

DC Cooke nodded, but still looked tense, aware of the implications of this discussion.

'Believe me,' Chandra concluded, 'I've no desire to stir up a hornet's nest, but I'm going to have to talk to him. We'd be failing in our duty if we didn't. Make the necessary arrangements, but do it *quietly* please.'

Nodding earnestly, Cooke hurried away to do her bidding. Chandra thought for a moment, her mind suddenly buzzing with numerous possible permutations and pitfalls to come in this fast-moving investigation, before following her colleague into the incident room. Scanning the sea of faces, she spotted DC Reeves rising from her desk, beckoning her over.

'Got some news, guv,' Reeves said, hurrying across to her.

'Me first,' Chandra said, cutting her off. 'I want us to get in touch with the Burnham family and the Armstrong family too.'

Her subordinate looked taken aback, so Chandra elaborated.

'They're the obvious targets for our perpetrator if they're contemplating further leaks, given that the offenders responsible for Jessica Burnham's and Billy Armstrong's murders were granted lifelong anonymity by the courts. Hopefully I'm overthinking this, being paranoid, but if we can I'd like us to contact them, to ensure they haven't received any unsolicited messages and to put my mind at ease.'

Reeves nodded, but looked even more concerned than before. Chandra didn't mean to alarm her colleague and sincerely hoped she was wrong, but the leaks appeared to be coming thick and fast now, so it wouldn't do to take chances.

'Sorry, you said you had news for me?' Chandra continued, dragging her attention back to the here and now.

'Yes, just heard from Hartlepool,' Reeves responded. 'The three brothers accused of chasing Willis to his death have been released without charge.'

'What?!' Chandra exclaimed, hardly believing her ears.

'Insufficient evidence apparently. Thirty locals gave them a rock-solid alibi.'

'So because of their lies, these three guys are going to get away with pre-meditated murder?' Chandra responded, appalled.

'Looks that way. They were careful, knew what they were doing and got the job done.'

'Well, it's disgusting,' Chandra replied, shaking her head. 'And it sets an incredibly dangerous precedent. But what do they care?'

Her eyes were drawn to the photo of Mark Willis's brutalized corpse, as she concluded:

'They're bloody *laughing* at us.'

Chapter 72

Olivia slammed the horn, but received only a single-fingered response from the courier who deliberately took his time as he sauntered back to his van.

'Fuck's sake…' Olivia muttered to herself, returning the favour.

Smirking, the driver hauled himself into his van, before slowly moving away. Olivia followed, cursing London more than ever. Not being a native, she still occasionally got lost in the capital and she had done just that tonight, losing her bearings in her desperate attempts to locate Jack. Google Maps had come to her rescue, but as she tried to find her way back to Tottenham Hale from Romford, she'd encountered the truculent courier, who seemed determined to delay her. How she hated this overclogged, overpriced city today.

She knew she was overreacting, her anger and anxiety about Jack's disappearance stoking her emotions, but try as she might, she couldn't quell her jangling nerves. Jack had been missing for hours now. Was he in Southend, London or beyond? Was he safe and sound, drunk and helpless, or even now being pursued down the street by an angry mob? She knew there was already profound alarm back at Petty France over his disappearance, but it was nothing compared to the distress she felt. This was a *major* fuck-up and on only the second day of his release. Whatever happened now, this would rebound on her, no question.

Spinning right on Tottenham High Street, Olivia redialled Jack's mobile once more.

'Hi, this is Jack. Leave a message.'

'Jack, it's Olivia again. Just call me as soon as you get this.'

Who was she kidding? She knew full well that her messages hadn't been listened to, that Jack's phone had remained off for the whole afternoon. Was this his choice? A desire to drop off the grid? Or had someone turned it off *for him*? Her ignorance was driving her mad, her imagination conjuring up all sorts of scenarios, and she cursed herself once more for her stupidity. She had moved too far too fast with Jack, should have bedded him in more slowly. In rushing things, in wanting to get him sorted and settled, she'd pushed too hard, undoing months, years of patient rehabilitation. Given her experience, she should have known better, shouldn't have been so impatient, failing in her primary duty of care. Unless he had always planned to do a bunk? This was certainly possible and made Olivia feel a tiny bit better, but in reality the outcome was the same, a vulnerable probationer missing, or on the run, at a time of real and pressing danger.

Pulling back onto Exeter Road, Olivia sped down the street. She had driven past Jack's house six or seven times tonight, the darkened gloom of its interior crushing her fond hopes every time. She didn't even know why she was bothering, except for the fact that she had no other credible plan, but now as she approached the modest two-up, two-down, she noticed a light burning inside. Slewing her car into the first available space, Olivia abandoned it and ran to the front door. She was tempted to hammer on it, to make a scene, but instead, she tugged out her key and slid it into the lock. Yanking the door open, she hurried inside, to find a bleary, unsteady Jack staring back at her.

'Why, Jack? Why would you do that?'

Olivia was apoplectic, stunned by what she'd just heard.

'I've told you why,' Jack moaned. 'Danny told me Mum was ill, so I went to see her.'

'You had to go back to Southend?' she replied, disbelieving.

'Yes, for all the good it did me. That fucking bitch hates my guts...'

'What did you expect? She never looked out for you in the first place and, after everything you've put *her* through, put the family through, is it any wonder you're not welcome home? You shouldn't have gone there.'

'Tell me about it,' the probationer returned, bitterly.

'I mean it, Jack. It's too dangerous right now, not to mention the fact that you have breached your licence in pretty much every way possible. By rights, I should send you to prison now, tonight.'

'It was one stupid trip.'

'And the rest. What have you taken?'

'Nothing.'

'What have you taken? Your pupils are as big as saucers.'

'Bit of weed, some speed. Just to take the edge off things.'

'Where'd you get it from?'

'A dealer in Southend.'

'Someone you knew?'

'No, just a guy I used to see around.'

'Did he recognize you?' Olivia demanded urgently.

'I don't know, maybe...'

'Jesus Christ, Jack!'

Olivia threw up her hands in despair, stalking across the room. 'Two days into your probation and you punch your boss, abandon your work, go back to Southend, row with your family, buy illegal drugs and potentially get recognized into the bargain.'

'All right, all right, you've made your point,' Jack protested, avoiding her eye.

'No, I obviously haven't, so let me make it perfectly plain. Look at me, Jack.'

Still her probationer stared at the floor.

'Look at me!' she shouted, shocking herself and making him jump.

Slowly, Jack looked up, guilt-ridden and unnerved.

'It is dangerous out there right now,' Olivia continued, eye-balling him. '*Really* dangerous. And I am the only thing standing between you and a baseball bat. Do you understand that?'

Jack shrugged, but it was clear her words were hitting home.

'There are people out there who would willingly tear you limb from limb. It is my job to make sure that doesn't happen, but I can only do that if I know where you are *at all times*, that you are never out of contact and that you are *where* you're supposed to be, *when* you're supposed to be. No ifs or buts or maybes. Any slip-up, any mistake puts that at risk, puts *you* at risk. Do you get that?'

'Yes.'

It was said quietly, begrudgingly, but it was the best Olivia could hope for.

'We're going to have to deal with the fact that you might have been spotted, recognized in Southend. We'll probably have to move you, find new work for you – and that's the *best*-case scenario. If the powers that be decide your behaviour warrants a spell behind bars, I won't be able to stop them. It might even be the safest thing for you right now.'

'No, please. I've told you I don't want to go to an adult prison.'

Olivia was surprised to see real fear in his eyes.

'I'll do anything you want, play by the rules. Just don't send me inside.'

'I can't promise anything, Jack, not after today.'

'I'm *sorry*, OK?' he insisted, tearful. 'I fucked up, I know that. But I'll do whatever you want, honest to God. I didn't want to freak you out, to make things difficult ... I just wanted to see my mum. She's sick, I haven't seen her for nearly two years and I might not get another chance. She's all I've got, her and Danny, so I wanted to say sorry, to tell her I loved her ...'

Olivia said nothing, surprised by his openness, his vulnerability. She suspected Jack hadn't got the chance to tell his mother how he felt, rocked by her naked anger and hostility.

'It was stupid, fucking stupid. She doesn't want me; Danny doesn't want me ...'

Tears were creeping down his cheeks, emotion overwhelming him.

'I'm bloody toxic. Nobody wants anything to do with me and ... it's hard. It's so *fucking* hard.'

He dropped his face to his hands, sobbing bitterly. Olivia regarded him coolly, still angry and annoyed, but surprised at how small, how broken the teenager looked tonight. Despite herself she felt a pang of pity, of sympathy, for the shitty, unloved life Jack had lived. Few things sting quite so keenly as rejection, as Olivia well knew herself.

'OK, we've said enough for now,' she responded calmly. 'Let's get some coffee into you, a bite to eat, then we can reset tomorrow. It'll take us a day or so to come up with a plan so—'

'Can you stay?'

For a moment, Olivia thought she hadn't heard him right. 'I'm sorry?'

'I know it's against the rules and that, but can you stay tonight? I don't want to be alone.'

It was completely of the question, a gross breach of protocol. But the way Jack was looking at Olivia strongly suggested that he might do something desperate if she *didn't* stay. So despite the pit of anxiety in her stomach, the nagging stress headache that was already brewing, Olivia found herself nodding her head. Instantly, Jack fell into her arms, crying like a newborn baby, clinging to her as if she was his last anchor to earth.

Chapter 73

He had cried himself to sleep.

Each quiet sob had cut through Emily like a knife, tears streaming down her cheeks in time with Sam's, but each attempt to comfort her son had been brusquely rejected. He had nowhere else to go, Marianne insisting mother and son stay together for security reasons, but that did not mean Sam had to communicate with her. Emily had managed to coax him out of the bathroom, the lure of a comfortable bed too great to resist, but Sam had not looked at her as he crossed the room, merely climbing between the sheets fully clothed and silently sobbing, face turned to the wall.

Emily had never felt as wretched as she did tonight. During that terrible time, nearly thirty years ago now, when she was spat at, abused, vilified, the furious crowds hammering the sides of the van as she was driven to court, a simmering, resentful anger had co-existed alongside her guilt and sadness. Now there was no such defiance, no fury, propping her up. Now she just felt total desolation. Her boy, her beautiful boy, the only good thing she'd ever done in her miserable life, could no longer bear to look at her.

He was at least asleep now, exhausted by the events of the day, but in truth this was cold comfort for Emily. For he would wake soon enough, and then the post-mortem would begin. Strange to say it, but today had been the easy bit, when shock and distress were his overpowering emotions. From tomorrow morning, mother and son would have to create a new relationship, a new life, one in which Sam knew exactly who his mother was and what she was capable of. In her own mind, Emily bore no resemblance to Janet anymore, physically, emotionally or morally, but how would she ever convince Sam of this? She knew full well he would have googled Janet Slater, drinking in the prurient articles and gossip that continued to inflame tensions in Bridgend, keeping the sainted memory of her baby sisters alive. She knew logically that she still deserved this punishment, this infamy, but she *wasn't* that person anymore. She was a committed, loving mother, entirely harmless, whose only desire was to do *good*. What chance of that now? When she would have to leave her chosen profession, abandon her home, perhaps even lose her son?

Emily suppressed a groan of anguish, biting down hard on her finger, desperate not to disturb Sam. Perhaps whilst he slept, he was at peace, oblivious to his misfortune, his tragic birthright. But when he awoke, he would remember and then it would begin – the anguish, the distress, the accusations. And who could blame him? She had killed her sisters, but she had also killed his aunties. Just as bad, she had lied to him his entire life, keeping this dark secret hidden from him, making him repeat a fiction that many people, not least the probation officers who often turned up posing as her friends, were well aware was bullshit. Tonight, this seemed like the grossest of deceptions, the bitterest of pills to swallow.

Would they ever recover their closeness? Could the trust between them ever be restored? She had had fourteen years to tell her son the truth about her real identity, her real past and she had failed to do so. She'd kept her counsel out of sheer self-preservation, out of a desire to abide by the terms of her licence, to embrace a new life and see if she could wipe the slate clean, erasing the sins of the past. And it had led her here, to this lifeless hotel room, where she now lay next to a fourteen-year-old boy who was disgusted by her.

The past decade and a half seemed like a dream now. Despite the failure of her marriage, they had been resoundingly happy years and Emily had never once felt alone in all that time, keeping Sam close and revelling in his company. Would she lose that now? Lose her lifeline? Back then, when she was a ragged little girl, with threadbare clothes and lice-infested locks, she had known what it was like to be lonely, overlooked, neglected. She had felt the keen smart of her father's belt, the sharp bite of his tongue, but even his presence seemed like a boon next to the gaping void left by her mother's departure, whose casual abandonment of her children still brought tears to Emily's eyes, the dull ache of incomprehension compounding the awful pangs of despair. She had not felt these emotions fully in years, but they were back tonight. Loneliness had always been the thing she feared the most and she had never felt more alone than she did this evening, despite the presence of the teenage boy slumbering peacefully just a few feet away from her.

Chapter 74

She looked up at him expectantly as he climbed into bed.

'Well, this is an unexpected treat,' Penny cooed. 'Get time off for good behaviour, did you?'

Christopher Parkes stared at his wife, sifting her words for signs of anger or suspicion, but found none. She appeared as warm, loving and welcoming as ever.

'Hardly,' Christopher sniffed. 'The whole place is going to hell in a handcart, but there's nothing to be done tonight, so I thought I'd call it a day at a reasonable hour.'

'Good for you,' Penny replied brightly, sliding across the bed towards him. 'What's the atmosphere like?'

'Toxic,' Christopher sighed. 'Firth suspects everyone, including me, of briefing against him. Plus, he's intent on conducting a witch hunt to root out who's behind these leaks.'

'You don't think that's warranted?'

'I don't think he'll find what he's looking for. Anyway, do you mind if we don't talk about work?'

'Of course. I just worry about you, that's all. You spend too much of your life in that place...'

Kissing him, she snuggled down, laying her head on his chest. Neither spoke, Penny sighing happily as she listened to the reassuring thump of his heart, whilst Christopher stared

upwards, his unhappy eye seeking out every tiny crack on the
ceiling. Many was the night that he'd lain awake in this very
position, fretting, agonising. Professionally so assured, he had
been in personal turmoil for the last three years, ever since Olivia
Campbell had come into his life. Though his pursuit of her
had been cautious at first, his attraction to her was instant and
lasting. She was the whole package – looks, wit, intelligence and
a sexual confidence that knocked him for six. He'd done things
with her, to her, that he'd never have contemplated with another
woman. Which is why it had been so hard to break off their
affair, despite all the tears and acrimony.

They had had it all – the early euphoria, the burning excitement, the golden period where everything seemed so easy.
During that time, Christopher had considered leaving Penny
and had told Olivia so, something he later regretted. It seemed
like madness now and her reaction to falling pregnant had
proved what a mismatched pair they really were.

'What are you thinking about, sweetheart?'

Snapping out of it, Christopher realized Penny was staring
at him lovingly.

'Just work,' he lied, faking a grimace.

'Well, let's see if I can take your mind of things…'

Underneath the duvet, Christopher felt her hand ferret inside
his pyjama bottoms.

'It's been a while, but I think I still know what to do,' Penny
teased.

In spite of himself, Christopher felt his body respond to
her touch. He didn't want to do this, but it seemed Penny had
made up her mind. Already she was pulling back the duvet,
sliding down the bed, taking him in her mouth. Closing his
eyes, Christopher resigned himself to the inevitable. He didn't
find his wife attractive anymore, and generally tried to avoid

intimacy, but there was no escaping it tonight, so best to submit with good grace. It would be diverting and, who knows, he might even orgasm, as long as he kept his thoughts firmly fixed on Olivia Campbell.

Chapter 75

She sat in the darkened room, staring at the tiny screen. Jack had sobbed in Olivia's arms for several minutes, clinging to her as he moaned in anguish, pressing his skinny body against hers. It was completely inappropriate and at first she'd longed to throw him off, to say she wanted no part of his unwarranted self-pity. But as the minutes passed, she'd relaxed into it, responding to the physical contact, an acknowledgment perhaps of how long it had been since anyone showed Olivia any real affection. Over time, Jack too had relaxed, his whimpering slowly petering out as he regained his composure, but as he raised his face from her shoulder, pushing his nose, his lips into her soft neck, Olivia finally had enough, pulling away from him sharply, calling time on their intimate tête-à-tête.

Jack hadn't lingered, hurrying off to dry his tears, embarrassed by this open display of vulnerability. Olivia had sat alone in stony silence, processing their strange communion, trying to work out what it meant. She fully expected him to return any moment, to apologise, or perhaps to pretend his collapse had never happened. But the minutes ticked by with no sign of him, so instead she'd reverted to looking at her phone, digesting the explosion of bile and glee that had replaced the news.

It was incredible. Every major newsfeed and gossip site

majored on the recent murders, poring over every grim detail and, in some cases, openly speculating about what would happen next. Most sites led with the news that Caitlin Rose had been charged with Andrew Baynes's murder, a decision that had provoked predictable fury in the tabloids and beyond. The wider public was clearly on Caitlin's side; already a petition had been posted online, demanding her immediate release and pressing for the charges to be dropped. It already had fifty thousand signatories and rising, the counter seeming to tick up constantly. The sentiment on social media was similar, vast swathes of trolls and armchair bullies revelling in the brutal deaths of Willis and Baynes, lambasting these boys' mothers for perceived failures of upbringing. Strange how the fathers were never mentioned in these things.

There was one more thread on social media that Olivia was particularly interested in, that really went to town on the Probation Service. This institution, which she'd worked for these last fifteen years, was now a national laughing stock, the target of endless 'piss up in a brewery' memes and jokes. The service, its management and officers were ripped to shreds in an avalanche of mockery and anger. Years ago this would have infuriated Olivia and she would probably have retaliated on line, earning yet more censure from her superiors, but now she was inured to it. In her view, the Probation Service should be right up there with the NHS, another vital public service attempting to keep the public safe, to maintain the fabric of a civilized society, but no one claps for probation officers, do they?

'Thank you.'

Olivia looked up, startled by Jack's appearance. He was framed in the doorway, looking sheepish but determined. Smiling tightly, Olivia ushered him over, the embarrassed probationer settling himself on the footstool opposite her.

'For what? Bollocking you?' she replied, keen to lighten the mood.

A fleeting smile came and went, then he responded:

'No, for looking out for me. No one's ever done that before.'

It was said with real sincerity, taking Olivia by surprise once again.

'They said that a lot in court, you know. They said that nobody had ever protected me and they were bang on. All that bitch cared about was where her next bottle was coming from, where to get her next hit. And God knows she didn't care *how* she got it...'

Pushing aside these grim images, Olivia said gently:

'Jack, I'm not sure this is very helpful. I know your mother was difficult, neglectful—'

'You don't know the half of it.'

'I don't need to. As I've said before, you have to leave Kyle Peters behind, all that heartache and misery, you have to blot him out and become Jack Walker, who had a decent upbringing, loving parents—'

'But how can I when it's in *here*?'

He pounded his heart with his fist, his voice shaking once more.

'I try and shut it out, but I can't forget. How she made me suffer, how *they* made me suffer.'

Olivia desperately wanted to shut this conversation down, could sense the approaching vortex of bitterness, but something in Jack's manner silenced her. It felt like he had to speak, had perhaps never articulated his feelings this honestly to anyone before.

'Sometimes she'd just... disappear. Be gone for days on end. We had no idea when she was coming back, *if* she was coming back. I used to stare out the window, waiting for her, praying she'd come. Eventually, she would, of course. Whoever she was shacked up with would get tired of her, boot her out, then she'd be back. Never said anything much, never said sorry, just battered us for making a mess. She didn't...'

Jack's voice faltered, his distress mastering him.

'...she didn't care about how upset we were, about the damage she caused. She never once put us first, *never*.'

'That must have been very hard for you,' Olivia sympathized. 'You must have felt very lonely, very afraid.'

'All those people in the house and I felt so alone,' Jack responded angrily. 'The one person I did want to notice couldn't have cared less and the others... well, they wouldn't leave me alone. Especially when *she* wasn't there.'

'Jack...'

'They'd always wait until I was asleep. I'd try and stay up as long as possible, but they'd find me, sleeping by the TV, hiding under Mum's bed. And then it would start.'

'I really don't think you should do this,' Olivia pleaded. 'It's only going to stir up difficult emotions, make it harder for you to move on.'

'Colin would always go first,' Jack continued bitterly, oblivious to her intervention. 'He was bigger and besides he said he didn't want Phil's "sloppy seconds".'

'Please, Jack...'

'I hated that bastard, really hated him. But Phil was worse. He just stood and watched until it was his turn. He didn't once think to pull Colin away, to protect me...'

Jack was ashen now, his pallid features gripped with righteous anger.

'It went on for months. And no one ever said anything about it. Not them, not my mum, not social services. She knew, by the way. My mum, she knew, but she didn't give a fuck. She'd take me to the bathroom sometimes, clear up the blood, the mess, but she never once helped me. Just told me to take better care of myself, not to be so "mucky". God I could have killed her when she said that.'

Olivia could well believe it, fury seeping from Jack's every pore.

'If I hadn't done what I did, I'd still be there now. Still suffering. They made… made my life an utter misery. They enjoyed hurting me, *humiliating* me…'

'But doesn't that make what *you* did even worse?'

It was a risky response, but Olivia couldn't sit there and let him get away with this crass self-pity, not without saying *something*.

'What you did to Billy Armstrong was no different to what your brothers did to you.'

Jack was shaking his head angrily, but Olivia persevered.

'All those emotions you felt, the fear, the pain, the anguish, Billy would have felt them too. Which is why I find it so odd that you have never acknowledged his suffering, or apologized to his family. I know facing up to what you did isn't easy, but it would have helped his parents so much to know that you regretted your actions and that you truly understood the terrible suffering you'd put Billy and their whole family through.'

'I'm not talking about him, I'm talking about my brothers,' Jack responded curtly. 'I was punished for what I did, *they* never were. Sure, they got banged up for other stuff, but not for the things they did to *me*.'

'And that was wrong, that was very wrong. They should have been, maybe they will be one day, but that doesn't change the fact that what you put Billy through—'

'Look, I'm trying to say thank you, all right?'

He virtually shouted the words, furious *and* beseeching at the same time.

'Don't spoil it, for God's sake.'

It was crazy, infuriating, shocking. Jack's desire to ignore his victim's suffering, to gloss over his crime, was appalling. Olivia wanted to take him to task for it, to hold a mirror up to him so that he could see himself properly for the first time, but to do so tonight risked a full-on argument, perhaps even a total meltdown. So she bit her tongue, saying nothing.

'I want to thank you, Olivia,' he continued, uttering her name for the first time. 'For trying to keep me safe, for looking after me. It means a lot.'

He only just got the words out, his voice shaking as he reached out and took her hand in his. It was a surprising gesture and part of her wanted to snatch it away, but Jack was so desperate, so close to the edge tonight that she let her hand rest in his, giving him what support she could, more a mother to this child killer than his own mum had ever been.

Day Four

Chapter 76

The attack was unrelenting.

Mike had been tempted not to turn up to work today. He was exhausted, hungover and ashamed, knowing full well that he'd be hauled over the coals the minute he set foot in the showroom. But there was no avoiding the reckoning, so he had showered and dressed, forcing three cups of coffee down his protesting throat, steeling himself for what lay ahead.

'I had to spend the rest of the night persuading the guy not to press charges,' Simon vented, his face purple after ten full minutes of shouting. 'And you can imagine what the area manager thought of it all. This was supposed to be a bloody *bonding* event.'

Looked at one way, it was darkly funny. But for Simon this clearly wasn't a laughing matter.

'Yet, you in your wisdom decide to spread some festive cheer by punching one of our up-and-coming stars.'

'That guy? *He's* an up-and-coming star?'

'Don't, Mike. Just don't.'

Simon was wagging a finger in his face, as if he was about to lose control himself, even punch Mike. Catching himself, his boss reined the emotion back in.

'I have stuck up for you, Mike,' he continued angrily. 'When others wanted to get rid of you, I fought your corner, because I know what you've been through, what you're still going through... but this time you've gone too far.'

He was working himself up slowly, trying to justify his decision, building to what Mike now knew was coming.

'You skip work, you lie about where you've been. When you do turn up, you're listless and disinterested, stinking of booze. It's not right, it's not *professional.*'

He landed on the final word with real conviction, as if stating God's own law.

'But punching a colleague? Assaulting a member of our wider family in front of *everyone?*'

Mike suspected that this was the root cause of his manager's fury, how his stupidity and rashness had made Simon look foolish. And despite Mike's anger at this dressing down, he understood his reaction. What he'd done was crazy, rash, inconceivable really.

'I wouldn't be doing my duty if I didn't act. So...'

He sighed heavily, a twinge of remorse puncturing his anger.

'...I'm going to have to let you go, Mike. I thank you for your service, but I think it's probably best if you leave straightaway – we'll put your P45 in the post.'

It was delivered gravely, sadly, but with real firmness. Perhaps Simon feared Mike would fall to his knees, begging for his job back and wanted to pre-empt any such unpleasantness. If so, he was sorely mistaken. Mike had neither the energy nor conviction to fight his summary dismissal. He had worked here for many years, had become part of the furniture, but this counted for little now. The last few days had destroyed his equilibrium, broken his heart and scrambled his brain. There was no question of returning to the comforting monotony of his old life, not whilst Courtney Turner was out there, living her life to the full. He would be no use to anyone here, he was an accident waiting to happen, which is why Mike didn't protest now, simply rising and walking away from the storeroom that had been his sanctuary for years, without once looking back. What was there to say? How could he possibly justify his actions? He had let himself down, he'd let his colleagues down and, as Mike had felt every day since his beloved Jessica's death, he knew he deserved to be punished for it.

Chapter 77

'I want this done properly, but I want it done *fast*.'

Olivia whispered the words, investing her command with real urgency. She was standing in the front garden with one of their vetted security experts, one eye on him, another keeping a close watch on passers-by.

'We need CCTV front and back, motion sensors in the house linked to a smart alarm and two panic buttons, one in the bedroom, one in the front room. Ideally, all installed and running by mid-afternoon. Can you do that for me?'

'Well, it's possible,' the technician replied, blanching. 'But I might have to call in more help.'

'No, just you. Quick as you can. Understood?'

Her tone brooked no argument, so her companion nodded meekly, picking up his tool bag to set to work. Satisfied, Olivia re-entered the house, pulling the door shut behind her. Padding across the hall, she slipped into the kitchen, keen to reassure her anxious client. But as she crossed the threshold, she ground to a halt. Jack was standing in the middle of the room, feverishly scrolling on her phone.

'What the fuck do you think you're doing?' she demanded, marching over to him and snatching her phone back. 'You know you're not allowed unsupervised access to any internet enabled device. What are you playing at?'

'I could ask you the same question.'

Confused, Olivia stared down at her screen. She had been expecting the worst, but now realized that Jack had been looking at the Justice Never Sleeps website, which continued to revel in the death of Mark Willis and Andrew Baynes and the outing of Emily Lawrence.

'You tell me to trust you, to have faith in you, but how can I if you don't tell me the truth?'

He was furious, but clearly scared too.

'Look, I was going to bring you up to speed, I was just waiting for the right moment.'

'Bullshit, you just want to keep me in the dark. This is what all this is about, isn't it?'

He gestured towards the front of the house, where the technician could be heard noisily drilling into the brickwork.

'You think they're coming for *me*, don't you?'

'No, I don't. Honestly, I don't. But given everything that's going on, we can't afford to take any chances.'

'"Everything that's going on!" Would you even listen to yourself! They're leaking *everything*. Names, locations, even bloody pictures of folk doing their shopping. I'll be lucky if I see the day out at this rate. Billy Armstrong's dad could be coming here right now...'

'There's no indication that you're in danger, Jack, that your cover has been compromised in any way. I am here to protect you, like you said last night, and I'll do just that. As you can see, I've got extra security being installed and as soon as a new safe house becomes available—'

'I want to move *today*,' Jack interrupted. 'I want a new

location, new name, new history that's known only to you and your immediate boss.'

Olivia stared at him, the technician's drilling seeming to mock her now.

'I mean it, I'm not spending another night in this place,' he insisted, clocking her reaction.

'With respect, that's not your call. We have much more experience of this stuff than you.'

'And look where it's got you,' Jack replied witheringly, nodding aggressively at the phone. 'You've got more leaks than the *Titanic*, and with respect, it's my neck on the line, not yours, so get it sorted. I want out of here.'

He pushed angrily past her, stomping out of the room and away up the stairs. Olivia wanted to reason with him, to make him see sense, but she knew there was little point. He was agitated, upset, scared and, in truth, he had every right to be. The image on her phone gave the lie to all her protestations, her vain attempts at reassurance. The Justice Never Sleeps website was celebratory, on point and particularly disturbing today. In big, bold letters, emblazoned above the mug shots of Emily Lawrence, Andrew Baynes and Mark Willis, was a simple chilling message.

Who's next?

Chapter 78

The next few minutes would be crucial. Emily knew that what she said now, and how Sam reacted, would determine both their fates. Either Sam would stay loyal to his mother, attempting to make sense of the past, present, and hopefully future, or he would reject her outright, sickened by her dishonesty, her duplicity, her crimes. Her sanity hung in the balance, so Emily had to make the effort now, she had to *try*.

'Sam, love, I know you must still be reeling from yesterday's events and that you probably have a thousand questions you want to put to me. Which is absolutely fine. I'm here for you, to talk about whatever you want, whenever you want.'

She spoke in hushed tones, aware that other guests were taking their breakfast nearby. Mother and son sat alone at a corner table, pushing toast round their plates, a picture of quiet misery. Marianne and a couple of other probation officers ate nearby, though in their smart suits they could easily have been mistaken for business people, easily blending in with the other travellers.

'You can run the show today,' she continued cautiously. 'You're in charge. We may have to chat to my probation officer later, think about moving to a less public place, but we're safe here for now, so we've time to talk things through. Whatever you're thinking, whatever you're feeling, I want to know. I want to *help*.'

Sam said nothing, toying nervously with his phone. Emily longed to take it away from him, to pull him away from the avalanche of bitterness and recrimination doing the rounds on social media, the scores of scathing, hurtful comments beneath that ridiculous snatched photo of her outside Tesco Metro, but she didn't dare exert any parental authority today. Instead, help-less and hollow, she picked up the toast rack, sliding it across the table to him.

'Come on, love, why don't you eat something, then we can chat? Starving yourself isn't going to do any good.'

'I'm not hungry.'

'You must be, you normally eat like a horse first thing. Here, let me do a piece for you.'

She picked up a slice of toast and started buttering it for him.

'Do you want jam or marmalade?'

The sound of his scraping chair brought her up short, Sam rising swiftly to his feet. Shocked, Emily rose too.

'I can't do this,' Sam whispered unhappily, before turning and walking away.

He was already halfway to the exit, tapping aggressively on his phone. Horrified, Emily turned to look at Marianne, who was also rising, then hurried after her son. By the time she made it into the lobby, Sam was out the main entrance, hurrying away across the forecourt. Desperate, Emily abandoned all caution, sprinting out through the open doors, the pursuing probation officers close behind.

'Sam!'

She screamed his name as she ran, but he didn't turn, continu-ing his determined march away from the hotel. Terrified that if she lost him now, she'd never see him again, Emily sprinted towards her son, catching him just as he reached the main road. As she snatched at his trailing arm, however, he pulled away from her as if burned.

'Stay, Sam,' Emily pleaded, tearful, bereft. 'Stay and we can sort this out…'

'No!' he barked. 'You don't get to tell me what to do anymore.'

'I only want to explain, love…'

'All that shit about me being a good citizen,' he continued, bitter, enraged. 'About making the right choices… and you do *that*?'

Emily was rocked back on her heels, his scorn too hard to bear.

'You're a hypocrite and a liar, *Janet*.'

Another hammer blow. Nobody had called her that in nearly thirty years. But Sam was not for stopping, his attack remorseless.

'You've lied to me my whole life. About you and Dad, about your family, about your "friends" who came to visit. Was anything you ever told me true?'

Emily couldn't look at him.

'Those marks on your back, those scars. Were they *really* from a car accident?'

He was goading her, deliberately twisting the knife, but she deserved it.

'No,' she confessed quietly. 'They were from my dad.'

'There you go then,' Sam exclaimed triumphantly, as if this abuse was something to celebrate. 'Everything you've ever told me is a lie, isn't it?'

He was shouting now. Worried, Emily turned to Marianne, who'd now caught up with them.

'We need to go inside now,' the probation officer hissed. 'You're creating a scene.'

Beyond them, Emily could see hotel staff watching the argument with interest, but they were not her concern right now. The only thing that mattered was her son.

'You're right, Sam. Everything you've accused me of, I did. And more besides. But I want to make amends, I want you to *understand.* Just please give me that chance and I swear we will get through this – we'll be happy again.'

'Oh really? How do you figure that? Way I see it, we either stay here, under armed guard night and day. Or we hide out in some arse end little town, cut off from friends, from family, living a lie. Those are our only options, no actually, they're *your* only options. I don't want any part of it.'

'Sam, don't say that, please ...'

'Get off me.'

He pushed Emily roughly away, as she clawed at him.

'I don't want to be with you. I don't even want to know you anymore.'

Emily fell to her knees, broken by this brutal rejection.

'I'm going to Dad's. Don't try to call me, I won't pick up.'

As he spoke, an Uber pulled up, Sam hurrying away towards it.

'Sam ...'

But it was too little too late. The car was already pulling away, Sam now safely inside.

'Can't you stop him?' Emily pleaded to Marianne, but the probation officer shook her head.

'He's free to go where he wants, but *we* need to go back inside now, Emily. A crowd's gathering.'

Her tone was urgent, authoritative, but Emily ignored her, turning back to watch as the car slowly drove away into the distance, her son vanishing from her life for good.

Chapter 79

'I'm very sorry for your loss. Andrew's death must have come as a terrible shock to you.'

Diane Baynes looked up sharply, as if startled by Isaac Green's words of condolence. She had been staring at her son's corpse for over a minute in total silence, her face rigid, her eyes dry. Now she peered at the probation officer, as if trying to find some hidden meaning in his words. Slowly, however, her features relaxed, as she eventually replied:

'I always worried that he would come to a sorry end, but...'

She petered out, her eyes straying back to her son's corpse. The mortuary attendants had tried their best, but there was no disguising the extent of his injuries.

'I know it's hard to take in and I'm sorry you have to see Andrew like this, but we have to go through the formalities, I'm afraid.'

'To think that someone could hate another human being so much that they would do *this*,' she responded distantly, as if she hadn't heard him. 'What must that be like, to carry so much *hate* in your heart?'

Isaac nodded, but said nothing.

'To be so angry? So vicious? It must eat away inside you...'

The elderly woman shivered, her voice cracking, the first hint of grief punching through.

'My son wasn't an angel. What he did to that girl, well, it could never be forgiven, could it? But it was such a long time ago and he *had* been making a go of things, hadn't he?'

She turned to Isaac, her expression entreating.

'He had a good job, a flat, some friends,' she continued. 'He was doing something useful, something productive, wasn't he?'

'He was certainly trying,' Isaac agreed.

Diane nodded absently, before adding:

'Do you ... do you think there was *some* good in him?'

For a moment, Isaac didn't know how to respond, ambushed by the question.

'Apart from family, you knew him best,' she continued, insistent. 'Did you see anything good in him? Anything at all?'

Her need was patent, heartfelt, but still Isaac hesitated in his response, choosing his words carefully as he replied.

'I'm not sure words like good and bad are very helpful in these cases. I think Andrew would have liked to have lived a useful life, to put his problems behind him ... and yet he never spoke about his victim, never seemed able to own the suffering he'd inflicted on the Rose family, which meant that some people found it hard to forgive.'

Diane Baynes nodded but said nothing, acknowledging the truth of this accusation – her son, the unrepentant killer, the tabloid monster. Isaac watched her closely, awaiting a response, but the grieving mother remained mute and still, looking as shocked and traumatized by her son's crimes as she had done all those years ago.

'Anyway, I'll leave you alone for a moment,' Isaac added tactfully, moving off. 'When you're done, come and find me and we can go through the details of where you'd like the body sent.'

'Oh, we don't want the body.'

Isaac turned back to her, surprised.

'I mean, we're not planning a funeral or anything like that.'

'I see.'

'I guess we were hoping that *you'd* be able to deal with all that.'

'Well, we can of course,' Isaac responded, surprised. 'But it would be in an unmarked grave, with nothing to denote—'

'I think that would be best, don't you?'

It was said firmly, determinedly, with only the slightest hint of emotion, a mother doing what was necessary to protect her family. And who was Isaac to contradict her? What other end *could* there be for such an individual? Which is why he now found himself saying:

'Yes, I do.'

Chapter 80

He stared down at the finely etched words, drinking in their familiarity, but felt only a crushing sense of emptiness.

Jessica Burnham, born 14th May 2002, died 2nd August 2013.
Beloved sister, daughter and granddaughter.

Mike knew that for many friends and relatives this simple epitaph was unnecessarily brief and stark. Alison had certainly thought so, arguing vehemently for a more fulsome tribute, but Mike had resisted all entreaties. What could they possibly say that could do justice to Jessica? And how could they reflect the awful reality of her death without resorting to lies, euphemisms or meaningless clichés? There was no place here for 'Gone to soon' or 'Happy in God's embrace'. Mike didn't believe in an afterlife, nor could any soft-soaping suggestion that Jessica had simply departed this life early obscure the fact that she'd been abducted and brutally murdered by two twisted girls looking for kicks. If they were going to write anything, they should write *that*, trumpeting their crime for the whole world to see.

Tearing up, Mike pulled a faded bouquet from the urn, replacing it with his own. He tried to visit Jessica once a week and had come here instinctively following his dismissal from work, hoping to find some respite in his daughter's company. It was true that sometimes he *did* gain some comfort from being here, tracing the gilt letters of her name with his finger, feeling close to her again, but today he felt no such relief.

'I'm sorry,' he gasped, tugging angrily at a stray weed. 'I'm *so* sorry...'

In truth, he felt ashamed. On previous visits, he'd cried like a baby, raged like a madman, offered drunken protestations of love, but he had never felt as low, as pathetic, as he did today. He had failed in his career, failed in his marriage, but worst of all he had failed Jessica. Failed her when she needed him most. The memory of his transgression killed him every day. He could still see himself running out of that travel agent, racing back to his car, excited to tell Jessica of the family trip to Disneyland he'd booked for the summer, only to arrive at her wheelchair aerobics class five minutes too late. Five precious minutes that had destroyed their lives forever. In trying to arrange the holiday of a lifetime, Mike had unwittingly condemned his daughter to a terrifying, violent death.

'Oh, God, Jessica...'

Mike clung to the cold marble, sobbing. He knew he was worthless, a fuck-up, but today he felt as though he had hit rock bottom. If Jessica's grave could have opened up to swallow him too, he would gladly have accepted his fate.

'Mike?'

Startled, Mike spun round to see Alison approaching.

'What's going on?'

Her tone was concerned, but accusatory too. As if Mike was defiling Jessica's grave with his display of self-pity and grief. Lost for words, Mike rose, wiping the tears from his face.

'Shouldn't you be at work?' Alison continued.

Mike's heart sank still further. Did he really have to confess all here?

'I ... I quit,' he muttered. 'Or rather, they let me go ...'

'Oh, *Mike*. You were good at that job. They liked you there.'

'Not enough apparently. According to Simon, I'm unreliable, distracted, a liability ...'

He tried to sound angry, but his heart wasn't it. He knew he was in the wrong.

'And so you decided to come *here*? Of all places?'

Her verdict was crushing, but correct.

'Isn't there someone you could call? Someone you could talk to?' she persisted.

A few years ago, Mike would have called *her*. Alison had been his closest friend, his confessor and mentor, but there was an insurmountable barrier between them now, a thick wall of anguish and recrimination. Alison had rebuilt her life, had a huge support network around her now, whereas Mike had no one. But he was not going to admit that here, so instead he hung his head, replying tersely:

'What's the point? What's done is done.'

'There's really no chance of talking them around? Persuading them they've made a mistake?'

'Have they? From where I'm standing, I think they've got it *spot on.*'

He knew he sounded bitter, but he couldn't help it.

'Mike, come on, that kind of talk won't get you anywhere ...'

Her tone was compassionate, revealing a glimmer of her past affection for him, but this only made Mike feel even worse.

'It's the truth though, isn't it? Everything I touch turns to shit.'

'That's not true. It was *never* true.'

'Isn't it? Have you forgotten what you said to me, Alison?'

Now it was Alison's turn to look away.

'Please, Mike, I really don't want to do this...'

'You *blamed* me for what happened, blamed me fair and square.'

'I was upset and angry, I didn't know what I was sayin—'

'Oh, you knew exactly what you were saying. "If you hadn't been so distracted, so determined to book that bloody holiday, our daughter would still be alive." Those were your exact words, Alison. Your exact *bloody* words.'

Alison said nothing, refusing to look at him.

'Do you deny it? Do you deny that you blame me for ruining your life, for breaking your heart, for torturing you every hour of every day?'

He launched the words at her, hostile and enraged, but now to his horror he saw her shoulders shake, as his ex-wife began to weep. The sound of her sobbing had always crushed him and it did once more now. What a worm he was to berate her. What right had he to accuse *her*?

'Alison, I'm sorry, I didn't mean to...' he blustered, taking a tentative step towards her.

'I just came here to lay some flowers, Mike...' Alison gasped between sobs, her eyes glued to the ground. 'To lay some flowers on *our daughter's grave*...'

She could barely speak, distraught, devastated all over again.

'Why do you have to attack me like this? What have *I* done?'

It was true. She'd done nothing, other than marry a man who was unworthy of her.

'Please, Alison, I didn't mean it. I've had just an awful few days and...'

He petered out as she waved her hand at him, desperate for him to stop talking. Every word seemed to hurt her now. For a brief moment, the two parents stood together, the heavy silence broken only by Alison's low sobbing. Then stepping quickly past him, Alison laid her flowers, pausing briefly to kiss her daughter's headstone, before straightening up and hurrying away down the path.

'Alison...'

He wanted to stop her, to hold her, to beg for her forgiveness, but he knew it was pointless. She had no need of him, no desire to share in his self-pity and pain. He was all alone here, with only his guilt, his desperation and his deep, deep shame for company.

Chapter 81

'Are you seriously telling me you'd be sorry if something happened to Emily Lawrence?'

It was bold, provocative, which is precisely what Guy Chambers had been from the moment Chandra Dabral set foot in his office. This tactic was equally ballsy, being interviewed in the Ministry of Justice, openly and unapologetically, without a lawyer or aide in attendance. Chandra was unable to tell whether this was the crafty ploy of a guilty man or the confident behaviour of an innocent one. Either way, it was two against one, DS Buckland by her side for the interview, yet the junior minister appeared supremely relaxed.

'I mean I know we all need to put on a sad face in public, to act solemn and concerned, but I don't mourn Andrew Baynes or Mark Willis, nor would I weep for Emily Lawrence, sorry Janet Slater, if justice finally caught up with her.'

'You call what happened to Baynes and Willis *justice*?'

'Some people might,' he replied, sniffing noisily.

'And you'd advocate the same for Emily Lawrence, would you? Even though she's a wife and mother?' Buckland asked.

'She was a child killer *first*. And I think you'll find she's an ex-wife. Not that I can judge her for that, I've been through three myself...'

He smiled at Chandra, revealing an immaculate set of teeth. This was emblematic of his whole persona – immaculate, manicured, untroubled.

'You think this is amusing?' Chandra asked, trying to conceal her rising contempt.

'I think *you're* amusing, coming to my office with your half-baked allegations.'

Chandra was about to interrupt, but Chambers talked over her.

'Look, I've been on record countless times saying that we are too lax in this country, too indulgent. Punishment has become a dirty word these days, the emphasis forever on the welfare of hardened criminals, rather than that of the victims and their families. I absolutely believe we need a sea change in government policy, to reflect what real people are thinking and feeling. Criminals need to understand the true weight of their crimes, pay for what they've done, but this doesn't mean that I'm going to jeopardise my career, my liberty, the whole shebang by handing these animals to the mob. How stupid do you think I am?'

Chandra was tempted to tell him, but instead she replied:

'That's a very pretty speech, but we're not on the hustings now, minister, so perhaps you could answer my question. Did you, or anyone acting for you, leak confidential information relating to the aliases or whereabouts of Mark Willis, Andrew Baynes or Janet Slater?'

'Absolutely not.'

'But you don't deny that you were pleased that someone did, that you were happy these three offenders were exposed?'

'What sensible person would?'

'Someone with a conscience perhaps?'

She was overstepping the mark, but Chandra wanted to provoke a response. Happily, Chambers rose to the bait.

'Well, isn't that interesting,' he replied knowingly. 'Your heart bleeds for the criminal, rather than the victim. Ironic really, given your profession. I've met *hundreds* of serving officers who share my views.'

'And what views are those?'

'That creatures like Baynes, Willis and Slater are evil, pure and simple. They were born bad, grew up bad, committed unspeakable crimes and are incapable of remorse or rehabilitation. The idea therefore that these creatures should be released back into the community under the cloak of anonymity, protected and enabled by an incompetent Probation Service is not only irresponsible and dangerous, it is immoral.'

He invested this last word with Old Testament certainty.

'I mean surely you agree, Inspector? Don't you feel there are some people who are just too far gone? Some crimes that should *never* be forgiven?'

'And what would you do with these "creatures"?' Chandra replied, avoiding the challenge. 'String them up?'

'If I could get the numbers in the Commons,' Chambers responded, smiling. 'But you know what the Centre Left are like. Don't dare have an opinion about anything these days...'

'So you admit that you want these offenders dead?'

'That isn't what I said.'

'One sure fire way to achieve *that*,' Chandra continued, 'would be to leak their identities and whereabouts to the bereaved families, letting Justice Never Sleeps pour fuel on the fire by publishing photos of their corpses, *plus* photos of offenders like Emily Lawrence who are now on the run. That way, you could let others do all the dirty work for you, whilst keeping *your* hands squeaky clean.'

'Well it's certainly an entertaining theory,' Chambers replied, smiling blithely.

'Let's see if you're still smiling when we pick up Ian Blackwell,' Chandra replied coolly. 'We've circulated his particulars to every police officer in the capital, so it won't be long before we have him in custody. Perhaps *he'll* be able to tell us who's responsible for these leaks?'

'Perhaps he will. But, in the meantime, as you have nothing concrete to back up these fanciful notions, may I suggest that—'

'Were you at your constituency surgery in Reading on Friday 5th December?' Chandra interrupted, determined to seize back control of his interview.

Chambers' smile began to fade now, the MP regarding Chandra with obvious distaste. Plucking a tissue theatrically from the box on his desk, he blew his nose and replied:

'If it was a Friday, then yes I probably was.'

'*Probably* doesn't cut it, I'm afraid.'

'Yes, I was.'

'What hours were you at your surgery?'

'Well, you'd have to check with my secretary, but it's usually 10 a.m. to 1 p.m.'

'After that?'

'No idea. I usually catch up with paperwork, then catch the last train back to London. But I'd have to dig out my ticket receipts.'

'So you were in Reading the whole day?' DS Buckland piped up.

'Yes.'

'Did you message Robert Slater whilst you were in Reading, revealing the current identity and whereabouts of his sister?'

'Don't be ridiculous.'

'Did you encounter Emily Lawrence that day? Specifically did you take *this* photo of her outside Tesco Metro in the town centre?'

Buckland slid the snatched photo of Emily across the table.

'As I'm sure you're aware,' Chandra said, picking up the baton, 'this photo was leaked by the Justice Never Sleeps website last night, just hours after Emily Lawrence narrowly escaped a violent confrontation with her brother.'

'No, I had nothing to do with that photo either. Are we done?'

'Not yet. You see, I'm keen to find out why you were present whenever these highly damaging leaks took place. You *were* at the Ministry of Justice conference at the ExCel centre on the seventh of November...'

'Scores of people were there.'

'You *were* at the BBC, near Oxford Circus, on the twenty-eighth of November when Andrew Baynes's details were disclosed.'

'Do you have any idea how many people pass through Oxford Circus every day?'

'And you *were* in Reading on the fifth of December when someone messaged Robert Slater, compromising Emily Lawrence's anonymity and revealing her current address.'

Chambers eyeballed her, saying nothing.

'You would have known Lawrence lived in your constituency, would have known where her house was, where she worked and shopped. Plus, you were one of only a handful of very senior officials able to access details of Willis's and Baynes's identities and whereabouts. So you may scoff, but let me be very clear with you, Mr Chambers. You are a suspect, our *prime* suspect, and as such you have some serious questions to answer.'

Chambers regarded her shrewdly, realizing perhaps for the first time how serious her accusations were. Then, leaning back in his chair, he asked:

'Do you know when the photo of Emily Lawrence was taken? I mean, *precisely*? The day, the time...'

Chandra's spirits plummeted. Chambers had zeroed in on a key hole in their investigation.

'Not yet,' she blustered. 'But we will soon. My officers are—'

'And can you link me, my email or phone accounts to *any* of the highly confidential information that you say was leaked to the relatives of the victims?'

'No, but we know they were all sent from the same pay-as-you-go phone, a Samsung Galaxy, and once we have that in our possess—'

'So, in fact, you have no concrete evidence linking me to *any* of these crimes?'

Chandra said nothing, simmering, prompting Chambers to thrust home his advantage.

'Can I suggest then, Inspector, that you get the fuck out of my office?'

Chapter 82

Chandra stalked away from the Ministry, DS Buckland struggling to keep up with her.

'Cocky little shit.'

'Fair dos,' her deputy replied, breathlessly. 'But he *does* have a point. I did say that it was a bit bold going in all guns blazing, given that we don't have anything solid to lay at his door.'

'Fortune favours the brave, DS Buckland,' Chandra responded, annoyed by this patent lack of support. 'I wanted to see the whites of his eyes, see how he reacted to the accusations.'

'Which is all well and good, but he's a powerful guy. He could make life very difficult for you, me, the rest of the team. Careers could be damaged, so we need to tread carefully.'

'You tread carefully if you want to. I'm more interested in saving lives than playing politics.'

Finally her deputy got the hint, swallowing his protests.

'So what now?' he asked, short of breath.

'Now we shake the tree. I want a full breakdown of Chambers' digital footprint in the last few months, chapter and verse on his movements, his communications, *plus* I want a search warrant for his office at the Ministry, his flat in London, his constituency home in Reading.'

'If you're sure...'

Typical of Buckland, wanting to push back, but not having the balls to do so.

'One hundred per cent. Best-case scenario we find the Samsung phone, or some *concrete* evidence linking him to the leaks. Worst case, we find nothing, but make life very difficult for this arrogant, unhinged … reactionary.'

'Not on your Christmas card list, then?'

It was a poor attempt at humour, designed to mask his discomfort at her passion. It was true she was probably crossing the line, letting Chambers get to her, but she couldn't afford to pussyfoot around when the stakes were so high and, moreover, she would enjoy making life difficult for the cocky junior minister.

This was personal now.

Chapter 83

He strode across the allotment, his boots crunching on the frosty grass. Here and there, a fellow grower hailed him, but Graham Ellis ignored them, maintaining a steady pace until he eventually reached his shed. Then, pulling his keys from his pocket, he unlocked the padlock and, darting a quick look around him, slipped inside.

Closing the door, he turned on his camping lamp and dropped the blinds. They were a nosy bunch around here, bored and inquisitive, assuming that every retiree had time to chat. They'd attempted to pry into his business before, pressing their noses up against the dirty window. Well, they could go hang. Today he needed to be alone.

Carefully, Graham set about removing items from the bottom shelf of the storage unit, which ran the entire length of the back wall. Pushing aside a box of old magazines, he shifted a barrel of weed killer, then pulled out a fork and spade, before eventually unearthing a large plastic box hidden beneath a dust sheet. Tugging off the ragged cloth, he slid the box out into the middle of the floor, before sitting down heavily in a nearby chair.

Catching his breath, Graham wiped the sweat from his brow. He felt light-headed, exhausted in body and spirit, but gathering himself, he teased open the box, revealing the contents. Instantly, he reacted, a photo of eleven-year-old Jessica Burnham staring up at him from the front of a tabloid newspaper. To most, this image would have appeared to be a sweetly tragic picture of a gappy-toothed little girl, but to him this photo held no such innocence. To Graham Ellis, her expression was accusatory and bitter.

Slowly, Graham Ellis began to sift the contents, pulling out newspaper articles and pages of correspondence until he found the file, concealed in a plain manila envelope. Even as he opened it, he felt a shiver of unease, of disquiet. He knew full well that he should have got rid of this box years ago. He'd told his wife he'd done just that, swearing blind that he'd burnt the whole lot on the same day that she'd threatened to leave him for good. How would he explain to her that it was all still here, every last crime report, press article or scrap of paper pertaining to the murder investigation, should she stumble across it? How to explain to the Force, to his old colleagues, that he still had all the original files in his possession, when they should have been safely tucked away in the police archive? This was his secret, one which could never be divulged.

He continued to leaf through the file, digesting the reams of material pertaining to Jessica, pausing to take in the bundle of post-mortem photos. Years on, they still sickened him to the core, her tiny, pale body brutalized almost beyond recognition. These awful images made him nauseous, upset, aggrieved, but they made him angry too, so replacing them, he moved on to the sections dealing with the perpetrators. Now the former officer slowed again, taking in Courtney Turner's mugshot, skim-reading her social worker's report before falling upon her prepared statement.

This was the real prize, the one item in this secret treasure trove that never failed to provoke a visceral response. Even before he'd read a whole line, Graham felt a dull rage rise within him, Turner's tissue of lies almost as obscene as the casual manner in which she'd delivered them. Jessica Burnham hardly warranted a mention in her testimony. There was certainly no concern for her welfare, rather a concerted attempt to distance both Courtney and Kaylee from the events at Highworth's quarry. Courtney Turner was a natural storyteller and an accomplished liar, embellishing her tale with all sorts of quirky digressions in an attempt to give her denials the ring of truth. Whilst Kaylee had sat mute and whimpering in *her* interview suite, Courtney by contrast had gone to town in hers, letting her imagination run riot. Some of his officers had almost been fooled by this bravura performance, such was Courtney's level of invention and conviction, but *he* had not been hoodwinked, not for a second. He knew that in this case the devil was in the detail.

Years had passed since they'd written down Courtney's wild lies, but they had the same effect on him now as they had back then, outrage and fury wrestling for supremacy. Had Courtney *once* thought about what Jessica had endured? Had it entered her head that her plaything that day was a living, breathing human being, with parents, a sister, friends? Graham knew the answer to that, which is why his fury, his hunger for justice, burnt keenly. Courtney, the ringleader behind Jessica's awful murder, had never once confessed to her crime, never acknowledged the extent of the suffering she'd caused. In fact, she continued to thumb her nose at justice, blithely unconcerned by the devastation she'd left in her wake.

Staring down at Courtney's photo, the cheeky ten-year-old gurning mischievously at the camera, Graham Ellis laughed bitterly. If Mike Burnham could see him now, what would he say? Would he rage, curse, lash out at him? Mike would be well within his rights to do so, the irony of the situation crystal clear.

Graham's deception, his hypocrisy, was total, a gross betrayal of their friendship. He'd urged Mike to move on countless times over the years, but what right had he to do so? Who, after all, was more obsessed with Courtney Turner? The bereaved, broken father or the police officer who'd taken early retirement as a result of this traumatic case? Graham knew Mike regularly had nightmares and so did *he*, Jessica's battered body appearing regularly in his dreams, setting his supposed recovery back still further, to his wife's evident despair. Mike, for all his faults, had his sanity at least. Staring down at Courtney's photo, his hands shaking, his eyes flooded with tears, Graham was seriously beginning to wonder if he retained *his*.

Chapter 84

He was like her shadow, dogging her every footstep, ever-present but unseen.

Angry and adrift after his confrontation with Alison, Mike had driven straight from the cemetery to Courtney's house in Colchester. Where else should he go now, when there were no other calls on his time, no one else who needed him? This was the only place he could be now. The only place he could do something *useful*.

It hadn't taken long for his target to emerge, pushing her buggy down the street whilst chatting on her phone, and Mike had immediately abandoned his car to set off in pursuit. His quarry was unaware of his presence, feckless and carefree as usual, which suited Mike down to the ground. Despite his simmering anguish and shame, it cheered him to think that Courtney was totally oblivious to the danger, that this time he was hunting *her*.

She turned the corner, pocketing her phone and pausing briefly to rearrange the baby's blanket, before continuing on her way. Walking tall, Courtney received the warm smiles of old ladies as she passed by, looking every inch the proud mum. It was a sight that still scrambled Mike's brain and clawed at his heart – he had never once conceived that Courtney Turner might be a young mum. She was a child killer, not a child maker.

Yet the evidence was in front of him, mother and child now coming to a halt at the local bus stop, exchanging a word with another young mum. It all seemed so effortless, like Courtney was actually *enjoying* motherhood. Did this make it harder to hate her, suggesting as it did that she was capable of love, of compassion, not to mention the fact that there was now an innocent child who might be dependent on her? Or did it make it easier to despise her, Courtney enjoying all the things – adulthood, motherhood, romance – which Jessica had been denied?

Mike kept his distance, pretending to read the headlines at a newspaper stand, but now a bus pulled up. Courtney manoeuvred the buggy on board, exchanging a cheerful word with the driver, before moving off down the aisle. Mike had a split second to make a decision. Should he continue his surveillance of her or abandon the whole enterprise? To follow her onto the bus would risk discovery, as it was possible she still remembered what he looked like, though of course he had changed greatly over the years. It was foolish, rash and yet something urged him forward, telling him to take the chance. He found the small change of her existence strangely compelling, the mere sight of her reviving old emotions, making him feel angry, vengeful, *alive*. And, anyway, if he gave up now, what else would he do? Stripped of his job, his sole reason for getting up in the morning, what was he *for*?

The doors hissed, as they started to close. Darting forward, Mike hopped onto the bus, turning his back to the passengers as he paid the driver. Looking up, Mike clocked the driver's mirror and taking in its view of the passengers, made out Courtney seated next to the buggy park, immersed in her phone. Taking his opportunity, Mike walked swiftly down the aisle, breezing past her without exciting any interest, seating himself in the back row. As the bus sluggishly moved away from the kerb, Mike stared out of the window, pretending to be interested in the world beyond, before slowly turning his attention back to Courtney.

She continued to toy with her phone, typing furiously, then pressing send, over and over again. He knew this was the modern way, to deluge friends with dozens of short messages, rather than writing one catch-all missive, yet it still annoyed him. It seemed frantic, ill thought through, reactive, an addiction rather than a means of communication, but perhaps this was his problem, not that of the younger generation, another marker of his increasing age and distance from Rachel's world.

Annoyed with himself, Mike pushed this thought away. Courtney did not belong in the same universe as Rachel and her friends. She was something altogether different, something malevolent and unnatural. Settling into his seat, Mike took her in once more, scrutinising her every move. If he was patient, surely he would see it eventually, some sign that Courtney *didn't* care for the child, hated it even? A scowl, a harsh word, perhaps even a slap? Yes, he would enjoy that, watching Courtney reveal her true self through a casual, thoughtless act of violence. Then the world – or at least the customers on this sluggish bus – would see the young killer in their midst. Then they would *know*.

He kept his eyes fixed on her, even as the city became the suburbs, yet still Courtney gave nothing away. She seemed relaxed and content, pocketing her phone to play peek-a-boo with her baby, blowing kisses after each reveal. The child gurgled happily, staring up at her mother, her young eyes shining with love. And Courtney responded, blowing on her face, stroking her cheeks, giggling with her. It enraged Mike, he was *sure* it was an act, a charade to fool others, yet it seemed so natural, so easy. Part of him wanted to cry out, roaring his frustration, his confusion, his anger, but there was no possibility of revealing himself, of giving the game away. So instead, as the bus continued its journey out of town into the Essex countryside, Mike sat perfectly still at the rear, his gaze fixed on the happy pair, desperately searching for a sign – one clear sight of Courtney Turner's evil.

Chapter 85

'He's going out of his mind. Honestly, I don't think we have a choice, we *have* to move him.'

Christopher Parkes looked up from his desk, clearly irritated by Olivia's assessment.

'With the best will in the world, we can't allow him to dictate what happens. We're the grown-ups in this relationship, Olivia. We tell *him* what happens.'

'Normally, yes, but this is a unique situation. Three high-profile probationers have already had their anonymity blown, two with dire consequences and Justice Never Sleeps and the rest of those muck-rakers are promising more revelations. The poor kid is going out of his mind, convinced that the mob are going to turn up with flaming torches at any minute and you know what, Chris? I can't promise him that they won't.'

'Is it any wonder with him buggering off back to Southend, looking up friends, family, old bloody dealers? Jesus, sometimes I think these people *want* to get caught.'

'Even so, he has a point,' Olivia persisted. 'And we need to respond.'

Christopher looked away, turning to tap a couple of keys on his computer, something he always did when he'd been bested in an argument or didn't have a ready answer. Olivia had seen this countless times, but wasn't prepared to put up with it now.

'Well? What shall I tell him?'

Still her former lover hesitated, avoiding her gaze. Why the hell was he being so evasive?

'Look, there's every chance that his identity, his whereabouts, have *already* been leaked,' she persisted. 'It's possible people are planning something even now, so I really think we need to do something. I know it's a lot of hassle, a lot of red tape, but someone's life is at stake, so we need to act.'

'Point taken,' Parkes replied, rising from his desk. 'Let me talk to Firth and get back to you.'

'Is that it?' Olivia replied, annoyed at this peremptory dismissal.

'I'm not sure what else you want me to say?'

'I want you to acknowledge that we have a very serious situation here. I want you to *do* something. Unless there's some reason *why* you want him to stay there? Why you *want* to leave him vulnerable and exposed?'

'Don't be ridiculous.'

'So what are you going to do about it?'

'I've said I'll raise it with him and I *will*. I can't sign off on these things – you know I can't – so you'll just have to be patient. Now if you'll excuse me, I've got to run.'

Olivia stared him, angry and resentful. Was he rushing from the room because they were in the midst of a crisis or because he disliked being alone with her now?

'What's so urgent?' she demanded.

'Well, any number of things, to be honest, but if you must know, Chandra Dabral's team have asked to speak to me.'

Olivia stared at him, wrong-footed. She hadn't been expecting *that*. Sensing her reaction, Parkes was quick to elaborate.

'It's nothing serious – they're talking to everyone with high-level access to Limited Access Only files, and between me and you, they seem much more interested in Guy Chambers, but even so I need to be prepared, just so there's no misunderstandings or confusion.'

He had one hand on the door handle, when Olivia spoke up.

'About that...'

The seriousness of her tone made him turn back.

'It's probably overkill, but if they are going to interview you, do you think I ought to ask them to interview me too?'

He looked at her as if she'd just announced she was an alien life form.

'Why on earth would you do that?'

Well, isn't it obvious?' Olivia replied, bridling at his hostility. 'What happens if Dabral finds out we are ... were an item? If it looks like we've deliberately concealed that from her, then she's going to ask some difficult questions.'

'Like what?'

'Like whether you told me things you shouldn't have.'

'Oh, don't be ridiculous.'

'I'm not saying I should ask, I'm just saying we should consider it – to cover my back as well as yours. If we're completely honest with her, then she can't misconstrue—'

'Have you lost your mind?'

The words erupted from him, terse and unpleasant.

'You do that and the whole department will know about us within the hour. We can't afford to risk it, we've been so careful...'

'Not careful enough,' Olivia shot back, glancing at her belly.

'Oh, so this is your way of punishing me, is it? Sabotaging my career, making me the butt of gossip and innuendo. Simply because you're angry and bitter?'

'Oh piss off, Christopher.'

'No, you piss off, Olivia. I'm sick to the back teeth of these conversations. You're a grown woman, you knew what you were getting yourself into. Now you'll have to live with the consequences.'

Spitting out these final words, Christopher snatched up his phone and left. Olivia remained rooted to spot, outraged yet crushed. The unfairness of this situation was devastating – Christopher had everything, whilst she had nothing – a fact underlined by the framed photo that stood in pride of place on his desk. Christopher, Penny and the two boys beamed up at her – smug, confident and victorious. Their arrogance, their superiority, their *happiness* made Olivia want to scream, to roar out her misery, her fury, but there was no way she could do so here, in front of her solid, judgemental colleagues, so instead Olivia turned on her heel and marched out of his office, slamming the door loudly behind her.

Chapter 86

He tugged hard at the door, but it refused to budge. Anxious, Jack double-checked the new deadlocks, the Yale latch and the bolt, ensuring all were in place. Satisfied, he moved away, checking the back door, the kitchen and living-room windows, before scurrying upstairs. His heart was racing, his mind conjuring up all sorts of phantoms, so he went from room to room methodically, checking latches and bolts, closing curtains and pulling down blinds, until he was convinced that he was invisible and, more importantly, secure.

Collapsing onto the bed, he pulled out his phone, opening the Ajax app that Olivia had helped him install earlier. He stared at it, the Face ID system vetting him, before allowing him in. Now a gloomy black and white image sprung up on screen, showing the front garden. Thankfully, all was peaceful, not a soul visible, so he flicked to the rear camera, but hard as he looked, he could detect no lurking danger. Relieved, he closed the app, before sinking back into the pillows.

So far, so good, but still Jack knew he wouldn't rest. The new hi-tech security equipment was a useful addition to the house, but if anything, its presence made him feel more nervous, not less. After all, why would they be installing it if they didn't think there was an imminent threat to his welfare? He wanted to be moved, to be given a new name, a new life to inhabit, knowing full well that he wouldn't feel safe until he was far away from here. But Olivia still hadn't called – he had no idea what was going on – and he knew he would be spending every waking minute religiously checking the security of the house.

His head was thumping now, tension racking his body, and he closed his eyes in a vain attempt to rid himself of the agony. If he could just sleep, even for an hour or so, then he might feel a little better, a little less wired. But it was hard to rest when even the slightest noise made you jump. Thanks to the Justice Never Sleeps site, Jack knew full well now what had happened to Mark Willis and Andrew Baynes, the first chased to his death, the other dispatched by a knife to the face. The thought of the latter chilled his blood, the idea of that cold blade slicing through skin and muscle. Was Emily Lawrence even now experiencing something similar at the hands of her brothers? And when the world was done with *her*, who would be next?

Try as he might, Jack couldn't resist conjuring up all sorts of scenarios, involving baseball bats, hammers, knives, Billy Armstrong's enraged father and vengeful uncles descending upon him, tearing his hair, gouging his eyes, smashing his teeth, mutilating his genitals, all the while raining down vile abuse on him in their thick, Southend accents. Every time these visions came to him, during waking hours or during the long nights, he felt it: pure, unadulterated fear, the kind of which he hadn't experienced in years. It was an emotion, a sensation that rocketed him straight back to a time, to a place he'd tried to forget. To that squalid bedroom. To his older brothers descending upon him, vicious and unforgiving.

He always knew when it was about to happen – hushed voices outside their shared bedroom, then the awful squeak of the hinge as the door swung open. Once inside the room, his brothers

never spoke, backing him into the corner quickly, cutting off
his cries with a rough hand, tugging at his hair as they forced
him down onto the dirty bed. He often pissed himself with fear
before they'd even overpowered him, the mere sight of them
enough to strike the deepest terror into his heart, but they never
cared, yanking down his pyjama trousers and roughly forcing
his legs apart. Then came the pain, the unbearable pain, their
violation of him violent and sustained. During his ordeal, the
agony kept him conscious even as he tried to blot out the rest
– the humiliation, the degradation, the shame. They showed no
mercy, no pity, just an animalistic desire to satiate themselves on
his misery. He hated them with all his heart, hated their power,
their control, their sadistic enjoyment of his subjugation, but
worse still, he loathed them for how they had *changed* him. For
even as he wept tears of abject desolation, even as he screamed
in pained anguish, he felt another emotion rise up in him too:
the desire to hurt someone *himself*, to dominate, degrade and
destroy *them*, to visit all his pain and rage *on someone weaker than
him*. He hadn't felt this way in years, had pushed that darkness
way back into his past. But as fear stole over him, as anxiety
gripped him once more, he felt it tonight.

Chapter 87

They were wrong. There was no forgiveness, no redemption, no happy ending.

Emily sat alone in her hotel room, staring at the unmade bed, where only hours earlier Sam had been slumbering. Then, although wracked with guilt and remorse, fearful for the future, she had nevertheless harboured fond hopes that perhaps the years of devotion, of care and love might soften Sam's judgement of her. That he would see that she had changed, that she had atoned, that Janet Slater was a different person. How wrong she'd been. She was tainted, a stain on society, forever disfigured by the mark of Cain.

How quickly and how shockingly things had unravelled. Yesterday, she had been an average mum, with a job, a mortgage, bills to pay and a child to raise. How glorious these challenges, these workaday duties seemed now. What she wouldn't give to return to her little house in Reading with its ill-fitting windows and frayed carpets, to her peaceful, insignificant existence. But there was no chance of that. Marianne had warned her not to go on social media, to avoid looking at any newsfeeds or websites, but the lure had proved impossible to resist. She'd hoped, prayed, that her exposure wouldn't be big news, next to the recent murders of Mark Willis and Andrew Baynes, but if anything, the outrage, fury and opprobrium surrounding her exposure was *worse* than anything they'd provoked. Was it because she was a woman? Because her victims had been so young? It was hard to say but what was clear was that the wider world detested her, many of them deeming a slow painful death too lenient a punishment, given the horror of her crimes.

Each comment was more vile than the last, yet somehow Emily felt compelled to keep scrolling through the tweets and posts, as if this outpouring of bile was her due. For some reason she had to read them all, had to digest every hideous comment, had to know how complete her disgrace was. She could imagine her colleagues and friends doing likewise, gossiping in shocked tones about the devil in their midst. Did they afford her any charity, any pity, any recognition of her services to her firm, to the community? Or were they as brutal as her family and the Bridgend hate mob, whose tweets made her feel physically sick?

Eventually, the collective assault had overwhelmed her and she'd switched to the BBC news app instead. To her horror, this was even worse. For there, next to their brief description of the fast-moving events, was mobile phone footage from her street in Reading. She couldn't believe what she was seeing at first, crowds of angry residents, some of whom she recognized, crowding round her house. They were hammering on the door, shouting insults and then it began – someone spray-painting 'Scum' on her front door in neon blue letters. Emily felt a surge of outrage; she'd painted that door only last year, but this was just the beginning. Further vile slurs were sprayed onto the front, then a huge cheer went up as a dustbin crashed through the front window. Soon after the police arrived and as they pushed back the crowds, Emily got a clear view of her home, her lovely little home, now daubed, damaged and disgraced.

It had been her life, but she could never go back there now.

Nor would she now ever be Emily Lawrence again. That woman, her resurrection, her penance made flesh, her second chance was gone, a hate figure to one and all. Thanks to social media, to that hideous vigilante website, everybody now knew what this fiend looked like, meaning that anyone was a potential threat, a lurking assassin. It was too much to bear, too nightmarish to contemplate, but it was true. She would have to change her name, her appearance, perhaps go on a crash diet, but would any of it be enough? She was a marked woman now.

Right on cue, Marianne appeared, knocking gently and entering.

'We need to go.'

'Five more minutes, please,' Emily pleaded, bone-weary and desolate.

'We can't wait, I'm afraid. Sam used your real name in front of hotel staff – I'm sure they're already looking at Twitter and joining the dots, so I'm sorry, we need to go *now*.'

What choice did she have but to comply? Emily had worked hard to forge a new identity for herself, a new existence where she could live free of fear, hatred and danger, where she could be a normal person. But that was over, the fiction of Emily Lawrence revealed, the comfortable anonymity she'd spent years building destroyed with the touch of a button.

Chapter 88

The bus lurched to a halt and the driver pressed the release button, the doors sighing as they opened. Mike reacted sharply, clocking Courtney rising and carefully manoeuvring the buggy off the bus and down onto the pavement. Now she was wheeling it away and Mike was on his feet, hurrying down the aisle, determined to keep her in view.

Stepping down off the bus, he looked around, discomfited by his surroundings. They were deep in the Essex countryside now, but where he couldn't say. Moreover, there was precious little cover here, the houses spaced out and the streets all but deserted. What should he do? Press on with his pursuit? Or wait it out, hoping that Courtney would return to the bus stop? Pulling up his hood, he carried on, keeping a safe distance between them. He knew it was risky, but something told him that if he didn't stay close to her now, he might never see her again.

Courtney was walking up a long road that flanked this modest village, but now turned, suddenly looking back in his direction. For a second, Mike faltered. Had she seen him? Was she turning to confront him? Relief flooded through him as he realized she was just checking that the road was clear. Now she was crossing, lifting the buggy up onto the adjacent pavement, before hurrying out of the village up a narrow footpath. Confused, Mike bided his time, then followed, eventually disappearing from view too.

The footpath was steep and uneven, Courtney struggling to keep up the buggy's momentum, apologising to her child with each violent lurch. Mike hung back, wary now, knowing that if she turned she would know she was being followed. Thankfully, she now crested the path, disappearing from view, and Mike made his way after her, pursuing her into a wide-open field. Now her destination became clear – a children's playground nestling in the centre of the wide, green space. Courtney hurried towards it, wheeling the buggy through the gate and away towards the swings. A friend was waiting for her, turning now to say hello. Head down, Mike had no choice but to walk on, passing the playground and disappearing into dense woodland beyond, as if out for a morning hike. Praying his presence hadn't caused any alarm, he now doubled-back, taking up a position on the fringes of the wood from where the playground was visible.

Settling in, Mike resumed his surveillance. The absurdity of the situation was not lost on him, crouching in a bush in a random village watching two friends coo over Courtney's baby. What the hell was he doing spying on this mother and child? What was he hoping to see? He knew he wanted Courtney to reveal her dark heart, to provoke his vengeful ire, but she appeared to live a thoroughly unremarkable, even tedious life. She was a young mum, buying groceries, collecting benefits, meeting up with friends. What could he possibly discover that would profit him? Did he genuinely think she would harm a child she appeared to love with all her heart? Or was this just the first stage of his unravelling, his obsession with Jessica's killer finally breaking his sanity?

Sighing, Mike continued his lonely watch. He was tired, hungry and increasingly beset by self-doubt, but there was no chance of heading back past the playground so soon without being seen, so he remained where he was. And now he noticed something. Courtney and her friend were chatting in low voices and, despite their apparently casual demeanour, seemed jumpy and ill at ease. Both kept their heads down and their hoods up, exchanging brief words, whilst tugging on cigarettes. More intriguingly, every time another mum or child passed by, they would turn away, as if fearful of being overheard. What could they be saying to each other that was so important, so secret? And why did they seem so apprehensive, so fearful of discovery?

A thought suddenly landed, a sickening, disorienting thought. It couldn't be, could it? Suddenly Mike wanted to push through the foliage and race down to the playground, to satisfy his burning curiosity. But what if he was wrong? He would look foolish, insane, and would have given himself away into the bargain. No, there was nothing to do but sit tight in the wood and wait. It was sheer agony, his frustration burning, his emotions churning, as other young families came and went, dawdling over the slide, swings and carousel. Finally, however, Mike got a break, the other mums dragging their children away to leave the secretive duo behind. Instinctively, Mike took a step forward. There was no way he could break cover, yet he was desperate to see what they were doing, perhaps even to catch a snatch of their conversation. And then it happened. Finally at ease, the pair removed their hoods, Courtney's friend turning to face her properly for the first time.

Mike stared, disbelieving, anger and outrage coursing through him. It was *her*. It was Courtney's partner in crime, Kaylee Jones, the girl who'd stood by as her best friend stoned Jessica to death. The one person Courtney was *absolutely forbidden* from seeing. Yet here they were, chatting like old times, secretive and conspiratorial, thoroughly at ease in each other's company. Did this mean they had met *before* today? And if so, how many times?

Mike was reeling, feeling light-headed and unsteady on his feet, his brain working overtime. When had they got back in touch? And to what end? Was it out of loyalty and affection to one another? Was it a rebellious fuck-you to the tight strictures of their release licence? Or was it possible that they were descending into that vortex of anger, sadism and violence once more?

Was it possible they were planning to kill again?

Chapter 89

'Many people write off ex-offenders. They regard them as damaged, untrustworthy, even evil. This has never been the view of the King's Trust. We believe that offenders have more motivation than most to make good on the opportunities they're afforded.'

Guy Chambers turned away, bored by the keynote speaker, annoyed by his piety. It was the lot of junior ministers to sit through countless fundraisers, anointing their efforts with the support and patronage of the Ministry of Justice. But he seldom found them interesting or illuminating, the same earnest faces saying the same earnest things. Stealing a glance at his watch, he realized that it was time to go, so rising quietly, he slipped away, smiling apologetically to the other dinner guests. Hopefully they'd assume he had urgent ministerial business to attend to, little guessing the real reason for his departure.

Leaving the ballroom, he headed back towards the main staircase. Smiling, he waited for a waiter to head past, then, satisfied the coast was clear, darted across the corridor. Pushing through the emergency exit, he was now on the fire escape, the chill of the winter air assaulting him. Shrugging off the cold, he glided down the stairs, making as little noise as possible. He descended one flight, two flights, three, then finally he was at ground level, picking his way between the giant refuse bins that reeked of rotting fish and ordure.

It wasn't a pleasant place to find oneself, but it would suit his purpose tonight. It was dark and shadowy, couldn't be seen from the hotel bedrooms and was seldom frequented. This was the side of the Park Lane Hyatt that guests never got to see, the only visitors to this sad space the kitchen porters with their bags of slop, and they seldom spoke English, making this the ideal place for a clandestine meeting.

He darted a look up the alley that led to Park Lane, but there was no sign of life. He took another look at his watch, concerned. It was not like Blackwell to be late. Hopping from foot to foot, Chambers tried to ward off the cold, but his pointless dance could not calm his nerves. Not when there was so much at stake. He'd been so careful, so discreet, yet still Chandra Dabral was on his scent, seemingly determined to bring him to book. He rather feared she would take personal pleasure in doing so.

The sound of quiet footsteps made him look up and he now saw Ian Blackwell approaching, hugging the wall, concealed in the shadows. Scanning the filthy courtyard, Chambers emerged from his hiding place, crossing fast towards his companion.

'You took your fucking time,' he hissed.

'Just being cautious. I had to make sure I wasn't being followed.'

'Are you serious? You're being tailed?'

'No, I don't think so. But it doesn't do to take any unnecessary risks.'

'My thoughts exactly, which is why I wanted to see you.'

'I *was* wondering...' Blackwell responded dryly. 'I'm not usually lucky enough to be afforded a face-to-face meeting.'

'Well, don't get used to it. This is the last time we'll meet.'

And now the ex-police officer's face clouded over, his heavy Manchester accent punching through as he demanded:

'What are you talking about? You giving me the brush-off?'

'I'm looking out for our interests. The risk is too great at the moment, the pressure too intense, for us to continue our association.'

'What do you mean by that?'

'I mean you need to get out of London and lie low for a while.'

'You've got to be kidding me?'

'Do I look like I'm fucking kidding?' Chambers fired back. 'I had the police in my office earlier – *in my bloody office* – formally interviewing me about the murders of Willis and Baynes, not to mention the exposure of Janet Slater. They seemed particularly interested in any connection I might have to Justice Never Sleeps, and to you in particular.'

'I see,' the ex-copper replied, taken aback.

'I'm glad to hear it. Which is why for both our sakes, I'm suggesting you disappear for a while, take a back seat until things have died down.'

'But this is our moment. This is what we've been working towards.'

'Be that as it may, we have to react to the situation on the ground. Because believe me, you will be next on Dabral's hit list and as soon as she gets a sniff of where you're hiding—'

'No.'

Blackwell's tone was low and menacing.

'I won't do it.'

'You don't have a choice,' Chambers hissed back. 'Not unless you *want* to end up behind bars with the scum you claim to despise.'

'Yes, I bloody *do* have a choice. As do you. And I'm not

running scared. I have spent the last two years building to this. I've sacrificed my job, my marriage, everything I hold dear to make sure that the public are protected, that they know what monsters walk amongst us, preying on the weak and the vulnerable. And now that we're finally getting somewhere, now that ordinary people are rising up and reclaiming the streets, you want to run up the white flag? You want to chicken out?'

'It's not about chickening out. This is about biding our time, making sure the job is done properly and not spending the rest of our fucking lives behind bars.'

'Dress it up how you like, it makes no difference,' Blackwell replied, witheringly. 'This is our time, Guy, our opportunity to make a real difference, like you said. If anything, now's the time to double down, not to retreat, so—'

Blackwell gasped, cut off in mid-sentence, Chambers' fingers clamped hard around his scrotum. Surprised, Blackwell tried to react, but his attacker was too quick for him, ramming his forearm under the ex-police officer's chin and forcing him hard up against the grimy wall, even as he continued to tighten his grip below.

'What're you doing? You're hurting me!'

'I'm glad I've finally got your attention.'

'Please, let go...'

But Chambers increased the pressure, crushing his fingers together and forcing a low whimper from his victim. Then, leaning in close, he whispered:

'This is the last time we'll speak, so listen up. You will do as you're told – you will leave London, lie low and never, never contact me again. If you attempt to contact me, I will ensure that your ex-colleagues in Manchester, who would love to be alone with you in a custody cell, pay you a little visit. You do not want to fuck with me, Blackwell, or I will destroy you. Is that clear?'

Writhing in agony, the police officer nodded his head meekly, gasping with relief as Chambers finally relinquished his grip.

'I'm glad we finally understand each other,' Chambers added grimly. 'Now get out of my sight before I do something *you'll* regret.'

Chapter 90

She stared out of the imposing casement window at the twinkling lights below. Warwick Square, with its handsome mansion blocks and perfectly manicured garden, was a world away from Chandra's own life and for a brief moment she wanted to breathe in the opulence, the privilege, the prestige. It would be the closest she ever got to it.

Turning from the window, Chandra took in the impressive interior of Guy Chambers' Pimlico flat. Many politicians had properties in this area, given its proximity to Westminster, but few were as well appointed and grand as the junior minister's residence. Chambers came from money, possessing the breezy confidence of a public schoolboy used to getting his own way. His casual dismissal of her yesterday had irked Chandra more than she cared to admit, yet standing here amongst the Chippendale furniture, William Morris prints and Joshua Reynolds portraits, she could *almost* understand it. From this high vantage point, everything must seem grubby and workaday, other people a tiresome inconvenience.

Everything here was just so, the tastefully designed, high-ceilinged apartment looking particularly resplendent tonight, enlivened by innumerable bespoke Christmas decorations. Even the vast Christmas tree in the corner of the room seemed to have been made for the room, just the right height and width, its twinkling lights perfectly matching the glinting illuminations that adorned the shared private garden in the square below. Indeed, the only thing marring this pretty festive scene was the phalanx of suited search officers currently rooting through the cupboards, desk and the dresser.

Searches were being carried out in all properties connected with Guy Chambers, even as the tech team probed his digital communication history. So far, they had turned up nothing incriminating and, as the teams from his constituency residence and Ministry office had already called in with a blank, this plush flat represented perhaps their last chance of uncovering concrete evidence linking the minister to the recent leaks.

The nearest officer, a handsome young Spaniard called Pablo, looked up as Chandra crossed the polished floor to him.

'Anything?'

He shook his head, before turning to his colleagues. But they too had nothing to show for their endeavours.

'Well, keep at it. There's a pint – several in fact – for the person who finds anything.'

Smiling tightly, Chandra left the room, heading swiftly down the stairs. Her nerves were on edge, her mind uneasy, desperate now for some break in this case. Was she wrong to have taken her eye off Isaac Green, in order to double down on Guy Chambers? Was this all an overreaction, caused by her instinctive dislike for the arrogant junior minster? The desperate punt of a police officer clutching at straws? It didn't *feel* that way, something telling her Chambers was implicated in the leaks, but where was the evidence? So far they'd turned up nothing.

Reaching the ground floor, Chandra headed into the kitchen to find two search officers taking the washing machine apart.

'Anything?'

'Two hair grips, a button and a fifty pence piece,' the female officer replied. 'But other than that...'

Chandra moved past them to the study, but the scene was the same here. The more they looked, the less they found. Chandra was now facing the very real prospect of ending this intrusive search empty-handed and was wondering how she was going to justify her actions to her superior, when DC Reeves approached. Her hangdog expression told Chandra all she needed to know.

'I've been through the refuse bins, the recycling, and there's nothing. So either he's very careful... or he's very innocent.'

Her attempt at humour cut no ice with her boss, who was feeling increasingly stressed.

'Is there anywhere we've overlooked?' Chandra asked anxiously. 'Is he still in touch with any of his ex-wives?'

'Absolutely not.'

'What about local friends then?'

'Doesn't really have any, I don't think. This guy lives for his career. When he's in London, he's either here or in Westminster. I've spoken to neighbours and it's the same every day, jogging from here to the Ministry first thing, then back again in the evening.'

Chandra digested this, then replied:

'That's his regular routine, is it?'

'Regular as *clockwork*, apparently.'

'Do we know what his route is?'

'According to the neighbours, he cuts through the communal gardens in the square, then onto Vauxhall Bridge Road. From there it's a straight jog, before you cut left onto Millbank.'

Chandra paused a moment, then made a decision:

'Right, grab a couple of search officers and come with me.'

Without waiting for a response, Chandra marched through the open doorway, heading fast in the direction of the communal gardens.

Chapter 91

She sat quite still, her chin resting on her knees, lacking even the energy or enthusiasm to smoke. Following her unpleasant conversation with Christopher, Olivia had made straight for the smokers' yard, the one place in the whole department that you could rely on for a bit of privacy. Top brass never visited this lepers' enclosure, nor the thrusting young things who neither drank nor smoked. No, this space was reserved for the beleaguered foot soldiers of yesteryear, the old guard who had never quite fulfilled their early promise.

To some extent, Olivia only had herself to blame. Abandoning the north-west for London had set her back a few years, having to earn the trust of her managers all over again, and refusing promotion on more than one occasion had marked her out as recalcitrant and odd, further marring her prospects of entering the inner sanctum. She had done this partly out of cussedness, born of her dislike of management generally, with their corporate speak, group think and blind loyalty, but also because she enjoyed flying under the radar, a handy place to be when you have a penchant for dating married colleagues. But, if she was honest, it was in part down to her natural self-destructive tendencies, her ability to sabotage any opportunity that came her way. Her mother had always said that she was never happier than when ruining things for herself and others.

Olivia was lost in these bitter thoughts when the door to the yard swung open. Olivia's heart sank, her solitude ruined, but turning she was cheered to see that the intruder was only Isaac Green. He was not a smoker by habit, meaning he was either desperate to escape the mayhem or had deliberately sought her out.

'Thought I might find you here,' he said, putting that argument to bed.

'Where else would I be? Pull up a memory, join me...' Olivia replied, gesturing to the cracked chairs that littered the yard.

Smiling, Isaac obliged, the aged chair creaking ominously under his weight.

'Everything OK?' he asked, settling himself. 'You shot off in quite a hurry. And the way you slammed that door...'

'Oh, you know. Different day, different shit, but just as bad.'

'Amen to that.'

'I wouldn't mind, but it's ageing me, Isaac. I looked at myself in the mirror the other day and saw a fifty-year-old looking back.'

'Don't be foolish, you're still a beautiful young thing.'

'Plus, I'm losing my hair.'

'You're not,' Isaac chuckled, shaking his head.

'I am. I was twiddling it the other day and a whole clump came out in my hand. I know it's just the stress, but even so...'

Olivia broke off, catching herself.

'Sorry, Isaac, I don't know why I'm talking to you about stress. You must have been through the wringer these last days, after what happened to Andrew Baynes.'

'I've handled worse. Besides, we're not here to talk about me, I want to know what's eating *you*.'

'Where shall I start?' she replied ruefully. 'My charge is going out of his mind, convinced he's about to be lynched. I can't reassure him he *is* safe because the whole system's unravelling, thanks to incompetent leadership and an endless slew of leaks. I'm also pregnant by a man who doesn't give a shit about me, who wants to pretend I don't exist.'

She stole a sideways look at Isaac, but he didn't react at all, underscoring her impression that he'd *always* known the state of play between her and Christopher.

'I'm old before my time, living in a crummy flat I can't afford and I'll probably be bald by New Year.'

'Is that all?' Isaac replied, earning himself a good-natured punch from his companion.

'I don't know, Isaac. Do you ever wonder what it's all for? Do you ever look at your life, at what we do, and just think it's all entirely pointless?'

'All the time.'

Olivia turned to her colleague. Isaac had never been the most upbeat colleague, but even so, the speed and sincerity with which he said this surprised her.

'When I started this job, I was so committed, so idealistic,' Isaac continued, choosing his words carefully. 'But with each little mistake, each failure, each re-offence, something was lost. They keep telling you you're doing the best job you can *in the circumstances*, but they don't believe it and neither do you. I think "Failing Grayling" did for this place. I mean what are we now? A bunch of overworked, underpaid firefighters, babysitting a pack of offenders who seem determined to re-offend. There is no point to it, no pay-off, no happy endings. I mean you work hard, follow the rules and what do you get for it? A knife in the guts. A knife that slashes your hopes and dreams...'

Olivia looked up, concerned, knowing how traumatized her

colleague still was by the brutal attack on him. She reached out, placing a comforting hand on his arm, as he continued:

'I mean you try to keep the faith, but it's hard, *really* hard ...'

Isaac toyed with his crucifix, lost in thought. For a minute, Olivia thought he was going to continue, to unburden himself completely, then abruptly he changed the subject.

'Anyway, listen to me, rattling on, when I'm supposed to be cheering you up.'

'You have in a way.'

'Well then, scratch everything I just said. I am useful for something.'

He rose, with a smile on his face, trying his best to be jovial. But there was something forced, even slightly pained about this bonhomie tonight.

'Talking of which, I'd better get back to the grindstone,' he added ruefully. 'Don't stay here alone too long, it's not good for you. And *no more cigarettes ...*'

Winking at her, Isaac departed closing the door behind him. Olivia bided her time, waiting until the sound of his footsteps had faded away, before tugging a cigarette from her pocket.

Chapter 92

Sam was staring at his phone in shock, still trying to process the images of his home being defaced, vandalized, then attacked by firebomb-throwing youths, when he heard a gentle knock on the door. Looking up, he saw his father approaching carrying two cups of hot chocolate. Paul's was unadorned, but his was piled high with cream and marshmallows.

'How are you doing, son?'

Sam shrugged. What was there to say?

'I know it's hard, that you must be reeling given everything that's going on, but I'm not sure watching it play out on Twitter is going to help you, so why don't I swap you this for that?'

He held up the hot chocolate, nodding at Sam's phone. Sam was happy to oblige, already sickened by the images of mob rule and rampant vigilantism.

'That was a lesson I learned a long time ago,' Paul continued softly. 'If something's beyond your control, if you're caught up in something you can't fix, it's best just to step away.'

'We don't need to talk about this now, Dad,' Sam replied, knowing full well where this was going.

'No, it's important,' he insisted. 'I mean, I've never really been able to tell you my side of the story, because ... well, because of the secrecy surrounding your mother.'

Sam didn't want to hear this. He loved his dad, but he couldn't bear to take on anyone else's pain tonight. But his father was determined, years of frustration compelling him to speak.

'There was no way round that,' he complained. 'Your mother's new identity was protected by law. Anyone casting doubt on that, or her fabricated personal history, could be prosecuted, so I had to keep quiet. I lied to you, son, I won't dress it up. I lied about why me and your mother split, but I hope you understand now that I had no choice.'

'Of course I do. I'm not angry with you.'

Paul looked so relieved, so cheered by this reassurance, that Sam softened. The situation must have been intolerable for his father.

'How long have you known? About her past, I mean?' Sam asked quietly.

'Since the moment she said she'd marry me,' Paul replied with a rueful smile. 'I met your mum at a house party, fell for her hook, line and sinker. She didn't want to know at first, so I had to work hard to get her to go on a date. One night out led to another, then another – I won't deny we clicked – then six months later I proposed. I'd never met anyone like her and was determined not to let her go. She said no, of course, just as she did when I asked her again three months later. But when I asked for a third time, she realized I was serious...'

He paused for a moment, looking up at his son.

'...and that's when she told me. About who she really was, about her past.'

Neither of them spoke for a moment, the weight of their shared history hanging between them, heavy and unyielding.

'What happened then?' Sam asked tentatively, torn between wanting to know and wanting to shut the whole conversation down.

'Well, I was shocked, of course I was. But in some ways it made me love her *more*. I felt sorry for her, was angry about the way she'd been treated. I'm ashamed to say that I thought more about *her* than those poor girls.'

He dropped his gaze, shifting uncomfortably on the balls of his feet.

'What can I say? I was in love. I wanted to make everything right for her, to wipe out the past, more fool me...'

A hint of bitterness had crept into his father's tone now, which immediately made Sam look away.

'Don't get me wrong, we had some good times. And she *was* a loving mum to you, no question about it. But I found it hard. Given her history I found it difficult to trust her with you. I guess I was a bit intrusive, crowding her, supervising her, but it was all done with good intentions. She was angered by it, *oh* she was angered by it, calling me out all the time. "Why did you marry me if you think I'm still that person?" And, honestly, I didn't have an answer for that. I was the only person, other than her probation officers, who knew the truth, you see, and I thought I could handle it. Turns out I couldn't. It wasn't just my worries about you, I was concerned for her, for myself, for all of us, wondering what would happen if the truth ever came out. It felt like we were building a castle on shifting sands, carving out a life for the family that might fall apart at any moment. I blamed myself when we argued, telling myself I used to be a bigger man, a better man; urging myself to be more forgiving, more optimistic, more hopeful. But perhaps you understand now that when you know that about someone, you can't unknow it.'

Sam nodded once more, but didn't make eye contact, his emotions still too raw.

'I found it hard to see her purely as Emily, this new happy, productive person, because Janet always lurked in the background.

It didn't help that her brothers were forever in the tabloids, promising to revenge themselves upon her. It was a hell of a thing to live with that hanging over your head.'

Sam looked up at his father, realizing now how weary he looked. He felt a pang of sympathy for this man he only half knew, realizing how much the sins of the past had affected him.

'Anyhow, it soon became clear that things weren't going to work out between us. It was your mum that called time on it, saying I wasn't being supportive enough, that I wasn't trying to understand her. That got my goat and I'm afraid things went a bit sour after that, with lawyers and so on involved. You were too young to understand it all, but it was all a bit of a mess. I wanted to take you with me, wanted full custody, but you were so young the judge was predisposed to side with the mother. Plus, she had a good job at the time and I didn't, so it was pretty much a done deal. Of course, the judge knew nothing of her history and I couldn't say anything.'

He exhaled heavily, the injustice of it clearly still rankled.

'That was the worst day of my life, when I found out she had sole custody. I was very bitter, full of regrets, wondering if I'd done the right thing walking away from my marriage, but here's the thing. Despite my loneliness, despite my deep sadness at losing you, it was still the right thing to do. I don't believe any man could have lived with that knowledge, that secret. It was slowly killing me, undermining my confidence, my happiness and my resolve. And, as difficult as it was after we split, it was honestly the making of me. I moved away, got a new job, found love again and, eventually, rebuilt my relationship with you. In the end, I was so much better for making the break.'

And now he looked up at his son, the import of this history lesson clear.

'Maybe you should consider doing the same. There'd be no

shame in it. You've been a loyal, loving son all these years, but under false pretences. Janet lied to you about who she was, what she'd done and that's hard to come back from. You love her still, I'm sure, and I understand that. It's all so raw, so fresh. But sooner or later you're going to have to think about your future, about what's best for you. I know it's tough, that you're confused and upset right now, but honestly I really do think it would be for the best if...'

He paused a moment, before taking the plunge:

'...if you finally cut the cord once and for all.'

Chapter 93

Emily turned off the phone and flung it across the room, the device landing with a dull thud on the shabby linoleum. The sight of fire crews battling to put out the fire ripping through the family home was too much to bear. Crowds still surrounded the property, cheering and clapping, revelling in the destruction, despite the desperate efforts of the fire crews to contain the inferno. What was wrong with these people? Couldn't they see how dangerous the situation was, how immediate the threat to her neighbours?

It made Emily feel sick to think that these lovely people – kind Mrs Singh and the scrupulously polite Frasers – were in real danger, their properties on the brink of immolation, even as locals celebrated the devastation. What must her neighbours be thinking? How confused, angry and bitter must they be to discover that they had been living next to a monster all these years? That *she* was the cause of this carnage?

Emily buried her face in the nylon sheet, but couldn't hold off the desolation stealing over her. With each passing minute, things seemed to be getting worse, the situation spiralling out of control as she descended deeper into this bottomless nightmare. She had started yesterday safe and sound in her home, then she had found herself holed up in a commuter hotel in Heathrow, now she was hiding out in a caravan park in Hertfordshire. Marianne had eventually broken Emily's resistance, cajoling her to pick herself up following Sam's angry departure and to race away from danger. Emily hadn't wanted to; her first instinct had been to go after her son, her second to lock herself in the bathroom and cry her eyes out. But the threat was real, the danger immediate, so she'd allowed herself to be bundled in a car and driven away at high speed. The journey had been bewildering, the car constantly doubling-back on itself to confuse anyone attempting to pursue them, before they'd suddenly arrived at the Colne Valley holiday park. The place was nigh on deserted, few venturing here during the cold winter months, only a couple of the many static caravans now illuminated by dull lights inside. It was a sight that Emily found instantly crushing. She had lost her son, her home, her job, her peace of mind and this was the reward – an out of season caravan park that was as lifeless as it was depressing.

Marianne had done her best to cheer Emily up, but she'd shut the door in the probation officer's face, before collapsing onto the tired bed. Reluctantly, Marianne had retired to a nearby caravan, leaving Emily alone with her despair. She had taken in her new residence with growing dismay – the stained lino, the mildewed curtains, the chipped Formica – before turning away in disgust, retreating to her phone once more. This had only made her more depressed, however, underlining with perfect, devastating clarity the destruction of her former life. The conflagration at her home was grim enough, but just as bad were the publicity seekers and turncoats who were already taking to the airwaves and social media – locals, colleagues, even friends enjoying their moment of celebrity, wallowing in their brief association – their close shave – with Janet Slater. How quickly people forget, how inadequate her years of good service and loyal friendship.

367

She was alone now, utterly alone in this decaying, lifeless box. How long would she have to stay here? How many days, weeks, even months would *this* sentence be? Marianne hadn't been able to tell her anything – she, like everyone else in her department, were simply reacting to events, desperately trying to keep their clients safe as the situation continued to spiral out of control. New identities, new histories, new documents took days, possibly weeks to create. Did that mean that she would be stuck here for all that time, with nothing but her despair, her agony and the overpowering smell of mildew for company?

Suddenly Emily was on her feet, barrelling towards the door. She had to get out, to get away, knowing she'd go mad if she stayed here a second longer. Teasing open the door, she stepped out into the night air, the cold pinching her and making her shiver. She cast around, trying to take in her new surroundings, picking out Marianne in earnest conversation with a colleague. Happily, she seemed not to have noticed Emily, so closing the door quietly behind her, she hurried down the path, ducking behind another mobile home. She had no idea where she was going, but she knew she had to get as far away from this decaying prison as possible, so she kept the pace high, pounding down the muddy path. She suspected her absence would cause a commotion, that Marianne would go berserk, but right now she didn't care. In truth, she didn't care about anything anymore.

The path was dark and shadowy, the camp lights weak and intermittent. Leaving the main park, she found herself in woodland, able to navigate by the light of the moon. The way was uneven and Emily stumbled several times, falling twice and badly jarring her shoulder. But picking herself up, she carried on, pushing through branch and bush, until eventually she broke cover into a large clearing. Now she ground to a halt, taking a moment to regain her breath and drink in her surroundings.

This was clearly the centrepiece of the whole holiday camp – a large lake with jetties and pontoons off it. In the summer, when lifeguards kept a careful eye over the frolicking families, it was presumably a joyful place. Tonight, however, it seemed sinister, deathly quiet, but also serene, the moon reflected in the lake's still surface. Emily stood staring at it, transfixed. It was disquieting, beautiful, but more than that, it was *hers*. Nobody else knew she was here, nobody could find her – it was as if she was finally cut off from a world that now despised her. The thought cheered her immensely. What if she was to stay here forever, hidden away from their hate, their judgement, their anger? Wouldn't that be lovely? To be safe, secure, untouchable. And wouldn't that be her revenge, to deny them the vengeance they so badly craved?

Smiling, Emily found herself walking towards the lake. Yes, this was the solution, the obvious way to protect herself and frustrate them. Why hadn't she thought of it before? She couldn't hide here all night, let alone all week, the temperature dropping fast now, but there was *another* way. Stepping off the bank into the water, Emily felt an immediate shock, the icy water swirling round her ankles, but then a strange calm descended upon her, the water a soothing balm. She took another step, then another, the water lapping at her calves. She stumbled, but pressed on, the water now up to her thighs, saturating her clothes, dragging her down. She shivered as the water crawled over her tummy, spilling onto her chest. As it finally lapped her chin, she paused, then whispered into the night air:

'I'm sorry.'

Then she plunged beneath the surface, swimming fast downwards, embracing the dark oblivion. It was overwhelming, it was exhilarating, it was terrifying.

But it felt *good*.

Chapter 94

It was decision time.

Mike had stood, transfixed, watching in stupefaction and horror, as Kaylee and Courtney huddled together, dragging on their glowing cigarettes, whispering, plotting, laughing. His first reaction had been to break cover, to tear across the field and hurl himself upon them, pummelling them into submission, letting them feel the full weight of his anguish and rage. Then he had wanted to flee, to put as much distance as he could between himself and the murderous pair, the sight of them laughing and joking, as they had done in the dock ten years ago, too much to bear. Kaylee still seemed to hang on Courtney's every word and, watching on, it seemed to Mike as if nothing had changed. The pair had grown, of course, and were both now statuesque, powerful young women, but their manner – secretive, knowing, conspiratorial – was exactly the same. It made him want to scream, to puke, to rage, but more than that, it made him want to run.

Thankfully, the pair had eventually moved off and Mike had seized his opportunity, half running, half sliding down the muddy path back to the village. Spotting a bus pulling up, he had raced to catch it. Half an hour later, he was back in Colchester and, minutes after that, was burning back down the

A12 towards Maidstone. He was fleeing, racing as fast as he could away from those awful creatures, yet they never left him, his mind ablaze with riotous, conflicting thoughts. He was still in shock, he knew that, but his brain was also processing what he'd just seen, wondering what their reconciliation meant – for them, for him, for the wider world. What were they up to? And why had they chosen to meet in such a remote, out of the way place?

A dark fear was growing within him now, visions of fresh cruelty, of fresh bloodshed assailing him. Parking up, Mike had hurried inside his house, barely registering the friendly greeting of the postman, his mind turning, turning, turning. Today he had discovered something truly shocking, something important. The question was what should he do about it.

The obvious thing to do was to call the police. Curiously, they had called him as he raced back to Maidstone, Mike declining the call as he didn't recognize the number. On listening to the voicemail message, he'd been surprised to find that the caller was a DC Cooke from Scotland Yard who seemed keen to have a word with him 'following recent events'.

It was a strange coincidence, the police calling him on his way back from this shocking encounter, which set him wondering. Was this just a courtesy call, given his history? Or was it possible they now knew he had been sent Courtney Turner's details?

The thought unnerved Mike. He could call Cooke back, confessing that he had received confidential information from an anonymous source, adding that he had news about Courtney Turner and Kaylee Jones that they might find interesting. But how to do so without revealing that he had received this information *two days ago*? And that during that time he'd walked out of his job in order to devote himself to stalking Courtney, watching her every move, even breaking into her house? He could imagine their reaction, their horror and disapproval, wondering if he might even face charges himself. Wouldn't that be the ultimate irony, Courtney Turner watching on as *he* stood in the dock, judged, humiliated, sentenced?

No, there was no way he could endure that. No way he could be open and honest with the police. What about the Probation Service then? There was clear evidence that Courtney and Kaylee had breached the terms of their licence. This was more appealing. He had snatched a photo of the pair of them on his phone, he could prove that they had broken the rules, could perhaps even send them back to prison, where they belonged. But how likely was that? The Probation Service was clearly in freefall and, besides, even when it was vaguely functioning, their default position was always to indulge the offender. If he told them what he'd seen – that he knew Courtney's new identity, her new address – then they would simply slap her on the wrist, then spirit her away to a new town, creating a new fiction for her. And then where would he be? He would lose sight of her for good and she would be free to return to her wicked ways without any sanction or oversight.

No, he couldn't tell the Probation Service. So what then? He couldn't just sit and do nothing, not whilst innocent lives were at stake. Was there anyone else he could talk to? Alison? Mike pushed that thought away; she already thought he was out of control. Graham Ellis then? This was more plausible, especially as Mike still harboured a suspicion that the ex-police officer was somehow mixed up in all of this. But what if he was mistaken? Graham would take Mike to task for his actions, insisting he go straight to the police ... and then Mike would be back to square one. It seemed hopeless, yet the more Mike thought about it, the more obvious the solution seemed. He couldn't rely on anyone else to help him, but there was no question of doing nothing, not when the stakes were so high. Courtney Turner needed to be called to account, especially if she was colluding with her old accomplice once more. She needed to be stopped and if no one else was willing to do it, then the way forward was clear.

He would have to deal with her *himself*.

Chapter 95

If you want something doing, do it yourself. This was a lesson Olivia had learned the hard way during her many years of service, but it had paid dividends tonight. Annoyed by Christopher's dismissal of her plea, she'd gone straight to the top. Jeremy Firth had been resistant, as she'd suspected he would be, but he was also scared, buckling when Olivia painted a vivid picture of the consequences if Jack's current whereabouts had already been leaked. Buoyed up, she'd raced round to Jack's house to give him the good news.

'They've agreed to move you. New location, new name, the works.'

Jack looked at her, surprised, wrong-footed.

'Right... what, tonight?'

'No, not tonight. But first thing tomorrow. I can't give you details yet, they're still being ironed out, and, besides, it's best I keep them under wraps, given what's going on at the moment. If you can just sit tight for one more night, then everything should be fine.'

Jack continued to stare at her, saying nothing.

'Jack, this is good news. This is what you wanted.'

'Yes, sorry, I know,' he replied, smiling sheepishly. 'I... I just didn't think it was going to happen so quickly, that's all.'

'If that's your way of saying thank you, you're welcome.'

'Yes, sorry, thank you,' he replied, flustered.

'So here's the drill. I'll pick you up around ten thirty, then we'll leave together. We'll probably head out the back way to rendezvous with transport a few streets away. If anyone is watching the front of the house, it's best they think we're still here, until we're long gone. We won't have any time to muck about, speed will be of the essence, so I will need you to pack tonight. Is that OK?'

Jack nodded, but suddenly looked uncertain.

'Are you OK to do that? Are you feeling up to it?'

Still he said nothing. Olivia hesitated, before continuing:

'If you want, I can stay with you. You know it's against the rules, but if you need me to stay the night...'

'No, you're OK.'

'I mean it – if that's what you'd like, it's fine. God knows I've got nowhere else to be.'

'Honestly, I'm feeling much better. Now that I know I'm being moved and all...'

He was smiling at her fixedly, his enthusiasm real, yet also somehow forced.

'Is everything OK, Jack?'

'Yes, I'm fine. Just tired, that's all. I'm sorry for freaking out, for being a pain. It's not easy, that's all, but it's all good now.'

'Well, if you're sure,' Olivia replied cautiously, a little unnerved by this sudden upturn in his mood. 'I've got you some things to keep you entertained until tomorrow. Some football magazines, a couple of Alex Rider books. You said you liked those, right?'

Jack nodded, but reddened slightly, clearly embarrassed by his reading age.

'And I even got you ten B&H, because I know you like a smoke. But try not to burn the place down, right?'

Jack took the gifts, shyly nodding his thanks.

'Right, I'd best be off then. Try and get a decent sleep, eh? Big day tomorrow.'

Jack reassured her, saying all the right things as he saw her to the door. Bidding him goodnight, Olivia walked back to her car, deep in thought. What was going on with him? Having lost the plot earlier, insisting that his life was in danger and that he needed to be moved *immediately*, he now seemed oddly distracted. Was that just his way? Was he incapable of expressing gratitude or pleasure, having received so few good turns during his life? Or was something going on? Something she was *missing*?

Uneasy, Olivia plonked herself into the driver's seat, tugging out her phone. Should she call someone, share her anxieties? Isaac? Firth? No, the person she always called in these situations, her sounding board, was Christopher. And even though their last conversation had ended very badly, perhaps this could be a way of bridging the divide, of showing him that they could have a normal, functioning professional relationship? That she wasn't intent on destroying his happiness, his equilibrium, his life?

Her hands were shaking and as she located his number and hit 'Call'. Clearing her throat, she prepared to put her best foot forward, to be calm, sympathetic, sane. The call connected, rang twice, then was abruptly declined.

Immediately, Olivia felt anger flare within her. Didn't that just say it all? Didn't that sum up their time together perfectly? She had given her heart to Christopher, given him everything and what had been her reward?

She had been seduced, impregnated, then brutally rejected.

Chapter 96

Christopher marched along the lonely corridor, his emotions in tumult. How typical of Olivia to call him now, when his head was still spinning from his interview with DC Cooke. Was his former lover deliberately trying to stick the knife in? Desperate to continue her verbal assault on him, despite knowing he was deeply concerned by the police interest in him? How stupid he was not to have seen this coming. Yes, Olivia was sharp, sassy and a great fuck, but she was a basket case, anyone could see that. Why had he not brushed her off at the first opportunity and found his pleasures elsewhere, with someone safer and more discreet?

The department was quiet, most of the exhausted probation officers having called it a night, desperate to grab a few hours' sleep before the mayhem commenced again. Christopher was glad of this, keen to find a quiet space to mentally replay his interview with Cooke, anxious to analyse whether he'd said anything that might have aroused her suspicion. The interview *seemed* to have gone OK, as far as he could tell. Cooke had been polite, open and straightforward, asking numerous questions about the Service's chain of command, the structure of the department, access to their IT systems and so on. Her enquiries didn't seem to have an edge, but then maybe that was her technique? She certainly scribbled a lot of notes as she smiled fixedly at him, notes he would dearly have loved to read.

The one point where he faltered slightly was when she asked him about his relationship with the press. Cooke had asked him outright whether he had ever discussed sensitive information with someone *outside* the department, whether he had any ongoing relationship with journalists or bloggers. A momentary pause from him was enough to intrigue her and whilst he'd worked hard to cover this minor slip, insisting that confidentiality was paramount in his position, he wasn't sure the young DC had believed him. Unpleasant though it was to acknowledge, Christopher felt sure that this would come back to bite him, that he would have to answer further charges on this count at a later date.

Right on cue, Christopher's phone sprang to life. It's tinny ringtone echoed around the deserted department and, aghast, he raised his thumb to kill the call. Bloody Olivia... Except the call wasn't from his ex-lover this time, but from Madeleine Barnes. Having already profited from their brief acquaintanceship, the journalist was no doubt returning for more, seeking out further damning information about Firth. Well, she would have to wait, he wasn't in the mood to be grilled tonight. The call rang out, then seconds later started up again, causing Christopher to swear viciously. Didn't that tell you everything you needed to know about women? Always wanting more than you could give. Angry, flustered, Christopher turned off the phone, stowing it in his pocket.

He marched on, picking his way through the desks in the gloomy, airless space. He wanted to retreat to his office now, to try to gather his thoughts. But as he approached his seventh-floor sanctuary, he spotted something that stopped him in his tracks. *Someone was in his office.* A figure was standing by his desk, rifling through his correspondence in the gloom. For a moment, Christopher froze, beset by the fear that this might be connected with Dabral's investigation, that one of her lackeys was searching for incriminating evidence, but he swiftly pushed this crazy notion aside. If the police wanted to search his office, they'd be here in force, with a warrant, not sneaking around late at night. It wasn't Olivia either, she was with Jack, and Penny was tucked away safely at home, so who...?

Marching to his office, Christopher burst through the door, flicking the main lights on. Startled, the intruder looked up sharply.

'Isaac? What the fuck do you think you're doing?' Christopher demanded.

The veteran probation officer was clutching a file in his hand, his torch trained on it, but quickly slid it back into Christopher's in-tray now.

'Just looking for Yusuf Bedlin's latest probation review. He's got a review coming up and—'

'In my office? In the dark?' Christopher retorted dismissively, hurrying across the room towards him.

'Anyhow,' Isaac continued briskly, 'I'm sure you've got a lot on, so—'

'You stay where the fuck you are,' his superior demanded, rooting out the file.

Flicking it open, Christopher wasn't surprised to see that it was Isaac's disciplinary report, a final copy of which had been placed in his tray for signature.

'I might have known,' Christopher said witheringly, snapping the file shut. 'Keen to know the verdict, were you? Keen to know what we're planning to do with you?'

'So what if I *was*?' Green replied, unrepentant. 'This whole process has taken months, months of stress and bad blood and innuendo...'

'And you think that entitles you to covertly access confidential personnel files *in my private office*? I ought to have you fired on the spot.'

'I bet you'd love that.'

'Too bloody right I would. You've been trouble from day one, seeing slights where they don't exist, inventing incidents of prejudice, all to explain your own pitiful performance.'

'Speak your mind, Deputy Director,' Isaac laughed bitterly. 'Speak your mind.'

'Jesus Christ, Isaac. Where do you get the brass neck to waltz in here and then make light of it?'

'Look, if I'm being thrown on the scrapheap after all my years of service, then I have a right to know. You can't keep a man dangling forever, torturing him like this, *humiliating* him...'

'You've brought it all on yourself, Isaac. This is your doing, not ours. But let me tell you this, we're reaching the end of the road, *my friend*. You're drinking in the last chance saloon...'

Christopher said this gleefully, expecting, hoping for a hostile reaction, but to his surprise Isaac broke into a bitter, world-weary smile. Holding his superior's gaze for a moment, he brushed past him, whispering darkly:

'You have no idea...'

And then he was gone, leaving Christopher angry, aggrieved and deeply discomfited. What else had Isaac stumbled upon whilst rooting through his office?

Chapter 97

They were searching, searching, searching … but still the break-through eluded them. Turning away from her weary officers, Chandra tried to conceal her frustration and disappointment as she cooed discreetly into her mobile.

'Mummy loves you too … but Mummy has to work. Perhaps Daddy can tuck you in tonight, sing you to sleep. You know how good at singing Daddy is …'

Her suggestion was met with a chorus of disapproval, which made her heart sink. Chandra felt guilty at not being home for bedtime and worse still that Nimesh's tender care of their girls was so frequently dismissed and disparaged. The wheels would have come off months ago if it wasn't for his patience and resolve, yet what thanks did he get for it? It was unjust, hurtful, and though he always insisted he didn't mind, she knew he did. Chandra longed to be back there, reassuring him and scooping her daughters up into her arms, but there was no question of that. Not whilst their investigation continued to falter.

They had crawled over almost every inch of the perfectly manicured communal garden, but so far had found nothing. What next? Would they continue down Vauxhall Bridge Road, perhaps head onto Millbank, rummaging through bins and pulling up drains all because of a hunch? It seemed pointless, misguided, a sure sign of their growing desperation, yet Chandra was so convinced that Chambers was involved, that he was hiding something from them, that somehow she couldn't let it go. But what if the search yielded nothing? Would the team continue to trust her, having followed a wild goose chase? Or would they start to question her leadership? She was sure Gary Buckland would be on hand to take advantage if they did.

Chandra realized she had zoned out of her girls' plaintiff grumblings, so sending love and wishing them goodnight, she rung off. She suddenly felt wrung out, tired and disconsolate, and a large part of her was tempted to concede defeat. But knowing that her officers were looking to her, aware that not *every* inch of the park had been covered, she rejoined the fray, snapping on a pair of latex gloves as she strode towards a nearby bin.

Wasn't this just perfect? Here she was, SIO on the most complex, high-profile investigation of her career and what was she doing? Standing in a gloomy garden after hours, rummaging through a bin, pulling out empty coffee cups, crisps packets and the obligatory bags of dog poo. Angrily, Chandra set to work, barely glancing at the detritus she tugged out, convinced she was making a fool of both herself and the team. She was keen to get this over with, to face down this defeat, so she upped her pace, tugging out a clutch of empty beer cans and a discarded half bottle of vodka. Scowling, she added them to the growing pile next to her, before diving down into the depths of the bin. And now she hesitated. For here, at the very bottom, she spotted something intriguing. Something small and oblong, wrapped tightly in a Boots bag. Curious, Chandra opened it, surprised to see a mobile phone inside.

Suddenly her heart was racing. The screen of the Samsung Galaxy wasn't cracked or damaged and the phone itself seemed to be in perfect working order, springing to life now as she turned it on. So why would someone throw it away, concealing it at the bottom of a dirty bin, unless...

Teasing off the back cover, Chandra held it up to the light, a smile spreading across her face. The phone's serial number was long and complicated but she recognized it instantly. This was the phone that had been used to leak compromising information about Mark Willis, Andrew Baynes and Emily Lawrence.

Finally, she had Guy Chambers exactly where she wanted him.

Chapter 98

Solitude usually scared him. But tonight it was his friend.

Padding through the empty house, Jack felt a surge of excitement and adrenaline. He had been on the back foot for weeks, terrified of his release, shocked by the reaction in the wider world, disoriented by his new life, but tonight he felt good. Better than good.

Checking the front door was locked, he completed one final circuit of the house before returning to the kitchen. Tugging the curtains tightly shut, he crossed to the fridge, kneeling down on the sticky floor. Running his fingers along the skirting board, he teased the edge of the linoleum up, revealing the floorboards beneath. Seeking out the one next to the fridge, he pressed down on it, the far end rising slightly. Tucking his fingers underneath the lip, he then prised the floorboard up to reveal his rucksack concealed in the void beneath. Reaching down, he hauled it up and out, before carefully replacing the loose board.

Now he moved quickly, settling himself at the kitchen table and pulling out his new iPad. Placing it on the stand, Jack turned it on, waiting impatiently as the Apple sign stared back, passive, immobile, taunting. His excitement was growing, as was his impatience with it, but now the machine sprang to life and he typed quickly. This was not a simple process – accessing the dark web was a difficult and hazardous process, with all sorts of traps laid for the uninitiated. One wrong move and the police would be onto him in a flash, so he took his time, patiently working his way through the various protocols, avoiding the obvious red flags. Then, suddenly he was in, the encrypted chat room opening up like a flower. Jack giggled nervously. He hadn't been sure whether it would still be active, if he would still be admitted, but here it was. His breathing was shallow, his body buzzing, but there was no question of rushing this. He had to get it right.

First thing he needed was a name. Daisy? Debby? Dawn? Yes, Dawn would do. His hands were sweaty, so he wiped them on his jeans, before laying his hands on the keys. He knew what he was doing, knew what he wanted to say and his eyes remained glued to the screen as he typed his first message:

'Hi. My name is Dawn. I'm a mum of a three-year-old girl who's ripe for fucking. Send me your clips and I'll send you some of her in return.'

Leaning back in his chair, one hand resting on his groin, Jack pressed SEND.

Chapter 99

Olivia's chest felt so tight she thought it would burst. Her nerves were jangling, her breath short, but still she kept moving, placing one foot defiantly in front of the other as she walked up the pristine front path. She had sat in the squalid smokers' yard for the best part of an hour, debating what to do, before rising suddenly, her mind made up. On her way over here, she'd been so determined, so angry, so resolved, yet the sight of the impressive three-storey mansion, discreetly tucked away in a hidden corner of St John's Wood, seemed to challenge her conviction. This wasn't a world she belonged in, nor one that would welcome her, despite the expensive wreath on the door and the candles burning brightly in the windows. Nevertheless, she'd come here with an express purpose and intended to see it through. Why should Christopher continue to enjoy all the trappings of a happy, successful life, whilst she was left out in the cold? His betrayal of her had been brutal, callous and utterly unforgivable and now he was going to pay the price.

There was no doorbell, the house too refined for that, so grasping the polished brass knocker, she rapped lightly on the door. What a find Penny had been for Christopher – devoted, supportive and, crucially, *rich*, providing the funds for them to live in one of the most exclusive corners of London whilst

Christopher carefully plotted his rise within the Service. No wonder he was determined to hang onto Penny at all costs, despite the fact that he found her dull in conversation and even duller in bed.

The door swung open, revealing the mistress of the house. As usual, Penny was immaculately dressed, radiating wealth and refinement. If she was surprised to find Olivia on her doorstep unannounced, she didn't show it, immediately breaking into a grin.

'Olivia, how nice to see you. Christopher's not back yet, but won't you come in?'

Smiling tightly, Olivia stepped inside.

Why hadn't she come here before? If she had, Olivia would have *known* Christopher would never leave. This place, which Chris always joked about as being a dowdy family home, was absolutely stunning, like something out of a film. It was especially impressive at this time of year, the whole house dripping with Christmas decorations, festive knick-knacks and a huge array of cards from their many friends and associates. Most impressive of all was the towering Christmas tree – what did *that* cost? – flanked by the imposing marble fireplace in which roared a lively fire, crackling and spitting with festive enthusiasm. Olivia took a moment to warm herself next to it – her hands suddenly felt like ice.

'Chris should be back soon, so why don't we have a drink and a gossip?'

'Sounds lovely,' Olivia replied brightly.

Penny padded across the floor, clasping two brimming flutes of champagne. Olivia took one gladly, half emptying it with her first swig.

'I don't hold out much hope for a peaceful Christmas,' Penny said, pulling a face, 'with everything that's going on, but we have to take our cheer where we can find it, eh?'

She smiled at Olivia, crinkling up her eyes in sisterly bonhomie, as they clinked glasses.

'Happy Christmas.'

Olivia felt decidedly gauche, realizing now that she'd taken a large swig before they'd toasted the season, but she needed the courage the chilled alcohol gave her.

'Same to you,' she replied firmly, her eyes fixed on Penny's.

'Have you got plans for Christmas? Are you seeing family or...?'

'Not really. My mum lives up north, and we're not close. How about you, Penny?'

'Oh, the usual. Scores of relatives descending, utter chaos, but some fun and laughter buried in there somewhere.'

Penny wasn't fooling anyone. Olivia was sure Christmases here were magical occasions.

'It's always a major operation, but the boys seem to enjoy it, which is the main thing.'

Penny sighed happily, then took a sip of her champagne. Olivia smiled back, letting her eyes wander over the interior, drinking in the finer details of the expensive styling. The pair now lapsed into silence and when Olivia turned back to her hostess, finishing her drink as she did so, she noticed that Penny was looking at her curiously, as if beginning to find her presence in the family home slightly odd, even a little unnerving.

'I can ring Chris if you want,' she offered. 'See how long he's going to be. Or perhaps *I* can help? Are you dropping something off for him, some files or...?'

Penny looked at her entreatingly, and once more Olivia felt a pang of nerves. She could lie now, turn around and leave, pretend that everything was OK. Or she could stay the course and get the job done. The thought of leaving this enchanted space to return to her draughty studio flat decided her, however, and she pressed on.

'Actually it was *you* I wanted to see, Penny.'

'Really?' her hostess replied, faltering slightly.

'Yes, I wanted to share my good news with you.'

Penny continued to stare at her, intrigued, but also unnerved by Olivia's forced jollity.

'Well, go on, don't keep me in suspense,' Penny urged.

'I'm pregnant,' Olivia replied breezily.

A momentary reaction, then Penny recovered, breaking into another broad smile.

'Well that's marvellous, Olivia. I had no idea you were seeing anyone.'

'No, we haven't really advertised it...'

Smiling, Olivia turned away from her hostess, drinking in the beautifully appointed interior.

'And?' Penny continued gamely. 'Who's the lucky guy? Anyone I know?'

Olivia said nothing in response, instead turning back to Penny and staring intently at her. There was a second's confusion and then she saw it. The moment of realization, of dreams crushed and worst fears realized, as her hostess's smile slowly faded, the blood draining from her face.

Chapter 100

He tugged the bank notes from the cashpoint, shoving them roughly into his jacket pocket. Turning away, Isaac Green pulled his hood up and moved off, heading down the busy high street. Losing himself in the crowds of shoppers, he limped silently through the throng, before suddenly changing direction, disappearing down a narrow side alley.

Now the probation officer slowed, leaning heavily on his walking stick. His leg was aching, but this delay also allowed him to check he wasn't being followed. He wouldn't put it past Dabral to have put him under surveillance, hence his caution. There could be no witnesses to this particular pilgrimage.

Happily, however, he appeared to be alone, so he continued falteringly on his way. As he did so, Isaac retrieved his mobile phone from his pocket, powering it down. This was probably overkill, but he did it out of habit now, determined that his visits to the less salubrious streets of Lambeth should not be traceable. Any sniff of criminality would result in instant dismissal from the Service, something Christopher Parkes would take great delight in facilitating. No, it was better to be safe than sorry, given the circumstances.

Isaac struggled on, cursing his useless leg, cursing his luck, cursing anyone and everyone who came to mind. His faithless wife was at the forefront of his thoughts of course, but there were others too – family members, colleagues and past acquaintances who'd proved themselves to be fair-weather friends, unwilling or unable to cope with his injuries, his mood swings, his burning sense of injustice. Their treachery, their selfishness had rubbed salt in his wounds, ensuring that over time, bitterness had seeped into his heart and soul. Now, when he felt like this, when it seemed as if nobody cared whether he lived or died, he came here, to feel alive again, however briefly.

He rang the buzzer and was swiftly admitted. Inside, the gloomy staircase led up to a first-floor flat and he struggled up them, pulling hard on the rail to keep himself from tumbling backwards. Exhausted, sweating, he crested the landing, just as the flat's front door opened to reveal a slender young woman wearing an imitation silk robe. Pausing to gather his breath, Isaac feasted his eyes on her long, tanned legs, his desire stirring.

'There you are, I'd almost given up on you.'

'Work,' Isaac grunted.

'Fair enough, but let's not hang about, eh? I've got a ten o'clock and, believe me, that guy's *always* punctual.'

It was deflating to be reminded that Isaac was just one in a line of visitors, but Isaac willed himself forwards, fixing his eyes on the contours of her supple body. He needed her affection tonight, needed the comfort she gave him, needed to pretend, if only for an hour, that somebody loved him.

Chapter 101

'Why can't we find him?'

DS Buckland looked offended by the brusqueness of Chandra's tone, bristling as he replied:

'It's not for the want of trying. DC Reeves visited Mike Burnham's house and I followed up with a phone message, but so far nothing.'

'Have you tried him at work?'

'Of course. Turns out he was fired yesterday morning. His boss wouldn't say why, but he sounded pretty pissed off about it.'

'And you didn't think this was worth following up?' Chandra replied, aghast.

'To be fair, guv, we've been a bit busy following up on *actual* crimes to start—'

'I should have been told earlier,' Chandra interrupted. 'Mike Burnham is an obvious person for our perpetrator to contact. Who knows, maybe he's already made contact.'

'There's no evidence of that,' Buckland protested.

'It doesn't strike you as odd, coincidental, that Burnham's suddenly been fired?'

'There could be any number of reasons for that.'

'Or it could be directly related to the current situation. I'll get DC Cooke to chase Burnham. I want you to get round to his showroom, talk to his boss, find out what happened. If you have any suspicions that it's related to the leaks, then I need to know ASAP.'

'All right, all right,' Buckland held up his hands, annoyed and aggrieved.

'I mean it, Gary. If we can get ahead of our mole, then maybe we can catch him in the act.'

'I've said I'm going...'

Chandra watched her deputy lumber across the incident room, annoyed by his lack of urgency or initiative. If the culprit, the source of these leaks, was intent on finishing the job, then the Burnhams and the Armstrongs, relatives of Kyle Peters' victim Billy, were the obvious next recipients of confidential information. DC Cooke had already made contact with the Armstrongs, who'd been at pains to reassure her that they'd received no unsolicited messages. Alison Burnham likewise, but her ex-husband Mike remained elusive, which worried Chandra, especially now she'd learned he'd been unexpectedly fired. What *was* going on? Was he too being sucked into this vortex of bloodshed?

Turning, Chandra headed back to her office, deep in thought. Stepping inside, her eye was drawn to the stack of files on her desk. They had just arrived via secure courier from the Probation Service HQ in Petty France and contained the personnel files of everyone involved in the monitoring and supervision of the very highest-profile offenders. She approached them now, removing Isaac Green's file from the top to reveal Christopher Parkes' just beneath. Should she start on them now? Or wait until they knew more about Guy Chambers? Her decision was made for her, however, by DC Drummond who now knocked and entered.

'Just heard from the tech team, guv. The phone you found is *definitely* the one used to send the photo of Emily Lawrence to Justice Never Sleeps.'

Chandra felt a flush of triumph. They'd known from the serial number that the Samsung Galaxy had been used to leak the ex-offenders' identities and whereabouts to the bereaved families. Now they could explicitly link the same phone to the Justice Never Sleeps group.

'How confident are we?'

'Hundred per cent. The photo had been deleted from the device, but it wasn't hard for the tech team to retrieve.'

Chandra felt her whole body relax.

'OK, bring Chambers in ASAP,' she said decisively. 'But let him stew in the cells for a night first, soften him up. We'll have a go at him first thing in the morning.'

'Yes, boss.'

DC Drummond was already on her way, summoning DC Meacher to join her. Chandra breathed out, long and slow, suppressing a smile. This investigation had been so complicated, so confounding, so unnerving, but now she sensed they finally had a chance to finish it, to bring this grim cycle of violence and retribution to an end.

Chapter 102

It was time to run.

Hastening across the concourse, Ian Blackwell was alive to everything and everyone, certain now that each passing stranger represented danger. Since his unpleasant encounter with Guy Chambers, the former policeman had been in a state of tumult, uncertain whether to ignore the MP's ultimatum or heed his advice and flee. Blackwell was determined not to be bullied into leaving the capital, especially not by a snake like Chambers, and yet there was no question that the net *was* tightening. Greater Manchester Police had visited numerous properties in his home city, shaking down family and friends in their search for him, and Blackwell knew from a loyal source in the Met that his details had been circulated to every ward in London. The pressure was rising, yet still he hesitated. It seemed unlikely that he could remain under the radar in London, as his details, his face became ever more widely circulated. But what if he drew attention to himself by making a break for it? He had no access to a car, nor could he hire one now, so he'd need to head for a train or a bus station. What if they were watching for him there?

Then he heard news of Chambers' arrest. This time Blackwell didn't hesitate, now seriously alarmed. Who knew what Chambers might say once they got him in the interview suite?

What tall stories he might invent? Blackwell had a small window of opportunity and he had to seize it. He would head to Glasgow, visit an old pal there who'd shield him for a day or two, giving him much needed time to think.

Clutching his ticket, Ian Blackwell marched through King's Cross towards platform 14. The train for Glasgow left in five minutes and if he could get on it, he felt sure he'd be safe. He hurried on, his stride seeming to grow with each step, straining to reach the platform as fast as he could. He saw faces coming at him, bodies brushing against his, the station rammed in the run-up to Christmas. Was it his imagination or were people staring at him, drinking in his features? Dropping his gaze to the floor, he pressed on, upping the pace, but almost immediately he cannoned off another traveller, staggering sideways.

'Watch where you're going, mate ...'

Blackwell didn't respond, holding up his hand in apology and hurrying on. Platform 11 passed by, then platform 12 ... he was nearly there. With a sigh of relief, he saw the barrier for platform 14 and beyond it the train, ready and waiting. Slipping his ticket into the machine, he passed through the barriers, breaking into a gentle trot. Behind him, he heard the barriers clatter open again, but ignored the noise, close now to salvation.

'Excuse me?'

The voice was close behind, but Blackwell hurried on, making for the train door.

'Ian Blackwell?'

The fugitive froze, then pivoted round, shocked to the core. The same 'traveller' who'd just bumped into him was closing in. Dressed in plain clothes, he was holding up a Met Police badge. Turning, Blackwell dropped his bag and sprinted down the platform, but he'd barely covered five yards, when two members of the British Transport Police began hurrying towards him from the other end of the platform. Blackwell only had a second to make a decision about what to do next – turn and tackle the plain clothes officer, jump on the train or leap onto the empty track next to him – and his hesitation cost him. The plain clothes officer was swiftly upon him, gripping his jacket, spinning him around, pressing his face up against the dirty carapace of the train.

It was all over in a second. Blackwell's great mission, his secret life undone in the blink of an eye. He was caught fair and square and would have to face the consequences. They would throw the book at him – there was nothing serving officers hated more than a rogue colleague – but a jail sentence was unthinkable. He'd be a dead man walking, convicted criminals lining up for a piece of the self-styled vigilante. No, if Blackwell wanted to survive, he'd have to be canny, to barter, to play the only card he had left.

He would have to give them Chambers.

Chapter 103

He glided down the deserted aisle, head down, eyes to the floor. Mike knew where he was going, had visited this store countless times before, and he was glad of it tonight. He didn't want to linger, to draw any unnecessary attention to himself – he just wanted to get the job done and leave as swiftly as possible. So he made his way without delay to the tool section, trying to appear as inconspicuous as possible.

On cue, his mobile phone started ringing, the annoying electronic melody echoing down the deserted aisle. Pulling it out, he answered it quickly, killing the tune.

'Mike Burnham.'

'It's me.'

Typical Alison. Straight to the point.

'Alison, this really isn't a good time. I'm in the middle—'

'What do you mean it isn't a good time. You're supposed to be here, now.'

'What?'

'Oh, please, Mike. Don't tell me you've forgotten?'

Mike tensed, racking his brains, but came up blank. What was she on about?

'You were supposed to be having Rachel tonight. We arranged it weeks ago, it's my work Christmas do.'

A stab of guilt now, as a vague recollection of this agreement punched through.

'I've got a taxi on the way. What the hell am I supposed to do?'

'Can't Dave look after her?' Mike goaded, bristling. 'I thought he was a model "dad".'

'He's coming too, as it happens.'

'Showing off your new fella, are we?'

'Don't be so bloody childish. When can you get here?'

A moment's hesitation now. Mike knew he was in the wrong, knew he should help out, but how could he?

'I'm sorry Alison, I've got to go.'

He hung up, swiftly turning the phone off. He knew that Alison would be going crazy, leaving messages, calling him everything under the sun, but he couldn't afford to get distracted, couldn't let his focus slip even for a second. Stopping at the end of the aisle, he reached down to pick up a large claw hammer, weighing it thoughtfully in his hand. Satisfied, he placed it into the trolley, next to the chainsaw and heavy-duty bin liners, then headed on his way, walking swiftly towards the checkout.

Chapter 104

It wasn't until his dad left that Sam let his smile slip. Paul and Sandra had been working overtime to cheer him up and he'd tried hard to show his gratitude. But in truth he found their remorseless positivity cloying and their constant digs at his mother difficult to stomach. Yes, she deserved it, but the alacrity with which they were trying to drive a wedge between her and Sam left a bitter taste in his mouth.

Tiring of their drip, drip, drip of recrimination, he'd jumped at the chance of getting a takeaway, offering to go out himself, until Paul had put his foot down, insisting that it was too much of a security risk. He insisted he would go instead, Sandra swiftly deciding to join him, clearly uneasy at the thought of having to make polite conversation with Sam in the interim. Sam hadn't been unhappy about this, partly because he found Sandra bland, but mostly because he wanted to be alone.

Sam felt as if his feet had hardly touched the ground since yesterday morning. It seemed like only five minutes ago that his mother had pulled him out of school and yet he'd endured a lifetime of nasty shocks and unpleasant surprises since then. He was not the same person, they were not the same family, his whole world seemed to have tilted on its axis, yet he had had no time to process this or even begin to work out how he felt. He had been *reacting* to events ever since – taking in his mother's confession, discovering the truth about that terrible time, lashing out at her, running to his father – and he still didn't know what it all meant. Was his mum safe? Would he see her again? Could he find it in his heart to forgive her? And if not, was this his future now, living in a strange village with a stepmother he barely knew? Or was this just another stopgap? Would he have to move on *again*, changing his name, his story, his past?

Sam felt unstable on his feet, the whole experience over-whelming him. What he really wanted to do was run back to Reading, hunker down with Gavin and cry his eyes out. But there was no prospect of that, not whilst there were people out there actively hunting them, burning for revenge. Perhaps the best he could hope for was a bit of solitude, a moment to reclaim some kind of composure. Crossing into the living room, he picked up the remote. Some mindless TV might distract him from his own predicament, as long as he could avoid the news channels. Perhaps a beer might help too. Yes, that was what he needed, something cold and powerful to take the edge off things.

Flicking the TV on, he tossed the remote onto the sofa and made for the kitchen. He didn't dawdle, the thought of a cool beer driving him on, but as he entered the darkened room, he paused. Something was wrong. He couldn't put his finger on it at first, simply knowing that something about the gloomy space alarmed him. Then he realized what it was. It was freezing in here. Sandra felt the cold, so the house was always well heated, especially the kitchen at the rear, where she spent much of her time. But it was distinctly chilly now and shooting a glance across the room, Sam understood why. The back door was ajar, moving gently in the breeze. Immediately, Sam tensed, knowing he'd heard Sandra shut it just a few minutes ago, having returned from putting out the food waste. But if Paul or Sandra hadn't opened it, then who...?

Spinning, Sam headed fast back towards the living room, but as he reached the doorway, he heard a voice behind him.

'Sam, it's me.'

He froze, not quite believing his ears. Slowly Sam turned round, confused and alarmed to see his mother emerging from the shadows, dishevelled, dirty and damp.

'What are *you* doing here?' he demanded.

'Please, Sam. I didn't mean to scare you and I don't want any trouble. I just had to see you.'

'You can't be here. You know that. Where are your probation officers?'

'They don't know I'm here. But it's fine, I wasn't followed, you're perfectly safe.'

Angry, unnerved, Sam instinctively took a step back, but his mother held up a hand, imploring him to stay.

'Please, Sam, just five minutes, then I'll be gone. I *swear*.'

She looked so desperate, so forlorn that Sam couldn't say no. Relieved, his mother took a tentative step towards him, stepping into the light that spilled from the living room. And now Sam saw how muddy and damp she was, her whole body shivering with cold.

'Jesus Christ, Mum, are you OK?'

'I'm fine. Thanks to you.'

'What do you mean?'

His mother looked up at him and Sam was surprised to see that she looked... ashamed.

'I... I did something crazy tonight. Something I never thought I would do.'

'What are you talking about, Mum? You're scaring me.'

'I was out of mind, wasn't thinking straight,' his mother

blurted out, tears threatening. 'I'd lost you, my job, my home, everything. I just wanted it all to stop, to blot out the pain I'd caused, the pain I'm *still* causing...'

Sam stared at her, mute with shock, slowly realizing what she was building to.

'It felt like my only option at the time, the only thing I could do to make things right.'

She was faltering, Sam's evident distress making every word hard.

'I walked into a lake, went right under, swam down as far as I could. I thought I wanted to stay down there forever, to just... disappear. Then I saw your face. In my mind's eye, I saw *you*. And I knew I couldn't do it. That I had to see you, if only for one last time.'

'Don't say that, Mum, please don't say that.'

He was crying now, devastated by the thought of his mother feeling so wretched, so alone, that she'd attempted to end her life. He desperately wanted to hold her, to tell her everything was going to be OK, even though he knew it wouldn't. But as he took a step towards his mother, she held up her hand, stopping him in his tracks.

'Please, Sam, let me speak. And then I swear I'll go. You won't hear from me; you won't have to see me ever again.'

She was breathing heavily, exhausted beyond measure, but resolved to say what she'd come to say without interruption. Although it killed Sam to hold off comforting his mother, he stood his ground, immobilized by her tearful, pleading expression.

'I... I don't want you to forgive me, Sam. I can't expect that and I don't deserve it. But I do want... want you to try to *understand*. The papers said that I did what I did for attention. Because I was lonely, bored and bad. And I thought that too at first. God knows, I thought that and I *hated* myself for it. But now I know that it wasn't attention I wanted, it was love. The one thing I'd never had.'

Sam desperately wanted her to stop – it was too much, too awful – but she pressed on, remorseless, even as tears filled her eyes and her voice cracked.

'Of course, what I did to those poor, innocent girls, to my own sisters earned me only hatred. And anger. The very opposite of what I wanted. I thought that was it for me then, that I'd got what I deserved. That I'd be despised for the rest of my life. That I'd never know a kind word or a tender touch…'

Emily dropped her gaze to the floor, overcome by guilt, by self-loathing. Sam watched as a tear crept down her nose. He longed to stem her sadness, to end her suffering, but to his surprise, his mother now looked up, love beaming from her tear-filled eyes.

'…but *you* changed all that, Sam.'

Sam couldn't meet her eye, utterly overwhelmed.

'It was only years *after* all that madness and misery, after I'd changed my name, my address, my whole life that I found what I'd always craved. *You* gave me love, gave it me in spades, the only person who ever really has.'

Sam stared at her, every word piercing his heart.

'I know I've ruined all that, ruined your life, which was the last thing I ever wanted to do. But I want you to know that I'm *not* who they say I am. I'm *not* that… that monster. I have changed, I have done some good things in my life, because of the love you gave me.'

How was she able to keep going? Sam was utterly undone, tears streaming down his face, but somehow his mother found the strength to continue.

'So I wanted to thank you, Sam. For helping me, for *saving* me. You've done more for me than you could ever know...which is why I wish you all the best now. I may not be around to witness it, but I wish you a happy life. I can't offer you anything more, I've already destroyed so much, but I can at least offer you my thanks and my love. Thank you, Sammy...'

Stepping forward, she leaned in, giving him a gentle kiss on the forehead, holding him tight one last time. Then as silently as she'd arrived, she departed, slipping out the back door, leaving Sam alone to cry his heart out in the darkness.

Chapter 105

She stumbled back along the road, blinded by tears. Everything had played out exactly as Emily had hoped, yet she felt even more desolate now than when she had stepped into that icy lake. Then she had been purely thinking of herself, of ending her suffering once and for all, but now she knew she would live and, worse, live without Sam. He had been her greatest joy, her only achievement; now his existence would torture her night and day, starved of his presence. Perhaps it was her due, but it was a cruel punishment.

Strange how bitter the pill should taste now. Having been consumed by self-hatred, her desire to see Sam one last time had filled her with energy and adrenaline. She had stumbled from the caravan park to a nearby village, ordering a cab from the local pub. The driver had seemed more interested in preserving the pristine interior of his car, never once questioning why she was so muddy, or why she avoided his eye. The journey to Maidenhead had taken less than half an hour and she had arrived at Paul's house just in time to see her ex heading into town, holding hands with his vacuous wife. Suddenly it felt as if the fates were on her side and Emily had taken full advantage, more relieved than she could say that Sam didn't turn and run at the sight of her. He had not rejected her, he had not chastised her, yet that only made the conclusion of their time together worse – her final image would be of her son, broken and distressed, his cheeks stained with tears. Was this her legacy? Was this the vision of Sam that would haunt her for the rest of her days?

Sobbing quietly, Emily staggered to the nearest taxi rank. Soon she was on her way back down the M40, her driver more solicitous this time, clearly worried that something terrible had happened. But Emily said little, stifling her sobs, whilst promising him an extra tenner if he put his foot down. He duly obliged and it was just striking midnight as they approached the entrance to the caravan park in Colne Valley.

'You can pull up here,' Emily said, commanding him to stop just short of the entrance.

She waited until he'd driven away, then struck for 'home', cutting through the undergrowth to avoid the main driveway. She made fast work of it and was soon on the path once more, darting between the static caravans. Here she paused, fearful that her absence might have been detected, that Marianne and the others would now fall upon her, irate, aggrieved, demanding an explanation. But to her immense relief, the caravan park was as quiet, as still, as she had left it. Emily offered up a silent prayer, thankful that one thing had gone right today – she had no appetite for a dressing down. Pleased, Emily covered the last few yards quickly, silently climbing the steps and gratefully teasing the door open.

But as she stepped into the caravan, she suddenly felt an unwanted presence, someone looming over her in the doorway. She tried to scream, to cry out, but before she could do so, she felt a crushing blow to the back of her head. Cannoning forward, she connected sharply with the door frame, barely registering what was happening, as a pair of rough hands grabbed her, forcing her inside.

*

Blood. She could taste it in her mouth, she could feel it clinging to her face. Opening one eye, her vision swam, but still she could make out a familiar shape ranged in front of her. As her eyes became used to the gloom, as the pounding in her head began to subside, she saw him clearly, seated on the chair opposite hers – her older brother Robert.

'Hello, sis, long time no see.'

She flinched in her chair, terrified by his voice, his bearing, the glint in his eye. Robert was so close to her, that he could have leaned forward and kissed her, but a loving reunion was not what he had in mind.

'I can crush your larynx before you get a sound out, so don't even think about screaming. Understand?'

Emily nodded, mute with terror.

'Good. That should make things go a lot easier.'

He smiled as he spoke, revealing his rotten yellow teeth. Suddenly Emily was rocketed back to a time in her life she'd fought hard to forget, where food, comfort and even basic hygiene was in short supply.

'I can tell you're pleased to see me,' he hissed. 'And I'm very glad to see you. Taken me ages to track you down. Might not have been able to if it wasn't for the boy...'

And now Emily realized the magnitude of her mistake. She had been so intent on seeing Sam, on justifying herself to him and saying a proper goodbye, that she hadn't stopped to think that Robert might be watching *him*, presuming perhaps that where Sam was, Emily would eventually follow. It sickened her to think that her actions might have put him in danger, that she could have been so stupid. Fortunately, however, Robert seemed more interested in her and she prayed that his revenge tonight would be the end of it.

'Well, you've changed. Made something of yourself, haven't you?' her brother sneered.

'I see you haven't,' she fired back. 'Still drinking Bridgend dry, are you?'

'Why change the habits of a lifetime, eh? The others say hello by the way, they would have liked to have been here, but this is *my* job. No need for them to get mixed up in it.'

'What a hero,' Emily scoffed. 'What a family guy.'

She was rocked back, his hand connecting with her cheek before she'd even seen it coming. She was seeing stars, but he was in her face, savage and enraged.

'Don't you dare talk to me about family, you little bitch. What do *you* know about family? All you've ever cared about is yourself, getting what you want, even if it means... if it means killing defenceless little girls. Burning them as they slept in their beds.'

Emily was shocked to see real distress behind his anger, his grief still fresh. Chastened, she gathered herself, spitting out some blood, preparing to beg for her life.

'Look, Robert, you've got every reason to hate me. What I did was beyond wicked. Not a day has gone by when I haven't thought of those girls, hating myself for what I did, wishing I could turn the clock back. I visit their graves every year on their birthdays and I pray for them, asking for their forgiveness...'

'Don't be obscene, woman.'

'I know what I did. And I know the cost of it. Not just for me, but for all of us. And I'm so, so sorry for that. But, Robert, please believe me when I say I never wanted any of that. I didn't hate them, I didn't hate you, it was just that place, that awful place. I couldn't bear it, couldn't bear him, couldn't bear Ma not being there...'

'You leave her out of it,' Robert replied, glowering.

'Oh, please, don't defend her. She was the *cause* of all this, if she hadn't walked out on us—'

This time she saw it coming, but couldn't move fast enough, his hand connecting hard with her nose, snapping her head backwards, sending her tumbling to the floor. Dazed, Emily struggled to her feet, backing into the galley kitchen, as Robert advanced on her.

'Don't you say another word about our ma, or any of us for that matter. You don't get to talk about us, you don't get to talk about *anything*…'

There was fire in his eyes, a dark vengeful fire. Her brother had not come to hear her confession, he had come to kill.

'Funny, isn't it, how you've plenty to say. Been quiet up until now, haven't you? Hiding out, getting on with your life, having a jolly old time, whilst the rest of us have had to live with what you did. To see Ma and Pa torn apart, to see the others drinking, moaning, fighting. To be singled out, spat at, abused all for something *you* did, you and you alone…'

He was right. She hadn't wanted to know what had happened to them, couldn't bear to think about what they said about her in Bridgend, how the survivors had suffered.

'There's not one of us that's right in the head, not one of us who's in a good place, because of what you did. Because you were lonely. Because you were bored. Because you wanted attention…'

'It wasn't like that.'

'Well, you've got the attention you wanted now, haven't you? The whole world knows about you, the whole world's looking for you, but I've found you. And now I have, I'm going to enjoy myself. You deserve to suffer, Janet, and I'm going to make—'

She opened her mouth to scream, knowing all was lost now, but he was too quick for her, clamping his hairy hand over her mouth. He was in her face now, his stale breath sickening, but his proximity presented her with an opportunity. He was leaning over, his weight pressing down on her, so she drove her right knee up with all her might, ramming it into his groin. Shocked, Robert moaned in pain and she spun away from him. He clawed at her, but she managed to wriggle out of his grip, making it to the knife block before he could stop her. Pulling out the longest blade, she turned to face him. To her surprise, he broke into a grim smile, as he straightened up painfully, closing in on her.

'You really think you're capable of that, girlie? You really think you can take me?'

'It's not for me.'

Taking hold of the blade, she offered him the knife.

'I know what you came for. And I'm ready for it. So let's get it over with.'

Robert smiled once more, surprised and amused by her offer.

'Fuck's sake, Robert!' she continued angrily. 'I'm handing this to you on a plate. Are you a man or a mouse?'

Still he made no move to comply, sucking on his teeth as he replied:

'Oh, it's not going to be that easy, Janet...'

And with that, he stepped forward, head-butting her hard in the face.

Chapter 106

She had never known pain like it. Searing pain, splitting her head in two, as wave after wave of nausea swept over her. Emily could feel a tooth loose in her mouth, knew her nose was broken, could barely see for the blood creeping into her eyes. She was alive, which surprised her, but was lying face down on the dirty floor, in a pool of her own blood. She tried to right herself, to breathe in some fresh oxygen, but she couldn't move her hands or feet. Craning round, she opened one eye, realizing now that she was tightly bound with some kind of cord. Confused, she turned once more, to find Robert standing over her. As she did so, it hit her, that sharp, metallic odour. Petrol.

'Please, Robert...'

She didn't have the strength to beg, but she had to try.

He ignored her, emptying the last drops from his jerry can, before producing a lighter.

'Robert, I'm begging you.'

'Too little, too late,' he rasped, smiling. 'See you in the next life, bitch.'

He let the lighter fall, huge flames rearing up as it struck the sodden floor. Through the blaze, Emily could see Robert departing, hear the door locking behind him. And in that moment, she knew that he had won. *This* was how her story would end, these flames her atonement for her past crimes. Poetic justice in death.

Emily lay on the floor, helpless, disorientated, as the fire danced wildly around her. Pain ripped through her, even as the acrid odour of burning petrol made her retch, vomiting violently onto the disintegrating carpet. The heat was intense, surrounding her, *attacking* her. She could feel her skin blistering, her hair tingling, then crackling, as it caught fire. She had only moments left now – in a few seconds she would be consumed by the inferno. By the time Marianne got to her, she would be a charred corpse, a hideous, smouldering mockery of the living, loving woman she'd once been.

Roaring in agony, Emily tugged desperately at her bonds, but they refused to yield, her hands clamped tightly together. Even as she struggled to free herself, another wave of heat tore over her, searing her eyeballs, singeing her skin. Emily clamped her eyes shut to avoid being blinded, knowing that her struggle was nearly over. She was operating blind now, barely conscious of which direction to head in, unable to contain the agony that gripped every part of her body, yet she knew she had to do something. She was seconds from death.

Drawing her knees up to her chest, Emily forced her body forwards. Fire reared up around her, but she hardly registered the pain, propelling herself forwards again. Her ragged knees slid over the smoking carpet, ripping the fabric off her legs, exposing the vulnerable skin below, but on she went, faster and faster, before suddenly coming to an abrupt halt, as she collided hard with an unyielding surface. Emily desperately wanted to tease an eye open, to see if she'd found the door or simply backed herself into a corner, but she didn't dare, terrified of instant blindness. Resting her head against the wall, she pushed down hard with her toes, slowly moving her body upwards into a standing position. It was exhausting, it was agonising, but finally she was on her feet. Then, rotating her body, she slid along the wall, using her backside to guide her, keeping herself tethered to her only chance of salvation. And now once more she came to another abrupt halt, something hard and painful digging into her left hip. Immediately, her hands scrabbled towards the obstacle, then instantly recoiled, the metal door handle red hot to the touch.

Emily moaned in agony, her hands singing with pain, but even so, hope sprang up within her once more. Now she knew where she was, which gave her a slim chance of escape, despite the inferno that continued to rage around her. Taking a step back into the blaze, she checked her momentum, then threw herself bodily against the door. It shuddered and groaned, but refused to yield, propelling her back into the fire. For a moment, she nearly lost her balance, toppling backwards into the conflagration, then righting herself she charged forwards, crashing into the burning door once more. This time it cracked and bent, but still the lock held firm, denying her salvation. Stumbling backwards once more, Emily felt the strength drain from her, her resolve shattered. She couldn't do it anymore, she couldn't take another step, overwhelmed by the smoke, the heat, the awful agony. Emily swayed on the spot, her head spinning, her throat thick, utterly overwhelmed, then with one last desperate surge, she screamed Sam's name and threw herself at the door.

Emily cannoned into it, her shoulder exploding with pain, her head connecting hard with the door frame, but as she did so the smouldering door finally gave way. For a moment, Emily felt herself falling, then a second later she connected hard with the ground, her clothes hissing and crackling as she rolled over and over in the crisp, frosty grass.

Day Five

Chapter 107

What the hell was happening? What was the hideous noise?

Olivia jerked awake, disorientated and alarmed. She felt like someone was inside her head, trying to punch their way out, but as she struggled upright after another terrible night's sleep, she realized that the sound was coming from her front door. Grabbing her dressing gown, she hurried over to the intercom, her heart sinking as she saw an irate Christopher staring directly at the screen, challenging her to ignore him. She was tempted to do just that. Her former lover looked bug-eyed with rage, almost possessed. But there was no avoiding this confrontation and better perhaps to do it here than at work.

Pulling her dressing gown tightly around her, Olivia opened the door and hurried down the stairs. Already she could hear movement above, the other tenants of this block no doubt angered by this early wake-up call, but she ignored them. They had no place here. Tugging open the door, she found Christopher poised to hammer on it once more.

'There you are,' he hissed aggressively, withdrawing his fist.

'This is where I live, Christopher, so—'

'Don't you dare make a joke of this, don't you *fucking* dare...'

He was wagging a finger in her face and for a moment

she wondered if he might actually strike her. He looked wild, unhinged, dark rings under his bloodshot eyes.

'Trust me, Christopher, there's nothing about this situation that I find amusing.'

'Bullshit, you're *enjoying* yourself. Forcing your way into my home, confessing to my wife, destroying my family.'

'Hold on a minute,' Olivia protested. 'Penny invited me in and I didn't say anything that wasn't true.'

'Don't say her name. You're not fit to wipe the shit from her shoe.'

'But I was fit enough to keep *you* entertained, wasn't I? Three times in one night, if memory serves. But guess what, Christopher, a man reaps what he sows...'

He turned away from her, clawing at the air in frustration, crazy with rage. For a minute, she thought he was going to explode, but when he turned to face her once more, he looked hollow, pale, defeated.

'It's Christmas in a week, for God's sake,' he said, his voice cracking. 'But Penny won't allow me in the house, won't let me see the boys.'

'You could always stay here.'

'Oh, go to hell. I wouldn't piss on you if you were on fire, you stupid cow.'

Olivia was rocked back, she'd never heard him speak like this to *anyone*, least of all her.

'What the hell were you thinking, going round there, telling her everything? We could have worked it out...'

'Except we couldn't, could we?' Olivia retorted acidly. 'You had your fun, then the minute things got complicated, you ran home. Well, it appears you're no longer welcome there...'

'You'll pay for this,' he ranted. 'Penny, my boys, they're all I've got in the world. And if I lose them because of your bitterness, your sadness—'

'Oh, get lost, Christopher,' Olivia replied calmly, slamming the door in his face.

A moment's silence, then the hammering resumed. Olivia leaned against the wall, exhausted and miserable, cursing her fate, each blow going right through her. Maybe this *was* partially her fault but, really, did she deserve this? Why was it always *she* who ended up on the losing side?

And why, despite everything, did she still love him?

Chapter 108

He stole along the corridor, hardly making a sound. Jack's naked feet kissed the floorboards as he flitted down the hallway, peering first into the kitchen, then into the living room. He was almost certain he was alone, but he had to be sure, memories of Olivia's unannounced visit the other morning fresh in his mind. He couldn't be surprised, not today.

Having explored every room, Jack hurried into the front room, teasing the drawn curtains apart to peer into the road. No sign of her battered Corsa, nor any sign of the woman herself, which came as a massive relief. In his mind's eye, Jack had visions of her bursting through the door, pointing the finger at him, exposing him. But the suburban street was quiet and still. The security cameras were rolling front and back, but they were facing outwards, of course, searching for intruders. Inside, he was safe from their scrutiny.

Pivoting, Jack retraced his steps to the kitchen, crossing the floor quickly and heaving up the loose linoleum. Moments later, he was sitting at the table, the iPad set up in front of him. He navigated the web quickly, disappearing ever deeper into its reaches, until he was once more in the chat room. Now he paused, his breathing short and erratic, his heart pumping. Would anyone have responded? Had anyone seen 'Dawn's' message? If so, had they gone for the bait? The anticipation, was almost too much to bear, so he opened up his inbox. A moment's delay as it buffered, then suddenly it sprang into life, Jack gasping as it did so. Overnight Dawn had received over five hundred messages, most of them with files attached. His fingers trembled as he opened up the first one, ignoring the message, immediately clicking play on the file. A mundane scene sprang to life on his screen – a gloomy bedroom in which a man and a woman stood over a young child who now turned to look up at the camera with wide, frightened eyes.

Barely able to breathe, his senses exploding, Jack leaned back in his chair, slowly sliding his hand inside his pyjama trousers.

Chapter 109

They were having the time of their lives. The toy shop was full of festive gifts, packed to the rafters with talking dolls, futuristic robots and cuddly dinosaurs that roared when you squeezed them. Courtney wandered past the endless displays, seemingly as transfixed as her baby girl, who cooed, pointed and shrieked. They seemed lost in the wonder – the lights, the colours, the Christmas music – but Mike saw none of it. He had eyes only for them.

For mother and child, Christmas had come early this year. They had already visited Primark and H&M, sending staff members off in search of unusual sizes whilst Courtney ferreted out items whose security tags were loose. Six, seven, possibly more items had been concealed in the bottom of the buggy; Mike couldn't be exactly sure of the number as he had to remain at a discreet distance, but he knew it was an impressive tally. Now the pair had moved onto the toy shop and Courtney was at it again, seeking out the smaller, non-tagged items, slipping them into her coat pocket. Even from a distance, Mike marvelled at her proficiency – the probationer knew instinctively where the CCTV cameras were and how to angle both the buggy and her body to conceal her actions. At this rate, all her Christmas shopping would be completed within a morning, with not a penny spent.

Her mission accomplished, Courtney now left the shop, smiling sweetly at the security guard. He clearly liked the look of her, smiling knowingly back and offering a wink, little knowing what manner of person she was, what barbaric cruelty she was capable of. To him it was all part of the day's entertainment and for Courtney too, it seemed, who threw a flirtatious look over her shoulder as she strolled away. For one terrible moment, Mike thought she might have clocked *him*, but then she carried on her way, apparently unconcerned. Reminding himself to take more care, not to get distracted, Mike continued his pursuit, following her into a men's fashion discount store, where she set about sourcing more items, presumably for her boyfriend. Once more she set to the task with alacrity, never giving a moment's thought to the fact that she was out with her child, that she might potentially be apprehended or arrested. She had a job to do and went to it with great enthusiasm and zero fear, searching diligently for a pair of designer jeans with a loose tag.

As he watched her, Mike was transported back to the trial, where her lawyers had made great play of the extreme deprivation and emotional neglect she'd allegedly endured as a child. They claimed that Courtney had had to steal to eat, to thieve school uniform from Asda in order to attend her local primary. Her lawyer had played on the jury's heartstrings, casting the young killer as a downtrodden artful dodger, surviving by her wits, doing what she had to to survive, even in the teeth of violence, abuse and cruelty. But she'd never appeared like that to *him*. To him, it seemed obvious that this was an act, that Courtney Turner was a bad seed. Someone who revelled in disregarding the rules that everyone else lived by, part of a family who, in a euphemism often used during the trial, were 'well known to the authorities'. The defence counsel had successfully woven their web, fooling the gullible, bleeding-heart jurors, but it was all a tissue of lies, a smokescreen. Courtney Turner was a born thief, liar and killer, who never showed any remorse for her wickedness, who knew how to play the system to ensure that she always got away scot-free.

From his viewpoint behind a rack of leather jackets, Mike watched as Courtney sauntered from the store, sharing a joke with a female member of staff, the latter utterly unaware that the young mum had at least three pairs of jeans concealed in her buggy. For Mike this exchange was emblematic of Courtney's entire life, committing crimes without conscience, then smiling as she evaded censure or punishment. She had sailed through life thus far, laughing at authority, doing exactly as she pleased, plumbing the depths of criminality and depravity without ever being called to account.

But that ended today. Someone was wise to her this time – finally this devious young woman was about to get her comeuppance. Mike smiled to himself as he watched her stroll along the street with her ill-gotten gains. Courtney was in good spirits, looking forward to the festive celebrations, high on life and love, little realizing that this year Mike had a very special Christmas present to give her.

Chapter 110

'Are you out of your mind? Do you really think I'm capable of plotting someone's murder?'

Guy Chambers was puce, outraged to find himself in the interview suite under formal caution, after a sleepless night in the cells.

'I'm a government minister, for God's sake. At the *Ministry of Justice*. I'd have to be stark raving mad to get caught up in something like this.'

'Well, insanity is a potential plea, but that's for further down the line,' Chandra replied, amused to see Chambers' shocked response. 'For now, I'd like to focus on the evidence.'

'I've told you I've never seen this phone before in my life.'

Chambers gestured dismissively to the table, on which lay the recovered Samsung phone encased in an evidence bag. Eyeballing Chandra, he blew his nose and pointedly tossed the tissue into the bin, as if suggesting she could do the same with her 'evidence'.

'So you're categorically denying that the Samsung Galaxy that we retrieved from a public dustbin near your flat in Pimlico belongs to you?'

'Absolutely.'

'You'll go on record confirming it's not yours?'

425

'Yes! How many times do I have to say it?'

'Then could you explain how we found your DNA on it?'

Chambers stared at her, aghast.

'That's not possible.'

'An attempt *has* been made to clean it, but we found traces of your DNA on both the battery *and* the battery compartment.'

'You're bluffing, this is nonsense...'

'Do I look like I'm bluffing?'

Cornered, Chambers turned to his lawyer, but the latter looked as worried as his client.

'If you want us to step outside, so you can consult with your lawyer, prepare some kind of formal statement...'

'I'm not going to give you any statement, except to say that I've done nothing wrong,' Chambers protested angrily.

'The evidence suggests otherwise. My working assumption is that you feared you were close to being exposed, were perhaps concerned that you were under surveillance, so you got rid of the phone as quickly as possible, cleaning it up, then dumping it on your run to work.'

Chambers looked stunned; the fact that Chandra knew his routine, the route he took to work, had clearly unnerved him.

'Do you deny it?' Chandra asked, pressing home the advantage.

'Completely. I have nothing to do with either these leaks or these crimes and you can't prove that I did.'

'Except we now have physical evidence to go with the growing body of circumstantial evidence, placing you in the frame. You were at the conference where Willis's details were leaked. You were near Oxford Circus when Baynes's were divulged. You were in Reading for the Emily Lawrence security breach.'

'You've been through all this already and it didn't wash then, so—'

'Plus, we now have information suggesting a link to *another leak,*' Chandra continued, ignoring his interruption. 'We've just learned that details of the whereabouts and identity of Courtney Turner were leaked to Mike Burnham three days ago.'

'So what?'

'So the message was sent from *this phone*, whilst the caller was in the vicinity of the Ministry of Justice.'

Chambers stared at her, poleaxed. Concerned, his lawyer attempted to intervene.

'Mr Chambers, I think it might be wise for us to take a break, discuss these developments...'

Chambers waved away this intervention, but seemed unsettled and distressed.

'Guy, I told you yesterday that you were a key suspect,' Chandra continued, keeping up the pressure. 'My conviction of your guilt, your complicity in these crimes, has only strengthened in the interim. Last night, Ian Blackwell, administrator of the vigilante website Justice Never Sleeps was apprehended at King's Cross Station. He is currently being interviewed by one of my colleagues, but has already told us about his arrangement with you, describing how you worked together to whip up public hysteria and incite mob violence.'

Chambers stared at her, stunned by this unexpected development.

'His testimony, plus the recovery of your phone, makes it an open and shut case as far as I'm concerned. We're talking misconduct in public office, conspiracy to commit murder, incitement, the list goes on. You're looking at the end of your career – a major, public scandal, not to mention a sizeable jail term. Whichever way you look at it, you're staring down the barrel, so I would suggest it is in your interests to be open and honest with us. Co-operation will be noted, reciprocated and will definitely make life easier for you. But if you fail to help us, if you hold out on me, I will throw the book at you.'

She let her words hang in the air, watching with satisfaction as Chambers stared at the table, fidgeting nervously. His macho posturing, his sneer of superiority had vanished. Now he looked like the world was closing in on him.

'Guy? What can you tell us?'

Her tone was deliberately softer now and it seemed to have the desired effect.

'Look, I want it put on record,' Chambers rasped, his voice cracking. 'That I had nothing to do with the recent leaks, these terrible murders...'

Chandra tried to intervene, but Chambers raised his voice, talking over her.

'...but, yes, I have had contact in the past with Ian Blackwell.'

There it was, the admission they'd been waiting for.

'He... we... well, we share the same world view. And he had a licence, an anonymity that allowed him to prosecute our shared agenda without any repercussions. As such I... I offered him snippets of information for him to publish on his site.'

'Information about probationers? Ex-offenders and the like?'

There was a pause, then Chambers nodded solemnly.

'And this information led to real world consequences? Attacks and so on?'

Another curt nod.

'Who? Who did you "out"?'

'No one major, no one well known. Sex offenders, rapists, people who should have been known to the community, but who'd gone off grid, or who'd fooled the Probation Service...'

'How long? How long have you been working with Blackwell?'

'Two years or so. He contacted me out of the blue one day and it went from there.'

'And this led directly to these latest leaks?'

'No.'

'You and Blackwell decided to step things up a gear, expose the very worst of society, those monsters that you felt had got away with it.'

'No, it wasn't me.'

'Guy, you admitted earlier that you felt these people – Willis, Baynes, Slater – deserved what they got, deserved summary justice. Now you've admitted to having active contact with a vigilante group who are directly linked to the exposure of these infamous criminals. Your DNA is on a phone that was used to reveal both confidential information regarding ex-offenders *and* a recent image of Emily Lawrence to Justice Never Sleeps and yet you're *still* denying that you are the source of these leaks?'

'Absolutely. Look, I should never have had any contact with Blackwell. I bitterly regret that I did. But I am *not* responsible for these attacks.'

'The science doesn't lie, Guy. We have your DNA on the phone.'

'It's *not* mine, I've never seen it before, I swear.'

'Look, we're going round in circles here,' Chandra interrupted. 'So I'm going to cut to the chase. Guy Chambers, I am arresting you on suspicion of committing misconduct in public office, specifically the passing of highly confidential information to members of the public and known vigilante groups. You do not have to say anything, but it may harm your defence if you do not mention something you later rely on in court.'

Chambers stared at her, mute, ashen. For a moment, Chandra thought he might faint, but as she rose to leave, the suspect rallied once more, grabbing her arm and whispering fiercely:

'It wasn't me, I swear. I've been set up. I'm *innocent.*'

Chapter III

Once the world has condemned you, there's no going back. You are branded for life, tainted by your crimes, forever a pariah amongst angels. Even when you've been badly mistreated, when you might expect a kind word or a modicum of sympathy, there is none. You are damned and your role is to suffer.

Emily Lawrence knew that she should feel glad. Against the odds, she was alive. Bound and helpless, the flames licking around her, she'd stared annihilation in the face, part of her seeing the justice in her fiery death. And yet, in those last moments, she had fought, throwing herself against the buckling door, crashing out onto the cold earth beyond. Her frantic probation officers had been on hand, throwing blankets over her, extinguishing the flames, tending to her wounds, keeping her conscious until the ambulance arrived. Miraculously, she had cheated death, but any elation she felt at her survival swiftly dissipated as the agony set in. She had burns from head to foot, and though she knew they were not life-changing injuries, the pain was still unimaginable. It was impossible to rest, impossible to lie still, her skin appearing to revolt against her, seething, protesting, blistering as if she was still being attacked by the flames. She was drugged up to the eyeballs of course, but this hardly helped, rendering her dizzy and nauseous to boot. Emily was a mess, battered, bruised and burnt, but it wasn't her injuries that really stung.

Emily had noted it when she first came round in the private recovery room; the nurses and doctors stealing surreptitious glances at her as they dressed her wounds and checked her vital signs. There was no pretence anymore – Emily Lawrence was gone, destroyed in that inferno. She was Janet Slater now. Evil Janet Slater. A figure of curiosity and intrigue, the baby killer who'd got what was coming to her. Faces passed by the door, peering inside, before being moved on by the uniformed officer outside. Marianne had insisted that his presence was to protect her from further attacks, as her brother Robert was still at large, but Emily saw through this charade. That officer was stationed at her door to protect the rest of the hospital from *her*.

It seemed preposterous, but it was true. The maternity unit was on the same floor, just a short walk away and there was no question of the hospital allowing a convicted child killer in their midst without some form of additional protection. It beggared belief; to take even one step would be exquisite agony for Emily, yet still she needed a guard? What did they think she was going to do? Run down the corridor and torch the maternity unit? It was outrageous, twisted, mocking her decades-long mission to atone for her crimes, yet the censure, the curiosity, the disgust was written on many of the faces that passed. She railed at them for their lack of pity, but in truth would have happily endured their silent judgement if Sam, the one person who really mattered, was on hand to offer her compassion, understanding and sympathy. Everything she'd done over the last two days, everything she'd ever done had been to secure his love, to help him flourish and grow. The rest of it was just noise, the jet wash of a life badly lived, which she could stomach, even dismiss, if her one true love showed her even a modicum of tenderness. She ached for his presence, just the sight of him, a simple smile or gesture enough to make all her pain, all her sacrifices worthwhile. But as yet there was no sign of him. On the nurse's last visit, Emily had summoned her courage, asking her if anyone had been in contact with the hospital, if she'd had any visitors asking about her condition. The middle-aged nurse, plump and judgmental, had taken great pleasure in looking her up and down, before replying:

'No. No one at all.'

Chapter 112

He couldn't believe his eyes.

Sam had risen late, after another poor night's sleep. His new room was strange, the bed uneven and he was plagued with visions of his mother, nightmares in which she came to him with a new story of deception and heartache. It was a horrific experience, his shock, hurt and anger feeling both real and powerful every time she unburdened herself, his pain constantly recycled and reinforced. Waking, he'd felt listless and unhappy, unsure in the cold light of day what he felt about his mother now, whether he wanted her fond farewell last night to be the final goodbye.

Rising, he'd descended to the kitchen to find the table groaning with shopping bags. His father had already been out and about, cutting a swathe through the men's fashion stores in Maidenhead and was keen to display the fruits of his labour.

'I think I got through seven or eight stores,' Paul boasted proudly. 'First person in most of them, so I had a clear run. Got jeans, t-shirt, sweats, some shirts, all the fashion items a young man about town needs.'

'It must have cost you a fortune, Dad. You shouldn't have.'

He meant it. Sam knew Paul and Sandra weren't flush and that this represented a considerable outlay.

'Ah, don't worry about it. Who am I going to spend my money on if not you? I know you had to leave a lot of stuff behind, and I didn't want you to suffer. None of this is your fault.'

Sam ignored the unsubtle dig, opening a JD sports bag and pulled out a hoodie.

'I wasn't a hundred per cent sure about sizes, so why don't you try them on? If any of them don't fit, or are the wrong style, we can take them back, make a little trip into town together. I'll clear out the spare room later, get my stuff out of the wardrobe so you can make the place your own, eh?'

'Thanks, Dad, that's really kind.'

Waving away his thanks, Paul gathered up the bags.

'Go on, then, take them upstairs, then I'll bring tea and toast up in a minute, if you like?'

Taking the bags, Sam padded back upstairs, slipping into the small guest room. Staying here didn't seem natural somehow, but he appreciated everything his dad was doing to make him feel welcome, so it was only right to humour him. Popping the bags on the single bed, Sam pulled off his pyjama top, tugging a Puma t-shirt from the nearest bag. He made to put it on, then paused, catching his reflection in the wardrobe mirror. He looked pale and gangly as he always did, his ribs poking through, but that wasn't what grabbed his attention. No, it was the long thin scar on his abdomen which caught his eye.

For a moment, he didn't move, staring at the pink scar tissue that stood out so clearly on his milky white skin. Now he found himself running his finger over it, taking in the ridges he knew so well, his mind awash with memories. He remembered being rushed to hospital, the terrible pain, his confusion and fear, but he also recalled the constant presence of his mother, clutching his hand, stroking his cheek, bathing him in her love…

The t-shirt fell to the floor as the young man suddenly crumpled onto the bed. Unbidden, his mum had come to him and now he couldn't resist, resting his head in his hands and weeping bitterly.

Chapter 113

They were locked together, bound by an invisible cord born of anguish, suffering and fury. Courtney had not been more than thirty feet from Mike the whole day, the pair of them locked in a macabre dance; murderer and victim moving with effortless synchronicity through Colchester city centre. As yet, the young woman appeared unaware that she was being tailed, though she definitely appeared more wary now, following a phone call which had clearly left her rattled.

The young mum had abandoned her shopping and was heading home, pushing the buggy fast along the streets, leading Mike away from the city centre. Occasionally Mike would cast nervous glances behind him, fearful that he was walking into a trap, that her burly boyfriend would descend upon him, pinning him to the floor, raining blows down on him. But there was no sign of any danger, nor any evidence that Courtney was wise to him, as he feared in his darker fantasies.

He kept his head down and his hood up, occasionally feigning interest in his lifeless phone, making sure to avoid the more obvious CCTV cameras. He had bought the heavy parka jacket and faded jeans from a charity shop, paying cash to avoid leaving a trail. As soon as the deed was done, he'd torch them, leaving no trace of the hooded figure shadowing the mother and child's every move. It was all going to plan so far, despite his persistent fears. Now he just needed the opportunity to strike.

This was proving more elusive, Courtney sticking to busy residential streets. Mike stuck close by, tense and alert, adrenaline coursing through him. He was getting impatient now, his stomach moaning, his mouth parched, but there was no question of relenting. He had received three phone messages from the police now, each seemingly more urgent than the last, urging him to contact them without delay. He had no idea if they knew anything, if they had discovered that he had received confidential info about Courtney Turner, but he felt instinctively that his window to strike was narrowing, given the marked change in Courtney's behaviour.

Continuing her escape from the city centre, Courtney made her way down the back streets, pulling away from the throng of Christmas shoppers. They were in a heavily residential area now, meaning his presence was more conspicuous, so he hung back, treading as lightly as he could, praying that his presence would remain undetected. Courtney turned one corner, then another, bumping the buggy over the uneven paving stones, humming happily to herself. As each street passed by, as they got closer and closer to home, Mike's fears grew. Would she confound him at this late stage, unwittingly foiling his plans? It seemed unthinkable that she could be so lucky, yet why not? Everything else had gone her way so far. Why should today be any different? Even so, the thought was too much to bear. It was as if the last ten years had been building to this moment, this day. Surely he could not return home empty-handed? And if he did, what then?

Mike was lost in dark thoughts, wracked with visions of failure and despair, but now he got a break. A pulse of adrenaline, of hope, surged through him as he saw Courtney come to a halt outside a newsagent. Arresting his own progress, Mike bent down to tie his shoelace, watching on surreptitiously as Courtney flicked on the buggy's brake, before hurrying into the shop, clutching a used scratch card. He couldn't believe it. This was it, the moment he'd been waiting for? But could he do it? Could he really go through with it?

His head was throbbing, his hands shaking with fear. But even though he could feel the sweat crawling down his spine, he did not hesitate, walking confidently forward, clicking off the buggy's brake and silently wheeling the gurgling infant away.

Chapter 114

'We have to leave now?' Jack asked, shocked.

Olivia stared at her charge. He'd been flustered when she arrived, distracted and ill at ease. Now he was having problems processing simple instructions.

'Yes, we need to go now, straight away…'

He nodded, but still appeared hesitant.

'Jack, we had an *arrangement*,' Olivia continued, annoyed. 'OK, so I'm a bit early, but you knew I was coming. So can we just get cracking? We've got to rendezvous with the team at Tottenham Hale Station in half an hour, so grab everything, clothes, books, toiletries, and toss them in your bag. You can leave your old ID and house keys here – we'll deal with those later. Well, come on, vamos!'

Olivia ushered him towards the door. He hesitated, a wan smile on his face, then turned to leave. But as he did so, he shot a fleeting glance to the other side of the room. It was so quick, blink and you'd miss it, but Olivia saw it plain as day. She didn't react, however, smiling and chivvying him along, frogmarching him into the bedroom. But as he pulled his holdall from under his bed and started packing, Olivia retraced her footsteps to the kitchen.

Hurrying over to the far side of the room, she yanked open

the fridge, checking out the shelves, the freezer compartment, the vegetable drawers, before giving up. Then she tried easing the fridge away from the wall, to see if anything was hidden behind, but here too she drew a blank. It was as she was pushing the fridge back against the wall that she spotted it – a small patch of lino that had come away from the floor. Instantly she dropped to her knees, clawing it up to reveal the bare boards below. Convinced she was onto something, she teased the nearest board open, lifting it to reveal a bag hidden in the void beneath. Sweating, tense, she removed the bag and, unzipping it, tipped the contents on to the ground. An iPad and stand clattered noisily on to the floor, the sound echoing off the bare walls. Instantly, anger flared in her; Olivia's suspicions, her convictions, proved right.

Now she knew why Jack had been so unwilling to leave.

Chapter 115

He hammered on the door, angry and frustrated. DS Gary Buckland was not a man known for his patience and he was starting to lose it now. He and his colleagues had been hunting Mike Burnham for nearly forty-eight hours now without getting so much as a sniff of their quarry. They had visited his house twice, left countless messages, gatecrashed a family gathering at his ex-wife's house and got chapter and verse from his former boss, Simon, about Mike's lack of focus and loss of drive. But still they were no closer to finding the man himself, which he knew would enrage Chandra Dabral.

Gary hammered at the door again, before pressing down on the bell, taking out his frustrations on the lifeless house. To his surprise, he suddenly heard movement and his hopes were momentarily raised ... but it was just Burnham's neighbour poking his head out of his front door, aggrieved and unhappy.

'What's going on, mate? If he's not there, he's not there.'

Gary stared at the man for a moment, then casually removed his warrant card, holding it up for inspection.

'It's a police matter, sir,' he replied witheringly. 'So if you don't mind ...'

'Sure, absolutely,' the man replied quickly, chastened. 'You carry on. Only he's not there, so you might be wasting your time, that's all.'

'You know for a fact he's out.'

'Yeah, he took off in his car early this morning, hasn't been back since. He normally parks right outside, so you can see he's not here. He drives a dark blue—'

'VW saloon, yes I know. Thank you, we can take it from here.'

'Just trying to help…' the neighbour grumbled, retreating.

Gary watched him go, then turned away. For all his brave talk, he was stumped as to what to do next. They could put out a search on his car, hope that maybe traffic cams had picked him up, but there'd been no sign of Burnham in the obvious places, which concerned him. For weeks, months now, Burnham had been a man of rigorous routine, colleagues confirming that he went from home to work and back again, with only the occasional diversion to the supermarket. So why had he suddenly disappeared off the face of the earth, arriving home late at night, only to burn off first thing? Why wasn't he answering his emails, returning their calls? He surely knew by now that they wanted to talk to him urgently, so why was he working so hard to avoid contact?

Gary headed back to his car, full of dark thoughts. They had pulled Burnham's mobile log, obtaining an extraordinary warrant to access message content, in the process discovering that their worst fears had been realized. Mike Burnham *had* been sent details of Courtney Turner's whereabouts and he'd told no one about it. Not family, not friends, not even Graham Ellis, who still took a paternalistic interest in him. Factor in his erratic behaviour at work and the picture seemed clear – a grieving, bitter man, whose equilibrium had been destroyed by the discovery that his daughter's killer lived less than a hour's drive away.

The team had immediately contacted Essex Police and a team was being sent round to Turner's new address now, but Gary was beginning to wonder if they were already too late. It was Friday today, yet Mike Burnham had received this information on Tuesday morning. What had he been doing ever since? What had he been plotting? Was it possible that he might be considering something dangerous, something reckless? It seemed crazy, as Burnham was not on the face of it a violent man, but his determination to avoid police interference, to remain below the radar, set Buckland's alarm bells ringing.

Where the *hell* was he?

Chapter 116

'Where's my baby? Where's my baby?'

Courtney scanned the street desperately, shrieking wildly as she searched for Jailan. She had been right here, just outside the shop and now she was gone.

She felt faint, giddy, couldn't believe this was happening. She'd only been gone for a minute, the buggy left securely parked on a safe, suburban street, yet in that split second it had vanished. Her first thought had been that the brake had failed. Her heart was in her mouth as she'd raced down the road, expecting to see her sweet baby marooned in her buggy in the middle of the road ... but the street was empty.

Panicking, Courtney had run the whole length of the street, checking between the parked cars, then back along the other side of the road. All sorts of possible scenarios presented themselves. Had Jailan somehow got out of her buggy? But, if so, where was she? She could only crawl so couldn't get far. Had some well-meaning old lady seen the buggy and wheeled it away to the nearest police station? That was possible, of course, but they would have to have moved like lightning to be out of sight by the time Courtney returned to the street. In fact, they would have to have taken the buggy almost immediately she

444

stepped into the shop and that didn't make any sense at all, unless someone had deliberately taken it...

Courtney felt giddy, panic overwhelming her, as a dark thought began to take hold. Still she screamed out, hollering for her baby girl, hoping for a response, for some sign of her, even if just a cry for help, but there was nothing. The street was deserted, lifeless.

What the hell should she do? Should she call her probation officer back? Ring the police? It was as Courtney was debating this that her phone started buzzing. Pulling it from her coat pocket, she stared at the number, hoping that this call would bring salvation, some answer to this terrifying riddle. She didn't recognize the caller, but the coincidence of the timing seemed too much to ignore, so she answered it without hesitation.

'Hello? Who is this?' she demanded, breathless, panicky.

There was a brief pause, then a man replied, hissing words that chilled her blood.

'Hello, Courtney. It's Mike Burnham.'

Chapter 117

'What name, please?'

'Margaret Withers. She was brought in from a house fire in Bedford last night.'

The receptionist checked her system, before looking up at Robert Slater, confused.

'You're sure she was brought to this hospital?'

Robert made a play of checking his phone.

'Lister Hospital, burns unit. That's what my brother said anyway...'

'Well, I can't see any trace of her on the system. You can try up on the ward itself, see if they know anything. Ask at the main reception on the third floor.'

'Thank you.'

Robert Slater was already on the move, keeping his head down to avoid the numerous CCTV cameras in the lobby of the busy Stevenage hospital. Crossing to the lift bank, he stabbed the call button, looking with distaste at the gaggle of visitors and patients waiting patiently alongside him. Normally Robert avoided hospitals like the plague – he'd spent far too much time in them as a kid, thanks to his father's violent rages – but he would make an exception today, in order to finish the job he'd started last night.

The lift doors pinged open and he stepped inside. As the lift slowly filled up, then began to ascend, Robert felt inside his coat pocket for his knife, running his finger along the nasty, serrated edge. It was a hunting knife, weathered but sturdy, the one thing he retained from his childhood that he had any affection for, a fleeting moment of generosity from his father. He was glad of its company now. At least you knew where you were with a knife.

How he now cursed his decision to use fire as his weapon of choice. At the time it had seemed a fitting method of revenge – Janet would suffer the same fate as Gwyneth and Susan. But fire was unpredictable, as were people's responses to it. He'd felt sure he'd done enough to ensure Janet's death – tying her up, locking the door behind him – but had watched on in horror, as his younger sister had exploded from the blazing caravan, tumbling onto the icy grass. Though her vocal agony was gratifying, Robert had known instantly that Janet wouldn't die, that he had *failed*.

Robert had fled the campsite in the darkest of moods. His family had entrusted this mission to him and he had let them down. Embittered, adrift, he made it to his car and sped away, eventually finding sanctuary in a remote layby, drinking whisky and cursing his luck, until the listless dawn brought him to his senses. Knowing Janet's burns must have been extensive, he had driven straight to the Lister, the nearest hospital to the caravan site and the biggest in Hertfordshire. The police presence in the car park and lobby had convinced him he was on the right track and immediately he'd felt his desire for revenge rekindle. All he needed after that was a strong coffee and a moment or two to sober up, before he abandoned his car, pulling his cap down low and moving purposefully towards the main entrance. Janet wouldn't escape him a second time.

The lift doors slid open and Robert stepped out onto the third floor. Following the signs, he made his way to the burns unit, waiting until the nurse was distracted, before slipping past reception into the ward. This was a large unit, with three corridors splitting off from the main junction, but Robert knew instantly where Janet was being treated, the solitary uniformed police officer standing guard outside her room trumpeting her presence.

Determined not to attract unnecessary attention, Robert peered down the middle corridor, pretending to check out the room numbers, as if attempting to get his bearings. All the while, he kept an eye on the corridor to his left, watching on as a couple of nurses brushed past him, heading on their break. Another darted look reassured him that the left-hand corridor was now completely deserted, save for the lone police officer.

Taking a deep breath, Robert turned, then groaning loudly, staggered down Janet's corridor. He clawed at the wall, swaying wildly on his feet, taking a couple of steps towards her room, before collapsing to the ground. Now he started to convulse, his limbs flailing wildly, as he began to choke. There was a moment's pause, a seeming lifetime in which Robert thought his plan had failed, then he heard urgent footsteps hurrying towards him. Moments later, he clocked the PC's concerned face as he bent down to check on him.

'Are you OK, mate?'

Instantly, Robert stopped convulsing, grabbing the startled police officer by his collar, and pressing the knife point hard into his belly.

'You make a sound and I'll gut you like a fish. Understand?'

The shocked PC nodded, white as a sheet.

'Do as I say and you'll be fine. If not...'

With this threat hanging in the air, Robert Slater clambered to his feet and, pushing the PC ahead of him, marched his helpless captive along the corridor. Ahead, Robert spied a storeroom and he made straight for it, wrenching open the door and shoving the police officer inside. Alarmed, the young man tried to turn, but Robert was too quick, striking him hard on the back of the head with the butt of his knife. Stunned, the policeman collapsed to the floor and Robert was swiftly upon him, forcing a handkerchief into his mouth, before yanking his arms behind his back. The young PC struggled but was powerless to resist now, as Robert pulled a length of nylon cord from his jacket pocket and began to bind his hands.

Chapter 118

'Do it, Jack. Do it or I swear I'll call it in right now.'

Olivia had dragged Jack from his bedroom, confronting him with the evidence, which now lay on the kitchen table. Her client stared at the iPad, as if seeing a ghost.

'I swear I'm telling the truth – I've never seen that before.'

'Don't. Just *don't!*' Olivia spat back, jabbing an accusing finger in his face. 'I have bent over backwards to help you. I've argued your case, stuck up for you, covered for you, when I should have reported you. And *this* is how you repay me? You didn't want to go this morning because you didn't want to leave this behind. I know it's yours, so just open it up.'

Still he hesitated, looking pale and sweaty, so Olivia lost it, grabbing his arm and dragging him towards the machine.

'Get off, you're hurting me.'

'I don't give a fuck,' Olivia replied grimly. 'Open it now.'

Slumping into the chair, Jack whimpered slightly, making no effort to comply. Enraged, Olivia slapped him hard on the top of the head, making him jump, even as he emitted a low groan. And now, finally, he leant forward, typing in six digits at lightning speed. Immediately a chat room sprung up, to the left of which was an inbox, which appeared to be rapidly filling with messages, the number of received items rising all the time.

'Is this you?'

Jack nodded morosely, staring at the table.

'So these messages are all for you?'

Another sullen nod.

'Go to Sent Items.'

'Olivia, please, I've opened it up ...'

'Get out the way, I'll do it myself.'

Shouldering him aside, Olivia opened Sent Items, to discover there was only one item there. Clicking on it, she began to read:

'Hi. My name is Dawn. I'm a single mum of a three-year-old girl who is ripe for ...'

She petered out. Humiliated, Jack turned to her, imploring:

'I'm sorry, Olivia, I didn't want to do it ...'

He didn't get any further, Olivia striking him hard on the cheek, knocking him off his chair and sending him crashing to the ground. Shocked, he struggled back onto his knees to find Olivia looming over him.

'What the hell have you done? All that money, all that time spent on your rehabilitation and you do *this*? Within days of your release? What the fuck, Jack?'

'I'm sorry, I'm sorry ...'

He was sobbing heavily now, his face in his hands, pathetic, defeated, exposed.

'I trusted you, you piece of ...'

She just about reined herself in, aware now that she was shouting. Gathering herself, she hissed:

'I am tempted, *sorely* tempted, to leave you here, Jack. To abandon you right now, let you take your chances on your own ...'

'Please, no.'

'But unlike you, I'm a woman of my word. So I will get you out of here, I will get you somewhere safe. And then we will deal with *this*.'

He remained on his knees, but reached out a hand to her, in penitence and submission, but she batted it angrily away.

'But be under no illusion, Jack, that things will be very different from now on. We have tried to help you, to offer you a fresh start in life, taken you at your word when you said you wanted to change, to be a better person. And now what do we find?'

Still he avoided her gaze, but she grabbed his chin, forcing him to face her.

'That you've been playing us all along.'

Chapter 119

Chandra Dabral paced her office, anxious and impatient. Following her interview with Chambers, she'd held a lengthy discussion with his lawyer, emphasizing the benefits to her client of a full and frank confession. Chandra's message had been stark, but the response from Chambers' lawyer had been disappointing, the latter confirming that her client continued to protest his innocence. Frustrated, Chandra had sent the brief back into the interview suite to talk her client round, but as of yet there had been no white smoke. What was taking so long? What was there to talk about? Detective Superintendent Draper had already called her twice this morning asking for progress and she was running out of excuses to stall him.

The sound of a knock on her door made Chandra look up expectantly, but her face fell when she saw that it was not the duty sergeant.

'Whatever it is, it's going to have to wait,' she told DC Reeves, as the junior officer crossed the room towards her.

'I'm not sure it can.'

'Later, DC Reeves. I'm at a critical stage in the interview with Guy Chambers...'

'Which is why you need to see this.'

A feeling of unease stole over Chandra, as her colleague handed her a fresh witness statement.

'Who's Sol Harrison?' Chandra demanded, reading the signature on the statement.

'A busker, who lives and works in Reading.'

'Go on,' Chandra replied, cautiously.

'So we've been trying to work out the exact date and time that the photo of Emily Lawrence was taken in Reading,' DC Reeves explained. 'As you suggested, we published the photo online, in the newspapers, asking the public if they recognized themselves in the image. Loads of people got in touch, but this guy spotted himself in the photo.'

'But there aren't any blokes in the photo,' Chandra countered impatiently. 'Just some old girl with her shopping trolley and a young mum.'

'It's not obvious at first,' Reeves countered, flipping over the statement to reveal a printout of the photo. 'But here in the shop window you can see someone reflected. He's got his back to the shop front, but—'

'You can see his outline, plus the neck of his guitar,' Chandra overlapped, spotting it.

'Anyhow, he moves around a lot, busking at different sites in Reading, but he knows for certain that he was busking outside Tesco Metro on the morning of 2nd December.'

'Is that from memory, or do we have anything more concrete? Parking receipts, travel tickets?'

'Better than that. He's got one of those tap and tip electronic card readers, as no one carries cash anymore. It links directly to his bank account...'

She produced a printout of his bank statement.

'...which shows the date, time and amount of all his tips.'

Chandra ran her eye down the line of transactions, zeroing in on the dates.

'So the leak was made on the fifth, but the photo of Lawrence was taken *three days earlier*. Meaning we need to put Chambers in Reading on the second of December.'

'That's the problem,' Reeves replied, sheepishly. 'Guy Chambers was in Paris that day, meeting his French counterpart. He didn't set foot in Reading on the second. That's why I wanted to talk to you.'

Chandra stared at her in shock.

'Are you *sure?*'

'Absolutely. His PA emailed me his schedule just now. It covers the whole of November and December, pinpointing exactly where Chambers was at any given moment. Plus, I looked it up online. There was a press release to coincide with his visit to Paris, a photo opportunity. Guy Chambers was *definitely* in the French capital on the second of December.'

Chandra slumped onto her desk, the air punched from her.

'I'm really sorry, guv, but I thought you ought to kn—'

'But it *must* be him,' Chandra insisted. 'His DNA is on the phone used to leak the info, to send that photo of Lawrence to Justice Never Sleeps. Are we saying someone's set him up?'

'Or he could be in league with whoever took the photo?'

Neither of which suggestion got them any further forward.

'Right, I'll talk to Chambers again,' Chandra found herself saying, even though her head was spinning. 'Tell the rest of the team – we need to go back to basics. Who was at the conference in Shepherds Bush, in Oxford Circus and in Reading on the days in question. Run the rule over everyone and anyone, I need *names.*'

As Reeves hurried off to do her bidding, Chandra leant heavily on her desk, staring down at her shoes. Was it possible that

Chambers was telling the truth? That he really *was* innocent? Breathing deeply, Chandra tried to gather herself, but her mind was doing somersaults and she felt sick. She'd wanted to finish the job today, to nail Chambers once and for all. But she was now more mystified and adrift than ever, the perpetrator of these dreadful crimes seemingly forever just out of reach.

Chapter 120

'Well, this is a sorry situation, isn't it?'

There was a glee in Jeremy Firth's tone that unnerved Christopher Parkes. He had been summoned to the eighth floor and had hurried there from his office, expecting to find Firth in foment about some fresh disaster, perhaps even about to throw in the towel. But, to Christopher's surprise, his boss seemed upbeat, even rather triumphant today.

'Have there been any developments?' Christopher demanded, trying to conceal his unease.

'In a way,' Firth teased, staring at his deputy intently.

'Is it Emily Lawrence? Has something happened?'

'No, she's perfectly fine. It's *you* I'm worried about.'

He flashed a toothy smile, which seemed to go right through Christopher.

'I had Penny on the phone this morning. She was very upset, making the most outlandish accusations.'

Christopher didn't react, but inside his nerves were jangling, his whole body pulsing with anxiety.

'According to her, you've been conducting an affair with Olivia Campbell for the last two years, as a result of which she is now pregnant.'

Christopher stared at his boss, then summoned all the shock and disappointment he could muster.

'Oh my God, I'm so sorry, Jeremy. There was no need for you to get involved in this foolishness. I'm afraid Penny has always been paranoid about Olivia, I've no idea why, and somehow has now got it into her head that we've been in some kind of relationship, which is categorically untrue. I would never be so unprofessional.'

'You deny it then?'

'Absolutely.'

'I thought you might, which is why I rang Olivia straight after. I caught her on her way to pick up Jack Walker. She confirmed *everything* your wife said.'

The blood drained from Christopher's face, as he realized that he had walked straight into an ambush.

'It puts me in a rather difficult position, Christopher,' Firth continued. 'It's not ideal timing given everything that's going on, but in the circumstances I'm going to have to ask you to consider your position.'

'You can't be serious?' Christopher blurted out.

'Oh, we don't have to make a song and dance about it. You can say you're resigning on grounds of ill health or to spend more time with your family, whatever you feel would play best for you and Penny.'

Firth smiled broadly, this pretence at sympathy paper-thin.

'You bastard,' Christopher spat back, enraged. 'You've been gunning for me from the get-go, haven't you?'

'No, Christopher, you've been gunning for *me*. Conniving with that bitch from the *Daily Mail*, trying to force me out, trying to take my chair at the top table.'

Christopher couldn't deny any of it and his mood wasn't improved as Firth concluded:

'But you've royally fucked that up now, haven't you?'

Chapter 121

What on earth was he going to say to her? What could he possibly say that would make up for the events of the last twenty-four hours?

Sam tried to keep his emotions in check as he marched along the hospital corridor, but he knew he was liable to break down at any moment. He had been riddled with guilt *before* the phone call from the Lister, alerting him to his mother's admission. Now he felt as if he'd never be able to look her in the eye again. How callous his decision to abandon her seemed, fleeing to his part-time father's house, leaving her vulnerable to an attack from her brother. Sam had run away because he'd felt overwhelmed, angry, confused, but if he'd stopped to think, if he'd *listened* to what his mother was saying, he'd have seen that she'd only ever done what she felt was best.

She hadn't wanted to lie to him, but was compelled to by the courts, by the Probation Service, and of course by her own crushing sense of guilt. He saw now how sickened she was by her past, how much she wanted to distance herself from that angry, violent little girl and who could blame her? She'd had a horrific childhood, whereas his had been warm, loving and stable. In spite of his parents' divorce, Sam had never once felt unloved or unwanted. He had said exactly that to his dad this

459

morning, whilst the latter pleaded with him not to seek out his mother at the Lister, but Sam would not be turned, his head full of memories of the tender care she'd lavished on him over the years. Being back in a hospital reminded Sam of his mum's bedside vigil before, during and after his appendix operation and he realized now how poorly he'd treated her, how badly he'd misjudged her, how dearly he wanted to make amends. He just hoped he'd be in time. He had no idea of the extent of her injuries and feared that fate might intervene once more, denying him the loving reunion he craved.

Tears sprang to Sam's eyes now, as this worrying thought took hold. Unbuttoning his coat, he wrenched it open, craving cool air. The hospital seemed so overheated, the atmosphere cloying and airless. Suddenly he felt utterly overwhelmed, the events of the last two days seeming almost unbelievable in their brutality and cruelty. The idea of his mother being attacked and left to die in that inferno was too much to bear. How terrified must she have been? How lonely and scared? And how much agony must she be in now?

Summoning his courage, Sam pressed on, guiding his uncertain steps to the reception of the third-floor burns unit. As he approached, the nurse looked up. Tugging his ID from his pocket, Sam offered it to her.

'Sam Lawrence. I think my mother's being treated here. Emily Lawrence, though it's possible you might have her down under another name...'

He hesitated to reveal her real identity, uncertain what the rules were.

'I know who you mean,' the nurse replied swiftly, studying his ID carefully, before looking up to take in his anxious features. 'But I'll have to talk to the police first, as access is restricted.'

Taking back his ID, Sam felt a small surge of optimism. If

access was being strictly controlled, then presumably his mum *must* still be alive.

'Is she OK?'

The nurse paused, arresting her progress to look back at him.

'How bad are her injuries?' Sam persisted.

'Just give me a minute, I'll be right back,' the nurse said evasively, hurrying off.

Sam swore under his breath. Did his mother have no rights anymore? Were her crimes so taboo, her existence such a closely guarded secret, that her own son wasn't allowed to know if she was dead or alive?

Sam shifted impatiently on his feet, waiting for the nurse, a police officer, someone to return and put him out of his misery. Thirty seconds passed, a minute, then finally the nurse returned, looking troubled. Fixing a smile on her face, she returned to her station, tugging her radio from her belt as she did so.

'Wait here. I just need to ...'

She didn't elaborate, talking rapidly into her radio as she hurried away towards the main body of the hospital. Her words were lost to Sam, but her manner seriously alarmed him. Something was wrong.

Once more, Sam found himself on the move, instinct propelling him forwards. Reaching a junction, he saw three corridors leading away to different parts of the ward. His mother could be in any one of these rooms, so which direction should he head in? Presumably there would be some kind of police guard in attendance, given that Robert Slater was still at large, but oddly all three corridors appeared to be deserted. Which one should he choose? Left? Centre? Right? And was he really going to go down every corridor, checking every room? Could he do that and find the right one, *before* the nurse returned?

Making a decision, Sam moved towards the central corridor.

But as he did so, movement in his peripheral vision made him stop. Someone had just stepped out of a door at the far end of the left-hand corridor. Taking a step back, Sam turned to face them, hoping they might be a police officer, a surgeon, someone who could put his mind at rest. But the figure opposite him was clearly not a professional, even though he had just exited a hospital storeroom. He was dressed in scruffy jeans and a stained parka and had a baseball cap pulled down over his face. Instantly, Sam was on edge, something about this man's appearance alarming him. The man was urgent in manner but furtive in bearing, seemingly determined to keep his face turned to the floor.

'Hello?'

Sam's voice echoed down the corridor, prompting an instant reaction. The man looked up and immediately Sam froze. The malevolent, haunted features that stared grimly back at him belonged to his uncle, Robert Slater. A man he had never met before, but whose face was now all over the news.

'What the hell are you doing here?' Sam demanded.

Slater didn't reply, clearly shocked by the sight of his nephew. Man and boy eyeballed each other, the length of the corridor between them, daring each other to make the next move. Then Slater made up his mind, tugging a blade from his pocket and racing down the corridor. Sam didn't hesitate, launching himself forwards, racing towards him. Slater was quick, skidding to a halt by the door to a private room and wrenching it open. Sam only had a split second to react and launched himself forwards, crashing into his uncle and sending them both flying backwards.

For a second the world turned upside down, then they both hit the ground, Sam crashing into the far wall. Winded, he pulled himself upright, only to see that Slater was already on his feet, waving a grim-looking knife in his face.

'Two for the price of one, eh?' he leered. 'Suits me fine.'

Slater lurched forward, thrusting the knife at Sam's throat. Darting left, Sam dodged the blow, the knife point driving into the plaster. Yanking it free, Slater lashed out wildly at him, catching Sam on the top of the shoulder. His victim had moved just in time, however, the blade slicing through cotton rather than flesh, leaving Sam unharmed. Slater blundered past, but turned quickly, swaying unsteadily on his feet, as he prepared for another attack.

'Just go,' Sam screamed. 'Go now and you might still get away.'

'But I don't *want* to get away,' Slater hissed unpleasantly. 'I want to kill that evil bitch. And unless you want to join her, I'd get out the way, sonny…'

'I'm not going anywhere,' Sam replied angrily, stepping in front of the open doorway.

'You'd risk your life for *that*?' Slater mocked, nodding towards the room. 'Don't you see it yet? Your mother is scum.'

Sam stared at his uncle, the anger inside growing with every word.

'Scum who should have been put out of her misery years ago. She killed two girls, two innocent little girls. If there was any justice, they'd have strung her up back then.'

Sam could feel his fury spiralling. Why would he not shut up?

'Oh well, better late than never, eh?'

Slater took a step towards Sam, raising his knife. He clearly expected the teenager to move out the way, to save himself, but instead Sam took three decisive steps forward and launched his head at his uncle's face. Caught off guard, Slater had no time to dodge Sam's forehead crashing into his nose. Howling in pain, Slater collapsed to the floor. Instantly Sam was upon him, batting the knife from his hand. Dazed, his uncle tried to wriggle free, but Sam had already pinned down his arms with his knees and, raising his own fist, brought it crashing down.

This time he felt Slater's nose snap, his victim screaming in pain. Adrenaline coursing through him, Sam didn't relent, raising his fist and bringing it down again, blood spraying from Slater's slack mouth.

'You're going to pay, you piece of shit!' he hissed.

Another blow landed, rocking Slater's head back against the floor.

'You're going to pay for what you did to her.'

Once more his fist connected and now his victim's eyeballs rolled upwards in their sockets, revealing a great expanse of white. Slater was clearly losing consciousness, but Sam didn't relent, roaring out his rage and agony as he rained down blow after blow. He didn't want to stop – *couldn't* stop – wanting to destroy the lowlife who had threatened his mum. But now Sam was suddenly yanked backwards, two strong arms hauling him away from the fight. Wincing in pain, Sam felt his wrists being wrenched behind him, as a breathless police officer spun him round, pressing the teenager's face hard into the wall.

Breathless, panting, Sam looked back over his shoulder, as the handcuffs bit into his skin. The pain seemed to bring him back to earth and Sam stared down at the unconscious, bleeding man on the floor in horror. What the hell had come over him? What had he *done*?

Chapter 122

The buggy bumped roughly over the uneven ground, shaking both the cheap metal frame and its unhappy occupant. Still Mike kept up the pace, wheeling it up and down the festering piles of refuse, bumping it over the discarded scrap, taking pleasure from each nasty jolt. The going wasn't easy, but there were numerous piles of mouldering rubbish on the abandoned refuse site and Mike made a point of covering them all. Years back this place would have been teeming with people, dutifully offering up their recycling, but now it was all but forgotten, deserted save for Mike and his reluctant companion.

The front wheel hit a concrete block, almost upending the buggy, but Mike dragged it back, manoeuvring it around the obstacle and onwards. If the crying baby had been unhappy before, she was distraught now, the shock of the impact doubling her growing anguish. Her cries rang out, piercing the deathly quiet of this desolate space, but they had no effect on her tormentor. Mike could hear the noise, process the ear-splitting shrieks, but it meant nothing to him, he felt nothing. Which was a good thing, given what he was about to do.

He was tiring now, sweaty and breathless, but still he didn't relent. Each time he was tempted to slow down, even stop, he saw Jessica again, being wheeled up and down those awful slag piles by a pair of gleeful girls. They had showed no mercy, no pity, delighting in Jessica's torment – filming it, for God's sake – so why should he? This anger, this hatred spurred him on and he continued to force the buggy over the rough ground even as the frame protested and the spinning wheels threatened to give way at any moment.

But now a noise nearby forced him to slow and listen. Taking his bearings, he scoured the site, spotting a solitary figure picking their way through the hole in the chain link fence. Panting, tense, he strained to see who it was. To his relief, he now recognized Courtney Turner, as she straightened up and sprinted towards him.

He made no move to descend, however, scanning the horizon for other intruders. Courtney had instantly complied with his request to join him, telling him over the phone that she would come straight away, but he wouldn't put it past her to double-cross him. Had she contacted the police? Called her boyfriend? It would be in her nature to betray him, to trick him out of natural justice, but to his relief she appeared to be completely alone.

'Please, give her back…'

Turning, he saw that Courtney was only thirty yards from the rusting pile of junk he was stationed on.

'Stay where you are!' he roared.

But still she came.

'I mean it!' he threatened. 'Stay where you are or I'll…'

Now the young mother ground to a halt, terrified of what he might do to her baby.

'Please, just let her go. She doesn't understand any of this, she hasn't done anything wrong…'

'Neither had my Jessica,' Mike hissed back. 'She'd done

nothing to you, yet you still killed her. Stoned her to death whilst she was *begging* for mercy...'

The words tore into the young woman, who flinched, as if in physical pain.

'Do you remember what she said?' Mike said, descending now, pushing the buggy roughly in front of him. 'Do you remember how Jessica *pleaded* with you to stop? I guess you must do. You and your little friend must have watched that video clip dozens of times...'

'Please, Mr Burnham, it wasn—'

'Don't you dare say my name. You've got no right to—'

'Honestly, it wasn't like that,' the young woman insisted, tearful, anguished. 'I *swear*.'

'That's *exactly* what it was like. The more Jessica begged, the more you got off on it.'

'No...'

'The more helpless she was, the more you enjoyed it.'

'I was just a fucked-up kid, I didn't know any bett—'

'Well, now you're going to feel what *she* felt,' Mike interrupted savagely. 'You're going to learn what it's like to feel utterly helpless, abandoned, tortured...'

Courtney looked up sharply, her shame, her anguish replaced by naked fear. Her eyes darted from her screaming child to her tormentor, then she took a step forward.

'I'm begging you. Don't hurt my baby. She's all I've got.'

'And what about *my* baby?' Mike screamed back.

'Please,' Courtney cried. 'I'll do whatever you want.'

She took another step towards him, desperate to be reunited with her baby. But as she did so, Mike tugged the hammer from his pocket, holding it high above the screaming child.

'Please, no...' Courtney shrieked, stretching out her hands towards him.

'You take another step and I swear I'll—'

'OK, OK...'

Whimpering, Courtney dropped to her knees, signalling her capitulation. Mike remained where he was, hammer raised, enjoying her anguish.

'What do you want? I'll do anything...' Courtney pleaded, her voice cracking.

'I want justice.'

Courtney looked up at him, wide-eyed, fearful.

'Someone must pay for Jessica's death. An eye for an eye.'

Courtney's eyes remained fixed on her screaming child, as Mike gripped the hammer hard, tensing his arm to strike.

'Not my baby, please not my baby...'

Mike raised his arm high above his head, brandishing the hammer in the air.

'No!'

Courtney lurched forward, prostrating herself at his feet, clawing at his trousers.

'She's all I've got. The only thing I've *ever* done right,' she pleaded. 'I'm begging you to take pity on her, to show mercy...'

'There's no mercy here, Courtney. We're way past that.'

'Then take me.'

Poised to strike, Mike paused, surprised by this sudden demand.

'If you have to hurt someone, hurt me. I'm the one that was responsible, I'm the one who hurt Jessica.'

Still, Mike hesitated, sensing a trap.

'You're right, she *did* beg me to stop,' Courtney continued. 'And you know what? I didn't give a fuck. In fact, I enjoyed hurting her. I'd do it all over again if I could...'

A low roaring sound was growing in Mike's ears. He knew

Courtney was goading him, playing him, but he couldn't quell his growing fury.

'I'd do anything to see that look on her face again. To hear her pathetic whining. Please stop, Courtney, *please*...'

Her words were blurring now, rage clouding Mike's senses.

'Is that what you wanted to hear?' Courtney goaded. 'Well, there I've said it. Now, do your worst...'

'With pleasure.'

Bellowing out these words, Mike stepped forward, slamming his hammer into the side of Courtney's head.

Chapter 123

They kept close to the wall, moving swiftly along the alleyway. So far, their progress had been unimpeded, the pair of them making it out the back gate of the house without a soul noticing. But both Olivia and Jack knew that the danger was ever present, so they didn't linger, walking quickly along the rear passageway that ran the length of the street.

'When are we meeting them?' Jack asked, breathing hard.

'Five minutes,' Olivia replied, shooting an anxious look at her watch.

'Where?'

'The car park at Tottenham Hale Station. It's a busy place, lots of folk around. We should be safe there.'

'Couldn't we have just got a cab, instead of creeping around like this?'

'Absolutely *not*,' Olivia returned quickly. 'No outsiders, no one we don't know. The best way to keep you alive right now is to keep this *tight*.'

Jack nodded, but said nothing, the thought of the danger he was in unnerving him, jumping now as Olivia's phone pinged loudly. He watched her closely as she read the message, her face clouding over briefly, before she slid the phone back into her pocket.

'What's the matter? What's up?'

'Nothing,' she responded curtly. 'They're running a few minutes late. But to be honest, so are we. Right, we're going to come out onto Glendale Road shortly. It's only a short walk to Tottenham Hale Station from there, but we'll be more exposed, out in the open. So keep your head down and stay close, OK?'

'Sure.'

It was as much as Jack could muster, his voice tight with tension now. The pair set off again, but almost immediately Jack ground to a halt, grabbing Olivia by the sleeve.

'What the hell...?' Olivia demanded, surprised.

Looking up, she followed his gaze. A figure had appeared in the mouth of the alleyway and was making his way directly towards them. Olivia's heart was beating sixteen to the dozen, as she screwed up her eyes, scrutinising the intruder. Who was this man? And what did his sudden appearance mean? Slowly she let out a long sigh of relief. It was just a pensioner out for a stroll, posing no threat. Tugging Jack onwards, Olivia hurried past him, ignoring his curious looks. Time was of the essence.

Reaching the end of the alleyway, they slowed once more. Olivia scanned left, then right, then left again, but Glendale Road was deserted, the school run long since finished.

'Come on.'

They hurried on down the street in silence, keeping away from the parked cars, their eyes scanning the way ahead. Olivia's phone sprang to life once more, but she ignored its urgent ringing, intent on her task now. Soon they reached the top of the street, and turning onto Nevis Road, saw the familiar sign up ahead. Tottenham Hale train station was now only two hundred feet away. Surely nothing could stop them now?

'Right, the last few yards are the most important. Stay alert.'

The pair moved forward cautiously, their senses attuned to

any possible danger. They were so close, but Olivia could feel how tense, how terrified Jack was. She glanced at him, taking in the sweat creeping down his temple. To her surprise, he now reached out, taking her hand in his, gripping it tightly. It was highly inappropriate and they must have cut a very odd couple, but Olivia didn't reject him, keeping hold of his hand until they had reached the entrance to the car park. Smiling encouragingly, she now withdrew her hand, checking her watch.

11.16 a.m. exactly.

'Right, the pick-up will take place in roughly two minutes' time. It's a Renault Movano van, registration number is OE16 VXL. The driver's name is Steve Fielding, OK? There'll be other officers present, but there's no need to talk to them. Keep yourself to yourself, right?'

Jack nodded, tense but relieved.

'Well, we've done it, Jack. This is as far as I go. Good luck.'

The probationer nodded, pale and emotional, before suddenly lunging forward, enveloping her in a hug.

'Thank you, Olivia,' he gasped, pressing her to him. 'I'm so sorry...'

'Me too,' Olivia replied evenly. 'Now come on, don't draw attention to yourself.'

Disengaging, Olivia turned and walked away fast. Their relationship was over, their time together at an end and she wasn't sad about it, though she sensed her charge felt differently. Though she didn't dare look back, didn't want to see him standing there alone, she had the distinct impression that his eyes were following her every step of the way.

Chapter 124

'I told you I was innocent.'

Guy Chambers glared at Chandra, his eyes blazing.

'That's what we're here to establish,' Chandra replied testily, annoyed by his tone. 'So perhaps you could drop the attitude?'

Chambers shrugged, but said nothing, still clearly deeply suspicious of her.

'Your PA sent us your schedule earlier. It covers the period of the first of November to the twenty-fourth of December of this year. Can you confirm that this is your diary?'

Chambers looked down as Chandra slid the printed pages across the table toward him. Chambers seemed annoyed by his assistant's disloyalty, but managed a curt nod.

'Following our discovery that you were in Paris on the second of December when the snatched photo of Emily Lawrence was taken, I've been poring over it, looking for connections to anyone else who either monitors high-risk offenders or has top-level access at the Probation Service or Ministry of Justice. And one name jumped out at me: Olivia Campbell.'

There was a moment's pause, then Guy Chambers burst out laughing.

'Liv? You've got to be kidding. She's a dedicated public servant – too bloody dedicated, if you ask me. Plus, she's a *friend*.'

'Even so, we've run the rule over her movements, specifically her phone use. Cell site tracking suggests she was in Shepherds Bush, Oxford Circus *and* Reading town centre on the days in question.'

'No, that's too crazy. It must be a coincidence.'

'I don't believe in them, plus she has a historic connection to Mark Willis,' Chandra continued forcefully, gesturing to Campbell's personnel file. 'We're still trying to piece it all together, but it appears she monitored Willis when he was first released from prison, when she was working in the Greater Manchester area. She was his case officer for six weeks, before suddenly going off sick, just prior to being transferred down south.'

'She never mentioned that to me,' Chambers replied hesitantly, suddenly much less cocksure. 'Which is odd, given everything that's been going on. I would have thought Liv would have dined out on that connection.'

Chambers seemed troubled by this revelation, so Chandra pressed home her advantage.

'According to your diary, you had lunch with her two days ago, at the Cinnamon Club?'

'Yes, that's right,' Chambers replied quickly. 'We were exchanging gossip about the total meltdown in our respective departments.'

'What do you remember about that meeting?'

'Nothing, it was just a regular lunch, we've had dozens of them over the years. We're old uni friends...'

Chandra digested this, her mind turning, before asking:

'Earlier you insisted that you'd been set up, that someone had framed you, planted your DNA on the burner phone. Is it possible Olivia Campbell could have done that?'

'I don't know see how…' Chambers replied, stuttering. 'We were together for less than an hour.'

'She didn't hand you a phone at any point, show off a new device or…?'

'No, nothing like that.'

Chambers stared at her, looking mystified and uneasy, before adding:

'Do you know what kind of DNA we're talking about? Blood? Sweat? Skin?'

'We're not totally sure, but we believe it was mucus or spit. Obviously you can spit when talking and when you sneeze you spread mucus, germs and so forth, but we're talking a decent amount, so…'

Chandra petered out, but as she did Chambers suddenly went white as a sheet.

'Fuck.'

'What is it, Guy?' Chandra demanded urgently.

'Well, it may be nothing, but I had this wretched cold then too. My nose was running like a tap.'

'And?'

'And I had a handkerchief with me, a monogrammed one that my brother gave me. I definitely had it at our lunch, but when I needed it later that afternoon, I couldn't find it.'

'But how could Olivia have got it off you? Surely it was on your person.'

'It was, it was…'

Chambers was racking his brains, then suddenly the penny dropped.

'But I remember now… I put it on the table when my phone rang. It was the department calling to tell me about Andrew Baynes's murder. I rushed off straight away, Olivia said she'd settle the bill. I must have left it on the table, she must have taken it then...'

Chandra stared at him. It sounded fanciful, but Chambers seemed totally convinced.

'But why, Guy? Why would Olivia do that? Why would she betray you, betray her calling, like that?'

Once more Chambers hesitated, looking deeply troubled, as he replied:

'I've absolutely no idea.'

Chapter 125

The van pulled up sharply, skidding to a halt just in front of him. Its arrival was so sudden, so startling, that for a moment Jack hesitated, unnerved by the speed and stealth with which it had approached him. But then he spotted the registration number – OE16 VXL – and suddenly his fears receded. This was it. His ride out of here, his route to safety.

The driver's door opened and a burly man in a waxed jacket and baseball cap approached. He kept his head down, seemed keen not to draw attention to himself, but nevertheless thrust out a hand in greeting.

'Steve Fielding.'

Jack shook his hand, flooded with relief.

'Good to meet you. I'm Jack Walker.'

'Course you are. Shall we go?'

He slid open the side door, revealing a bare interior, empty save for three men in tracksuits crouched inside. Jack took a step forward, then paused, curious as to why these men also kept their gaze turned to the floor, rather than looking up at him.

'What's up?' Fielding demanded angrily. 'We need to go.'

'It's nothing, I just …' Jack stammered, flooded with foreboding, picking out the driver's Southend accent now.

'Spit it out, Kyle. We haven't got all day.'

The use of his real name stunned him. Seized with panic, Jack tried to turn, but before he could, a fist crunched into the back of his head, sending him reeling forwards into the van. Now hands were grabbing him, hauling him inside. Dazed, confused, he tried to scream, but his anguished cry was cut off as the heavy metal door slid shut.

Moments later, the van pulled out of the car park, indicating dutifully before heading sedately away from the station, only speeding up when it reached Glendale Road. From her high vantage point on the passenger footbridge, Olivia watched the van drive away, watched Jack disappear from view for good, then slowly turned and walked away.

Chapter 126

She crawled over the rough ground, her cracked nails clawing at the cold, hard dirt. Disorientated, reeling, moaning in pain, Courtney moved clumsily over the discarded rubbish in a desperate attempt to avoid the blows now raining down on her. Mike shadowed her, choosing his moments to strike, raining down abuse on his victim, even as he rammed the hammer's blunt head into her ribs.

Crying out, Courtney collapsed, her face colliding with the icy ground, before struggling back onto her hands and knees. She had no idea which direction she was heading in, but she knew she had to try to escape her attacker, who was circling her even now, scenting blood. Her breathing was short and jagged, her vision blurred, every limb and bone ached, but still she lurched forward, trying to fend off the punishment she knew were coming. She knew she was bad – a worthless piece of shit – but she didn't want to die here, face down in filth, just another discarded piece of rubbish.

'How does it feel, Courtney?' her attacker goaded her, real glee in his voice. 'How does it feel to know that you're all alone? That there's no one coming to save you?'

Anger flared in Courtney, despite her pain. Spitting out a tooth, she scrambled on, determined to keep going.

'That you're going to suffer, *really suffer?*'

Courtney's right hand hit something sharp, tearing at her skin, but she swallowed down her agony, pushing herself onwards. But now she felt her pursuer grab her by the shoulder, brutally arresting her progress. Shocked, she barely had time to react, as he bent down, hissing viciously in her ear:

'How does it feel to know you're going to die in this awful place?'

'Fuck you.'

Blood sprayed from her mouth as she spoke, anger punching through her pain.

'No, fuck you, Courtney.'

The hammer blow connected squarely with her rib cage, punching the air from her and sending her crashing to the floor. For a moment, she lay entirely still, assailed by the most incredible pain, before some vestige of self-preservation forced her to attempt to rise once more. But it was futile, she had neither breath in her lungs nor strength in her limbs and she collapsed back onto the ground, fractured and defeated.

Mike Burnham's boots crunched as he placed one foot either side of her head. She heard his knees click as he bent down, grasping her by the hair, raising her face from the ground to meet his.

'You've reached the end of the road,' he hissed, spraying her with spittle. 'I'm going to kill you now, while your little girl watches on.'

Courtney coughed up blood, a great racking cough, before spluttering her defiance.

'Go on then. Do it. See if I care ...'

It was pathetic, hopeless, but it was the best she could do.

'Oh I will, don't you worry. But first I want you to tell me why.'

'Why what?' Courtney blustered, confused.

'Why Jessica?'

He was so close to her that she could feel his hot breath on her face.

'There were thousands of other kids out there. Why did you take her? Why did you take my little girl?'

His voice was shaking with emotion, dire distress punching through. His agony, his vulnerability undid Courtney instantly, a wave of misery, shame and self-hatred assailing her, snuffing out all resistance. But instead of answering him, she started to sob.

'No, no, no. You'll answer me,' her attacker warned.

Courtney shook her head fiercely, even as her vision swam and pain arrowed through her.

'You laughed through the bloody trial, never said a word to the police, but you'll talk to me. Even if I have to break every bone in your body.'

The hammer ripped into her flank once more, causing a torrent of blood to erupt from her mouth. Retching, Courtney tried to turn away from him, but he grabbed her hair, yanking her head up, so she was looking directly at him.

'Tell me. Why did you take her? Why did you kill my Jessica?'

She could see the pain etched in his features, despite the madness that gripped him. And she knew she had to respond, even though she felt sure he would kill her now, whatever answer she gave.

'Why?'

He screamed the word at her, finally breaking her resistance. Sobbing, Courtney opened her mouth to speak. She desperately wanted to end her suffering, to end *his* suffering too perhaps, but she knew the truth would hurt more than it healed.

'I don't know...' she gasped.

He stared at her, horrified.

'I don't know why I did it, I'm sorry...'

He glared at her, his eyes two dark pin pricks now.

'I just wanted to hurt someone. It was never about *her*...'

He dropped her like a stone, her face smashing onto the ground. For a moment, her vision swam, then through her half-open eye she glimpsed him, pacing back and forth, screaming and crying. Even from her prostrate position, her attacker appeared quite mad, driven to distraction by her words. For a moment, Courtney thought she might have broken him, that against the odds she might survive this wretched ordeal. But the next moment, her fond hopes were dashed as the grieving parent suddenly turned back to her, a dark anger in his eyes. She barely had time to react as he crossed the ground to her, sank to his knees and, pinning her face to the floor, raised his hammer once more.

Their conversation was at an end. Now it was time to die.

Chapter 127

'Tell me everything you know about Olivia Campbell.'

Christopher looked up to find Inspector Dabral marching towards him. He'd been holed up in his office for the past hour, staring at the wreckage of his life, convinced things couldn't get any worse. But now Chandra Dabral was bearing down on him, eyes ablaze.

'What do you mean? I don't understand ...' he blustered, playing for time.

Dabral didn't react to his obfuscation, pulling up a chair and seating herself in front of him.

'Guy Chambers has told us all about your affair, so cut the crap,' Dabral demanded, getting straight to the point. 'We know you've been intimate with her for over two years, that the relationship only ended recently ... so I need you to tell me where she is, what's going on and why she tried to frame Guy Chambers for the recent leaks?'

Christopher stared at her, dumbfounded.

'You can't be serious?'

'Deadly. Where is she?'

'I've no idea.'

Dabral eyeballed him, saying nothing.

'Honestly, I don't know. We had a bust-up this morning, but I haven't seen her since.'

As Guy Chambers had clearly dropped him in it from a great height, there seemed no point dissembling. The whole department already knew that he'd been kicked out of the family home, and would no doubt soon know about Olivia's pregnancy too.

'When was this?'

'At around half past eight.'

'And this was at her flat in Tooting?'

'Yes, Flat A, 83 Chandos Place. I assumed she was still there, to be honest, as she hasn't been in at all today, as far as I know.'

'She left her flat shortly after nine,' Dabral corrected him. 'Hasn't been back, according to neighbours. What was your bust-up about?'

Christopher looked at the police officer, then continued dolefully:

'Last night, Olivia visited my home. She spoke to my wife Penny, telling her that we'd been conducting an affair and that she was carrying my child.'

'Well, that was a nice Christmas present,' Dabral replied evenly.

'You can imagine how that went down. I spent the night in a Premier Inn in King's Cross, then went round to Olivia's first thing to have it out with her. That woman has destroyed *everything*...'

'And what was her reaction?' Chandra asked, clearly uninterested in his distress.

'She was totally unrepentant. We argued for a couple of minutes, then she slammed the door in my face.'

'And how long has all this been going on for?'

Christopher stared at his hands, examining his fingernails.

'We'd been seeing each other for a couple of years or so. We'd agreed it was over, that that was best for everyone. But then she changed her mind, wanted to renew our affair and was using the baby as leverage to try and force me to leave Penny.'

'But you wouldn't have it?'

'No, I love my wife, I love my boys.'

'So she went for the nuclear option.'

Christopher was surprised to see that this was said with no sense of triumph, no joy at the philanderer's comeuppance. If anything, Dabral looked concerned by this development.

'Tell me about her career history. She's had a good deal of experience monitoring and reintegrating high-level offenders, right?'

'Yes, she worked for while up north, then transferred to London about three years ago.'

'And Mark Willis was one of hers, when she was employed up there?'

Now Christopher paused, a sickening feeling creeping over him.

'Yes, she did monitor Willis for a while. She worked all over Lancashire, so Bolton came under her purview. She should never have been given him really, she was overstretched as it was...'

Why was he making excuses for her? It made no sense and yet for some reason he felt honour-bound to defend her.

'What happened?' the police officer demanded briskly.

'Things went OK at first, I think, but Olivia grew increasingly worried about Willis. He wasn't sticking to his curfew, was using drugs and alcohol, disappearing at night for long periods...'

He paused once more, the idea of airing the Service's dirty laundry to another agency unthinkable. Then again, his career was already ruined, so what did it matter?

'There was an incident in Bolton. An old lady was attacked in her home at night. A young man wearing a ski mask tried to sexually assault her. Fortunately she fought him off, screaming the place down, clawing at him. Olivia got wind of this, knew Willis had been out all night, so went round to confront him. He was evasive, hostile, but had scratches all down the side of his neck. She asked him directly if he had anything to do with the attack and he went mental, launching himself at her. She was in hospital for a night, then went straight to her manager's office. She demanded Willis be red-flagged, perhaps recalled to prison, but her boss was reluctant, said there was no *proof* that Willis was involved in the attempted sexual assault. Olivia was a hundred per cent convinced that Willis *was* a danger to the community, but she got a firm push back from her boss, so she resigned on the spot.'

Dabral stared at him, shaking her head in disbelief.

'What happened to Willis?'

'Not a lot. A new probation officer was assigned to him and things carried as normal.'

'And Olivia? I didn't realize she'd ever left the Service. There's nothing about that in her file,' Chandra added, flicking quickly through the pages covering her career history.

'There wouldn't be. The powers that be persuaded her to take extended sick leave, then accept a transfer to London.'

'Ensuring the whole thing could be neatly swept under the carpet,' Dabral concluded grimly.

'Something like that,' Christopher admitted, feeling oddly ashamed, even though it had nothing to do with him. 'She stayed up in Manchester for a while; I think she was basically having some kind of minor breakdown. But she had to stay with her mother, which didn't work at all, because she's a Class A bitch...'

Christopher said this with real venom, remembering with a

shudder the many nights Olivia had spewed out her hatred for her mother.

'Then she came down here and met you?'

'Not straight away. She was very focused on trying to resurrect her career at first, of forging a new life for herself here.'

'But it didn't work out?'

'It was a struggle from the off. London was too busy, too expensive, she never really felt at home here. She missed Manchester, if you can believe that. Plus the workload was horrific. Too many cases, not enough time, pointless box-ticking, minimal supervision. She struggled, like we all do, because we're not funded properly, because probation officers are consistently undervalued...'

Dabral held up a silencing hand, cutting off his rant.

'Anyway, we got on well and she used to confide in me. That's how our relationship started.'

'And during the time you were close, did she ever express any dissatisfaction with her job?'

'What do you think?' he replied scornfully.

'Specifically, though, did she suggest that offenders weren't being monitored properly, that they might be re-offending because of lack of detailed supervision?'

'Yes, on many occasions, but we *all* did,' he insisted. 'You wouldn't be human if you didn't. The whole system is on the brink of collapse.'

'How strongly did she express these views?'

'What do you mean?' Christopher countered warily.

'I mean, did she denigrate her clients in your presence?'

'Sometimes.'

'Did she suggest that they were committing crimes that were going undetected, breaking the terms of their licence, playing the system?'

'Yes.'

'And what was her response to that? What did she want done about it?'

'There was nothing she *could* do. She wanted a couple of them red-flagged, but what was the point of that? The prisons are full, can't take them. She asked to have one offender removed from her list, but who had the capacity to take him off her hands?'

'Did she ever suggest that she might take matters into her own hands? That she intended her probationers harm?'

'Not in my hearing,' he answered truthfully. 'But she was... she was in a dark place, I suppose. Because her mother didn't care for her. Because her clients were playing her. Because her managers were ignoring her warnings...'

'And because her lover got her pregnant, then dumped her,' Dabral concluded.

Christopher didn't respond, silenced by her obvious judgement. Was it really true? Was *he* part of the problem? Had he sent this sensitive, troubled woman over the edge? Was his brutal rejection of her the final straw? It seemed impossible, but laid out like that, one crushing rejection on top of another, it suddenly made total sense.

Chapter 128

He stumbled forward, his feet catching tree roots, his arms snagging thorn bushes. Jack had no idea where they were, no idea where they were heading or when his ordeal would end. All he did know is that his captors wanted blood.

He had fought tooth and nail in the van, kicking out at his assailants, scratching their faces, throwing wayward punches, but it was three against one. Soon he'd found himself pinned to the floor, his hands bound, a dirty rag stuffed in his mouth. Then the van had lurched away and he was hauled roughly upright. But his respite was brief, a sack placed over his head, even as one of his kidnappers punched him hard in the stomach.

The next thirty minutes were bewildering and terrifying. Jack was thrown around endlessly, as the van sped on its way. He lay on the cold floor, choking on his gag, trying to breathe, the lack of oxygen and sheer heat inside the rough sack rendering him faint and dizzy. No one came to his aid, no one tried to help him as he struggled to his knees. All he received was the occasional kick, sending him back onto the floor, accompanied by screeds of abuse. Each vile taunt, each barb that came his way struck fear into his soul. Their accents were clearly from Southend, which meant only one thing. Billy Armstrong's relatives had abducted him and were about to take their revenge.

As they cursed him, revelling in their power, Jack huddled on the floor, sobbing quietly. He hadn't believed it possible, had thought that he, out of all of them, would escape this sudden wave of retribution, but Olivia had betrayed him. He had no idea why. Even in his darkest hours he'd never imagined that *she* would be the one to turn on him, but there was no doubt now that she had colluded with his abductors, abandoning him to his fate. It made his blood boil to think how she'd chastised him, suggesting that he was a pervert, a stain on society, but it also floored him, sucking the fight from him. She had set it up perfectly, delivering him right into the hands of his enemies, and now he would pay the price.

He cried gently, not wishing to give his tormentors any more satisfaction, praying that he would die here and now in the sack, that he would suffocate, have a heart attack, anything to ensure he avoided the pain that he knew was coming. But as ever, there was no release, no relief, and after thirty minutes or so, the van braked suddenly. Moments later, the door slid open and he was yanked to his feet.

Within five minutes they were deep in woodland, well off the beaten track. His abductors had removed his hood now, so that he could walk, and he desperately scanned for signs of life, anyone who might intervene to save him, but they had chosen their spot well. They were quite alone in the dense woodland.

With each passing minute, Jack's anxiety rose still further. The men walked in silence, their good humour evaporating as they began to focus on the task in hand. Jack recognized some of them from court – the driver was Billy's father, one of the others an uncle of his. All wore the same expression, grim, determined, bitter. Dropping his head, Jack began to drag his feet, trying to string out this forced march for as long as possible, but they were wise to his tricks and he was hauled along the path, barely providing any momentum himself. Borne along, his mind started to flit back to Southend, to Danny, to his mum, to a little mongrel puppy called Chip that they'd had as a kid. He clung to these memories, seeking out moments of happiness, those few rays of sunshine he'd experienced before that dark day in October. But they were hard to summon and he was now yanked from his reverie by Billy's father, who gripped his shoulder, forcing him down onto his knees. Gripping Jack by the chin, he raised his head, forcing his captive to look at him.

'Take a look at this handsome face, Kyle. Because it's the last thing you'll ever see.'

Jack moaned, howling out his anguish, but the gag sucked up his agony, choking off the sound. Bending down, Billy's dad tugged it from his mouth. Jack gasped, sucking in the air, then turned to his attacker.

'Don't do this. I know you hate me, I know what I did was wrong. But please I'm begging you, don't do this. I never meant to hurt Billy, I was just a stupid kid—'

The mention of the boy's name seemed to electrify his father, who angrily stuffed the gag back in his mouth. Jack continued to scream, to writhe, looking beseechingly at his assailants, but it made no difference. The four of them calmly took off their coats and rolled up their sleeves, arming themselves with hammers, a wrench and a baseball bat. Jack could shout and scream, could beg to be spared, but it would all be in vain.

There was no mercy here.

Chapter 129

'Is that her?'

'I don't know, it could be.'

'Not good enough. Is that Olivia Campbell?'

Chandra Dabral glared at Christopher Parkes, who looked ever more disorientated. Having heard his mea culpa, she'd dragged him back to Scotland Yard, to the heart of the incident room. He looked bewildered and, in all honesty, so was she, leads coming in thick and fast now that they had a prime suspect. Slowly a picture was starting to emerge.

'Was she definitely in Reading on the second of December?' Parkes queried, looking edgy and unhappy.

'One hundred per cent,' DC Cooke explained. 'Cell site tracking places her at Shepherd's Bush, Oxford Circus and Reading on both the second and fifth of December, picking up a parking ticket there on the latter date.'

'Sounds like Olivia,' Parkes muttered grimly.

'So? Is it her?'

Chandra stabbed angrily at the CCTV image on the screen. It showed a tall woman in a bulky winter coat standing by a Vauxhall Corsa, which appeared to have a parking ticket on the windscreen.

'Well, it certainly looks like it could be her car, though I can't see the number plate. Can you go in a bit closer on her?'

Chandra obliged, watching with interest as Parkes deflated, recognition punching through.

'Yes, that's her. I bought her that coat. I remember she really liked the belt on it.'

'OK, and the other one? Take another look...'

She pulled up another CCTV still.

'This was taken two days ago in Pimlico, a stone's throw from the square where we believe she planted a mobile phone in an attempt to incriminate Guy Chambers. Is that her?'

Parkes leaned in, scrutinising the image. The woman in this image looked different, hair up, puffa jacket, trainers, clutching a cigarette, a far cry from the sophisticated city professional in the previous image. But once again Chandra saw Parkes react with dismay.

'Yes, it's her. I mean, obviously she's dressed very differently here, but you can see that she's lighting one cigarette off another. A nasty habit of hers.'

He said it bitterly, knowingly, as if this was somehow indicative of a dark heart.

'You're positive?' Chandra queried.

'Yes,' Parkes replied quietly.

'Good. Right, DC Cooke, pull everyone off what they're doing, top priority now is to locate Olivia Campbell.'

'No sign of her or Jack Walker at the safe house in Tottenham Hale, I'm afraid.'

'Send a couple of DCs down to Petty France, talk to her colleagues, anyone who knew her well. Also, circulate her particulars to uniform – let's get as many boots out on the street as possible. With any luck, cell site tracking might give us an idea where she's headed and then maybe we can get ahead of her. Also, get her car registration out, see if the traffic cams can pick her up anywhere...'

DC Cooke nodded vigorously and hurried away, calling fellow officers over to her. Anxious, Chandra turned back to Parkes, the pair now alone.

'What kind of access would Olivia Campbell have had to the Delius system? Would she have been able to read Limited Access Only files?'

'No, she's too junior.'

'So how did she find out where Baynes, Lawrence and Turner were living? What their new names were? Could she have accessed those files from any of *your* devices?'

'No, they can only be viewed within the department. She wouldn't have been able to log in to them, even if she had been on my computer, as it would have left a trace.'

'How then?'

Parkes suddenly looked crestfallen, dropping his eyes quickly to the floor. Now Chandra had her answer.

'Did *you* tell her where they were?'

'No. Well, not in the way you mean... I... we... often discussed cases when we were alone. I needed someone to talk to about them. And I suppose... over time, she could have built up an idea of where they were living, who was monitoring them, even what they were called...'

'So all this,' Chandra exploded, 'is because of bloody *pillow talk*?'

'Please believe me, I never thought she'd use that information like this. We were just two colleagues talking, that's all...'

He petered out, crushed, ashamed. Chandra stared at him, aghast.

'Well, I hope it was worth it,' she replied witheringly. 'Because your lack of professionalism, your indiscretion, has *cost lives*.

Olivia Campbell may be responsible for these crimes, but make no mistake, Mr Parkes...'

He looked up at her, ashen.

'You've got blood on your hands.'

Chapter 130

It was over. Helpless, broken, Courtney Turner lay curled up in a ball, coughing blood onto the icy ground. Mike had long dreamed of this moment and now it was here. All that remained was to finish the job.

His victim had offered little resistance, knowing she was no match for her attacker. Did she *want* to be punished? Did she know deep down that this was the price of her evil? It made no difference to Mike either way, she had submitted and he had taken full of advantage. Many people would have been tempted to dispatch her brutally and swiftly, but Mike had resolved to take his time, memories of Jessica's lengthy ordeal seared in his mind. For nearly an hour he had used boot, fist and hammer to pummel every inch of this pathetic animal's body, smashing teeth, cracking bone and tearing skin. He had roared with pleasure and triumph at each strike, knowing that each blow was sweet revenge for his beloved daughter. Years of anguish, frustration and rage seemed to fall away, as if all that suffering had been building to this moment. This was it. This was justice. A settling of accounts. And Mike was enjoying it to the full.

Courtney had stopped howling some time ago, her distress exhausted. She was beyond pain, at a point where the blows barely registered. Her body was broken, her face a bloody, fractured mess. She was in and out of consciousness, sometimes alert and cowering, other times passed out in a heap, overwhelmed by the pain. On those occasions, Mike had had to drag her up by her collar, slapping her hard on the cheeks to rouse her. Then he had set to again, his attack relentless and savage, as she slumped to the floor. But even Mike was beginning to tire now, his arms weary, his face caked in blood, his breath short. He had poured all his bile, all his rage into this savage beating, seeking catharsis, but the storm had blown itself out. Fearing exhaustion, terrified that he would be unable to complete his revenge, Mike gathered himself, preparing for the final act.

'Well, Courtney, this is it,' he rasped, gripping the hammer tightly. 'We've had our fun, but the show's over.'

He grabbed her hair, pulling her up onto her knees. There she remained, head down, staring at his blood-spattered shoes, waiting for the coup de grace.

'Is there anything you want to say to me? Any last words?'

She didn't react, didn't move, patiently awaiting the end. Mike gripped the hammer, adrenaline pumping through him.

'Then let's do it. But know this. This is not for me. This is for Jessica.'

As he spoke, Courtney lifted her head. Steeling himself, Mike raised the hammer, tensing his arm to strike. To his surprise, Courtney now raised hers, stretching out a hand forlornly in his direction, appealing for mercy. Mike shook his head angrily, gripping the hammer tighter – there could be no mercy for the likes of her. Still she gestured at him, flapping wildly at the air, moaning gently. What did she think he was going to do? Give up now, at the very moment of his triumph? Taking a deep breath, he picked a point on her forehead and took aim.

But then he heard it. A gentle whisper.

'Jailan.'

And again.

'Jailan.'

And now he understood. She wasn't reaching out to *him*, she was trying to connect with her daughter, who remained in her buggy, mute, exhausted, but awake.

'Jailan...'

Blotting out her gentle entreaties, Mike refocused, picking his spot once more.

'I'm sorry, baby. Mummy loves you...'

She breathed the words, quietly but powerfully, wanting to reach her child, to feel her love, to be with her daughter at the very end. But what did Mike care? He hadn't been with Jessica when *she* died. Gripping Courtney's hair, he raised the hammer again, this was a time to be brave, to be bold, to see it through.

'I love you, my sweet baby...'

And now Mike suddenly broke, howling out his anguish and anger, as he released Courtney, who crumpled to the floor, sobbing. Part of Mike was tempted to fall on her, smash her into oblivion... but he couldn't do it. He'd wanted to, he'd wanted to with all his heart, but now, faced with murdering this young mother, he found he was incapable of hardening his heart sufficiently to strike home. He had failed Jessica, he knew that, but he could not find it within himself to destroy their love.

Screaming out his frustration, Mike tossed the hammer onto the rough ground and hurried away, tears streaming down his cheeks.

Chapter *131*

The buzzing was insistent and intrusive, demanding her attention. Angrily, Olivia tugged the phone from her pocket, surprised to find that it was Isaac Green calling. Intrigued, she was tempted to answer it, but thought better of it. She had only just reached her car and needed to get back to base ASAP, in order to raise the alarm about Jack's 'baffling' disappearance.

Flinging open the door, she seated herself in her tired Corsa and fired up the engine, sliding her phone into the cradle. No sooner had she done so, however, than a text message from Isaac sprang up on the screen. Curious, she opened it, taking in the contents.

> The police are here. They want to talk to you about the
> leaks. Wtf's going on?

Short and sweet, but a hammer blow. Olivia stared at the message, disbelieving. How on earth had they got onto her? Chambers was still in custody and, besides, she'd been so careful, so cautious. How was it possible that *she* was now in the frame?

She had only a split second to make a decision. She could return to base, front it out, but the coincidence of Jack's sudden disappearance on the same day they'd got onto her made this impossible. It would be a fruitless endeavour that could end only with her incarceration.

'Shit's sake...' she cursed, slamming the steering wheel.

This was *not* how she had intended it to finish, not the promised end. But there was no doubt that she'd been rumbled, that Chandra Dabral was onto her. Tugging her phone from its cradle, she opened the window and tossed it out, before slipping the car into gear and speeding away. She never wanted this, had never planned for it, but she had no choice now.

It was time to run.

Chapter 132

Graham Ellis stared, shocked and horrified, before hurrying to help him.

'Jesus Christ, Mike. Are you OK?'

'It's all right, I'm fine.'

'But you're covered in ...'

'It's not *my* blood.'

The ex-inspector ground to a halt, confused. It took a second to register, but Mike now saw the creeping realization in his friend's eyes. His voice thick with shame, Mike added:

'Can I come in, please?'

They made a strange sight, sitting across from each other at the table. They had done this many times before, but never like this – Graham ashen and in shock, Mike exhausted beyond measure and covered in dried gore. Graham had insisted he touch nothing, clean nothing off, guiding him to a chair, and commanding him to stay put, whilst he retrieved his phone.

He held it in his hand, but hesitated to dial, instead staring at Mike with an expression of dire regret and crushing disappointment.

'Did you ... did you kill her?'

He hadn't mentioned Courtney's name so far and neither had

Mike, the ex-copper knowing instinctively what had happened, as if fearing all along that this might come to pass. Mike shook his head dolefully, suddenly overwhelmed by a wave of sorrow and humiliation. He felt beyond awful to have ever suspected his old friend, of having blatantly ignored his well-intentioned advice in committing an act of unspeakable brutality.

'Where is she?'

'Drayton Park refuse site, it's the old—'

'I know where it is,' Graham interrupted curtly. 'Is she conscious?'

'I think so.'

'And the baby?'

Mike could tell from Graham's expression that he hardly dared to ask, so he was quick to reassure him.

'She's there too. Unharmed.'

Relieved, Graham nodded, rising now as he dialled 999, instructing an ambulance to attend the scene. He turned his back to Mike, talking low into the phone, as if shielding him from the terrible consequences of his actions – a young mum gasping for life in a horrid, forgotten place – before ringing off and returning to the table. Seating himself, he looked at Mike earnestly.

'I'll have to call the police now, Mike.'

Mike nodded, staring at the table, too ashamed to even look at his friend.

'I think it's best we go in together. I can explain the context, do my best for you, but there's no getting round this. What you did today was unspeakable. And you will have to be punished for it.'

The brutal irony hit Mike like a train. For years, he had despised Courtney, the offender, the sadist, the murderer. And now he would be marched through the police station, printed, photographed and eventually presented to the world as a brutal, pitiless thug.

'We're talking abduction, GBH, probably attempted murder too. That's proper jail time.'

His voice was so anguished, it brought tears to Mike's eyes. He felt utterly ashamed, gripped by deep despair, now realizing all that he stood to lose.

'Why, Mike? Why did you throw away your life? What was it all for?'

Mike didn't answer, staring at his hands, even as a tear slid down his cheek.

'I mean, did it make you feel any better? Are you *happier* now?'

And now Mike did look up, unable to ignore Graham's searching question. Locking eyes with him, Mike shook his head slowly. He felt no better. In fact, he felt worse. It was the response the ex-officer had been expecting, but still it seemed to hit him like a punch in the guts.

'What a waste, what a waste...' he intoned, visibly upset.

It was more than Mike could bear, reaching out to his friend.

'I'm sorry, Graham. I'm so sorry.'

'It's not me you should be apologising to,' Graham replied bleakly. 'It's Rachel. And Alison. They love you, they *need* you. How will they cope with all this?'

'Please, Graham, don't twist the knife...'

Graham stared at him, sorrowful, hollow. Mike was aware he had to say more, but how to explain the temporary madness that had gripped him?

'I... I didn't think she was human,' he mumbled eventually. 'I thought she was an animal, a monster. And she *was* cruel, violent, sadistic... but she was also capable of love, *real* love. I've spent the last ten years hating her, living off my anger... and what was it all for?'

His desperate appeal received no answer, though he could tell from his friend's expression that there was no judgement here, just sorrow and regret. This made Mike feel even worse; he would have welcomed it if Graham had torn a strip off him, lambasting him for his stupidity and brutality, but the ex-officer was a wiser man, a kinder man than him. So instead he simply rose, offering Mike a hand up.

'Come on then, let's get this over with.'

Chapter 133

It was time to end this. To bring this case to a close. But still the perpetrator eluded them.

'It was found on the pavement near Jack Walker's safe house apparently,' DC Reeves reported breathlessly. 'It's definitely Campbell's phone, looks like she tossed it. I've got uniform bringing it over now.'

'Someone must have tipped her off,' Chandra replied angrily. 'Somehow she got wind of the fact that we wanted to talk to her. There's no other reason for dumping her phone.'

'Either way, she's going to go to ground now,' Reeves agreed. 'Either lying low or making a break for it.'

'My money's on the latter. She hasn't got a partner or family to speak of and not much in the way of friends, so who'd hide her? We need to get onto the local CID – let them know what's happened, tell them Jack Walker's vanished, possibly abducted, and that they should get themselves down to Tottenham Hale ASAP. Our priority is to find Olivia Campbell.'

Reeves hurried away to do her bidding, whilst Chandra marched over to DS Buckland.

'Any sign of Campbell at Heathrow, Gatwick, Luton?'

'Nothing yet. We've also got people at King's Cross, Euston,

Liverpool Street, Paddington, but they haven't seen hide nor hair of her.'

'What about the roads? We know she has her car with her, drove off in it this morning. Anything from number plate recognition or on the traffic cams?'

'Nothing yet, but to be honest we're not really sure where to look, she could have gone anywhere ...'

'Yeah, but if she's smart, she'll try and get out of the country. Which suggests to me she'll aim for the ferry ports, so that's the M3 or A3, depending on whether she opts for Southampton or Portsmouth ...'

Buckland typed furiously, before shaking his head, disappointed.

'Or she'll try the tunnel, via the M20.'

'I just tried that.'

'Try it again.'

Reluctantly, Buckland complied, then sat up in his seat as something flashed up on screen.

'Vauxhall Corsa, LK14 TFV, registered to Olivia Campbell, was clocked near junction 3 of the M20, three minutes ago,' he said breathlessly.

'Heading in which direction?'

'Towards Folkestone.'

'There we are,' Chandra replied, adrenaline coursing through her. 'Call it in.'

As Buckland hurried to oblige, clumsily snatching up his phone, Chandra added:

'We've got her.'

Chapter 134

Olivia kept her eyes glued to the road ahead, pressing down hard on the accelerator, as she bullied the cars out of her way. She knew she risked drawing attention to herself by driving so aggressively, but she had little choice. She had no idea how intense the police search for her would be, how convinced they were of her guilt, but she knew her best bet now was to get out of the country as fast as she could. She had her passport, two hundred pounds in cash and a bunch of credit cards. It wasn't much, but it would serve her for now and might buy her some time to find a place to hunker down in France or Spain. It was desperate, it would be hand to mouth, but those were the cards she'd been dealt. Now it was all about survival.

She hadn't meant it to pan out this way. Perhaps it was fanciful to believe that she could ever have got away with it, she was no hardened criminal, but things had been going to plan. Willis had got his comeuppance, something that had been *long* overdue, as had Baynes too, both perishing in a way which seemed entirely appropriate to her. Jack Walker was even now reaping the harvest of *his* crime, whilst Janet Slater was laid up in hospital with serious burns, her life in tatters. The only question mark was around Courtney Turner, but as Mike Burnham had clearly *not* contacted the police regarding the sensitive information Olivia had sent him three days ago, she felt sure that he was taking care of business, as she'd been confident he would. Burnham, who was often in the press bemoaning the light sentence handed down to Turner, had always struck her as a tinderbox ready to ignite. She raised a smile now as she passed junction 6 for Maidstone, Burnham's home town, giving a silent, respectful nod to the last of her covert executioners.

Only at the last had things gone awry. In her mind's eye, she'd seen herself getting away with it scot-free, whilst Firth resigned, Christopher succeeded him and Guy Chambers took the fall for it all. His incarceration and disgrace would have pricked her conscience, as she had once been fond of the preening loudmouth, but to some extent he'd been asking for it, with his outspoken views and reckless attitude. Besides, when the opportunity to frame him presented itself, it had simply been too good to pass up. Once all that had been achieved, once she'd resigned from the service, perhaps Christopher might in time have forgiven her, realizing it was better to start a new family with a woman who truly loved him, than spending Christmas after Christmas alone? It was impossible to know of course, but it was all moot now.

Strange how life lets you down. Olivia had always tried to do the right thing, to be what people expected her to be. Hard-working, conscientious and dutiful as a girl; optimistic, idealistic and fervent as a young woman; committed, determined and industrious as a professional, yet what had been her reward? Belittled and neglected by a mother who wanted a son, seduced by a charming liar who wanted to have his cake and eat it, betrayed by those on whom she thought she could rely. Even when she'd fought to do the right thing, demanding that Willis be sent to prison, she'd earned only resentment, mistrust and career reversal. At first she'd been surprised by this, shocked to learn the painful lesson that no good deed goes unpunished, but over time it started to make sense to Olivia. *She* had been the aberration, not everyone else. They knew that you could transgress at will, without sanction or comeback, repeatedly proving the maxim that nice guys really *do* finish last. This was the fruit of her education within His Majesty's Probation Service.

Olivia raced on, the junctions flitting by. She was zeroing in on Folkestone and, once there, a whole new vista would open up to her. She would make it to the continent, lie low for a few months, then resurface in a new town under a new identity. How ironic, how pleasing that idea seemed now, given recent events. It would be the cherry on the cake and she would enjoy it to the full.

She was still musing on her future plans, smiling to herself, when she noticed something. Looking in her rear-view mirror, her smile faded as she clocked flashing blue lights behind her. Keeping her speed steady, she strained to make out four cars racing down the M20 in her direction. A spike of fear arrowed through her and returning her eyes to the road, she floored the accelerator. The car lurched forward, straining as it roared on, propelling her away from danger. It was the middle of the day and the traffic was light, so Olivia made good progress, weaving in and out of the lanes, desperate to stay ahead of her pursuers. Shooting another look into her rear-view mirror, she was alarmed to see that they were gaining on her and started casting around for a slip road, a turn-off, anything by which she might leave the motorway and try to lose the following cars in remote country lanes. Here too she was disappointed, as there were now no junctions before Folkestone. What then? She would have to make it to the port and hide out there as best she could, whilst coming up with a new plan. It was far from ideal as a plan, but it was all that remained open to her.

Even as she thought this, however, her final hopes were dashed. The cars in front of her had been slowing and now Olivia realized why. Up ahead was a police road block, straddling the width of the motorway. Stingers had been laid out in the road to burst tyres and behind them sat a phalanx of police vehicles. All around her cars were slapping on their hazard lights, their incessant flashing orange seeming to trumpet the danger she faced.

The pursuing vehicles were drawing nearer, the trap slowly closing. What now? She could give up the ghost, surrender here and now. She could pull the car off the road, make a break for the verge and see if she could escape on foot. But this escape attempt would be both foolhardy and short-lived, a point underlined by the menacing whirr of the police helicopter, which hovered overhead. Which left only one option. It wasn't what she wanted, nor was it fair, but it was all that remained to her now and in some ways it was fitting. She was many things, but not a coward.

The following cars were nearly on her bumper, so time was short. The Corsa continued to speed towards the roadblock, but Olivia now pushed the accelerator flat to the floor, watching greedily as the speedometer hit 100mph. Almost immediately her tyres hit the stinger's sharp teeth, all four blowing simultaneously, the car skidding wildly out of control, careering forwards at breakneck speed.

Closing her eyes, Olivia took a breath then yelled aloud in triumph, as her tiny car smashed into the stationary vehicles with a sickening crunch.

Day Six

Chapter 135

The frost was thick on the ground, the grass giving way beneath her feet with a satisfying crunch. Ellen Townsend felt exhilarated this morning, full of optimism and cheer. Stocking presents had been opened, the turkey was roasting in the Aga, her family were all around her and, to top it all off, it was the most glorious Christmas morning she'd ever seen. The sky was blue, the sun glowing in the sky, yet the frost was thick and hoary. A more perfect festive scene you couldn't hope to see and Ellen felt profoundly glad to be alive.

As always, the morning had been hectic and fraught, but things always calmed down once the family got out on their traditional morning walk. Max, her Border Collie, was certainly happier when bounding through the woods rather than stuck inside, and she hurled his ball for him once again, happily watching him race off into the thicket. He soon disappeared from sight, but this didn't worry Ellen. He could be boisterous and overfriendly at times, but as she always picked out of the way places for their family walks, she felt sure he wouldn't bother anyone.

Striding along, breathing in the crisp, winter air, Ellen listened to the chatter of Gerry and the others. All was silent, save for their happy conversation, which meant she could hear them clearly and she eavesdropped happily. She and Gerry always loved having the girls back, though of course the dynamic was different now that they both had boyfriends. Different and in some ways better, she thought. She loved company, loved cooking for large numbers and Gerry seemed to enjoy the addition of some men to the mix, which was a bonus. Many people out there were less fortunate than they and Ellen always remembered to spare a thought for them on Christmas morning, but still she couldn't deny her own contentment, even excitement. Today was going to be a good day.

The others were catching up with her, so she slowed, noticing now that Max had not returned. Puzzled, she called his name, but this elicited no response. Letting the others pass, she set off after him, calling again and whistling twice. This usually did the trick, whistling inextricably linked in Max's mind to doggy treats. But still there was no sign of him.

Sighing, Ellen made her way through the thick foliage. She was intrigued rather than alarmed, as Max did occasionally wander off before suddenly reappearing, bounding out of the bushes towards her. But now as she ducked the thorn bushes, she heard something that sent a shiver of alarm through her. Whimpering. Quiet, high-pitched whimpering.

Had he hurt himself? Trapped his leg down a rabbit hole? Got himself tangled up in briars? Upping her speed, she hastened towards the sound, pushing between two large oak trees before emerging into a small clearing. As soon as she did so, she ground to a halt. Max appeared unharmed, but was clearly agitated, whining as he danced around a man, who lay prone on the freezing ground.

Ellen hesitated, suddenly scared. Who was this man? A

drunk? A vagrant? What if Max woke him and he suddenly rose, angry and hostile? She turned to leave, to call out to Gerry, but then she noticed that the man was not moving. In fact, he remained stock-still, despite Max's growing noise, almost as if...

Unnerved, Ellen took a step forward, then another. And now she saw it. Blood. Lots and lots of blood, congealed in a small pool around the motionless man. Had he fallen? Injured himself? If so, how long had he been here? It was seriously cold yesterday and she didn't much fancy his chances if he had spent the night here.

'Gerry, come here quickly.'

Her cry echoed through the woodland, eliciting an instant response, then footsteps haring in her direction. Emboldened, Ellen took another step forward.

'Hello?'

Still the man didn't move. Ellen was close to him now and could see his torn clothing, his blood-stained tracksuit and his badly broken right arm, which hung limply from the elbow joint. Clapping her hand to her mouth, Ellen took another step forward, so that she was now almost on top of the man. She knew he was almost certainly dead, but she had to try to help him, to see if there was anything that could be done.

Reaching out a trembling hand, she pulled on his shoulder, turning him over. The man's body rocked, then rolled over onto his back, looking up at her. Instantly, Ellen let out a scream that echoed through the woods. Suddenly she couldn't stop screaming, the horror of what lay before her too much to bear. The man was not simply dead, he had been *destroyed*. His limbs were shattered, his skin viciously bruised, his clothing ragged and torn. But worst of all was his face, which possessed no features, no distinguishing marks at all, being now merely a bloody pulp, having all but collapsed in on itself.

It was a sight that Ellen knew would haunt her for the rest of her life, that of a young man so brutalized, so defiled, that even his own mother wouldn't recognize him.

Chapter 136

Mike stared at him in utter disbelief, unable to believe his ears.

'Are you having me on?' he stuttered, finally finding his voice.

'I wouldn't joke about something like this,' Graham Ellis chided. 'I heard it direct from the SIO himself. Courtney Turner is refusing to say who attacked her, says the incident was *her* fault, flatly contradicting everything you told them.'

'But the police have evidence – the photos they took at the station, my clothes with *her* blood on them. Surely that's enough for them to bring charges?'

'Maybe, but if the victim is denying the attack ever happened, what are the chances that it'll go to court?' the police officer countered forcefully. 'Besides, if I'm being honest, I'm not sure the will is there to push this through, given the circumstances.'

Mike stared at Graham, stupefied.

'Don't misunderstand me,' the ex-policeman continued. 'What you did was profoundly wrong, but everyone understands the context, knows what you've been through. They also appreciate that you walked away from it, that Courtney *will* recover in time.'

'How is she?' Mike asked tentatively, crushed by guilt.

'Not great, as you'd expect,' Graham replied carefully. 'She's had emergency dental work, both her arms have been pinned and she's going to be in hospital for several weeks, but her boyfriend is on the scene, her sister too. She has a sufficiently robust support network to get through this, though the attack will leave a legacy.'

'For both of us,' Mike said soberly.

Graham nodded, adding:

'You've had a fortunate escape, Mike. Courtney has decided not to push for charges, has spared you many years behind bars, so now is the time to put her behind you. To move on and embrace your new life with Rachel, Alison, your family and friends. I know you blamed yourself for Jessica's murder, but it was only ever Courtney and Kaylee's fault. Courtney knows that, which is why she's shown you mercy. But this *has* to be the end of it, Mike, this has to be a fresh start for you.'

Mike suddenly felt a rush of emotion, fighting back tears.

'You're right. And I'm sorry for not coming to you earlier, for not trusting you to help me through this. I won't make that mistake again.'

'I'm glad to hear it,' Graham replied warmly, opening up his arms and pulling Mike into a hug. 'You need to make the most of this, Mike. This is a lucky break.'

'Lucky break?' Mike queried, his voice choked with emotion. 'It's a bloody Christmas miracle.'

Chapter 137

Emily leaned forward, straining to hear their voices. Instantly, she was riven with pain, even the slightest movement causing flames of agony to rip through her. Crying out, she fell back onto the pillow, gasping. And now, lying there, silent and still, she heard Sam's voice again.

'I don't care what your orders are. I want to be alone with my mother.'

There was a mumbled but persistent response from the uniformed officer, which Emily couldn't make out, before Sam cut in again, strident and insistent.

'Fair enough. Arrest me if you have to. But I want some privacy.'

Now the door opened and Sam stepped inside, closing the door firmly behind him. His manner was serious, his face creased with a frown, and immediately Emily felt herself tense up. She hadn't seen Sam since the fire and had no idea how he felt about her, especially as he'd been injured himself in a desperate struggle with Robert Slater, an incident that had led to him being held in police custody for several days. However you looked at it, she had ruined his life, turned it upside down, which is why she felt alarmed by his sudden appearance. Both his presence and his manner suggested he had something important to say.

'Hello, love,' she croaked, her lips cracking as she spoke.

'Hello, Mum,' Sam replied, looking visibly shocked by the extent of her injuries.

'Not much to look at, am I? But at least I'm alive,' she joked, wincing in pain.

'You'll be fine,' Sam replied, seating himself next to her. 'The doctors said most of the burns are minor and will heal in time.'

'It could have turned out very differently, for sure,' Emily responded. 'But I wasn't ready to give up on life just yet. It was the thought of you that gave me the strength to fight.'

Sam dropped his head, staring at his hands, clearly still distressed by the idea of his mother at the heart of a roaring inferno.

'I guessed I must have passed that gene on,' she continued quickly. 'I heard about you and your uncle.'

She shivered at the thought of her teenage son grappling with her thug of a brother. True, Robert Slater was now in custody, out of harm's way once and for all, but she wished to God they had never encountered one another.

'You shouldn't have done that, sweetheart, he could have *killed* you.'

'Or he could have killed *you*,' Sam replied quickly. 'And I couldn't let that happen, not after everything you'd been through. I ... I think I understand now a little better the rage you felt back then. I think I felt it too a bit when I—'

'Don't say that, Sam,' Emily interrupted passionately. 'What you did was entirely different. You were trying to protect someone. Whereas I ... well, what I did was unforgivable.'

'I understand that. I'm just saying I get it now. I can see how lonely, how angry, how helpless—'

'No, Sam. I won't have it. I'm glad you came today, *really* glad, but I don't want you here out of pity or a sense of duty.

I meant what I said the last time we met. I'm damaged goods, toxic, which is why you'd be better off without me. I love you Sam, love you with all my heart, so I only want what's best for you. You have the chance to start over without me now. Seize that opportunity, put yourself first for once, chart a new course.'

Easy enough to say, but much harder to swallow. Emily would be devastated if Sam turned his back on her, but she knew she had to give him the chance to escape the dark shadow of her legacy for good. For a long while, Sam said nothing, wiping away his tears. Emily yearned to comfort him, but she knew she didn't have the right to, even if she was physically able to do so. Finally, Sam looked up, his reddened eyes seeking out hers.

'I'm not going anywhere, Mum. I'm going to be with you every step of the way.'

Emily gasped, her heart bursting.

'I've had a lot of time to think about what you did, what happened in Bridgend. I know there's a price to pay for it, a price you pay every day and you ... *we* can never make up for the deaths of those little girls.'

Tears slid down Emily's ravaged cheeks, the memories still painful and fresh. Sam reached out and wiped them away, as he continued:

'We can't change the past, we can't wipe it out, but we don't have to repeat the same mistakes. There's been enough rejection already.'

Now Emily started to sob, his wisdom, his maturity, his kindness overwhelming her. Taking her hand in his, he cried freely too, cradling her damaged fingers in his.

'I guess the only question,' he managed between sobs, 'is what I am supposed to call you. Janet? Emily?'

Emily managed a smile, then gathering herself, replied:

'Emily. You can call me Emily.'

Chapter 138

She heard them whispering her name in the corridors; nurses, doctors and porters darting brief glances through the tiny glass panel as they passed by. Olivia had no doubt that her arrival had caused a major stir at the William Harvey Hospital, that they seldom had such high-profile offenders in their midst, cuffed to the bed and on display for all. Some daring souls had even tried to take a photo of her through the glass, before being roughly manhandled away by uniformed officers. It amused Olivia to think that, having remained under the radar for so long, she was now a minor celebrity.

In truth, it was a miracle she was here at all. She had hit the police cordon at full speed, expecting instant immolation. Against the odds, however, her battered Corsa had saved her, the airbag deploying instantly, rescuing her from serious harm. She had a fractured ankle, a dislocated shoulder and nasty whiplash, but otherwise she was largely unharmed. That was certainly the view of Inspector Dabral, whom she occasionally glimpsed outside. The police officer was desperate to question her and could be seen arguing with the doctors, but the latter's caution had kept her at bay so far, which had given Olivia time to think.

At first, she had been furious, then distraught that her attempt to take her own life had failed. But later, as the medical team were running tests, checking both her health and that of her baby, she'd had a change of heart. She didn't really believe in fate or karma or any of that nonsense, but to her it seemed that her survival, and particularly that of her baby, was a sign. Having been determined to end it all, now she was determined to embrace her situation, using her interrogation, arrest and trial as an opportunity to serve up a few home truths – to the police, the judges, the public. She would be unrepentant, defiant, holding up a mirror to the world and daring it to gainsay her. It was clear she would be convicted of multiple offences, not least incitement to commit murder, so there was no point obfuscating or mincing her words – she would hold nothing back. But that didn't mean she needed to spend the rest of her days behind bars, paying for her honesty.

That was where the baby came in, its fortuitous survival the spur she needed to continue the fight. Whatever the judge and the jury thought of her, they couldn't ignore the fact that she was now a single mum-to-be, with no one to help her raise or nurture her little one once the happy bundle of joy finally arrived. Sending a mother to prison, separating her from her newborn, would weigh heavily on their minds and Olivia intended to take full advantage of this. There was no question that her back was against the wall, that the criminal justice system would do its best to punish her, but the foetus growing inside her was a means of granting them only a pyrrhic victory, of avoiding the punishment that many would see as her due. She had a trump card now and she intended to use it.

After all, if anyone knew how to play the system, she did.

Chapter 139

His police radio chattered insistently, as DC Fulford hopped briskly from foot to foot, slapping his gloved hands together. This was partly to ward off the perishing cold, but also to dispel his nerves. This was not a home call he wanted to make at any time of year, let alone on Christmas Day.

Glancing nervously at Lindsey Hall, the accompanying FLO, he knocked again. This was the third time he'd tried to raise someone and now, finally, he heard movement within. Moments later, the door crept open, a haggard female face staring at him over the chain.

'What do you want?' the strange vision demanded, her Southend accent punching through loud and clear.

'Mrs Peters?' DC Fulford replied. 'Mrs Pam Peters?'

'Maybe. What of it?'

Her hostility and suspicion was palpable, which made Fulford's task all the more difficult.

'Could we come in? It'd be best if we chat inside.'

'On Christmas Day? You've got to be kidding. I don't want the filth in here, today of all days. Honestly, I don't care which one of the little beggars has got himself in trouble, that's their lookout. So just say your piece, then do one.'

'No one's in any trouble, but there has been an incident,'

Fulford replied calmly, ignoring her insults. 'So please can you at least open the door so we can talk properly.'

With a sigh, Pam Peters unchained the door, opening it a touch further, revealing a glass in one hand and a smouldering cigarette in the other.

'Well?'

Clearing his throat, Fulford continued:

'It's about your son, Kyle. I'm afraid he was found dead this morning, in woodland in Essex.'

'Essex? What the hell was he doing there?'

'We're still piecing that together, but it seems likely Kyle was taken there against his will, then attacked. I'm very sorry for your loss.'

The middle-aged mother stared at him, gimlet-eyed, displaying no emotion whatsoever.

'I thought you'd come calling one day,' she said coldly. 'I just didn't expect it to be on bloody Christmas Day.'

'I appreciate that and we're so sorry. I'm here with a family liaison officer, Lindsey Hall. If you'd like us to come in and sit with you for a while ...?'

'No, thank you,' Pam Peters shot back quickly. 'You've done your job, now you can piss off.'

And with that, she slammed the door in his face.

Chapter 140

'Tell me more, love. Tell me *all* about it.'

Mike watched Rachel intently, fearful that his daughter would clam up, even reject him. She knew nothing of the attack on Courtney, Alison thankfully having decided not to tell her yet, but Mike had done enough damage over the last few years, let his daughter down enough times, to warrant outright rejection. He'd half expected Alison to bar the door to him and had certainly been prepared for Rachel to call time on their Christmas chat before it got started. But to his enormous relief and joy, she began to talk.

'So, it was nothing special. Just me and a bunch of other sixth-formers from Beaumont doing the rounds of the local care homes. We did a few barbershop numbers, then went straight into the carols. They really loved that. A few of them said it really made their Christmas.'

'That's wonderful, darling,' Mike responded, proud and emotional.

'Anyway, that's not the interesting bit. The interesting bit, that Mum told me not tell you about, is that someone asked me out on the way home.'

'Right, I see...'

'Don't look so shocked. He's a nice guy. His name's James and he's in my history set. I didn't think he liked me ... but he does.'

She giggled as she spoke, blushing heavily, raising a smile from Mike.

'Well that's great, sweetheart. But I'm going to have to hear more about him, before I give you my permission to see this guy.'

'Dad!' Rachel moaned, pulling a face.

'Go on, tell me everything about him.'

Rachel obliged, talking with real excitement about her new boyfriend, her New Year plans, her hopes and dreams for the future. Mike drank it all in, hanging on her every word, more grateful than he could say to have such a vivacious, funny, caring child. She was a blessing, pure and simple, someone to be cherished, loved and supported every step of the way. In the years ahead, Mike would do just that, working hard to change, to be the father Rachel deserved.

For now though, he was happy just to sit and listen, drinking in all the tiny details of her life. Where once he'd been distracted, tortured and unhappy, now he was relaxed and content, gazing at Rachel's animated face as she chatted away to him. Jessica was somewhere in the ether – how could she not be, especially on Christmas Day? – but it was Rachel he saw now, and Rachel alone. There was no space for rage or bitterness here; today Mike was at peace, happier than ever to be spending some quality time with his lovely daughter.

It was the best Christmas present he could ever have asked for.

Chapter 141

'Well, isn't this nice?'

Propped up in her hospital bed, Olivia smiled warmly at Chandra Dabral. Standing at the foot of the bed, the detective inspector did not return the compliment, staring at the patient with disgust.

'I am sorry to have dragged you away from your family on Christmas Day,' Olivia continued brightly. 'But, hey, comes with the territory, right?'

'I'm not here to play games, Olivia, or make jokes,' the officer responded sternly.

'You surprise me.'

'I'm simply here to hear your version of events. The how, when and why.'

'Surely you know all that already,' Olivia replied, laughing. 'You must have spoken to Guy, to Christopher, you must know how *easy* it all was.'

'Not a word I would use, in the circumstances.'

'Well it *was*. Getting the necessary information was a doddle. Christopher gave me most of it, the rest I gleaned from Isaac and the others. Spreading it wasn't hard either; no, the tricky part was ensuring the leaks provoked the right reaction. But I needn't have worried on that score. The Bridges, the Armstrongs, the Slaters, even Mike bloody Burnham were chomping at the bit to get stuck into those lowlifes. And who can blame them?'

'Is that why you did it, Olivia?' Dabral fired back, unamused. 'To ensure that "justice" was done?'

'Absolutely. And I make no apologies for it,' Olivia said proudly. 'Some people are born evil, end of story. For them, death is the only remedy.'

'That's not your call to make.'

'Except in this case, it *was*, wasn't it? Olivia countered assertively. 'And my only regret, if you can call it that, is that Janet Slater and Courtney Turner survived.'

'It was your job to *protect* them,' Dabral protested. 'To rehabilitate them.'

'It was my job to protect the public. And as for the idea of rehabilitating those animals...'

Olivia dismissed the notion with a wave of her hand, as if amused by the very suggestion. Outraged, Dabral was about to hit back, but Olivia cut her off.

'They can't change, you must see that. Willis, Walker, Slater... they'd always be a danger to the public, so what choice did I have? The judges, the Probation Service indulge them of course, forever forgiving the unforgivable... but thanks to me those creatures will never prey on the weak and vulnerable again. Some people might judge me for what I did, but to my mind their deaths were justified, necessary and *entirely moral*. In fact, in many ways, they were mercy killings, because those creatures couldn't stop offending even if they wanted to.'

'When did you become so twisted?' Dabral asked, shaking her head in contempt. 'Such a disgrace to your profession?'

'Twenty years in the Probation Service will do that to you. But, hey, it's been an education.'

Olivia stared at the police officer, who seemed horrified by her relaxed demeanour and clarity of thought.

'Don't you get it yet, Chandra?' Olivia continued, laughing. 'We are *all* born bad. A child killer, a faithless lover, a neglectful mother – they are all different points on the same scale, because the truth is that all human beings are selfish, careless and cruel. Once you realize that, the whole idea of a Probation Service becomes a joke, a wicked, obscene joke, the idea that people *want* to rehabilitate themselves as much a myth as the idea that they actually *can*. Jack Walker proved that in spades over the last few days, but it was a lesson I learned long ago. People cannot be tamed or cured – we are what we are. So we must act to please ourselves. That's what Mark Willis did, it's what Jack Walker did. And it's what I did too, I suppose, though of course I was on the side of the angels.'

'Keep telling yourself that. But I don't believe a word,' Dabral replied darkly. 'I think you did all this because you were angry and bitter. You betrayed, you *killed* these people, because you wanted to, because you gained some kind of warped pleasure from it.'

'Oh, I can't pretend that my actions were entirely selfless,' Olivia replied, shrugging. 'I *did* enjoy the chaos, the moral panic, the total meltdown of liberal commentators everywhere. And yes, maybe I enjoyed the secrecy too, playing Chambers, Isaac, Christopher, fooling the whole lot of them. It would have been fun, I suppose, to be around when they realized the extent to which they'd been duped, but a girl can't have everything, can she?'

'You honestly feel no guilt about what you've done?' Chandra countered.

'For the suffering of those animals? None at all. They had it coming.'

'They were beaten to death, for God's sake,' the police officer cried. 'Their heads caved in with baseball bats and hammers. Their teeth smashed. Baynes had a knife driven through his face. All thanks to you. Yet you can seriously look me in the eye and tell me you feel *nothing* for them? No pity? No remorse?'

'Not a bit of it,' Olivia smiled. 'I guess you could call it my life's work, my contribution to society. And do you know what the best bit is, Chandra?'

Olivia beckoned the police officer towards her, leaning in close, as she added:

'If I had the chance, I'd do it all again.'

Credits

M.J. Arlidge and Orion Fiction would like to thank everyone at Orion who worked on the publication of *Eye for an Eye*.

Agent
Hellie Ogden

Editorial
Emad Akhtar
Celia Killen
Sarah O'Hara

Copy-editor
Claire Wallis

Proofreader
Linda Joyce

Editorial Management
Jane Hughes
Charlie Panayiotou
Tamara Morriss
Claire Boyle

Audio
Paul Stark
Jake Alderson
Georgina Cutler

Contracts
Dan Herron
Ellie Bowker
Alyx Hurst

Finance
Nick Gibson
Jasdip Nandra
Sue Baker
Tom Costello

Inventory
Jo Jacobs
Dan Stevens

Design
Nick Shah
Joanna Ridley
Helen Ewing

Production
Ruth Sharvell
Katie Horrocks

Marketing
Lindsay Terrell
Helena Fouracre

Publicity
Leanne Oliver
Ellen Turner

Sales
Jen Wilson
Victoria Laws
Esther Waters
Group Sales teams across
    Digital, Field, International
    and Non-Trade

Operations
Group Sales Operations team

Rights
Rebecca Folland
Tara Hiatt
Alice Cottrell
Ruth Blakemore
Ayesha Kinley
Marie Henckel